Stealing Glass
Tales of Bones and Roses 1
Liv Strom

SM Press

Copyright ©2023 by Liv Strom and SM Press

All rights reserved.

No part of this publication may be reproduced, distributed, or transmitted in any form or by any means, including photocopying, recording, or other electronic or mechanical methods, without the prior written permission of the publisher, except as permitted by U.S. copyright law. For permission requests, contact author on https://www.livstromwrites.com.

The story, all names, characters, and incidents portrayed in this production are fictitious. No identification with actual persons (living or deceased), places, buildings, and products is intended or should be inferred.

This book is not to be used to train generative AI models.

Book Cover by 100Covers

Map by Chaim Holtjer

Contents

Tales of Bones and Roses Series	VI
Epigraph	VIII
City of Bones and Roses	X
1. Vanya	1
2. Vanya	10
3. Vanya	23
4. Dimitri	40
5. Vanya	47
6. Vanya	63
7. Dimitri	78
8. Vanya	88
9. Vanya	97
10. Vanya	105
11. Dimitri	118
12. Vanya	122
13. Vanya	132

14.	Dimitri	142
15.	Vanya	147
16.	Vanya	163
17.	Dimitri	178
18.	Vanya	191
19.	Vanya	201
20.	Dimitri	215
21.	Vanya	223
22.	Vanya	235
23.	Vanya	243
24.	Dimitri	251
25.	Vanya	263
26.	Vanya	279
27.	Dimitri	288
28.	Vanya	296
29.	Vanya	312
30.	Dimitri	326
31.	Vanya	335
Epilogue		350
The Tale of Cinderella		353
About Liv Strom		355
Acknowledgements		356

Tales of Bones and Roses Series

Chronological order

- Ansa & Alexei – Unlocking Fire: A Bluebeard Retelling Novella (2023)

- Vanya & Dimitri – Stealing Glass: A Cinderella Retelling #1 (2023)

- Vanya & Dimitri – Claiming Glass: A Cinderella Retelling #2 (2024)

- Helia & Koshka – A Puss-in-Boots Retelling

- Ansa & Alexei – A Rumpelstiltskin Retelling

- Lumi & Damyon – A Snow White Retelling

- Mariska & Kazimir – A Little Red Riding Hood Retelling

- Lana & Nikolai – A Beauty and the Beast Retelling

FREE Short Stories

Ansa & Alexei – Returning Home – takes place after the events in *Unlocking Fire* (2023) **Download NOW**

Returning Home
An Ansa and Alexei short story

"Perhaps the greatest risk any of us will ever take is to be seen as we really are."

Cinderella, Disney (1950)

City of Bones and Roses

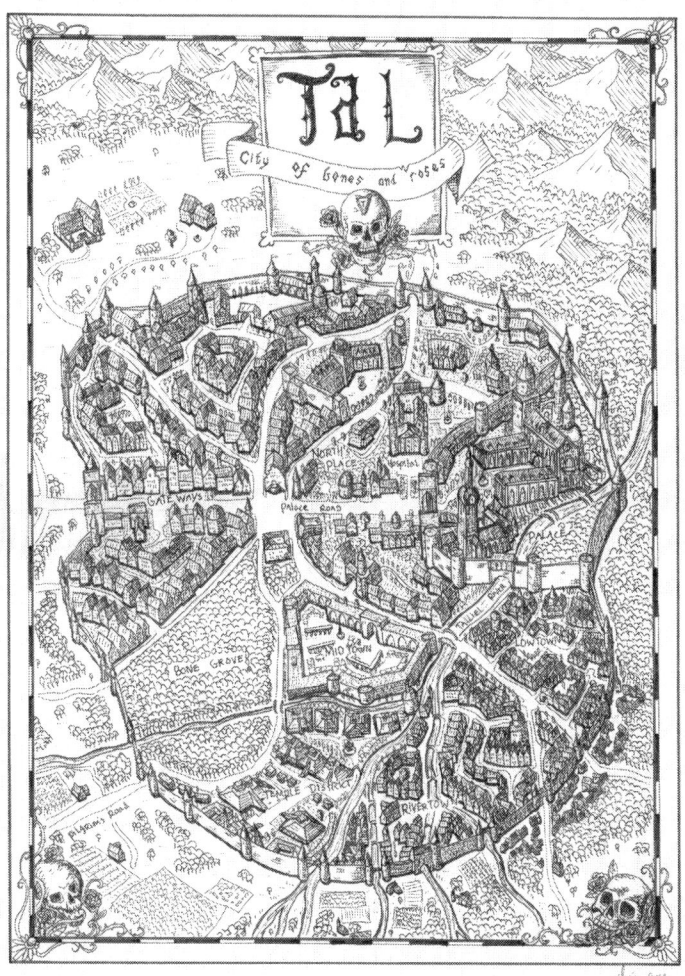

People, Places, and Magic

Royals

- Dimitri Alexandre Ivanov – Crown Prince of Tal

- Nikolai Alexandre Radanov – Prince of Tal

- Mariska Yelena Radanova – Princess of Tal

- Yelena Solovyova – Dowager queen of Tal

- Ivan Gregorious III – King of Tal

- Inessa Yustina – Queen of Tal

- Helia von Heskin – Princess of Oberwalden

- Flora von Heskin – Oberwaldian noblewoman

Nobles

- Alexei Semyon Yurievich – Second son of a Talian country lord

- Von Mekelns – Talian noble couple

- Ekaterina Kuznetsova – Talian noblewoman

- Stasia von Lemerch – Talian noblewoman, councilor

- Savva Novikov – Talian nobleman, councilor

- Mar Heridan – Talian nobleman, councilor

- Urs von Uster – Talian nobleman, head of the Roja, councilor

Commoners

- Vanya Komovara – Thief

- Lumi Komovara – Thief

- Komara Gorgiana Hereova – High-priced courtesan

- Kirill Anatolievich – Moneylender

- Svetlana Kirillovna – Kirill's daughter

- Grigori – Kirill's enforcer

- Popova – Lowtown business owner, suspected mage of unknown variety

- Fyodor Popovanov – One of Popova's sons

Others

- Morovara – High Priestess of the Death Goddess

- Gennady – Royal healer

- Zakhar – Former palace guard

Important historical figures

- Ealhswip – Last divine ruler of Tal, High Priestess of the Death Goddess

- Eydis – Ealhswip's daughter, not by Herebov, first High Priestess to not rule

- Herebov – Vsadnik clan war chief, first King of Tal

- Yelena – Herebov's second wife

Neighborhoods of Tal

- The Royal Palace

- North's Place

- Gateways

- Bone Grove

- Temple District

- Midtown

- Rivertown
- Lowtown
- Ramparts (outside city wall)

Recorded Mages

- Fire bearer – also known as known as explosions
- Wind whisperer – also known as weather mages
- Water seer – also known as seers
- Earth mover – also known as growers
- Sigil crafter – controlled by the Sigil Guild
- Matter manipulator – also known as telekinetics
- Hope holder – also known as healers
- Heart turner – also known as mind witches
- Death keeper – also known as necromancer

Chapter One

Vanya

I danced along the path to the familiar *tock-tock-tock* from the bones hitting each other high above, imagining myself at the crown prince's engagement ball.

The swarms of white-dressed pilgrims filled the Bone Grove—visitors to our cursed city, ready to pay anyone for an imaginary conversation with their lost ones. Maybe, like me, they knew it was a scam, but when you had nothing left, even a lie rang true.

Normally, they spoke quietly to their dead and sang laments in foreign tongues. Tonight, every conversation centered on tomorrow's ball and the Oberwaldian bride who had yet to be seen. Even the opaque Spirits illuminating the night were largely ignored.

All dead came to Tal sooner or later, and here they stayed in the form of Spirits—clouds in vague human shapes, some smaller than a fist, others larger than me—stealing the warmth from those careless enough to touch them. The bones of the dead hung from every tree, playing to honor them.

On the edge of the Grove stood the ancient tree I had climbed and hung my mother's finger bones in five years ago, while Lumi, my identical twin sister, stood watch.

I rested my hand on the smooth bark and sought my mother's blessing without expecting anything.

Still, I whispered a prayer.

Mother would never have approved of her daughters' new life, though I told myself she would have understood. After all, it was the debts and stepfather we inherited from her that put us in this position.

I pierced my thumb on the iron needle I carried for protection and left a smudged, bloody fingerprint as payment to the Death Goddess.

Lumi would laugh at me if she knew I still came here. That I talked to the Spirit of a woman who had barely been able to help us while alive.

The tree absorbed my blood, and after one last look at the black foliage high above, I hurried past the pilgrims. The moon was up, the streets packed, and Lumi probably already in place, cursing me for my tardiness.

At the ancient, black, stone gate separating the temple from the rest of Tal, a stick figure painted in blood made me take an alternate path. The crude drawing appeared everywhere lately, calling for the blood of our rulers—calling for trouble, more like it. Lumi and I needed to be out before the city erupted, because there was no way the poor would come out on top. If only I could make Lumi agree.

I shook my head. If tonight went well, we would have more than enough money to leave. We had a plan.

Exiting the Grove close to Midtown, I hurried my steps to avoid the brightly lit peddlers of charms, wards, and holy items; the seers claiming to speak to the dead, drawing the pilgrims into the fabric-clad booths. If the Bone Grove was a contrast of black and white,

Pilgrim's Road, dividing the Grove and Temple District, was a riot of color guiding the grieving into Rivertown—a trap for the living coming to Tal to pay their respects to their ancestors.

The peddlers and scammers called summer *high season* and laughed when they counted their coins each morning, but I longed for the calm winter brought.

After the diversions of Rivertown came Palace Road, the main thoroughfare from the outer wall to the palace, dividing Tal's six neighborhoods in half. Crossing it was a near-death experience.

I threw myself between coaches and horses, my heart pounding in my ears. They would not stop for one such as me, and a hoof could split my head like an egg. The richest of all rode proud griffons, whose sharp beaks could tear off an arm. Luckily, they rarely traveled on land.

On the other side, the merchants' houses were replaced by grand homes with walled gardens, street lanterns, and sweet-smelling roses, bursting through the gates.

The tension in my shoulders grew as I continued, my nerves strung tight like lute strings. The streets were quiet, though music and laughter from wild summer parties escaped from the manors.

As a highly-paid courtesan, Mother had gone out in the evenings and returned at dawn to tell us of the beauty and magic hidden behind the walls of the nobility. Lumi and I loved those stories until we learned she was a product to be sold, not an invited guest. Still, we lived off the nobles. In Tal, you robbed them or the pilgrims, and we preferred to target those who had enough to spare.

Finally, sweat sticking the many-times patched shirt to my back, I arrived on 3rd Street. Surrounded by quiet manors and parks, it seemed strangely forgotten; the former grand home on one side many years abandoned. Above, the bats squeaked and chatted.

The residents of the manor across the road, Lord and Lady von Mekeln, were to arrive tomorrow for the crown prince's engagement ball, and the house had already been readied for them, though only a few guards and staff had arrived. According to the maid Lumi bribed, one of the things already prepared was the lady's evening ensemble, including her diamond tiara and necklace, both fine enough to normally be kept in the impenetrable Talian royal bank.

But Lumi was nowhere to be seen.

This was her plan, damn it. Our stepfather added a higher interest each year that passed. If we did not pay now, we would never be free of his mark, and we both deserved better than serving him and our spoiled stepsister. We deserve freedom, even if we had to steal it from others.

The moon inched up the sky, and when halting steps approached, my nerves transformed every bush into a guard.

I sank further into the rambling roses. This was not a place to loiter; the guards here were a different kind than the ones west of Palace Road.

The shadowy figure stopped as if listening.

"Vanya?" she whispered, and the breath I had been holding left in a whoosh.

I crept closer. "Where have you been?"

She jumped, not as at home in the dark as me, despite all we had done to survive these last few years. Not that anyone would look at us—identical, too thin, short, curly-haired, barely into adulthood—and think we fit on the streets. Lumi belonged behind a desk, or in charge of an empire. Instead, she only had me to command while scrubbing pots and floors during the day and stealing at night. Her one-woman army. I had no idea if I belonged anywhere.

"I got held up," she said, avoiding my offered hug.

I barely flinched—she had kept her distance, emotionally and physically, since the attack. *It will get better*, I reminded myself. We just had to escape Tal.

"One last job, Lumi," I said with a forced smile. "Then we can pay off Kirill. Get away…"

She grunted noncommittally and fingered the knife that never left her belt. "I'm not running, V."

"It's not—"

"We are losing the night."

I nodded, ignoring that she was the one who had been late, and turned toward the wall opposite the von Mekeln estate. After we were free, she would tell me what the problem was. I would force her to open up and convince her we needed—no, must leave. *Tomorrow*.

The wall opposite our target was crumbling, the vines covering the ancient stones providing easy handholds. I cringed at the *skrrch* of my threadbare shirt catching on the rose thorns and ripping. Our stepfather or his spoiled daughter would add the inflated value of its mending to our outstanding balance.

Even with clouds blanketing the moon high above, the remaining climb was smooth. The next part was what Lumi called *my usual idiocy*, though this time, she had proposed it.

Heaving my leg over the wall, I took a moment to study the von Mekeln mansion. All was quiet. A lone light shone in the third window on the second floor. No sign of patrolling guards. More Spirits, untouchable and unidentifiable, than I had previously noticed drifted down the street and into the abandoned, overgrown garden behind me—*where had they come from?* They were unavoidable in all of Tal, but it was unusual for several to gather so far from the Grove and temples. My neck tingled, as if someone was watching. I shook my head. It was time to focus—a distracted thief was a dead thief.

The wall I clung to was as wide as my forearm and as high as a one-story building, and the alley below spanned the width of a tall man. Falling meant a broken leg, if not a skull. I grinned into the night.

Crouching, I found my balance. The moment I stood, my silhouette would be outlined against the city that never slept. Before doubts could dig their claws in, I released my breath, rose, and pushed off in one smooth motion. The air rushed around me, and for a moment, I was flying through the night sky, completely alive. Free. A laugh wanted to escape.

The other wall hit me in the chest, knocking the air out of my lungs as my arms clamped around it instinctively, and I threw myself down on the other side.

A bush broke my fall with a noisy crunch, but after silently singing "the Undead Queen and the King" twice under my breath, and no one showing up to investigate, I got up and unlatched the garden door for Lumi.

Besides what was bound to be a remarkable bruise, part one had gone as well as could be hoped. *We can do this.* One last theft, and we would walk away free from the debts we had worked four years to clear. Another year, and Kirill might sell us to the brothels to recuperate his funds, as he so often threatened.

We flitted from one tree to the next across the private park, with only bats and birds rustling the leaves. While the garden gate had been barred from the inside so that an invader would have had to break it down, the back door to the four-story manor had a more elegant lock. Lumi approached it and pulled out the required tools from the bag strapped to her chest, while I kept watch. Her tension was like an itch between my shoulder blades, followed by satisfaction the moment a click sounded behind me. No matter how she pulled away, she was still my twin, my other part.

The maid had given Lumi a rough description of the house, but it was unnecessary. In Tal, the richer you were, the higher up you lived.

We snuck across the dark, abandoned entry on the carpeted runner to avoid echoing steps. At a creaking sound on my left, I froze, but not even the curtains—a deeper black against the windows—rustled. Lumi, already at the stairs, waved for me to hurry. Usually, I was the one to rush into danger. But with freedom close enough to taste, each step seemed to carry more weight.

After a last searching look, I forced the unease away, and together, we hurried up the wide staircase. It spiraled through the manor, ending in a circular landing.

The fourth floor only had three doors. Simultaneously, Lumi opened the door on the right and I, the one on the left, searching for the lady's chambers. Heavy drapes covered the windows, the escaping sliver of moonlight revealing rows of books in an otherwise-empty chamber. *Wrong room.*

Closing the door silently, I saw Lumi outlined across the hall, shaking her head as well. As I opened the last door, Lumi a few steps behind, bright lights blinded me and panic closed around my chest. Two more steps and my iron needle rested against the lady's throat, my dried blood still coloring its tip. She opened her mouth, but I pressed harder in warning.

She was alone, a green silk robe thrown over her nightgown. But if she was here, others were inside the building. Only blind luck took us this far undiscovered. Lumi rushed inside and locked the door behind her. A picture was removed from above the desk, a closed safe visible behind it. *Damn the Death Goddess and her three-headed mate.* Couldn't they have given us this? Why had the maid not mentioned the safe was secured with magic sigils?

"Do it, V," Lumi said, and I stared at her blankly, feeling the warmth of the lady's body pressed against me as close as any lover. "We cannot let her scream. It's her or us."

Her meaning sunk in, and my previously steady hand wobbled against the pale throat. I'd never hurt anyone outside self-defense. The ice in Lumi's eyes transformed her from my twin into someone I would cross the street to avoid.

"She won't scream," I said, and all three of us must have known it was a lie. Everyone screamed when thieves burst into their chambers, but I could not slide the needle into her trembling neck. I had sworn to bring the warmth back into Lumi, not join her in the dark. The world needed kindness, not more death.

"She wouldn't hesitate to kill us. Would not think to help us if we starved. You're too weak for this life."

I shook my head, knowing Lumi was right; I still clung to the girl I had been. But after this, we could have another life. Lumi scowled at me before tearing through the lady's chamber.

She emptied a pearl studded jewel box into her bag, not that the lady would keep her finer pieces out when she had a sigil-protected safe. Maybe it was my nerves, or a sound my subconscious registered, but I turned, certain that someone was approaching the door. Lumi's head snapped toward me at the same time I opened my mouth to warn her.

"We need another way out."

She sprang into action without question. That was how we were: connected since before birth, a hidden bond strong enough that I might not have had to say anything for her to know what I thought. Maybe not as strong as before her face was cut and her Spirit seemingly twisted two years ago, but true when it mattered. Before, she would never have asked me to kill. She had come back harder, stronger, and unable to tell me what had happened to her. What I had allowed to happen by being too busy flirting to walk her home.

A raised man's voice snapped me back from the ever-present guilt. Lumi desperately tore down the curtains, brushing her fingers along the walls, searching for a way out. *Nothing*. There was only the door we entered through and the balcony. She cursed as the man on the other side of the door threw himself against it while calling for the guards.

One option left.

Improvising, I decided for all of us. Pushing the lady hard, I spun, grabbed Lumi's hand, and threw open the balcony doors. Lumi—afraid of heights, though she denied it—would never have gone this way, but I had seen the roses all Talian nobles loved grow all the way up to the roof. They were attached to a metal lattice that might just carry two malnourished women.

Unwinding the rope I carried around me like a belt, I tied the other end to Lumi, while the lady screamed at the top of her lungs behind us. With a final jerk, I tested the knots. Our fate was joined—either both or none would make it.

We swung out on the trellis as the door burst inward, and a bearded man in nightclothes stumbled in. Our eyes locked, his widened in surprise; then I climbed.

Lumi started on the long way down, but I jerked the rope and pointed up. The roof was much closer, and there was a good chance no one would search it.

The rose thorns scratched my hands, snagging on my clothes until they were beyond repair. I stayed above Lumi, the rope between us taunt, moving first to ensure I had a firm grip if she slipped. Twice, I thought she would fall and take us both down before we reached the roof.

Sitting on top of the chimney, I watched the house light up. Below, servants searched the park and called for the City Guard. I lifted my eyes. The City of Bones and Roses spread out before us, illuminated by the Spirits of the dead.

In the wind, or maybe in my mind, I heard our mother whisper the words she told us every night. *Be kind, for tomorrow will be a better day.*

Chapter Two

Vanya

We lay tied between the two grand chimneys so as to not slide off the steep roof while we dozed through the next day, soot and smoke staining us black. The contents of the jewel box would not even cover the interest. The gold and small gemstones spoke of years more emptying chamber pots, serving our stepsister, and beatings. Or worse.

When the sun set again, we rested on the edge, parched and with rumbling bellies. Even the early summer sun could scorch the earth in Tal.

"We could take the jewels and run. Go far away from here," I said into the last rays of light, watching the palace—a foreboding, black monolith overlooking the bustling Tal, the Taliell river's many arms, and Palace Road. It was not the first time we had this discussion—not the hundredth either.

"Even if we could escape the debt sigil, we would arrive broke again, begging, and no better off. All roads lead back to Tal." Lumi shrugged. "I'll do whatever I can to be free of Kirill, and then you should run, V, but I'm staying. Tal can change. We only need to discard those who would rather throw a ball than feed the people."

A ball would have the dancing and dresses I dreamt of, not that one such as me would ever be allowed to attend. Unease clenched my chest, and stick figure images calling for rebellion flickering in my mind. The blood dripping from the mark was message enough for those who knew what it meant.

"Death never changes, Lumi. How can Tal?"

"Blood," she answered, echoing my thoughts while keeping her gaze locked on the distant palace. "There are more of us, and they need us. The problem is that we fight each other. Look at you and me, never able to save enough because it benefits Kirill to keep us. There are places in the world where the masses decide. Tal can be that. Better. It's in our bones and Spirits; even if you run, you cannot leave it behind. We have power, V, they just need to bleed enough to see it."

The palace cupolas caught the last rays of the sun, burning bright enough that I had to close my eyes. Or maybe I closed my eyes to hide tears, because I no longer recognized my sister. *How can I protect her from herself?* The Roja—elite enforcers and spies—would crush all of Lowtown if they believed it a threat.

"It's a long climb down," I said with a sigh. A long way back to how we used to be.

The last Talian plague, a bloody cough, had killed our mother and hundreds of others, while a preventable fever had killed our little brother before his first birthday, neither's passing leaving a mark on the world beyond what we carried inside us. No one had saved them, and no one would save us. In Tal, the poor's troubles were as easily swatted away as the flies picking at the leavings on the nobles' tables. Later, I would make Lumi see that no matter how poor we would be, anywhere was better than here. In one if the free coastal cities, I could dance while she reserved her scheming for business. We were not the kind of people who brought change; we were the collateral damage of others' plans.

But none of it mattered unless we were free to choose. Kirill would sell us to the highest bidder to recoup the money our mother borrowed to dress us and train us to live another life than the one we were born to. We were bodies for Tal to consume until only our bones remained in the Grove, our Spirits eternally rattling them, together with the untold generations who came before.

When it could be put off no longer, we untied ourselves with soot-stained fingers. I smiled at Lumi's unrecognizable face. We looked like two cinder girls, lighting the streetlamps for pennies.

The climb down was uneventful and slow. Enjoyable for me, if not for my sister's unsure movements and hisses until she finally had solid ground under her feet.

Silent, like mice, we waited in the bushes until the coast was clear, and snuck out of the mansion's garden and back across North's Place, unseen. Perhaps those behind the decorated fences and walls were too busy coiling their hair and arranging their dresses to care about the trinkets we stole. In a few bells, the rich would converge on the palace for what was sure to be the ball of the season—the decade—to celebrate the upcoming wedding of the crown prince to a foreign princess, yet to arrive.

We walked in silence, spending precious coins in Midtown's bazaars on spits hot enough to burn our tongues, and confectionery sweet enough to calm the ache, despite the ever-increasing food cost—a feast, or perhaps a wake, to get us through the coming days. Sharing dirty smiles, I could imagine we were girls again, drifting between the long, narrow shops—like caves, filled with treasures drawing you in. In back rooms, where the only daylight came from clever holes in the walls, sat the seamstresses and carvers, and the pounding of the metal workers and the regular clap of the looms. Honorable people taking the wood and stone from the mountains, and the wool and hides from the steppe tribes, and transforming them into things of beauty to sell to the pilgrims and caravans.

Once, upon seeing our pretty dresses and coiled hair, the hawkers called us inside. These days, hard eyes met ours and smiles turned into frowns as if they saw not only the dirt, but our thieving ways. With the exorbitant prices they charged, perhaps we would have had more luck stealing from them than the nobles, though the idea of taking from those who labored for their gold twisted my stomach around the heavy meal.

Crossing the southern arm of the Talliel using one of the hundreds of bridges, I watched the show floats with longing. Last summer, I danced and played the queen on my one night off. It had been frivolous—they paid me only in food and drink and a good time—and I had wished it would not end with the turning weather. On the colorful, awninged barges stretching down the waterway, the crowds drunkenly cheered in the prince's honor, though some raised their glasses wishing the missing bride would stay gone. Everyone enjoyed seeing the rich rejected, and no one was richer than the Talian royals.

Lumi and I, like most of the city, had lined Palace Road two days ago to get a glimpse of the crown prince finally returning home. People had chanted blessings and thrown flowers—women had even bared their breasts—as the processions passed. Not once had the prince turned to look at his people welcoming him home. His uncaring face chilled me, as did the great, black griffon he rode on. The prince was handsome though, with hair as dark as his ride brushing his wide shoulders, and features like chiseled marble.

I do not remember anyone who rode on his sides, but his face was seared into my mind. There was something besides being the crown prince, something compelling, that made me unable to look away.

Not even Lumi, who had been mumbling curses at the royals, had denied it.

As we walked further into Lowtown, cobbles became dirt roads, the paint chipped, and cultivated roses ran wild. I paused to smell one, a rueful smile pulling on my lips. It held a beauty the perfectly manicured mansions did not. At some point during the last five years, this had become home, its people my people, despite my determination to leave. If someone gave us suspicious looks here, it was because they did so with everyone.

Passing the mothers washing clothes and children in the fountains, I exchanged greetings despite my heavy heart. Everyone here carried sorrows, but managed to share smiles. When you have nothing left to give, kindness became all the more valuable.

Moving as one, Lumi and I finally stopped before the grandest house on Mandible Street—one of the poorest streets in the poorest neighborhood. The shop on the bottom floor, with narrow, barred windows and drawn curtains, did not require a sign. Everyone knew the moneylender of Lowtown.

My hand found Lumi's and, instead of pulling away, she clenched it tight as we entered through the unlocked front door.

Inside, we walked directly to the front study. Better to get it over with fast. The debt sigils on our thighs made it impossible to hide.

Kirill—tall and muscular despite his age, his ochre skin crisscrossed with fine scars from his fights on the streets before he stole enough to dress as fine as any lord and have several in his debt—scowled when he saw us stain his precious carpet. He was as much a ruler in Lowtown as the king in the palace. Our mother, delicate boned with dreaming eyes, had probably looked ethereal on his arm. Not that we ever saw them together. The last years of her life, she left us for days, probably coming here to play the doting wife and be handed around to his flunkies and rivals like a treat. Did he see her when he looked at us?

Lumi poured our glittering findings onto the desk without a word.

"You upset the whole North's Place. City guards scourge the streets and disturb all kinds of nefarious activities and deals, and this is what you bring me."

Svetlana, his blond, rosy-cheeked, richly dressed daughter, always quick to agree with him, sneered. "And when you were supposed to be home, preparing the feast in the Prince's honor. You look like you rolled around in the hearth."

Our stepfather pulled up the ledger, already open on our mother's page. I knew it well. Upon her death, the debt sigil automatically transferred to us—only after Kirill found us wandering the streets had we learned of her loans to pay for our clothes and classes. She had repaid in services and secrets, often on her back. At least, Lumi and I had been allowed to pick which kind of currency we paid in. Since then, we lived in this house, given all the most menial and dirtiest tasks.

It was the additional loan I took two years later to pay for Popova's help—when Lumi came back beaten and bleeding, at risk of infection during the spring rains—that my sister had never forgiven me for. We might have been able to pay what was left on our mother's debts, but with the additional one, the interest, and Kirill charging for our upkeep, only stealing from nobles gave us a chance. At the time, Lumi had been delirious with fever, raving about the dead, and I, ready to give anything, including myself, to save her. I had never questioned the decision. Death was irreversible, life carried hope.

"Let us help with the business instead of cleaning, Stepfather. We want to repay you," I tried, while Lumi watched impassively. We both knew he thought we were good for nothing more than what our mother had been and should be glad he had not taken us to his own bed. I called him stepfather every chance I got to remind him we were no older than his own daughter.

"The Rivertown brothels would pay well for twins, though at seventeen, you are getting old to be properly trained," Svetlana said, stroking her fine, silk dress as if imagining how many more she could buy by selling our flesh. "That's the only way a man would stand your deformity anyway," she continued, pointedly staring at the scar marking Lumi from temple to chin, twisting her lips into a permanent sneer. Even with it, Kirill would triple his investment, and we all knew it.

"Not yet." He slammed the ledger closed and stood, filling the small study. "That doesn't mean you don't have to pay your dues. A client saw you and has made a special request. Please her, and I will consider the debt paid in full."

"Father, you cannot let them—" Svetlana protested, but Kirill silenced her with a look.

"If you return before midnight, I remove the debt sigil tonight. Shame me, and you'll be sold. I've had enough of you bringing trouble to my door."

I clutched Lumi's hand with my sweat-slick one. It was strange. Suspiciously convenient, even. I should have found joy in Lana's obvious displeasure, evident in the way her fists crinkled her dress, but it only deepened my apprehension.

"What is it?" Lumi asked, her tone cold, but I could hear it even in her voice. *Hope*. No matter the risks, we would never turn down a chance for a clean break.

"You're already late." A shadow of a smile touched Kirill's wide lips. "You're going to a ball."

Two worn-out women with Madam Jian's chained heart sigil on their forearms, both barely covered by flowy, green dresses, scrubbed me and Lumi in the rainwater barrels, our soot-stained appearance deemed too dirty for the indoor tub. If we failed, these women's lives could soon be ours.

Even the cobbled inner courtyard and impeccable, pale-yellow façade, decorated with climbing roses I had used more than once to quietly leave the house, were signs of wealth among Lowtown's mud streets.

Without a word, I was handed one of Svetlana's finest bronze dresses, as revealing as anything our mother had worn, and Lumi received a black and gray servant shirt, coat, and pants. My hair was oiled and coiled; Lumi's was chopped off. Neither of us protested. Instead, our minds were on what we had been asked to do. Our fingers brushed against the other's in silent support. Despite the stifling summer night, goose bumps covered my skin. I was crashing the crown prince's engagement ball. The nobles of Tal protected their own. If caught, the best I could hope for was a short trial and swift hanging. A night in Tal's prison was said to make you long for death.

Steal right under the noble's noses. That was what Kirill's mysterious patron wanted—for us to take an item as legendary as Tal itself. The glass crown, only used for coronations and weddings, would be displayed, but guarded.

Why would someone ask for us? I could not imagine Kirill or Svetlana touting our strengths. The customer must have offered him more than he could resist, and the danger was such that he would only send someone expendable.

Few of Lowtown's residents could blend with high society even for a night, but our mother—insisting we came from noble blood and would marry well—had taught us how to move and talk, calligraphy and history, dances and greetings. Part of me was surprised our stepfather had not tried this earlier. Maybe he knew we would have said no, but this time, I had seen the truth in his eyes. His patience was running short. If we failed, he would sell us or marry us off.

The prostitutes painted swirling noble sigils up my left wrist, marking me as a lady of the court. Fear settled in my bones as I watched the flowing pattern take shape; impersonating nobility was an automatic death sentence. *How accurate was the forgery?* At birth, each noble babe was permanently branded with their House sigils. No matter what they did in life, who they married, or what crimes they committed, it remained. The magic it carried forced them to obey their Head of House and allowed for them to be tracked no matter where in the world they went. The debt sigil on my upper thigh, a reduced version of the noble one, prevented us from intentionally hurting Kirill and forced us to serve until we repaid the money or died.

I ignored it as often as I could, as if it was a noose around my neck that tightened when acknowledged. It only enforced small, direct commands, but if we ran, Kirill would hire a hunter to bring us back, no matter where in the world we hid. You did not rise to his position by allowing debtors to skip.

The dark-skinned courtesan who dressed Lumi offered us her water skin. I drank deep and the burning liquor brought tears to my kohl-lined eyes and calmed my pounding heart.

When the women loudly announced we were ready, Kirill, who, true to his role as stepfather, had been blessedly absent while we washed and dressed, approached with a lanky healer dressed in their formal dark-red, knee-length coat over red pants. With surprisingly delicate fingers, he brushed over our visible injuries, and the scratches on our hands and arms disappeared as if we had never climbed the roses.

Instead of relief, I wished the injuries back; wished I did not know what that touch cost. If Stepfather paid for a healer without complaint, this job was worth more than all Lady von Mekeln's sigil-protected jewels. Worth more than our lives.

Our stepsister watched it all with disapproving eyes that blanked when her father looked in her direction. He might dress her up and spoil her, but there was no question who the master in this house was.

Lana leaned closer and adjusted the bodice of my dress.

"There are people you can disappoint and those you cannot. If you fail tonight, run and pray the Goddess finds you before Father," she said, barely moving her lips, before twisting them into the usual sneer and eying us both. "And don't dare ruin my dress."

Kirill patted her head like doting on a pet. "Don't worry, darling. After this, I'll buy you a hundred more. By fall, you'll be the envy of all."

The *clop, clop, clop* of hooves was followed by jingles from the bell at the back gate.

Kirill himself checked through the peephole before opening the gate to a black, unmarked carriage. The silent driver looked neither left nor right.

Our stepfather waved us forward.

"In and out. Follow the plan and return here directly on your own. Blend in, but talk to no one. I promised your mother I would look after you, and I've fed and clothed you, and kept you off the streets. But I bartered for a wife, not two useless girls. Succeed tonight, and we can all be free of each other."

He clearly expected no answer, pointing for us to get inside. Still, his words fed the hope inside my chest. He would not send us if it was impossible.

The door swung shut behind us, and with a lurch, the carriage moved away from a house that was home and prison both.

We sped through the Spirit-illuminated city, crossing the bridge back into Rivertown, then through Midtown before turning onto the bustling Palace Road that would take us to our final destination.

I sat opposite Lumi, as was appropriate for a lady and her maid, watching her instead of the familiar city on the other side of the sheer, lilac curtains. Her shortened hair curled up around her ears, leaving her pale neck exposed. Her face relaxed in thought, softening her features. Never had she and I looked more different. She was beautiful in the stark, forgettable clothes, though I knew she no longer believed it.

I brushed my sparkling, slipper-clad foot against Lumi's worn, leather shoe.

"You don't have to do it," I said when she met my eyes. "If they catch you, they might not waste time on questions."

"I'm sneakier than you think, and you're the one who'll be in the middle of them." She studied me with narrowed eyes, the previous ease whisked away. "You certainly look the part. Just like Mom would have wanted."

"It's just clothes. One night, Lumi."

Memories of our mother in her finery flashed before my eyes. Because of her facial scar, Lumi was too memorable to play the lady. Was that why she looked at me with suddenly cold eyes? Or because our mother had been too trapped in her delusions to see her life for what it was: that of a prostitute? Our neighbors in upper Midtown certainly had known and treated us accordingly, but mother had sold herself, then borrowed more to raise us into little ladies, all in deference to an imagined noble heritage. It was probably true for our father, as most of her clients had been noblemen. But nobles did not care about blood. It was the breeding that mattered, and no matter the clothes, fine manners, or dance classes, we would never be more than the bastard children of a prostitute, then reviled stepdaughters of a moneylender.

Still, excitement filled me as we got closer to the palace and the ball, where colorful nobles flittered like butterflies, dance and music filling their days in the inaccessible Women's Tower.

I refused to fidget under Lumi's always-observant eyes, though my feet and fingers wanted to move. *It is only a costume*, I reminded myself. *A means to an end. Nothing more.*

Our old lives had been a lie, and even if I could go back, I would not. Though, living as Kirill's stepdaughters and thieves felt no truer. This was a once in a lifetime opportunity in all possible ways—the last engagement ball was a quarter of a century ago. Only then, and at the much more private royal wedding, were the legendary glass crowns of Tal taken out of the treasury to be admired, but never touched by anyone outside the royal family. If all went well, tonight, I would be the exception when I took it from right under their eyes.

The carriage jerked to a halt and lanterns illuminated the world outside the curtain-covered windows. Lumi got up and smoothed her skirt, as if she was the one dressed in silk. With her hand already on the door, she turned and wrapped me in a tight hug. Before I could overcome my surprise and hug her back, she released me and removed her sturdy shoes.

"You need them more than me. The dress will hide them."

I hesitated. "Are you sure?"

"No one will see me. Steal the crown on my signal, follow Kirill's instructions, and then run. Get back before the midnight bell, and we are free."

She slipped into Lana's delicate slippers while I pulled on her worn but serviceable boots. When the dress covered them, Lumi nodded, took her sleek knife out from her deep pocket, and slid it into my wide waistband, where the shimmering copper fabric concealed it. "Don't hesitate this time, because I won't. There is no one here worth your life."

Before I could answer or return her blade, she was outside, holding the door for me with downcast eyes.

For another breath, I stayed in the dark, imagining my mother transforming at a client's knock on the door, transporting myself back to the floating stage in Rivertown, where I had played Queen Tatiana for the pilgrims.

Straight as a spear and proud as a goddess, I left the imagined safety of the carriage and strode through the obsidian palace gates, past the grand statue of the first king and queen of Tal, and became one of the nobility.

Careful not to gawk, I passed the sigils painted in ochre on the ancient, obsidian palace walls. They blocked Spirits from entering the compound, and, for the first time in my life, I stood outside at night without the dim haze of the dead nearby. Instead, there were people everywhere—guards, servants, nobles, and soldiers—working and celebrating, sometimes both at once. Some bowed to me, but no one questioned my presence. The strange coach driver must have presented our forged invites for us to get this far.

Lumi had already slipped away.

Time for me to get into position.

Chapter Three

Vanya

Hundreds of eyes slid over me as I slipped through the glittering throng of celebrating nobles, all the while, fearing they would spot the dagger chafing against my left hip. But for once, Svetlana's extravagant fashion taste was of use. The light dress exposed more of my chest than anyone outside the brothels in Lowtown should, and the transparent, bronze sleeves covered most of the fake sigil. No one would notice my face or that I did not belong.

A man at least double my age asked me to dance. Remembering polite phrases Mother taught me, I declined, though, despite having no interest in him, I would have liked nothing more than to say yes. The music already tugged at my every step, pointed my toes inside the hidden shoes as if readying for a spin. Unfortunately, there was no way of knowing how long it would take for Lumi to create the needed distraction, and Kirill had instructed me to blend. Midnight was only two bells away.

On the stone-plated dance floor, paired nobles swirled in intricate patterns, while at least double that consumed the king's food and drink. I forced myself to look away before the expert flutists and violinists made me forget why I had come. My heart already beat in time with the drum.

The crown prince's engagement ball took up most of the ornamental palace gardens. Lanterns dangled from tree branches and shimmering globes of glass fractured the light, turning the guests into magical beings of light and shadow. Or maybe it was real magic, such as only the nobility possessed and guarded as much as their riches.

It was a thief's dream setup—rich, inebriated guests in their best jewels, congregating in the dark. If Lumi and I were free, we would already have pockets full of enough gold to leave Tal. But if we were free, we would never have dared walking into the palace in the first place. Maybe I could still snag something on the way out, though that would probably count as not following Kirill's instructions.

Instead of robbing those who fixated on my chest, I stayed in the shadows until I reached the well-lit, empty podium. The curving lines of the four golden chairs reflected each candle flame. The royal family presumably mingled with their sycophants, drinking and making merry, as only those who never worried about food or funds could.

Light skirts swayed under stiff, short coats, the polished buttons and precious stones shone brighter than stars. Lords and ladies as pale as me and red-haired westerners mixed with the amber hues of Vsadnik—the steppe people most of the Talian nobles descended from—and even a few black-skinned Sorachians from the faraway coastal cities I dreamt of visiting. Due to generations of intermingling, for most, only the inherited names remained as clues to their origins. Skin color made no difference in Tal, perhaps because of the ever-present reminder that in death, we were all alike. Rich and poor traveled to the city and some stayed, to remain close to their ancestors, or profit from the next believer.

While many still carried the names of those who once roamed the steppes, what set the nobles apart was wealth, privilege, and magic—each tended like an ornamental garden.

I studied the crowd while waiting, wondering if I could spot the prince, remembering his stiff face when he entered Tal, like the cheering masses who lined Palace Road offended him. His black military uniform had stood out in the sea of palest purples and softest greens. Tall and imposing, he had stared straight ahead, only occasionally stroking the griffon he rode, a beast with a beak and claws as sharp as any blade.

Did such a man ever smile?

Luckily, there was no sign of him.

Around me, most of the guests laughed and celebrated, but some gathered with serious faces. The same question was on everyone's lips: *Where was the bride?*

She had been expected for months, but according to the rumors reaching the Rivertown drink halls, first due to spring storms, then the fragile health of her mother, she had yet to appear. The whispers grew until it was said openly that she was not coming.

But the party invites had gone out, food was going bad, and soon, the pressing summer heat would come and the nobility would escape to the countryside. The king had decided the celebration would happen with or without her and, listening to the group closest to me, people wondered if there would be a wedding on the Day of the Dead—the last day of summer and the Talian day for unbreakable vows—with an absent bride, or if another would be found to take her place.

Frowning, I switched my attention back to my target.

In front of the golden chairs stood two black pillars, each one carrying a crown. *Magic glass,* they called it, the smallest amount of it worth at least ten times our debts. My mouth dried while my hands itched in readiness.

I inched to the edge of the light.

Restlessly, my feet moved to the distant music. At Lumi's signal, I would take the smaller female one and run to the back of the garden. There was a three-hundred-year-old oak from which Kirill's mysterious associate had assured him I would be able to use to scale the palace wall. I would have to get there unseen, as after the guard's inevitable alarm, they would lock the gates and search every corner of the palace.

Never put it on, don't get caught, Kirill had instructed before we bathed. Then, our debt would be wiped clean, the sigils on our thighs removed.

My chest wanted to swell with hope, but after last night's failure, part of me waited for the axe to fall. Hope is a fragile thing. Kick it too often, and it will not dare return.

Sweat stuck the silk to my lower back while I waited, my eyes flickering between the crown and the castle.

Someone stepped up next to me, and I slunk further into the shadows. About to make clear again that I was not interested in dancing, I spotted a blinking light in one of the palace windows. *The signal.*

A moment later, the first cries sounded. Soldiers and nobles alike dashed toward the palace, and I prayed to the Goddess no one would be hurt and to the Wishmaker all would leave, while counting my heartbeats. By fifty-two, all seemed gone.

I darted into the light surrounding the thrones. There was no room for hesitation.

My hand closed around the smooth, glass circle as I let my momentum carry me past the podium. Three steps and I would be back in the shadows on the other side.

One.

Two.

The darkness closed around me like a friend, feeding the hope in my chest, before thick arms grabbed me from behind. My elbow snapped back in reflex, and a man cried out.

I sprinted for the tree line, daring a quick look behind before the foliage blocked the view. Flames streamed out of the upper palace windows and my fear reached a new high, imagining Lumi trapped inside. Then I saw the tall, dark shape throwing himself after me, and there was no more time for worries.

As I ran, the garden transformed into the king's private forest, the underbrush creeping over the well-maintained path and trees closing in from above. Only the distant fire lit the sky behind me.

Branches tore at Svetlana's fine dress and my borrowed shoe caught on a root, tearing at the worn lacing, pulling it free. Despite it being Lumi's only pair, I did not dare stop. The stones and needles dug into my bare foot, and the crown burned in my hand. My blood sang in my veins. I could feel the eyes of my pursuer—like an ancient dance of prey and predator.

I rushed through the night, pushing my body and senses. Joy leaped in my chest, the emptiness that had been growing no longer noticeable. Warm night air caressed my skin and the scent of night blossoms filled my nose. Never did I feel more alive than on the brink of falling.

The snap of a branch behind me was all the warning I got before I was slammed into a tree, and a man's firm body forced me into the rough bark, not letting my lungs refill. I twisted to ram my elbow into him again, but this time, he deftly caught it. The oak and escape had to be close, but freedom had never seemed further away.

What will they do to me? Torture, to give up my accomplices, probably. When you torch the palace and steal the sacred crown of the future queen, they do not go easy on you. Not in a place where they could throw you in prison for touching a noble without permission. Given a choice, I would never have taken this job. Given a choice, there were many things I would never have done.

I remembered Lumi's last words and twisted, not to get away, but to reach for the knife. If I did not get the crown to Kirill, he would blame Lumi. Maybe I could cut the guard holding me without hurting him too badly.

A cold, blue globe suddenly lit the woods, and I froze as any chance of escape evaporated. *Magic.* How unfair that those who had everything also got the gift of the gods. It was a small light, barely enough to see the next tree, but you never knew what a mage could do—would he set me on fire with a thought? Read my heart or manipulate matter itself? Each tale told of more incredible powers than the last. One thing they all agreed on: mages played by their own rules, becoming erratic and dangerous as magic twisted their minds.

The pressure on my chest lessened, and I was yanked around. Trapped between his muscular arms, I found myself looking up at a stormy face I had not been able to forget. A face everyone in Tal knew. I was, after all, still clutching the crown of his betrothed.

Crown Prince Dimitri Alexandre Ivanov's remarkable brown and blue eyes widened, as the mage light came close enough to illuminate my face. His painful grip slackened before he withdrew his hands as if burned and stepped back. Though I should not—though it made no sense—I missed his warm hands on my arms.

I could only return his stare, fear freezing me in place. *What was he doing? Could I run?* He had all the advantages, but at least he was not manhandling me anymore. Maybe in the dark, he had not known I was a noblewoman—some nobles had strange ideas of how their women should be treated.

Stall until I can use the blade or see a chance to escape, I decided. *Until then, deny and always stick to the lie. He's seemingly unarmed.*

In the distance, the firelight had died down. Soon, the guards would return to their posts and notice the crown missing. Cold sweat coated my palms, but I refused to let it show.

Instead, I made my body relax, a smile playing on my lips. Like in the theater, you only had to convince yourself to convince others, and I was great at lying to myself.

With the bow my mother taught me as a child, I swept the ruined silk dress and lowered my head, without taking my eyes off the prince. He was, if anything, both more beautiful and sterner up close: the jet-black hair braided away from his face, the wide jaw clenched, and his nose broken at least once. Cheekbones sharp enough to cut if I dared a touch. Lush lips pushed together in judgement. Fast enough to catch me, and strong enough to hold me. The famous eyes, one blue one brown, equally piercing. He stood tall enough to loom over me, though several steps away now.

He looked like the people in Lowtown with nothing left to lose—*dangerous*. Threatening and tricking a noble was a capital crime. Touching a royal... With a raised eyebrow, I ignored all I knew and did what Kirill and Lumi had told me not to do. I improvised.

"You don't really want to marry a foreign princess, do you, my prince? Without the crown, no marriage. It is better for all, no?"

It was a wild guess, but he had not seemed happy to be riding to his own wedding, and instead of celebrating or getting his bride, he had been lurking in the shadows with me.

Even in the artificial light, I could see his cheeks redden and fists clench. Instinctively, I pressed up against the tree again, and inched my hand toward the hidden knife. I could tear it out and thrust it into him in one motion. At close to double my weight, most of it muscle, and in possession of magic, I would have little chance in close combat. Not unless I was willing to go for the kill.

"I don't wish to drag anyone into marriage against her will, but this time neither party has a choice. It was decided before we were five years old."

I hesitated as he held out his hand for the crown. My chance of escape would greatly increase without it. He might even let me go. Better for me and Lumi to remain in debt than dead. Alive, there was always a chance for a better future.

With a sigh, I placed the circlet in his hand. Joined by the glass, a jolt surged through me, pulling at something inside, as if it wanted to eat my very Spirit. The throbbing bruise from when I hit the wall the previous night flared in pain, and my coiled hair must surely have stood on end. As one, we let go, and the crown landed on the ground with a dull clang.

The prince pulled his hand through his hair, loosening the careful braid, and looked at me with inscrutable eyes.

"And that, Princess Helia von Heskin, is why they want us to marry."

I stared at him, his words repeating in my mind without making any more sense than when they left his mouth.

"What?"

He scowled, his face all sharp angles in the cold, magical light. "Don't lie. I don't understand why you would not announce your arrival, but your court painter captured your likeness well enough, Princess. You are even wearing your own colors."

In no fantasy could I have invented this. Pretended this. *Princess*. He was nuts. Bat-bitten. He thought I was his bride.

The prince picked up the crown from the ground and offered me his free arm, his back straight as a spear. My eyes flickered to the dark trees. Maybe he was crazy enough to let me go. Surely, he would not hurt *the princess*.

Quick as any street thief, he grabbed my arm. "I don't want to lock my bride up like a common prisoner, but I will if you force me. We were both raised to this. It's a matter of contracts, if you want to break it, you'll have to negotiate with my father. And good luck to you." He had tried; I could hear it in his hard voice. "Though, stealing your own crown was certainly inventive. Without it, perhaps even he would delay the wedding."

The prince led me back through the forest, and soon, calls could be heard from across the grounds. The guards knew it was gone.

I had failed.

I pressed my eyes closed, praying to the Goddess that Lumi had made it out. We had agreed years ago that if only one returned, the other should run and never look back. Take what little we'd hidden, and forget debts and familial bonds. Truly live for as long as she could until Kirill found her. But I could never have left Lumi behind, so how likely was it that she would feel differently? Maybe she still thought all had gone according to plan. Maybe running would never be an option. *How long until midnight?*

At the edge of the outer lantern light, the prince halted and let the mage light dissipate. His mismatched eyes traveled back and forth between me and the crown, seemingly undecided what to do with either. I faced him silently, refusing to show how sweat gathered on my lower back and how my legs threatened to give way as I waited for his decision on how to proceed.

As he took in the torn dress, tangled hair, and missing shoe, he looked like he wished for a free hand to mess up his braid even further. Or maybe that he had not caught me after all. Guess this was not how he expected to meet his future bride.

"We cannot walk through the ball. They will think I...We..." He shook his head. "What were you thinking? They told me you are a sensible person. Calm. Normal. What else did they lie about?"

Who? I wanted to ask, but the real Helia would know. He did not sound crazy, though. Maybe in the dark, I resembled her, and it was clear that the prince had never met his bride-to-be. Lumi and I both had the pale skin and wild curls of the Oberwaldian mountain people, but in the light, one of the nobles would surely know the princess and expose me. Then it would be torture and death.

I itched to reach for the knife, but he was not threatening me. *Could I cut him any more than I had Lady von Mekeln? Kill the crown prince?*

Something inside me rebelled at the thought of bringing more death to Tal. The finality of an ended life. *There is always another way*, that is what I told Lumi. I just had to make my own *other way*.

I looked up at the prince through my eyelashes, the fake tears coming too easily, and placed my hand softly on his much larger one. His heat soaked into my clammy skin and I remembered the jolt of the crown.

"I just needed to do something. To be given a choice." I bit my lip and wondered if I was overdoing it, but the prince's locked jaw relaxed. "Is there a back door we can use? I came all alone and I cannot bear for them to see me like this for the first time. To believe that we..."

I could not fake a blush, the situation too outlandish, but it was enough. He nodded once, mostly to himself, it seemed, and led on dark paths toward the towering palace.

We moved between gigantic stone structures that made up the Talian center of governance, as well as housing most of the nobility. Overlooking it all stood the square Women's Tower, an ancient, black monolith surrounded by a walled garden. The parts of the palace built in the same black stone as the temple ziggurats ate the torch light and were said to predate most of Tal. The newer parts had been built with lighter stone on top of the old. In Tal, we lived on the bones of what came before. The building Lumi set fire to was only three floors high, and seemed newer than most.

As the prince and I neared the building, I noticed the soot stains climbing over the white facade. Lumi had been told to overturn a few candles and torch the curtains, but the damage seemed extensive; I was not the only one who had improvised. Remembering Lumi's talk of blood and uprising, I prayed to the Goddess no one had been hurt. If we killed a noble, they would tear apart the city searching for the culprits.

The prince's fingers clenched around my hand hard enough to bruise.

"Should we take this out of your dowry, Princess? But that would mean telling my people that their future queen tried to burn down her new home." He gave me a sideways glance, the distant lantern light reflecting in his eyes. "The lengths she would go to avoid marrying me."

"I…"

Empty excuses died on my tongue and shame burned my skin. This man, who seemed no worse than most, thought his future wife did this. I swallowed the feelings. If he learned the truth, maybe he would feel a fool, but if I was still around, he would surely take it out on me. Still, I could offer no answer to his accusation.

I dug my nails into my free palm, letting the pain remind me of Lumi's arguments. Due to him and the nobles, people like me were forced to do anything, give anything, to survive, while he sat on golden chairs and threw balls. I did not agree with her talk of blood and death, but that did not mean I should lose any sleep for hurting the crown prince's feelings.

The silence stretched while we walked, passing the griffon stables with their piercing whistles and the smell of manure, and entered the massive, black stone structure through what must be a servant entrance.

The prince marched us down the corridor and rapped on the first door he saw. As he raised his hand again, the door swung open. A woman the age my grandmother could have been, if I had ever known her, stared down the dark hallway. Standing behind the prince's towering form, I only caught glimpses of her fearful face.

"I need a cloak. The lady lost hers in the chaos outside," he announced, annoyance coloring his words.

A weak excuse, as no one would wear a cloak in Tal's summer heat. The woman shrank back from him, studying me.

"My dear," she said, grabbing my free hand despite our presumed difference in station, and avoided looking at the crown prince. "You can tell me what happened."

I snatched my hand back before either could see the smudged sigil decorating my wrist.

There was a suppressed terror in the woman's brown eyes and wrinkled face, but also determination, and she did not seem upset by my standoffish behavior. Reading people was something you quickly learned on the streets of Lowtown, or you never got any older. This woman would not give up the cloak without trying to help, but why would she think I was not safe with the prince? Midnight was coming ever closer.

I stepped around the frowning prince while hiding my arms in the torn sleeves, and pasted a nervous but open smile—the kind you forced to avoid crying—across my face.

"It was awful. There was a fire, and then guards came running and several pushed me over." I batted my eyes at the prince like a lovesick fool. "Then he saved me. But I cannot leave like this. What if someone sees me and jumps to the wrong conclusions? I'll be ruined. *Please*. I would be forever in your debt."

Her expression softened. She even smiled at the prince before going back inside. He leaned down behind me, close enough for the heat from his body to press against my back, his breath tickling my ear and sending a shiver down my neck when he whispered, "What was that?"

"People need more than a command."

He bent even closer to hear my barely audible words. The hairs on my arms stood up, and, for no sensible reason at all, I wanted to lean into him and soak in his warmth, despite the threat of torture and death hanging over me. It was the closest I had been to a man since the night Lumi was attacked two years ago, and something in the absurd situation held the same exhilaration as leaping from a great height, knowing the ground was coming, but momentarily flying. He could have hurt me in the woods or taken me directly to a cell, but instead, he was doing his best to preserve my reputation—or that of the foreign princess. Instead of the flowers and expensive perfumes I would have expected of a royal, he smelled of leather and iron and something wild.

The woman returned with a brown, homespun cloak, and I guiltily jumped, noticing I had been leaning too close to him.

"It's not much, my lady, but it will cover you."

I thanked her and promised that the prince would reward her for her help as he steered me away. Once we rounded a corner, he let me put on the cloak and pulled up the hood. The glass circlet gleamed in his hand—so close, but so far away.

We continued upward through the mostly-abandoned servant's stairs, and my hope of escape shrank. The few people we encountered bowed to the prince and gave me furtive glances. I could imagine the rumors that would fill the palace by morning, though this might be a common occurrence. He certainly knew the passages well enough, despite only returning to Tal days ago.

After what felt like a thousand steps, I was struggling. The last two days had contained too much adrenaline without enough food or sleep, and I could feel the crash approaching. I needed to get out of here, preferably with the crown, before I collapsed.

The prince stopped before a narrow door and spoke without facing me.

"I cannot fathom going to the lengths you did tonight, but neither of us volunteered for this. You have the money, and we have the soldiers, and"—he gestured between us—"you know. The wedding will benefit everyone." I nodded, assuming the real princess would have understood what he referred to. "Do nothing rash. Tomorrow morning, we will announce your arrival. Where are your luggage and servants?"

Distracted, I blinked up at him, replaying his question in my head, and conjured an image of a princess traveling a great distance. "Oh, I went ahead of them. Should arrive any day. I was too impatient to spend another day carted around in a wood box."

He turned to frown at me, jaw clenched like he swallowed several cutting remarks.

My breath hitched as I noticed his fine lashes and the raven hair slipping free.

In the half-dark, empty hallway, we stood closer than any nobles courting would. For a thief and denizen of Lowtown, this was nothing unusual. He seemed to realize it at the same moment I did, but instead of closing the gap between us, he opened a hidden door into a world of light and color.

Black stone walls with intricate drawings of bones and skulls, and swirling old language I could not read, stood out against the woven, crimson carpets and golden chandeliers. Ebony doors, double my height, rose before me. The prince checked that we were alone, then pulled them open without a look at the opulence, and pushed me into a dark room.

"We are on the royal floor, in the guest wing," he said while closing the doors softly behind us. "Your chambers have been ready since early spring. I cannot post guards outside without alerting anyone that you're here, but there will be several searching the building after what happened earlier. Stay the night, clean yourself up. I'll arrange for a trusted servant to come in the morning and dress you. Then we introduce you, Princess, to the king and court, and hopefully, forget this entire episode."

The enclosed room was stuffy and overheated. The princess might have been expected, but not tonight.

Confident that he could see me no better in the moonlight streaming in through the window than outside, I let the hood slip back. He was all shadows and angles, standing in the middle of the room. For the first time, I noticed his black uniform, only golden embroidery on the collar setting him apart from the soldiers. No wonder I had mistaken him for a guard when he chased me through the woods. At least he was not wearing the sigiled bones Tal's soldiers were famous for. Studying his broad frame, the tension clear even in the low light, I found myself drawn closer.

Another step and only a hand's breadth separated us.

When would I ever meet a prince again? This was so far from my reality that surely, another moment of lapsed judgment would not matter. Years of suppressed longing to be near someone roared awake, as if it had but waited for my permission.

With confusion written across his dark features, he backed up, like he had when he thought he recognized me in the forest, but this time, I grabbed him. I might die tonight. Or be sold into slavery tomorrow if I managed to return to Kirill. I would not waste my last moments of freedom, of feeling completely alive, on wishing for something standing right before me.

"Princess?" he asked, his voice rougher than before.

She would be one lucky woman indeed, but I must be the most confusing bride-to-be. It did not matter. With my fingers against the warm skin on his neck, I pulled his face down until only a breath of air separated us. I had never been able to turn away from danger, no matter what was good for me. There was nothing to lose anymore—tonight, I was already lost.

If I could not steal the crown, I would take a kiss.

The same strong arms that caught me held me in place as he tilted his head. His lips almost touched mine, our bodies as close as they had been in the woods, ragged breaths mixing. Time froze.

For once, I had no desire to run.

Again, the crown clanked to the floor, but neither of us moved. His eyes held a challenge all of me longed to match.

All the pressure of the last days urged me on. I wanted to remove his tailored coat, dig my fingers under the starched shirt hem, and feel warm skin against mine. Wanted to confirm, through touch, that I was alive. His hot breath fanned my lips. My eyes involuntarily closed. But instead of connecting in the kiss I sought, he pulled away, leaving me dazed and grasping the empty air.

"What is this, Princess?"

His low voice made me reach for him again. With hungry eyes still locked on me, he backed away another step.

"Will you say in the morning that I defiled you to break the contract? I'm not a boy to fall for such tricks, no matter what the rumors say, and I would never have expected this of a princess. Much less the woman who is to be my queen."

I blinked at him, my mind struggling to remember that I was pretending to be a princess, trying to prevent her marriage and follow his logic. *Was this how court politics worked?* Ignoring the convoluted situation, my tired mind focused on the sudden rejection, and my cheeks heated in anger.

"I was willing, as I'm sure you noticed, and would have told no one." To my surprise, the words were true. *This*, I would have taken to my death, like a small treasure, an unimaginable night, that was just mine. A moment of being a princess, of having a future, before I ended up in prison or was sold to the highest bidder. I mean, who would have believed me, anyway? It seemed I could not even steal a kiss. "Now, I would like you to leave, as my passion seems to have fled."

Rather, my sense had returned. Lumi would be waiting. Worrying. She could never learn of what had just almost happened.

Echoing my thoughts, the bell outside rang eleven times, dashing my hope for freedom with each clang. I turned to hide my growing desperation, and pointed at the door.

"Leave. Now."

Crown Prince Dimitri, future King of Tal and my captor, spun on his heel and left the room without a final look or argument.

When the door closed, I sank to the floor, and my hand brushed against cold, solid glass. *He left it.* But instead of pride, hot shame made tears burn behind my eyelids. He would think it all an act. The trick he had accused me of. Already the prostitute Stepfather threatened to make me.

I might be too late to secure our freedom, but if I could deliver the crown, it might stay Kirill's hand a while longer.

One day, tomorrow *would* be a better day.

Chapter Four

Dimitri

I stared into the crackling fire, no longer flinching at each snap as the flames ate the wood, no longer hearing Ekatarina's screams. The time away had given me distance. But the dry heat helped me remember why I had agreed to return. Tonight, I needed the reminder.

Above the mantel, the portrait's seemingly angry, green eyes met mine, drawing my mind back to my thieving bride. There was none of the deference I had imagined in the brush strokes yesterday.

The painter had enlarged Helia's eyes, giving her a childlike innocence. Dark curls were tied back in a strict, but probably fashionable, arrangement. The lips seemed thinner, less inviting than those I almost devoured earlier, though that could be my imagination. Nothing hinted at the curves I pressed against before I knew who the thief was. The painting showed the same woman, but they had failed to capture the fire that threatened to burn through my cold facade. If the ice was not the only thing keeping me together, I might have welcomed it.

She was the first woman I had been alone with in three years; the first who had dared step close. Surely, that was the only reason she was getting to me. I did not know her. Should not care, no matter that she looked like a dream and adventure or how forward she was. How she, in the space of two bells, challenged every social rule.

The wind called to the magic in my blood through my ever-open windows. I could not bring myself to listen to its joyous tales as I had in the mountains. That way lay peace, and I could not afford to lose my edge.

The intricate clock, a construction of exposed cogwheels and weights, ticked incessantly, reminding me I was back in civilization, where each minute was measured. Where it carried me closer to a wedding I had avoided for years.

Draining my second glass of wine, I turned the worn, leather shoe I had retrieved from the garden over in my hands. If I had not known better, I would have thought it a working child's. At least the princess had acquired practical footwear for her attempted theft. It was strangely enticing, like under the delicate surface of lace and silk, another creature hid.

I placed the shoe at the bottom of my closet, and for the hundredth time this night, tried to run my hand through my hair. It was a tic I picked up while letting it hang free the last three years. Now, it brought back the feeling of her fingers as she pulled me close. Fool that I was, I wondered where my future wife had gotten the experience that made her so forward, because she did not act the meek maid I had been led to expect. I should have been angry—they had promised a woman ready for marriage and children. A pawn I could use as leverage against my father. Instead, a reluctant smile refused to leave my lips.

It changed nothing. Three years ago, I was banished from Tal, swearing never to return. I was not falling into my father's plans like a dutiful son. Not after what he did. My eyes flickered to the sharp, green eyes staring down at me.

Letting out a long breath, I filled my glass for the third time.

The outer doors swung inward without a knock; few would dare such an entrance. Fortunately, this time, it was not my father or one of his goons.

"I hoped to catch you in a compromising position, Dimi. You have seen my naked ass enough times. Instead, I find you drinking alone," Alexei, my closest and oldest friend, said, theatrically searching for a hidden woman. "After the years you left me with these vipers, the least you can do is share."

He swung his lank frame down next to me and reached for the bottle without an invitation. Not that I would ever object. I might be the crown prince and he the second son of a country noble, but he was the closest thing I would ever have to a brother.

I sighed and drank deep. "Gossip already, then?"

Alexei filled his glass and raised it in mock salute. "The good prince, at his own ball, is seen dragging a serving woman through the palace. Even took her in his future wife's chambers. Considering how you left Tal, it's the story of the year. I know you want to piss off the king, but this seems a bit direct. One could think you've learned nothing."

She did this, I reminded myself. But I would get the blame. Maybe she meant to ruin my reputation, or her own, but even she could not have planned for me to catch her, could she?

"That was my future wife."

Alexei took in my serious face, and the laughter melted away. "You have been meeting with the princess in secret? Is she in on the plans?"

I shook my head and considered how much to tell him. His loyalty was without doubt, and while I had languished in exile, he had joined the Roja—something I was still wrapping my mind around—so he knew how to keep a secret when needed, but still, something guarded my tongue. Embarrassment at my lack of restraint, possibly. I should never have entered her chambers at night. He was right, I should have known better by now. Passion had been my ruin once before. I needed to keep my insides frozen. Play the part until the end. But I owed him something and it would be public news soon enough.

"She arrived tonight, ahead of her entourage due to troubles on the road," I said. "It'll be announced tomorrow, as the party was a disaster."

"Then it starts. Three months until the Day of the Dead and the wedding. Are you sure your father needs this marriage enough to abdicate the throne and his position as Head of your House?"

"The marriage contract is signed by him, and there is something else, something he isn't telling me. It doesn't matter. I will only marry if he steps down, and the first thing I sign after the marriage contract will be his death warrant. I'll wear the crown during the ceremony, the rest are only formalities. Until then, I play the dutiful son who has reconsidered his wayward ways."

The crown of Tal could only sit on one head at a time, passing as a new generation of rulers swore their vows to the city and each other. I would never accept being the crowned prince, still under my father's thumb. I would be king—if only long enough to achieve my own ends. Alexei saw my eyes flicker to the painting on the mantel and approached it, brushing his finger over her cheek. His light touch awoke a possessiveness that should not be there. She might be mine in name, but I would claim nothing more. Desire nothing more.

"But why insist on this specific girl? The marriage will be binding no matter why you enter it. She has barely been seen before, even by her own people. Mortally shy, or disfigured, they say."

I clenched my jaw. This should have been the easy part. She had been trained for this her whole life. "She will do."

Alexei raised an eyebrow in response, and I knew he saw more in my impassive face than I wished to show.

"She indicated she is not as enthusiastic about the marriage as we expected. She might seek to argue the point when she meets the king," I admitted.

"A match made by the gods." He snickered. "You'll have to convince her. If she breaks the contract, you have nothing on your father. His many vices are already known by the court, and I've found no other leverage. Build up her expectations. Charm her and ease her fears of married life. I know it has been a long time, but surely, she can't be that bad."

The feel of her warm body, the challenge in her eyes, replayed in my mind, and I wondered who was getting false expectations. In a matter of bells, she had stained a reputation my father had gone to great lengths to recover, burned down part of the palace, and made me forget myself enough to leave the crown on her sitting room floor. Getting it tomorrow seemed the safer option than entering her bedchamber now. With extra patrols in the royal wing, she was not going anywhere tonight.

The thick, stone walls pressed against me, my magic longing for the great mountains and whisper of the wind. Freedom beckoned just out of reach. I could manage playing the good prince for a summer.

"Enough," I snapped. "We have business before the sun rises. If I'm to clean house, we need the names before I ascend the throne. When I sign the first death warrant, the other rats will disappear. Everyone involved will pay, Alexei, one way or another. That is the only thing that brought me back. The only thing that matters."

Worry flickered across my childhood friend's face—for me or the plan, or maybe what the night held in store.

"Shouldn't you give the curse more time to work?" he asked.

"You told me you have found no signs of my father suffering in the last three years. Time is up. It was a fool's hope that kept me going when I could not act. I'll not rely on unseen magic not even the seers understand fully."

"It might not be obvious from the outside. Curses are fickle. I haven't been able to find Zahkar and the priestess. It could have gotten to them."

I nodded reluctantly. Every mage could speak three curses in their lifetime; though they were often unpredictable and had unexpected side effects, it was generally accepted their power was proportional to the mage's and how close the effect was tied to their affinity. When they forced me on the griffon, flying away from Tal after that fateful night and barely seeing the Spirits shine over Tal, I had gathered the little magic I had and spoken the simple words with as much force as I could, hoping my intentions would shape the magic. *May those who hurt mine, be hurt in kind.*

The power, like a piece of me, had surged toward the disappearing Tal, but I should have known better than to believe someone with as little magic in their blood as me, and a wind whisperer at that, would be able to bring down the king with words alone. Perhaps if I had desired to summon a sudden storm or drought, something would have manifested. Instead, the wind might have ruffled my father's hair or wrapped his coattails around his legs during a public appearance, proving him right. I'd been nothing more than an inconvenience, and foolishly reduced the little power I'd had for nothing.

Magic was not the solution when a blade could do the job.

I finished my glass and, with a last look at the flames to strengthen my resolve, rose. "Someone will know what happened. Time to make them squeal."

Alexei emptied his own wine and squeezed my shoulder in support. He might question this path, but I knew he would stand by me until the end. He had seen what they did. Had known both me and Eki since we were children, and understood like few could.

I would never enjoy torture and bribery, but I was done hiding from what needed to be done. The men who stayed silent would spill the names and locations of everyone involved with their blood, including the Council members who voted to condemn.

My father might have been proud—finally, he'd succeeded in teaching his only child that when it came to ruling Tal, nothing was sacred. No act too dark. But if he found out I did not plan to become the dutiful king after taking the crown, he would find a way to escape our agreement. To lock me up like the murderer I intended to become. He could not be allowed to suspect that my coronation would be the end of our House and line.

Chapter Five

Vanya

After pushing a dresser to block the outer door, I inspected the suite as the minutes ticked away on the mantel clock. The princess had been given four grand rooms: bedchamber, sitting room, servant's room and bathing chamber. The attic Lumi and I shared in Kirill's house could have fit twice over in the bedchamber alone. Everything seemed to have been provided for the princess's comfort—except an easy escape.

Pacing back and forth, I drummed my bruised fingers against the cool crown. Nothing remained of the strange energy it contained when the prince and I touched it together. Instead, its presence settled something in me. It meant success. Freedom.

If I got away, this would all have been worth it. Kirill might well write off most of the balance, even if I was late. Soon, Lumi and I could leave and build a new life. Forget the politics of those above us; forget the death that hounded every footstep and filled the coffers of Tal.

Midnight was approaching too quickly, but there was still a chance to make this right.

In the bedchamber, I pulled the curtains and let the new moon shine in. A floor-to-ceiling mirror reflected the light across the room.

Despite time running out, it drew me in. I had never seen its like, the glass clear as water—*did the princess really look like me?*

My too-pale skin came from leading a nocturnal life, not being shut indoors, the slim figure a result of eating my stepfather's scraps, and my main advantage when slipping in through a narrow window, rather than the result of a corset and overbearing mother. The noble sigil on my wrist was fake and smeared beyond recognition. The charcoal-lined eyes too large, reminding me of the soot often staining my hands. The red lips reminding of blood filling my mouth when too slow to duck Kirill's backhand.

My fingers brushed against the reflection, careful not to damage the pure glass. The crown glinted in my hand, blood from a scratch running down my forearm staining the bright surface. Lana's finest silk dress, such as I could never afford and would not wear again, hugged my curves. Luxurious despite its bedraggled state. *Princess Helia of Oberwalden.* Wealthy beyond measure, life planned out. *Safe.*

Though Kirill had ordered me not to, I raised the gleaming circlet over my head until it caught the moon's glow, illuminating the sigils covering the inside. Strings played in my mind, begging me to move with them. This night had gone wrong since the prince pursued me through the woods, but it had felt so right. So free and wild. I needed one more moment of being *her*, one moment to treasure.

Lowering the crown onto my head, I let it sit on my untamable dark curls atop my pale, drawn face, an impossible silvery halo, and waited.

Nothing changed.

The jolt from earlier did not return, my dress did not transform. I was still me. This was, after all, not a fairy tale.

The countless sigils decorating the inside shone through the glass. Despite having no knowledge of such things, I itched to study it further. The clock chimed once for the half bell, reminding me of my circumstances.

I stepped out on the balcony that ran from sitting room to bedchamber. As usual, the higher your status the higher you slept. If only they had mistaken me for a scullery maid. At least I was not locked in one of the towers. I counted six rows of bright windows below. A floor down, roses climbed a trellis, their sweet smell synonymous with Tal—rich or poor, death and roses were ever present. The descent would hurt, but I had managed worse. Or so I told myself.

The stone on the outer walls was rough, climbable for someone with a death wish. I silently thanked the Goddess that it was me, and not Lumi, who had played the princess. Though, had it been her, she would not have hesitated to stab the prince in the back. I could have killed the sole heir to the Talian throne tonight; instead, I had tried to kiss him. There was more than one reason I would take this tale to my end.

I used strips from my already ruined dress to tie the crown to my waist, then wrapped the rest around my hands and feet for protection. I would soon need it.

With regret, I tossed Lumi's remaining shoe through the nearest door and settled on the balcony railing. The shoe was too stiff to climb in, and I would need every sense to make it down.

The mild wind brushed my bare feet, and my courage wavered. Maybe the front door was better. The prince had said guards patrolled outside, but I might slip by. I could not stay here. The prince would surely see his mistake in daylight—what would he think when he found one worn shoe, and no princess or crown? Nothing good, that was sure. Dead or gone were the only options—and if I was found dead, Lumi might finally run. She had friends I knew nothing about, rebels who might be able to hide her for a while.

Smoke from a thousand chimneys rose from the streets far below, and more stars dotted the sky than I had ever seen through the Spirits' lights. No matter what happened, they would continue to shine. To the large, wide world, my life was meaningless. Luckily, I did not want to change the world, it was bad and always had been. I would settle for not adding to it.

Only Lumi would miss me if I fell, and maybe even she would be better off.

With that uplifting thought and a prayer for the Wishmaker to grant me safe passage, I tucked the cloak into the corset, climbed over the railing, and sought the first foothold. Being light and wiry since childhood, I had often climbed high to get away from our mother's customers; later, I used my skills to break into homes and businesses. *This is no different*, I told myself, then started down. A drop from four floors would kill as surely as the seven below me now.

Too soon, my muscles shook from holding my body in place while seeking the next hold. Each one forced me to stretch precariously, nearly falling, until the roses finally stung my feet. Two floors down, the trembling started in my calves, traveling up my thighs, through my clenched stomach muscles, and into my arms, increasing until I was ready to let go.

I'm never doing this again, I promised my screaming body when the silk wrapped around my hands and feet could no longer protect my skin.

Three floors left.

The thorns clung to me, tangling the cloak and tearing my flesh. I squeezed my eyes shut and clenched my jaw to silence the involuntary whimpers threatening to reveal me to anyone inside the rooms I passed. Each time my foot pressed down on a thorn or my fingers struggled to find the iron trellis beneath the flowers, something inside me cracked a little more and it was harder to will myself to search for the next hold.

Two floors.

Despite a light breeze, sweat coated my body, stinging my eyes as it made its way from my forehead to my chin, dripping into the ridiculous neckline. Despite facing the dark stones and leaves obscuring my vision, pinpricks of color danced before my eyes as I struggled to control my breathing and descent.

Leaning out as far as I dared, I stared at the dark soil below where the floor-length windows illuminated the night.

One floor.

My vision swam. My arms screamed. Blood and sweat mixed, and I knew I could take it no longer. A chosen leap was better than an unintentional fall.

Before I could second-guess myself, I pushed away.

By twisting in the air, I hit the ground shoulder first, rolled to absorb my momentum, and ended up on my back in a flower bed.

The scent of lavender embraced me. Muscles quivered and tears joined the sweat on my cheeks.

I was alive. Impossibly, wondrously *alive*.

Heart racing, breath catching, a laugh bubbled up through the pain. Finally, I had done something fitting for the lorists, and I could never tell.

As if to knock me out of my elation, distant bells rang twelve times, each *clang* saying, *Too late*. It felt like a lifetime since I entered the palace with Lumi, though only four bells had passed. Would returning before they struck one count?

Staggering up, I made my way toward the palace wall. Despite the party ending bells ago, torches lit the guard post next to the closed gate. No one was leaving unnoticed.

In the shadows, I hesitated. Would it be better to search for the oak or talk my way out? What was the chance of making it to the palace forest without being searched? The twinge in my muscles decided for me.

I brushed crushed leaves and petals from the dress. There was little else I could do—torn and bloody, I looked a fright and anyone who saw me would stop me.

A messenger approached the gate, and I watched the guards pat him down and empty his satchel. No way I could walk out with the crown. The outer palace wall was smooth stone and, by the moving lights, patrolled by guards. *Was it the same around the whole perimeter?* Kirill and Lumi were waiting while I stood frozen in indecision. I needed a third option. If I could not take the crown with me, I could at least ensure the royals did not find it either.

Impressive trees grew here as well, their foliage invisible in the dark. *Perfect*. With the crown still securely tied to my waist, I gathered the last of my strength and ran under the lowest branch. With a jump, I caught it and let the momentum swing me upward.

My bruised shoulder screamed, already exhausted muscles quivering as I climbed until I was completely hidden by the summer leaves. There I hung the crown on a branch. The glass seemed ice-cold, the sigils on the inside only slightly warmer. My fingers lingered.

Here it would be safe until the leaves fell. Once the security relaxed, I would return for it. With a nod to myself, I left the comforting shelter.

Safely on the ground, I wrapped the cloak around me and considered what story to tell. What could have happened to a woman who looked like I did. The image came too easily, as it was not that different from how I found Lumi after the attack.

I approached the guards at the gate with my head down and body shrinking in on itself.

When the light hit me, they placed their hands on their swords. These were not the old drunks patrolling Lowtown, or the relaxed easily bribed men and women at the city gate. They were the reason Lumi and I would never have attempted to sneak into the ball without help.

Their bone armor clanked like the Grove when they marched, with helmets shaped into the likeness of skulls hiding their features.

"Show yourself," the taller one said, while the other yanked off my hood.

With a trembling lower lip, I watched them through dark eyelashes and fought the instinct to run. The fear was not faked.

"I need to get home, I'm already late. Please."

My cloak opened to reveal the ruined dress.

"My lady, what happened to you?"

The guard searched the dark, as if my assailant was hiding just outside the circle of light.

"He didn't mean to. Please let me leave. My parents—" I let a sob out, loud and weak. "I should have listened."

The guards faced each other, something passing between them.

"We are on duty, my lady, but I can summon someone to help." His soft voice almost made me believe him. But everyone knew if you told a guard, they would tell the one who hurt you so that he would know who to shut up. Never snitch. I pressed my lips together and shook my head. Not that it mattered in this situation. I could not tell him the Crown Prince of Tal tackled me into a tree, locked me up and, by the way, thought I was his missing bride.

The guard sighed. "We have to search you before you pass."

When I removed the cloak completely, he snapped his teeth together, and the other cursed. Seeing myself in the light, I could not blame them. Shallow wounds covered arms and legs, the fine dress torn to shreds. Lana would kill me even if Kirill did not. The shoulder I landed on was stiff enough that I knew it was turning blue. At least the sleeve covering my smeared noble's sigil remained mostly intact.

"My lady—"

I jutted out my chin. "Can I pass?"

The guard briefly searched me, missing Lumi's still hidden knife.

"Was he trying to skin you? No, don't answer. If you need help... I have three daughters..."

The resignation was thick in his voice. Maybe he knew I would never take him up on his offer, or that if a high noble had done this to me, there was nothing a guard could do. My only answer was to wrap the cloak around me and scurry away. No one stopped me as I left between the black pillars.

On Palace Road, the luminous Spirits, busy merchants, and awestruck pilgrims kept me company. At the first crossing, I turned toward Midtown and ran.

I had made it, survived, and the crown was at least half stolen. *Goddess, let me not be too late. Let Lumi be safe*, I prayed with each slap of my bare feet hitting the cobblestones, the day's heat still trapped below. The Spirits stayed out of my way, and I crossed the floating bridge into Lowtown without feeling their cold touch.

Images of how Lumi might be punished for my presumed failure spun through my mind every time I paused to catch my breath.

Narrow wooden houses, one built on top of the next, replaced stone structures as paved streets turned into mud. Each district in Tal had its own texture and my feet could read them better than any map.

At Kirill's apartment building, the grandest in Lowtown, only a lone light filtered through the shuttered windows. Despite sweat covering me, I shivered. Closed shutters meant violence and secrets.

I tapped the locked door, praying to the Goddess Lumi was alright. The third time I lifted my hand, the door swung open and before I could register what was happening, a hand lifted me up. Barely inside, a thick forearm squeezed against my throat. I clawed and kicked until the scent of vanilla tobacco revealed the assailant's identity.

"I got it," I wheezed out with my last air, my head swimming.

The pressure on my throat lessened, and an oil lamp illuminated the hallway. Grigori, Kirill's enforcer and guard, double my age and missing at least three teeth, grinned before setting me down on the floor. Only my will, and the wall, kept me on my feet.

Kirill approached holding the lamp high. The bright light blinded, but it did not stop me from reaching for Lumi's knife. It was gone.

Grigori waved the narrow blade before my nose and Kirill *tsked*.

"Surely you would not stab your stepfather, girl," he said. "I cannot see my crown."

Easing away from the wall, I kept searching the shadows for Lumi. "I had to stash it inside the palace grounds, but it is hidden."

"Oh, Vanya, do you want your sister to hurt again? Or desire your own matching scar, perhaps?" He waved his hand, and a sudden thump was followed by a scream I knew too well. Her pain burned through my veins before I even saw her.

Huffing and puffing, Svetlana dragged Lumi behind her by the shortened hair. When Lana saw the state of her dress, one of the few things she cared for personally and kept in impeccable condition, she let out a *screech*.

"What have you done, street rat?" She half lifted Lumi in her anger. "Even if Father removes your debt, you will owe me for this."

I ignored her as I sought Lumi's eyes. One was swollen shut, the skin around it turning blue, and her arm unnaturally twisted, dislocated, I hoped. Still, fire burned when her eyes met mine.

She mouthed, *It'll be fine*. But nothing was fine. Our mother had tucked us into bed at night, whispering, *Tomorrow will be a better day*, and until this moment, I had believed it. Something inside cracked, and my last hope escaped. I had let Lumi walk home alone when she got attacked. I had agreed to the additional debt. I could not escape with the crown. Instead, I had almost lost myself in the prince's arms. I should be the one broken on the floor, not Lumi, who would have done what was needed. I should carry the scars of failure.

Kirill's fingers squeezed my jaw and forced my eyes back to him. His scowl was familiar, but there was fear in his narrowed eyes.

"This was a special job, girl. A last chance. You have disappointed me and a very important client. Let's hope the whorehouse pays enough for her to forget this incident."

The last embers of anger flared inside me. "I hid it and can get it back. Watch the guards and Roja. They will be searching."

"The secret police? Murderers and spies. The day I go near them, or onto the palace grounds, the Taliell must be running gold and the Spirits talking."

I should have cried, thrown myself at his feet, or reminded him how useful we could be to him on future jobs. A normal person would have. Instead, I pictured the Roja seeking the crown, the prince seeking his princess, all for naught until the leaves fell. By then, the real princess would have arrived and there, in the middle of the palace courtyard, they would find their missing crown. Laughter edged with desperation escaped my lips.

Everyone watched me, my chortling the only sound, until a cane rapped against the floorboards. The madness inside me stilled as an older woman strode down the hall.

Kirill stepped away with a bow, and she took his place, studying me like one might a bug. I returned the look. The ebony cane and embroidered stiff dress, so long out of fashion that it became a statement, screamed money and power, and something in her gray eyes communicated great age. Despite resting heavily on the cane, she projected mastery over us in a way only those born to unquestionable privilege could.

Another step, and she was close enough to touch me. Kirill and Grigori backed up at the wave of her hand. I tried to follow, but her eyes flashed with blue fire. I froze.

Only a trick of the light. But knew it was more. When the prince summoned a mage light, I had seen magic for the first time in my life. In my bones, I knew this was the second.

Lumi, who had been calm until now, channeled icy terror into me.

The woman's eyes, returning to storm-cloud gray, did not let me look away. Her face, smooth despite her age, seemed strangely familiar. Perhaps she had visited Kirill before, because how else would I have met such a woman?

"She speaks the truth," she said, wrapping her bony, icy fingers around my wrist. "Tell me everything that happened tonight. I'll know if you lie. Then, I'll decide what to do with you and your sister."

So, I did—though I did not mention how well the prince had treated me, skimmed over the almost kiss, and how he came to leave me with the crown.

"When I climbed down, the guards were searching everyone. To get out, I hid it. As soon as it quiets down, I will get it for you."

She pursed her lips, which had twitched once when I described how the prince bowed to me, and otherwise remained a thin line. Her tilted head reminded me of a bird of prey studying its next meal.

"With the cursed crown in my hands before midnight, I could have crafted a copy and returned it before they guessed it had left the palace. Now I have neither crown nor time." Fire gleamed deep in her eyes. "But the Prince noticed the distinct similarity between you and the Princess of Oberwalden. Bring more lamps. I need to inspect the girl closer."

For the first time, I saw my stepfather and Lana hurry to obey someone else. As they lit everything with a wick, I shivered under the woman's locked gaze. *She believed me.* Maybe Lumi and I would be free after all, but instead of hope, icy fear gnawed at my bones.

The woman waved for me to stand on the brightly lit landing before the grand staircase, then circled, her cane *rap-tapping* with each measured step.

Those who show their pain teach others how to hurt them—a truism of the streets I could testify to—so despite how all eyes brushed my injuries and naked flesh, I did not cover myself. Did not acknowledge them. Replaying the orchestra from the ball, I imagined myself dancing to it instead of standing here. I locked eyes with Lumi and smiled with too many teeth, like an animal uncowed.

When, despite the bruising, her lips curved in return, I felt closer to her than I had in months. Separated and beaten, we had each other. Would always have each other, and I would do anything to get her out of here.

This woman wants me for something, hope whispered as it wormed its way back into my heart like the parasite it was. *It isn't over until the Death Goddess rises.*

Lumi nodded, as if she had heard hope's voice as well.

The woman pulled my chin to face her again. Reluctantly, I let go of Lumi's green eyes.

"I had the privilege to meet the princess two years ago, and with a bit more fat, you could be her twin. Who are your parents, girl?"

"Our mother was a courtesan who died in the last plague."

"And your father?"

I hesitated, but her demand for truth made me continue. "A customer. Only her Spirit now knows his name—if he even gave it. Our mother claimed he was noble and would one day come to take us all away."

Thus we bore our mother's name, Komarova, like an eternal mark of shame. Despite Mother marrying Kirill and him taking us in, he had never offered his name. That would have been a mark of approval. Of family.

The woman tapped her fingers against the cane's bone handle. "Dead for five years. It would be hard to trace now, but I would bet that you have relatives in Oberwalden. Few have met the princess, especially in recent years. There are rumors she is sickly, which could explain any difference in looks. Even in daylight, there is a very good chance no one would challenge you." She turned to Kirill with a smile on her pointy face that sent shivers over my back. "The crown wasn't delivered per our agreement. I will take the girls in payment."

Kirill smiled back, regaining his confidence. You did not rise in the Talian underworld by letting chances slip by. "She is my stepdaughter. I cannot possibly part with her or her sister. My daughter would be left all alone."

"You were about to sell her to the whorehouse. You know who I am. Change is coming to Tal, and you would do well to work with instead of against me." She paused. "I'll throw in two silvers."

Kirill gave her a long look. "You are well informed about the cost of whores, Councilwoman von Lemerch, and make a salient point, but I don't get involved in politics. It's bad for the health. Makes the Roja come sniffing around. Besides, the girls owe me."

Von Lemerch. I had heard the name before but could not place it. Still, hope grew, and the music returned. Working for her must be better than our stepfather and the ever-present threat of the whorehouses.

"I require them until midnight on the Day of the Dead. Then I will either be a very good friend to have, in which case the girls go free, or I will have failed, and they return to your guardianship," von Lemerch said. "Keep the debt sigil as security. It is not like they can leave."

Free. The Day of the Dead was only a summer away, a blink of an eye compared to the years spent hustling to barely get by, debts always growing.

Kirill turned to Lana. "Draw up the contract."

She nodded and kept her mouth shut. While Svetlana could be a spoiled terror, she did not let anything get in the way of business.

"Leave me with my new property," von Lemerch said, and again, Kirill and Lana obeyed without a further word, Grigori following on their heels like the dog he was.

When the door to the sitting room silently closed behind them, von Lemerch stood straighter, no longer relying on the cane, and swept her gaze from Lumi to me.

"I own you, but I'm not an unkind mistress and believe the best motivation comes from positive reinforcement. Tell me what you want and, after we are done, you will have it."

I knew what I wanted. What I had always wanted. What we needed no matter what Lumi thought. For once, I was the one in charge.

"You pay the debts for me and my sister. We get passage from Tal and enough gold to start a new life."

Von Lemerch smiled. "Twenty gold, and your names registered with a caravan leaving Tal the morning after the Day of the Dead."

The astronomical sum set off warning bells, but maybe she was wealthy enough that gold were pennies.

"I'll do whatever you need."

"Good girl, we will get along just fine, and if we do not, I will have your sister to ensure obedience. You'll continue to impersonate Helia von Heskin. There are rumors the prince isn't happy about the match. Many did not expect him to return to Tal. You're to ensure that the wedding takes place as planned and no one suspects the crown is fake when you return it. Get close to the prince. The princess's rooms are in the royal wing, this gives you access that few have."

I nodded to each statement, head bobbing up and down, while my stomach tried to escape through my throat. She expected me, a thief from Lowtown, bastard and street rat, to play a princess in front of the entire court. *For three months.* The summer had never seemed so long.

"I'll marry the prince?" I choked out. "What if the real princess arrives?" Marriage contracts were for life, and if performed by a priestess, said to be enforced by sigil magic.

"Don't worry your pretty head. Our only problem is the missing crown, if you were not to play the princess, I would have left them searching until I planted the replica. Instead, you'll have to bring it to me."

Like pretending to be a princess from a land I had never seen would not be hard enough. "What if I tell you what it looks like? I studied it before leaving."

She smiled and her gray eyes swirled, fire consuming the pupil, then the whites until I looked into a blue inferno. She yanked me close with a strength she should not have possessed and placed her mouth on mine. It was more a brush of lips than a kiss, and a coldness similar to touching a Spirit spread from her mouth to mine.

"The Ruling Crown of Glass." Swirling images of the cold glass and strange sigils, the feel of it under my fingers, flashed through my mind. "It'll take longer than anticipated, but I'll make do with your recollections. Don't think of betraying me. My touch is death, and I cursed traitors long ago." She smiled. "Though it doesn't hurt repeating, *May those who wish to divulge my secrets, choke on their words,*" she whispered the last sentence, the barest sliver of air separating us.

The words sank into me, and I heard myself repeating them, felt them imprinting on my Spirit, while shivers racked my body. Von Lemerch let go and my legs finally gave out. Lorists told of curses in hushed voices, telling of the terrifying side effects and price to break them. How they rarely worked as intended. Her words rolled in my mind. The mere wish to talk could now kill.

"What if the prince doesn't believe it when he sees me?" *What if he asked questions I could not answer?*

"With your looks, you should have no problem leading him on until the wedding. After that, he'll no longer matter. No royals will. Dimitri Ivanov will not survive his wedding night."

Cold wrapped around me and a gasp escaped. She spoke of treason and murdering the man who held me in his arms only bells earlier. And I could no longer tell anyone, even if I had wanted to. This was different than Lumi wishing death on the royals. Von Lemerch's voice held stone-hard certainty. She spoke of a tomorrow she knew was coming and now I would be part of bringing it about.

"Why does she get to be the princess?" Lana asked, having snuck back while I was distracted, breaking the tension. "I should be the one living in the palace. Vanya knows nothing about being a lady or talking to a prince."

Von Lemerch, eyes gray again, smiled at her. "I'm so glad to hear you volunteer, because she'll not be going alone."

Chapter Six

Vanya

When Lana understood the role von Lemerch had in mind for her, she marched off to find her father. Von Lemerch followed at a more sedated pace. No one needed to guard us—as long as the debt sigils remained strong and with an opportunity to be truly free, no matter the cost, we were not going anywhere.

I staggered to Lumi and hugged her, her warm skin chasing away the lingering cold from von Lemerch's words. Later, I'd linger on them and my role, on a future further away than the next bell. Never had Lumi and I been separated more than a three-day, now months without my second half loomed before me. Our father left before we were born, our younger brother died before he turned one, our mother before we became women. Lumi was my everything and I wanted to wrap myself around her and never let go.

"Vanya," she whispered, "if anything goes wrong hide in the Bone Temple. The High Priestess will help."

"Why would she—"

"There's no more time. There are things you don't—"

Steps and cane echoed down the hall, like a countdown.

"Nothing will go wrong," I said, "Don't worry about me. I will do my part. We will be free, Lumi."

She pressed closer, so unlike her. "I'm sorry, V."

"I'm the one who failed to get the crown. To stand by your side."

Our stepfamily, followed by von Lemerch, reentered the landing, everyone except Lana smiling.

"I love you. If you think someone guesses who you are, run. Tomorrow *will* be better." Lumi whispered our mother's words before Kirill pulled me into his study by the ruined dress.

He threw me onto the yellow brocade sofa I normally was not allowed to touch and von Lemerch settled next to me.

"Time to transform you into a princess," she said and cleaned my smeared noble's sigil with a prepared cloth. "Dawn approaches, so there's no time to train you, but there is one thing we cannot do without."

With a finger as cold as ice, she traced new lines around my wrist. When she finished, the sigil stretched like a tattoo from the back of my hand to my elbow. It was a magic I had never heard of, a touch I was somehow sure could reach far inside and stain my very Spirit.

The blue and black lines moved in the flickering lamp light with a life of their own.

"Are you really marking *her* permanently as noble?" Lana asked, unable to look away.

Von Lemerch admired her work. "Not noble, royal. This is the family sigil of Oberwalden. It will not activate without a sigil crafter completing it so she is not forced to loyalty and servitude to the royal house, but it should pass any tests that can be done in Tal."

"It can't be removed after the wedding?" I asked.

Von Lemerch met my eyes and I fought not to flinch away. "A small price for freedom, no?"

Mutely, I nodded. Even a fool would not have thought I could get through this ruse without marks, let this be the least of them. No matter how beautiful, I would need to hide it for the rest of my life or find someone to cover it as soon as we were free. *Free.* I focused my whole mind on that small word. The hope inside me grew flapping wings. *Free.*

My fingers brushed over the lines, finding my skin sensitive but not painful. If von Lemerch had not claimed us, a slave sigil, harsh and black, might have marked me inside the three-day. *This is better*, I told myself. At least there was no magic enforcing it.

That von Lemerch was nothing natural did not matter. She had promised freedom, the way out of Tal I had longed for as long as I could remember. But her words returned again and the knowledge that the death of the prince I had almost kissed only bells ago would be the price, that I would lead him to it, left me as cold as von Lemerch's touch.

I don't owe him anything, I thought, trying to convince myself. If he discovered who I was before the wedding, I would be the dead one.

I met Lumi's eyes one last time as von Lemerch led me and Lana away. Dawn was coming and with it, a new, borrowed life.

Von Lemerch took us back to the palace in her carriage. She spoke to the guard at the gate too quietly for me to overhear while Lana refused to meet my eyes.

"Your father has an arrangement. For the next three months you will report everything and go where *the princess* cannot," von Lemerch said to Lana when she returned, and turned to me. "Try to betray me and your sister will pay the price."

We both nodded, scared and exhausted.

"The man outside will show you the way to the royal wing and the princess's chambers. He will say your maid servant arrived in the night."

I hesitated. Until now, someone else had been in charge and there had been clear instructions. Could I truly trick a prince?

"You're not coming?" Lana asked, for once in sync with me.

Von Lemerch pointed outside with her cane, clearly done with us, and I pushed my stuttering stepsister ahead of me. For the first time, I was glad for her presence.

A different guard than the one who had let me out held a smaller side gate open. Without a word, he led us inside.

No one stopped us as we walked through abandoned corridors and stairs, returning to the chambers I had so painstakingly climbed out of only bells ago. We seemed to enter through another door, our guide slipping something into the hands of the final guard, but my tired mind and body was beyond caring.

Inside the chambers, I ignored Lana's complaints. For once, she could not deprive me of food for not listening. Instead, I secured the rooms, then climbed into the enormous feather bed, and fell asleep in sheets finer than any dress I had ever owned.

Exhaustion swept all worries away.

The first sunlight colored the curtains red when a fist pounded on the door of my new chambers. It seemed my stepsister did not appreciate her assigned role.

The pounding came again, like a landlord who found out you had paid in chipped coins. *That could not be Lana.* She might hate pretending to be my maid but would not want to draw undue attention to us.

The last sleep fled. Only the prince knew I was here, and as far as he knew, I still had the crown. I scrambled out of the bed, almost falling on my face.

In the room-sized closet I found a robe to cover the tragic remains of the dress that I had fallen into bed wearing, but without water there was no way to scrub my face. No time anyway, as the prince seemed on the verge of breaking the door down. Avoiding looking in the wall mirror, I hurried into the sitting room.

"Princess! Why is there a dresser blocking the door?"

I had pushed it there last night after we had returned though a door in the servant's chamber I had not known existed, though presumably there so the royals did not have to see their own dirty laundry pass them in the halls. How much easier the previous night could have been if I found it then? Perhaps I could have slipped past the guards after all.

The prince hit the door again, and the dresser groaned. Grunting, I pushed on it before the intricate carvings of griffons cavorting were further damaged. Lana watched from the servant's chamber before turning away. The message was clear, she would not lift a finger to help, but I was sure she would report my every word.

"Princess," a harsh voice called from the other side of the door, snapping me out of my thoughts and back into action. Finally, the dresser now moved, the doors flew open.

The prince strode in like it was his suite instead of mine. He stood taller in daylight, his presence filling the room up to the high ceiling. Last night, playing the princess had seemed infinitely preferable to any other options, but now the permanent sigil stood stark against my pale skin—skin that suddenly felt too tight.

"You seem to have something of mine, Princess. Return it now, and we don't need to speak of it again. I'm protecting you, but the palace is in an uproar."

He had changed into a new stiff uniform and rebraided his black hair, but the dark circles under his eyes made me wonder if he had gone to bed at all. There was a wildness to his features, a barely contained violence.

Cold sweat coated my palms. I retreated behind the green sofa and swallowed my nerves. I was a princess, his bride, and had faced much worse than him—what did a royal know about the challenges of real people? He was not talking to me like this the entire summer, no matter how it ended.

"Invading my chambers when the sun has barely peeked over the horizon, Your Highness? Have you no manners?"

He clenched his fists, and I smiled internally; the need to get under his skin was like an itch I could not keep from scratching despite his hard looks. Part of me had always resented authorities, as most had treated us as lesser—from dancing instructors to calligraphy tutors, and later, our stepfamily. Some part of me needed to test the prince's limits, to know how far I could push before I found a real person.

"You know what I mean. You intentionally distracted me, then lied. Why I even find that surprising after catching you stealing, Princess, I don't know, but I need it back."

I refused to blush. Besides the theft, I had done nothing malicious last night, no matter what he implied.

"Distract you? Surely not, Your Highness."

Breath flaring through his nostrils, like a horse before a race, he stalked around the sofa separating us. I was supposed to get close to him, play the obedient well-bred wife-to-be, but somehow, his judgmental stare and haughty posture made it impossible. Also, there was no way for an obedient wife to not return the crown.

He stopped before me with a sinister twist to his handsome face. "Yes, Princess. You must be well practiced."

This time I did blush.

There was no shame in sharing yourself in love or lust, at least not in Lowtown, but what he implied... Two years ago, shortly after I added to our debt to help Lumi, Kirill had ordered me to find and set meetings with men derelict in repaying their debts. When they arrived at the prearranged spot, his men would beat and rob them—or recoup his losses in flesh and coin, as he put it. Twice, I acquiesced before refusing. I had sworn to not sell my affection like my mother, but what was the difference? I spent sleepless nights turning it over. I had not been paid for what was between my legs, but I had used it. Implied it. As long as I had a choice, I had sworn to myself I would never go down that road again.

Both von Lemerch and the prince assumed I did the same last night. They thought me a whore, and now I was supposed to marry knowing von Lemerch planned to murder my husband. Not even my mother had sunk that low. She lived in her own world, pretending her visitors were lovers bringing gifts, but never had she betrayed them. *I cannot do this.* I struggled to catch my breath, and the world spun. *I promised to be kind and now I'm trapped.* The weight on my chest expanded, squeezing the air out of my lungs. Images of Lumi's beaten face flickered before my eyes.

One moment I was swaying on my feet, the next, the prince carried me to the sofa.

"If this is another act, Princess—" Then the robe slipped to show my blackening shoulder and scratched chest. "By the Spirits, what happened to you?"

The world continued to spin, and my shame grew. *Von Lemerch would approve of you removing your clothing*, a dark voice snickered inside, but as I did the first time I stole, I forced it far, far down. *Lumi*, I reminded myself. Von Lemerch will kill the prince either way. He was supposed to marry a stranger who had not even bothered to show up. I was just a stage piece, useful, but replaceable. I would ruin and sell myself to not give von Lemerch a reason to hurt Lumi. Something inside shriveled up. Maybe if I had done what Kirill wanted from the start, we would already have been free.

The world stopped spinning.

I scooched away from the prince and forced a light smile, raising an eyebrow. I could do this. I had dreamt of becoming a dancer, standing on the Royal Theater stage, but this would be my only and greatest role.

"A brute pushed me into a tree."

He blinked. "I did this? You need a healer."

He seemed truly appalled. While there were women in the Guard and most other professions, noblewomen were different. They lived separate, barely seen lives. *Protected baby makers*, Lumi had called them behind our mother's back. The prince had probably never seen a scratch on a lady's perfect skin.

I tried to shrug and instead winced in pain. "I collided with a few trees before you caught me. It's worse than it looks. If you summon someone, they'll have questions."

"Let them have questions then. I'm not letting my bride walk around in pain to save face. I'll make sure it is someone I trust, but, Princess, I need the crown."

The tired honesty in his voice tried to worm its way into my treacherous heart. He did not want me to be in pain, despite what he assumed about me. Maybe he truly was not as bad as most nobles. Did he desire this marriage despite how he sounded last night? Von Lemerch would be pleased but it fed my own guilt until it was a choking ball in my throat. This would have been much easier if he was evil.

I rose and strolled to the windows. Despite my still racing pulse, I needed to distance myself before I blurted out the truth. At that thought, von Lemerch's curse wrapped around my already clogged throat, as if waiting to clench it shut. Only when I had recited each word silently, did it stop.

"It's not here anymore." The cold magic closed around my throat, as if testing each word. "I gave it away but can bring it back. You wouldn't want to cause a scene on the day your bride arrives. Give me time and we can start over. It was a mistake..."

I did not specify what the mistake had been, but the suffocating feeling subsided until only a tingling remained to warn me to think before I spoke.

The prince's mismatched eyes darkened, but beyond tearing the rooms apart or arresting me, there was little he could do. *For now.*

"Two days, then I must tell the king. I'll volunteer to lead the investigation and keep the Roja away. After that I'll bring them here myself."

At my nod, he pulled a string hidden behind a wall panel. A moment later a servant knocked on the outer door and the prince summoned a healer from the hospital and food.

Taking advantage of his distraction, I murmured an apology, and closed myself in the bedchamber. I sank down on the floor and leaned against the door. Von Lemerch must understand that if she expected me to trick the man in the other room into marriage, she would have to provide the fake crown in a hurry.

Surveying the room for anything that could betray my identity, my gaze snagged on the single, worn shoe by the still open balcony door.

A soft tapping sounded behind me, the opposite of the prince's previous abrupt invasion. Again, not what I would expect of Lana.

"Yes?" I answered as I pulled myself up from the floor, tossing Lumi's shoe as far as I could into the closet and summoning a carefully blank face.

A willowy female servant in a gray and blue starched coat buttoned up to her neck slipped inside and sank into a deep bow despite the pile of dresses in her arms.

"Your Highness, the Crown Prince informed me you had trouble on the road and arrived in secret ahead of your luggage. I brought dresses I hope will please you."

Her voice was barely above a whisper. No one had ever spoken to me with such deference; it made my skin crawl. I had spent the last years serving Kirill and Svetlana, swearing if I was ever in their position, I would be better. But I could not afford to be myself. So, instead of telling her to stand straight and call me by name, I put on the face I wore when playing the queen on stage—time to become the princess of Oberwalden.

"Show me and prepare a bath. Indeed, I had trouble on the road and will need to contend with whatever you have until my dresses make an appearance. Leave them and my maid will sort it later."

Lumi would hate it if she saw me like this.

The girl jumped and, without meeting my eyes, held up one dress after the other. With a dissatisfied scoff similar to Lana's, I dismissed each one while inwardly longing to run my fingers over the starched linens, minute embroidery, and silk that flowed like water. Colors—mostly pale blues, greens, and yellows—were popular, as were deep necklines, tight corsets with polished metal clasps, chopped-off coats, and skirts with more fabric than even my mother had been able to afford. From the six shown, only one would cover my shoulder blade and arms, which, in addition to last night's scrapes and scratches, showed a scar from a knife wound last fall.

"The blue painted silk will do." And, thank the Wishmaker, the exposed corset snaps also sat in the front, enabling me to dress myself. The accompanying coat barely deserved the name, not even reaching my waist, and instead of closing in the front, the sides were attached with delicate golden chains. The floor-length skirt with enough silk to ruffle was ivory with a painted navy pattern that reminded me of sigils and the face paint of the steppe tribes. Though she had never let me inspect it, I was sure Lana's closet held nothing half as fine.

The servant nodded and whispered she would provide a better selection for the evening. I wanted to shake my head—more than one dress a day, an unheard-of luxury in Lowtown unless you counted changing into dark clothes for a night of crime.

In the private bathing chamber, the woman reached for my robe, and I realized what was to come. I should have thought further ahead. The rich could not even clean their own asses.

"I wish to wash myself. Leave."

She stared at me. "But His Majesty is waiting. I'll help you."

He, I might have let wash me. But he was indeed waiting so I had better get back outside. There was no time for discussions.

"Please ensure that His Majesty has everything he requires and let him know I will be out shortly. Leave the clothes on the bed."

Seeing she was unsure how to proceed, I gently pushed her out of the room, then closed the door in her face. No way she was seeing my fresh bruises and old scars; what gossip that would make. Or it could ruin the ruse before midday, because surely, nobles had healers available for any scrape before it left a permanent mark. Better she believed me eccentric, or with an odd deformity.

When the bedchamber door clicked shut, I threw off the robe, ignored my injuries, and peeled the ruined dress off. In its intact state it would have been hard to remove on my own, but half of the clasps in the back had snapped during the night.

Naked, I stuffed it into one of the decorative vases in the back of the room. Later, I would have to get rid of it but for now, it would have to do.

Like in the public bath halls, the pool was sunk into the floor and covered in mosaics. There, the similarities stopped. In the public ones you only got clean water if you arrived before sunrise, the mosaics were simple checkered blue and white, and many of the tiles were cracked. And it was full of children playing, women gossiping, and the elderly playing games while avoiding the summer heat. Here, my private pool large enough for five beckoned with clean water brought for only me to enjoy.

I submerged myself in the welcoming heat and let it infuse my aching muscles. Never had I felt anything better. If this is what it meant to play princess, I would not mind the coming months, for I would just remain in the bath. If I did not have the prince waiting, I would have stayed until it grew cold.

Dirt and blood drifted off me, the fine cuts from the thorns stung before settling. On the rim, stood a block of soap and intricately shaped colored glass bottles. I let my nose guide me, memories long thought forgotten of my mother washing me with the gifts she received from customers surfacing. Lavender, mint, and roses. Happier, innocent times.

I allowed myself to slip under the surface one last time before leaving the grimy water. It was probably the dirtiest a lady had ever left it—no way to disguise that because for the life of me I could not figure out how to let the water out.

There was another knock on the outer door, and I dried myself as best I could before donning the robe and opening it an inch. A young woman even shorter than me, in a tailored red healer's coat with its tails reaching her knees to cover a matching dress, stood on the other side. Her curls were arranged into like a cloud around her head, perhaps to disguise her lack of height. Her straight teeth shone against her dark skin when she smiled at me and pushed inside, closing the door behind her.

"The prince summoned me. You can trust me, Princess von Heskin. He said you had trouble on the road and need healing. We are so glad that you finally arrived." Her words ran out like water, emphasized by smiles and moving hands. As she bounced in place, everything from her hips to the tips of her hair swayed. It was impossible to not smile in return. She must have been older than she seemed to be a fully trained healer.

"Thank you for coming so quickly," I said, fighting against the awe instilled in me since birth. Healers were revered. In a city that lived off death, they alone brought life.

"I'm Mariska. I'm still in training, but physical injuries are not a problem. Please let me see you. I'm also Dimi's cousin."

"Dimi?"

"Dimitri, of course." She herded me to the bed and pushed down my robe. I let her, only losing my smile as she gasped at my shoulder. "What did they do to you, Princess von Heskin?"

As she brushed her fingers over the injury, vibrations spread through my shoulder.

"Call me Helia. I fell from my horse and hit the ground with my shoulder, it seemed preferable to my head," I said, unsure what the prince had told her, but assuming that despite her being his cousin, he wanted the theft of the crown to remain secret. He had, after all, told me I have two days to return it.

The vibrations increased to a deep tingling, strange but not unpleasant, as her magic sought out other injuries. Mariska was much stronger than the healer Kirill had employed, and the pain seeped out of me. She was the kind of healer Lumi and I had begged the hospital to send when our mother became sick with the plague, her coughs sounding through the walls as she begged us to stay away and prayed to the Goddess to protect us. Watching one child die had been enough. Mariska was the kind of healer that could have saved her if we had had the coins. The buzzing under my skin was the feeling of true wealth in Tal.

An image of Lumi with the bruises from last night marring her face flashed before my eyes. How I already missed her. It had not been a day, and I already obsessed over what could be happening to her.

Mariska wiped sweat from her brow and stuffed her trembling hands into her pockets.

"All better, Princess von Heskin—Helia. I won't say anything, you hid the pain well... if you want to talk, or need me again, send word to the hospital." She smiled the brilliant smile again. "I hope you will like Tal, and Dimi, despite the unfortunate start." She hesitated, biting her lower lip. "Give him time... he is still not back to his old self, but I'm sure he is trying."

Maybe he had told her more than I thought. I rose, my body lighter than it had been in months.

"I'll keep that in mind. Thank you."

She nodded and showed herself out while I dressed and pinned my still wet hair into a bun, piercing it with the golden sticks laid out on the dresser. Leaving, I avoided the mirror and the lie I had created—the image of the lady my mother had dreamed I would become.

Instead, I silently repeated the words I had been telling myself in the carriage this morning and imagined myself dancing on a stage. The crowd would be watching, waiting for a misstep as I leapt through the air. Fortunately, I never fell.

I would play a princess with the confidence of a thief, deceive the people around me, and deliver what von Lemerch needed.

I had wished for a chance at freedom. And my stepsister ordered to play my lady's maid already proved wishes came true.

Chapter Seven

Dimitri

I wanted to pace, to drum my fingers, though the anger I entered the princess's chambers with had mostly dissipated. A prince did not apologize, but I should not have raised my voice, not when I needed her to agree to the marriage. For the second time in less than a day, I let my feelings control me in her presence. The thought left a sour taste in my mouth. It needed to stop.

My father's summons, emblazoned with the royal sigil, had waited for me when I returned to my rooms before dawn, exhausted to the bone. At least the court scribe had spilled two names with his blood—councilors who left the chamber with my father on the night everything changed—before we ensured with threats and gold he would never return to Tal. Mar Heridan and Savva Novikov, both long friends of my father, were not surprises, but I would not have executed them without proof. My father would have needed at least two more votes out of the Council's eight to legally condemn us—only when neither side reached majority did the king decide. When I had their names, as well as the priestess and the guard, who I once would have called a friend, I would be ready to take the throne.

In a fresh uniform and with rebraided hair, but without a moment to rest, I had obeyed my father's orders. That was what you did when the king and your Head of House called upon you. At least, I successfully hid my personal feelings before him, and the revelation of the princess's arrival distracted from the missing crown and where I had been all night.

Surely, he knew I left the palace, for my father had known just when to summon me to keep me off-kilter, and in my sleep deprived state, I had said too much. At least I had not mentioned her involvement in the theft, or her reluctance to marry. He would want to see her before noon, and by then, I needed her to stand behind the engagement.

Two servants, including the maid Alexei had sent with dresses, waited by the door, ready to act at my slightest indication, though none dared to look my way. They feared me like they would my father. No doubt they had heard how I flogged a valet at fourteen for tearing my coat. The story left out that it had been in my father's chambers. That he handed me the riding crop. That he quietly ordered me to swing it, and even a crown prince must obey the Head of his House. Perhaps especially a crown prince. It had built on the reputation my father wanted me to have. Not that I could fully blame the noble's sigil on my arm and the magic behind it—the past three years without distractions had provided ample time for introspection. I had wanted my father's approval. Wanted to prove myself outside the Women's Tower.

Next to the Talian servants stood a sullen light-haired woman with the Oberwaldian bronze sash around her shoulder—had she come with the princess? How had she entered the rooms and I heard nothing of it? Somehow, the princess had managed to secret away one of our most recognizable relics and smuggle in whole a person. I had questioned the guards in the royal wing personally before coming here. Each one swore no one had left the princess's rooms last night, but where had the new maid come from? Either they had grown incompetent in my absence, or they were keeping secrets on behalf of my bride. Could she already have a guard in her pocket? The famed Oberwaldian riches could be enough to twist allegiances.

Again, I wanted to pace, to move and fidget as I could not.

With only a quick greeting, Mariska had disappeared into the bedchamber, and her bright voice could be heard through the door. The sound was a familiar balm to my nerves. How I had missed my little cousin while away. She had risen to senior healer assistant in my absence, and I trusted her implicitly, no matter what else had changed in her life in the last three years. Hopefully, the princess felt the same as Mariska's quick hands removed bruises I could not believe I caused. They had stained her pale Oberwaldian skin like spilled ink.

I opened my notebook only to stare at the blank page with tired eyes, then study the room. The princess had the crown and gave it to her accomplice. Why would she do that when she knew I knew?

I could not believe a word out of the woman's mouth, still, when we were alone... She argued with me like a person, not someone to be feared or used. Completely inappropriate, and enough to make me forget my grief and thaw the ice.

The bedchamber door opened, and I was halfway to my feet when it closed behind Mariska, not the princess. It was a pleasure to see my favorite bubbly cousin—I only had two, and she was far preferable to her brother—but she would excuse me for not standing in her presence.

Mariska threw herself on the sofa next to me, and patted my knee like only family would. "She is all good, Dimi. Seems nice."

I tried returning her grin, but it, like the rest of me, was a shadow of who I had once been. "I'm sorry I haven't come to see you."

Her shoulder leaned against mine, and I imagined wrapping her in a hug, like I had when we were younger, but while I had been banished to languish and grieve, she had turned into a woman, so I held back. It would take time until we returned to how it had been, if we ever could after what happened and what I planned to do.

She did not seem to notice my hesitation. "Do you know where Alexei is? I wanted to visit while I'm in the palace."

I shrugged. "Sleeping, most likely. It was a long night."

When we were younger, she'd had a crush on my charming best friend. After three years away, I had no idea how their relationship had developed, but it was hard to imagine the carefree healer entertaining the Roja I had spent the night with.

"Have you seen *her* since you returned?"

I stiffened and discreetly watched the servants. The last thing I needed was more gossip. I owed Eki more than I could ever repay, certainly more than to pull her name through the mud. Satisfied no one was could enough to overhear, still I lowered my voice before answering, "I tried the first night. She refused."

"She wasn't the same *after*—still isn't. Talk to her when she is ready, Dimi." Silence stretched between us, and my dark mood returned together with shame at momentarily forgetting the debts I carried while alone with the princess.

Mariska squeezed my shoulder again before leaving. At the door, she threw the servants an uncharacteristic cautious look, then met my eyes.

"The princess seems good. Be nice to her," she said with sorrow in her voice. "Be better."

And again, I was alone with the servants, the empty page, and too many thoughts.

Maybe Alexei had told Mariska more than he should have. The princess was a means to an end. I would be nice because it was needed, after that, she would be on her own—based on last night, she would be glad to see me go.

The bedchamber doors opened again, and I retreated behind the princely mask I had perfected during bells of court, where a raised eyebrow could cause rumor. It was time to behave like the prince I had been born to be, not the broken mess I had become.

With an extravagant court bow, I offered the princess my hand while studying her in daylight for the first time without the distraction of rage and injury.

The midnight-blue painted dress with the elaborate jacket was better suited for winter, and none of the other ladies would have worn such a thing at the start of summer. Though I could not object to how the silk wrapped around her, showing the curves on her lithe frame I knew would haunt my dreams. Still-wet hair escaped the rushed bun, water-heavy curls framing her face. They should dismiss the Oberwaldian court painter, for he had captured none of this woman's spirit. There was a wildness in her eyes, a creature who did not belong in silk and jewels, who made me remember how I left her last night. How easy it would have been to close the distance between us.

I turned away, smoothing the emotions from my face, and led her to the prepared breakfast in the corner. After asking the lost gods to bless the food, I sipped my tea. Maybe the powerful mint brew could sharpen my sluggish mind and distract me from the lips I had almost kissed. She smiled as if she knew my thoughts, and I imagined the table between us a shield because this was a battle.

The princess ate with delicate, economical movements, a bird picking at crumbs, rather than the wild cat I had imagined, and I relaxed. Maybe we could put our previous encounter behind us.

"Majesty, you have my most sincere apologies for inconveniencing you last night. Hopefully, I can repay your kindness soon," she said, eyes downcast. "After the long arduous travel, I was too enthused at seeing a friendly face."

Enthused? My tea passed the wrong way, reducing me to an unseemly coughing mess. *Was she referring to stealing the crown, or what came after? Was that how she greeted each friendly face?*

I already dreaded and dreamt of any kindness returned by her, though these were the most ladylike words she had said so far, and that was saying something.

"Majesty, is there anything I can do?" she asked and handed me a cloth napkin, the picture of meekness and soft nobility, while I regained my breath and composure.

"When you asked to start over, I had not imagined it would be with a different person."

"I'm sure I do not know what you mean."

I wiped the tears from the corners of hard eyes, giving her a look that had made grown men shake. She did not even blink. Well, if she could pretend nothing out of the ordinary had happened, so could I.

"In private you may call me Dimitri, we are after all to be married," I said with what I hoped was a charming smile.

She blushed, and somehow that threw me even more. I had clearly underestimated her or dreamt last night—maybe that creature was a figment of my imagination. My eyes flitted to the servants, who avoided my gaze, as was proper. To them she seemed normal. There was nothing normal about this woman. Though the Oberwaldian maid stared at the princess in what I could only call affront. Which side of herself would the princess show to my father? The thought returned the ice to my blood. Based on her actions last night, she did not understand how far he would go to ensure the marriage took place.

She picked up a grape with callused fingertips, the only sign of the fighter inside.

"Then you may call me Helia." Her forest-green eyes met mine with none of the discomfort most displayed at their mismatched color. Though maybe she had studied my portrait long enough to become desensitized.

With a nod, I returned to the food, knowing I would not use her given name. It felt too intimate, like an acceptance of a future we would never have.

I had never been great at polite chitchat, and the years in the mountain fortress seemed to have robbed me of the little skill I had. Compared to the freedom when we were alone last night and this morning, the silence felt unnatural, like in the dark we had been our true selves and now we acted the roles we had been born into.

The silence and stolen glances also sent my mind back to what I had been avoiding since I left this room in the night, to what she had proposed before I threw it in her face. With cause, I had to remind myself, as she had been angling for the crown all along. Why else would she share herself with a man she ran from? The thought pricked my pride in a way that had little to do with any larger plans.

In that moment, I had wanted her—let myself want her—despite who she was, as I had not with anyone besides Eki. *How could I feel passion knowing what it had resulted in?* And worse, entertained the thought of acting on it since I first saw her in the flickering mage light, her unapologetically defiant eyes meeting mine? Despite her much smaller size, I had known I was in for a fight.

"What do you enjoy, Dimitri?" she asked, effortlessly breaking the silence like it had not been a wall between us, and licked the crumbs off her lips in a most unladylike way.

I blinked. "Enjoy?"

"What do you do when you have spare time?" She made the question sound genuine.

Raising my hand to pull it through my hair, I caught myself and clenched it. A shadow of a smile danced over her lips.

"What most nobles enjoy, Princess. Reading, riding—" *and the arms of a friendly woman*, that is how you would complete that sentence in a drink hall or camp. The classic male pursuits the lorists called it in the tales, which usually ended with the man learning a lesson or two. It was a joke, and a sentence that should never be uttered in front of a lady. "—and swordplay," I spurted out, blaming my lack of sleep on how my mind had wandered while she spoke. I could feel the lady maid's disapproval, her eyes cutting onto my back. Her duties included protecting the princess's virtue. I did not envy her the job.

The princess's eyes were locked on mine, her face unreadable. There was no way a properly raised lady would know the saying, especially not a foreigner.

"Maybe someday I could come and watch your...swordplay."

I choked for the second time. Her voice was shy, her eyes downcast, the words in themselves innocent. *But...* Again, I looked at the servants, and saw the smile the lady maid tried to hide. The princess might be oblivious, but the maid certainly knew.

"I do not think it would interest you," I grunted out.

"But if I am to be your wife, surely watching you engage in your passions would help me know you better."

The wish to push, to know if she knew what she was saying, buzzed through me. I felt more awake than I had in years. A smile tugged at my lips. My heart rate picked up.

Instead of engaging, I turned to my tea.

She had a way of making me forget myself, which I could not afford. This was the closest we would get before the crown was on her head and the vows said. Even then I would not take it further. Our engagement was the reason for the death and destruction my father ordered when he learned of my relationship with Eki. If Oberwalden had broken it when I asked, I would have been free to marry and there would have been nothing the king could have done about it. The woman before me might not know it, but she and her family carried part of the guilt. And no matter how engaging, she was far from trustworthy.

Abruptly standing, I smoothed my uniform. *Running away. Again,* part of me whispered.

"Despite your journey, we cannot delay introducing you to the king any longer. Anything after the tenth bell could cause offense, Princess."

She followed my lead without argument, despite her teacup still half full and my sudden interruption of our meal breaking at least three social rules. Perhaps this really was a new start.

A moment later, we were walking through the corridors, the Oberwaldian maid trailing behind, supposedly to ensure we did not hide away alone. I would have denied ever needing a chaperone but after last night, I offered no objection.

As we passed from the guest rooms into the royal hall in the opposite wing, I leaned closer to whisper in the princess's ear, inhaling lavender and her, and spoke as much to her as to myself, "Tell the king nothing of the crown. Instead of breaking off the engagement as you hope, he'll lock you in a cell until the ceremony, or send you back to Oberwalden in pieces."

How well did I know that mercy was not something my father was capable of? I needed her to go along with this. Needed the proper princess, not the version that heated my blood and melted my ice.

I studied the expressions flickering over her face, unable to guess her intentions. There was no fear, but a wariness I could recognize in myself. Her smile was hard when she placed her hand on my arm.

"Of course, I wish to marry you, Dimitri. That is why I'm here, after all."

The false sweetness of her words, compared to the honest passion last night, sent a shiver of unease down my back.

With a prayer for the Death Goddess to stay away until I needed her, I stopped before the royal chamber doors and waited for the guards to announce us.

Chapter Eight

Vanya

I could not tear my eyes from the bone soldier guarding the king's double doors. He was one of the elite, rarely seen in the city, but stories told of the terror they unleashed on the enemies of Tal when they descended upon their griffons. A gold mask in the shape of a human skull covered his face, and bones of the great predators living in the high mountains decorated the breastplate. What abilities would such a man have? Under his watchful eyes, I could not appreciate the black floor polished to a mirror sheen, nor the golden great doors depicting scenes of worship.

My heart beat like a Rivertown drum, and I could feel my stepsister's piercing stare between my shoulder blades, her constant presence a reminder I did not belong. It did not help that the prince's face had darkened as we approached the king's chambers. Presently, he looked like Lumi when Kirill tallied our outstanding debt. Even had I not been ordered by von Lemerch to play the proper princess, his words would have scared me enough to not disappoint the king.

The doors swung outward, and the guard saluted the prince before stepping aside. With my arm resting on the prince's, I entered a room more ostentatious than I could have imagined—like a lorist's dragon hoard, glimmering and glittering. Maybe a discount on a gold mine came with the marriage contract. It would explain why the king was so set on marrying his only child to the princess of a small, mountain nation.

Even against the backdrop of velvet walls, gold furniture, and emerald mantel, Ivan Gregorious III, King of Tal, drew my eye. He sat at a breakfast table not dissimilar to the one his son and I had just left, an older man with the same hard face as the prince, and even wider shoulders despite the gray in his braided hair. A silver-embroidered silken sapphire robe hung open to show his hairy barrel chest. As he studied me from top to toe, he made no effort to cover himself.

The similarly underdressed woman next to him slowly removed her hand from his thigh, and I could feel the prince tense beside me, his arm rock-hard under my hand. Considering that the woman appeared my age, with painted, plump lips and loose, red hair, long enough to touch the seat of her chair, she was clearly someone other than the queen. Perhaps someone paid, like my mother, or a noble lover rewarded in other ways. Nothing in the scene before me spoke of the love matches the Talian nobles claimed publicly.

She raised a mocking eyebrow at the prince, who turned toward his father and bowed, ignoring her. I followed his lead as I had no idea how a foreign princess greeted a king, especially when he was to become her father-in-law. Only halfway down did I realize the low-cut corset did not accommodate bows. For the second time this morning, I blushed and quickly straightened.

"Father, may I introduce Princess Helia von Heskin of Oberwalden. She arrived during the night," the prince said, his firm arm somehow reassuring.

"And luckily missed that fiasco of an engagement party." The king narrowed his eyes, a permanent scowl marring his stern face. "Better late than never, I suppose. A royal wedding should silence the rabble who questions us. We had all started to worry you ran off with a lover, making us all look like fools, despite the many letters from your mother assuring me Oberwalden is as committed to the marriage as Tal."

I faced the floor, outraged on behalf of a princess I had never met that her future father-in-law would speak thus in front of staff and his son. Though the prince, who was convinced his bride wanted out of the engagement, might believe the same. Clearly, Helia's mother had no objections to selling her daughter into a family she had never met.

This time, my cheeks blushed with anger, which the king must have mistaken for shame as he continued. "At least you came to your senses in time for the Day of the Dead." He turned to the prince, seemingly done with me. "Have you found the crown yet? When you deigned to arrive this morning, you assured me you have a lead."

My hand, still on the prince's arm, grew clammy. *What would happen if he exposed me here?*

"The situation has not changed in the last bells, Father. Two days, and you will have it," the crown prince answered, his tone relaxed, despite the tension that seemed a living thing, worming its way from his arm into me.

"Remember, the world holds a king to his word."

"And you have my word."

The king grunted and resumed eating dates from the dry east and flaking pastry that watered my mouth after trying to appear the well-raised princess at my earlier breakfast. Crust and red jam stuck to the corner of the king's mouth and the woman bent over his lap to lick it away.

Dimitri steered me out of the room without another word. Apparently, we had been dismissed.

I had not imagined myself marrying, but if I did, it would have been for love and belonging. This family could never have been the family I secretly wished for. The king spoke with his son with nearly as much derision as my stepfather did with me.

The prince had been correct the previous night; he and Helia's marriage was for country, duty, and gold. The princess was probably lucky she was marrying someone her own age. And handsome, I had to give him that.

As the door silently closed behind us, my breathing eased. The summer heat returned and there was a renewed urgency to get a message to von Lemerch. Two days and I had to return the crown, and when I did, I needed her not to punish Lumi for it.

The prince's tight grip force-marched me down the hall. Only the clitter-clatter of Lana's shoes followed us. We passed no windows, even the light was reserved for the king's expansive chambers on the other side of the wall. When far enough away to not be overheard, Dimitri swung around and aimed the death glare I had felt him suppress around his father at Svetlana.

"I don't know where you came from, but you're dismissed. Unfortunately, the princess and I have things to discuss, and I've learned better than expecting loyalty from strangers."

"I serve the princess and go wherever she goes. I have a job and intend to do it." Lana stared daggers back, less concerned with status than I had assumed she would be. It seemed looks could not cause my stepsister to cower.

Despite the pleasure of seeing them stare off, not being reported on sounded perfect. "You heard the prince. I'm sure he can find someone to summon you if I have need."

I had to bite my lips not to smile. Her posture as she stalked away said I would regret this later, but I could not bring myself to care.

When we were alone, the prince's features relaxed slightly.

"She does not like you much, does she?"

I snorted as we rounded the first bend, out of the sight of the bone guards, and ran straight into a man. The prince stumbled and let go of me with a startled curse.

The stranger was tall enough to tower over the prince but leaner, his previously broken nose hawkish, skin like warm copper marking him as Vsadnik—one of the people of the steppes—with a roguish grin that only widened as he looked me up and down. He'd caught the prince's arm and somehow, simultaneously bowed in my direction.

"Went that well, I take it?" His smile widened further at the prince's frown. "I'm Alexei, childhood friend of our dear Dimi, and I have already heard so much about you."

"Greetings, friend of a friend." *Had he heard about the crown? The almost-kissing? Something about the real Helia that I should know? Smile, nod, and get through it, Vanya.*

"The Talian words already roll off your tongue. You'll do fine." Alexei offered me his arm, as I cursed myself inwardly for revealing too much.

"I was returning the princess to her chambers," the prince said. "It's for her own safety until we have caught the thief from last night."

He gave me a sidelong glance, seeming to say, *Give me the crown, and you'll be let out.*

Ignoring him, I placed my hand on Alexei's arm. "Actually, I would like to stretch my legs and get to know my future people." And fill in any gaps in my knowledge as quickly as possible.

Alexei grinned. "I came to share news with our prince, but you will soon be queen. Dimi, you wouldn't want her to feel like a prisoner." He winked at the prince. "It is important to make her happy in her new home."

The prince stepped close to me, ignoring his friend, and I could only focus on the storm clouds gathered in his mismatched eyes. Unspoken words flickered between us as the silence stretched, until finally, a slow nod broke the tension.

"Fine. You'll be meeting the court tonight, Princess, and you'll need all the preparation you can get. You wouldn't want to do anything *ill-considered.*"

Last night, before we entered the princess's chambers, he said, *Do nothing stupid.* It was strangely similar to what Lumi always told me. If I moved an inch, our lips could touch. *Would I feel as alive as last night?* Would his icy mask break? Just being close was clearly ill-considered.

Maybe he read something in my eyes, because he flinched back and shifted his gaze to his friend. "News, you said."

With no further word, Dimitri led the way to the next, only slightly less elaborate but unguarded door, and unlocked it with a key hanging on a chain around his neck.

Like a servant, he held it open for us. I entered on Alexei's arm.

If asked how the Crown Prince of Tal lived, I would have guessed his chambers similar to the king's—gold and the finest of everything.

Instead, a sparse but still somehow cluttered sitting room split by a giant sofa facing a fireplace greeted my curious eyes. Two armors hanging on delicate, metal frames reflected the light—a leather one for flying and a heavy metal-plated one for horse riding. They were not the ceremonial ones worn when nobles rode through town, but practical and brutal. More mismatched pieces of armor, sketches of mountains, and endless maps covered most of the onyx walls, as if he'd rather imagine himself anywhere else. A row of red- and orange-stained floor-to-ceiling windows stood open to a wide balcony and unblemished sky. When closed, the room would be a perpetual sunset.

The prince settled stiffly in a high-backed chair at a round table covered in books, loose papers, and unfinished maps weighed down by rocks, paperweights, and gold trinkets, while Alexei pulled out the opposite chair for me, then leaned against the wall.

Sure Helia von Heskin would have been interested in her future husband's rooms, I allowed myself to unhurriedly examine the papers. Military studies were mixed with horse breeding and royal history. Ignoring them, I reached for a beautiful map drawn in sure strokes. It spoke of a world beyond Tal. Rivers and mountains. Cities and seas. I brushed my fingers over the edge of the map where a tiny creature flew. How I wished to leave all behind and discover if there truly were dragons beyond the edge of the map. Somewhere there must be more than death and struggle.

"That's the Jorian Sea, supposedly blue like sapphire."

Startled, I looked up, and found the prince studying the map from across the table with the same wistfulness as me. *How could the voice of someone so different, with all the resources in the world, contain a longing so similar to mine?*

I touched the unfinished edge, hinting at undiscovered wonders, and asked, "Did you draw this?"

He cleared his throat and turned to Alexei with a frown, as if I had found something too true and he wanted to move on before I discovered more.

"What news do you have?" he asked his friend, all business again.

"I reached out as you requested, and found the guard still in Tal, but Dimi, the city..." Despite his circumspect speech, ice filled me when Alexei paused as if gathering himself. There was dread in his previously cheerful tone. "Instead of food only refugees arrive from the outlying farmsteads and pilgrims tell of robbers on the holy roads. Only the quiet words of the priestesses keep them calm. Tal is filling with the disgruntled and desperate, and with no one to gather the fall harvest, it'll get worse. If you could talk to your father—"

"You know how well he listens to me. And what do you want me to do? The royal coffers are not endless, and without trade there are no taxes, and the steppes belong to no one. The clans would not welcome our interference out there." The prince paced; his face cold again. "But you found him, that's all that matters."

I stared at him. *How could I have thought we had anything in common?* "He says that Tal will starve and it does not matter?"

The prince gave me a blank look. "The poor always starve. They should have stayed on their farms. Those who work hard will succeed by next year. They should have planned better."

Fury simmered through me. Even while I dismissed Lumi's desire to bring down our rulers, and wished I could run from it all, I never believed those who could make a difference simply did not care.

"And how did you plan? Why are the royal coffers not enough? Why have you not been with the army ensuring peace instead of hiding in the mountains?"

The crown prince's enraged face and Alexei's waving hands brought me back to my situation, but how could I even pretend to care as little as him? If this is what it meant to be a princess, I was already a lost cause—pretending to want to marry such a callous man would be challenging enough.

"Hiding? Is that what they say in Oberwalden, Princess? Surely, they told you my enforced isolation in the mountains was due to your mother refusing to abandon this sham of a marriage. That, on what would have been my wedding day to the woman I love, my father arrived with soldiers. Separated and punished us. All so I could be free to marry you and uphold a marriage contract made before I was old enough to read. I might not know what is happening in my own city, but what do you expect when I've been isolated and forced quiet to save face? Who are you, but a traded bride, a commodity to be placed in the Women's Tower after the Night of the Dead, to speak of plans and change? You, who cannot even act like a princess."

The loud, angry words filled the high-ceilinged chamber as I struggled to understand. The stories told of the prince in the city said that he had gone away to perfect his magic and learn from ancient texts. None had mentioned a wedding or tragic love story.

I realized I was also standing, facing him across the table, breathing hard like I was already running away. Tears of anger and helplessness gathered in my eyes. Too much had changed too fast, and I was trapped with people I barely knew. Not that I could let either of these men see that.

"They are still your people," I said, hoping the plain truth could build a bridge between us.

"And soon they'll be yours, and yet neither of us has the power to change the world. I'll rule a city built on death, and death does not change."

"I'm sorry I'm not the princess nor the woman you expected. It's not like I chose this either. But lacking the ability to act, doesn't mean you shouldn't care. People with much less power than you try every day." Each word burned of truth as it exited my mouth. At once, I was Lumi and Helia and Vanya, then the confidence fled and tears overflowed.

I spun and rushed unseeing from his chambers and through the palace halls to escape the prince and royal expectations. At each staircase, I got closer to the outside world and freedom.

Give me a way out of this. Show me an escape, I prayed to the Wishmaker and the forgotten lesser gods decorating the ancient black palace walls. No one answered, for true to the prince's words, the gods of Tal brought only death.

Chapter Nine

Vanya

When I stepped out through the great palace doors, servants, workers, and nobles streamed past. Lost among them, I could finally draw a full breath. The princess's arrival had yet to be announced. No one here knew or cared about me—I was just another noble or merchant girl, too irrelevant for them to recognize. Tonight, the safety of anonymity would be ripped away as I was introduced to the court.

The courtyard appeared different in daylight; message boys and girls in the plain gray and blue of the Talian royals, and ladies with delicate sunshades, guards in black and bones on patrol, merchants with meetings in the palace complex, and civil servants whose business I could only guess at, rushed in all directions. The clang of the smithy rang from the far side, and in the middle stood a row of ancient trees, offering shade and peace in the bustling crowd—grown here before we were all born and would remain unchanged when our Spirits drifted through Tal, noble and servant equal in death. The greenery calmed my breath. I did not mind feeling small, returning to a life where my actions impacted only me and Lumi would be a blessing.

Strolling from tree to tree, I arrived under the one carrying the crown. An iron bench previously hidden by the dark sat in the shade as if waiting for me. Here, no one gave me a second look. The grand fountain before the palace sounded the same as smaller ones in Midtown. With closed eyes, I could imagine myself back in the Tal I knew.

Today, I snapped at the crown prince, speaking my mind when I was not even supposed to be me. I almost kissed a man who did not care about those he was to rule. I was set to marry a doomed man who loved another. Every word out of my mouth was a lie. *Why had I thought I could do this?*

Yesterday, I had risked everything, but I had known the stakes, been familiar with the risks of a life as a thief. I did not belong here. Even the stable boys walked with a confidence I could not even pretend. I longed to pull my feet up under me. To run and jump and laugh. To hear Lumi's voice. Her absence was like a hole in the world. I had been mistaken when I thought life under Kirill's thumb was empty.

I clutched the silk dress, then let it run through my fingers. Not since I was a child had I felt something so fine. Even then, Mother had only been able to afford small swatches for collars and hems. She had called us her princesses, insisted we were nobles, and no matter how the other children mocked us for how she earned her money, we held our heads high. That was before we understood our mother lived in her own world. Despite having a fine apartment in Midtown, schooling, and dance classes, we were the illegitimate daughters of a whore. Shortly before she died, her men started looking at me and Lumi differently, whispering, *Like mother, like daughter*.

And here I was, living my mother's pretense. Flirting and fighting with a man who was most certainly not mine.

"So you're the one set to marry our Dimi."

A woman drawled the prince's name like a lover, tasting each syllable. I jumped, shocked to have been so lost in thought that I had let someone sneak up on me and settle on the other side of the bench.

She gave me a once-over not dissimilar to how Lana viewed me after a particularly dirty job. "Oh, don't look so surprised. You have been introduced to the king, and I am *very close* to the royal family."

She seemed noble perfection next to my surely puffy eyes and disarrayed clothes—tall and slim enough to make an excellent climber, with midnight hair and golden skin shining against a pale silver dress without a covering or coat—but I knew malice well enough to read it in her eyes. Despite her smile, this woman was not happy to see me.

"And you are?" I asked, unable to formulate anything more princess-like.

Her smile widened to predatory proportions. "Ekatarina Kuznetsova, childhood friend of Dimitri. He might have mentioned me."

"We haven't talked much."

She smirked. "That's to be expected in an arranged marriage. What would you two even have to talk about?" If she was upset at my curt tone, she hid it well behind her obvious derision. Turning toward the central fountain, she continued. "Herebov and Ealhswip, the original rulers who made Tal into a nation instead of a remote temple complex. It's said that even in death they would not let each other go; the first love match."

The summer heat invaded my every breath as I took in the onyx stone woman staring out over the city below us, and a marble man embracing her from behind. He held a spear in one hand, ready but not threatening, while she gripped a skull. Ealhswip had been the last divine ruler of Tal, first among the priestesses, our tutor had said. When Herebov came from the steppes, they had fallen madly in love, and she had taken his tradition and married. So Tal became a monarchy and when Ealhswip died, Herebov and his heirs continued to rule. Some still argued three hundred years later that the Talian royals had no right to the throne and had damned Tal for they were the children of Herebov's second marriage to Yelena, but I was not sure life under a temple dedicated to death would have been any better.

Ekatarina leaned in closer, as if bringing me into her confidences. "Many question the king in secret," she said. "Why would he break such a long tradition of honoring love? What do you think, *Princess*?"

Helia von Heskin might know. Any princess would have a clear answer, straight back and commanding voice, but I was no princess. I shrugged, and Ekatarina seemed to grow taller while I shrank. She knew the prince belonged with someone like her, and if I let them introduce me to the court, everyone would know. It was a miracle that no one had called me out so far. The confidence from when I was alone with the prince this morning became as solid as a Spirit.

"Are you sure you should be here?" She could have meant the bench in the courtyard, but she made it sound like more.

"I need to..." I started, unable to finish the sentence. *I needed to get away from here. This is not me. After how I spoke to the prince, he must already doubt me.*

"Have you seen the Women's Tower yet, Princess? Solovyova doesn't let just anyone in. I, like all women of good standing, grew up there. Now I'm trusted with the Goddess's night garden. Do you even know what is required to be a lady of Tal?"

I jumped to my feet. While the boys I grew up with had often been oblivious to my standing, the merchant's daughters had always known I was a fraud. No one needed to tell them. This woman had the same look. The same certainty. *She knew.*

"I'm meeting someone" was all I managed before I fled into the sun, past the fountain, and through the open palace gate. Ekatarina's laugh haunted my every step. There stood no searching guards this time, no one to offer a reassuring word no matter how meaningless, or stop me leaving the palace grounds. With each step into freedom, I felt more trapped, knowing I would have to return.

Outside, Tal spread out below—the Talliel and Palace Road divided the neighborhoods, grand houses on my right, Midtown becoming Rivertown and then Lowtown on my left, too far away to make out individuals in the moving masses. This is what we looked like to those on top of the hill. Ants drawing their straw to the stack. *Interchangeable. Irrelevant.*

I was needed down there. Needed to find Lumi and run before my anonymity was completely lost. Someone must have seen where she was brought last night. I could sell the dress I was wearing, and maybe if I could take the rest of the princess's clothes with me, it would cover our debt to Kirill.

I climbed the public walkway that lined the palace wall. The height made my blood flow faster, transforming anxiety into exhilaration. More of the lower quarters unfolded before me. Familiar squares and bridges in miniature. At my back, workers repainted damaged sigils on the outer wall under the supervision of a green-coated Sigil Guild member. The man mumbled mundane curses at the gods for allowing anyone to damage the ancient lines. On the side, I saw the crudely drawn bloody stick figure. Only the palace could boast of sigils strong enough to keep out the Spirits. It seemed someone had taken offence at the nobility distancing themselves from the very meaning of Tal.

This time, I saw the other woman approach as if summoned by my thoughts, though I had hardly dared to consider her. My muscles tensed each time her cane hit the stones. I had wondered how a princess arranged a meeting with a councilwoman. It seemed, the councilwoman found her.

Von Lemerch stopped closer than comfortable, but I did not dare to move. There was nothing unnatural about her today, still the hairs on my arms and neck stood up, and my mind screamed to run before it was too late. But it already was.

"I should have expected you to fail to follow the simplest of instructions," she said after ensuring no one was close enough to overhear. "Princesses do not walk about on their own. They do not give their hosts any reason to question their provenance."

"I just needed a moment. There is no way they'll believe me. Please—"

Von Lemerch continued as if I had not spoken. "If I let this slide, how will you take anything I say seriously? I just left your sister, now I'll have to return. How should I punish a first offense? Remove a hand, perhaps."

The blood drained from my face and new excuses to cover my intentions spun through my mind. "The prince asked after the crown.

He knows I took it, and if I do not return it in two days, he will expose me to the king."

She scoffed. "Do you take me for stupid, girl? I am older than I look, have seen more than you can imagine, and you want me to believe that you left the palace because of the crown?"

"I'll do anything." I should have known better than to rush out in daylight and think no one was watching. She could not hurt Lumi for my lack of strength.

"Lucky for you, I received urgent news and was coming to find that stepsister of yours to deliver something to you. I didn't imagine she would lose you the first day." Von Lemerch pulled out a letter from a pocket hidden in her skirts and surreptitiously handed it over. "I'll know if you opened it, so don't even think about it. The king received a letter this morning with the same stamp. He cannot be allowed to open it. Exchange it for this one. You should have time tonight as they are read to him before he breaks his fast each day."

How could I get to the king's correspondence, and in a day? "But—"

"Prove that you can be useful—that you are a better thief than princess—or your sister pays the price for your insubordination. Perhaps if she lacked an ear, you'd listen better next time."

I swallowed the protests running through my mind. She was right. I was a thief, and though Lumi usually planned our heists, I could do this. I had been inside the king's chambers today. I knew the way. The sun was still high in the sky, giving me the rest of the day to find a solution.

I nodded and hid the hand holding the letter in the folds of my dress, careful not to wrinkle it. "You'll leave Lumi alone?"

"For now." Von Lemerch's inscrutable face remained stern, but her stance relaxed fractionally. "Behave like a princess, and everyone will see one, girl. Leave the palace grounds, and they'll ask questions better left alone. Someone is always watching."

I did not know if she meant herself or someone from the court, and did not dare ask.

"What about the crown?" I said instead.

"A duplicate will arrive with your luggage."

She strode away before I could ask when that would be. At least it gave me something to tell the prince.

Leaning against the low gray stone parapet, watching the workers paint white sigils, I wished I was one of them. Poor but purposeful. Truthful. Then I turned around, straightened my back, and returned to the palace, feeling a thousand hidden eyes watching my every step.

Tonight, I would be a princess for the prince, and a thief for von Lemerch. For me, I needed to remember that I was Vanya, a person with her own dreams and thoughts. That if I stopped making rash decisions, I could find a way out of this. I was not living in the dream world of my mother, but waiting for the right time to strike.

Passing the embracing statue of Herebov and Ealhswip, their colors reflecting the palace behind them, I wondered if they had experienced the true love Ekatarina had spoken of. Because if such a thing existed, I had yet to see it.

Chapter Ten

Vanya

I swept through the front door, past Lana's complaints, and into my bathing chamber. She pounded on the door, demanding to know what had happened.

"Ask von Lemerch," I called back. "She watched me herself."

Svetlana grumbled something about how I could not even behave one day as instructed but left me in peace.

Without Kirill to enforce her threats, my stepsister's ire was the least of my concerns.

Despite being only midday, sweat had stuck the silk to me. I threw it off and entered the bath. Through trial and error, I got the water running, and when high enough, dove under the surface. Pressure and weightlessness combined like an embrace. Today, I argued with the prince, almost fainted, was healed, met the king, argued with the prince again, escaped outside, was questioned by a noblewoman, and then von Lemerch's threats. And the sun was still high in the sky. Was this how each day would be?

The warm water relaxed my muscles as I floated to the surface and let my problems momentarily go with a long exhale. Time moved, and I thought of nothing more than washing my hair. If I was to be the princess before the entire court, I would at least be clean.

The mosaics covering the walls, floor, and bath painted pictures of winged creatures—griffons most likely—flying on the bottom. One edge ended in snow-topped mountains, the opposite sea blue, and the left forest green. The seemingly endless steppes around the city were done in gold. I sat with every place within my reach. Until now, the city of Tal had been my entire world, but how I longed to seek the horizon. The mechanical wonders of Ceeto and Sorach in the south, the endless harbor of Mjors where each sail displayed one's family colors and sigil, creating a kaleidoscopic forest, or even the mines of Denyev and glaciers of Oberwalden.

In the bath, I dreamt I could visit them all, dance on their stages, and learn the local songs. Reinvent myself each day if I so chose. Be as free as the wind.

When I could not delay it any longer, I dried and dressed in the robe from this morning and settled cross-legged on the bed to think. Last night's theft had been a mess, the same could not happen tonight when exchanging the king's letter. For von Lemerch to risk exposing me the day after she made me play the princess, it had to be important. What would I learn if I read it? My fingers itched, but she said she would know if it had been opened. *This is my chance to prove my dedication*, I reminded myself. *Lumi's limbs are on the line.*

My fingers beat out the cane's rhythm instead. Music and movement had always helped me focus. While Lumi had dreaded the dance lessons due to the other girls' whispers, I had lived for them because when the melodies started, the world fell away. After Mother died and Kirill became our stepfather and guardian, the lessons ended but deep inside me the music never stopped.

Alone in my chamber, I mentally added fiddles and flutes as the beat moved from my fingers to my tapping feet, then swayed my whole body. I would never been a strategist like my sister. I lived for the now, but within the dance, something resembling a plan came together.

With a little help from Svetlana, some improvisation, and a lot of luck, it might even work.

I dismissed Svetlana at the entrance to the great hall. There would be enough going on without her looking over my shoulder. She opened her mouth to protest, but channeling my nerves into an imperious expression, I stared her down. I needed to remember that when we were not alone, I was a princess and the future queen—in public, she could not challenge me.

She muttered, "I've better things to do anyway than stand at your side. You wouldn't see an opportunity if it struck you in the face."

Without waiting for me to respond, she spun and walked away. "Don't forget the preparations we talked about," I called after her and she raised a hand in a dismissive wave. At least she did not want to draw von Lemerch's ire any more than I.

Men and women in evening finery drifted through the colossal, gilded doors before me. This was a place for giants in glittering gowns, chandeliers and mirrors illuminating the black stone cave inside, and I had never felt more of a peasant, despite my blue and silver dress, decorated with black corset clasps and chains hanging around my bare shoulders like epaulettes, the fake, Oberwaldian sigil exposed on my arm for all to see. Kohl lined my eyes and powder glittered on my skin. Lana had insisted I could not hide behind cloth despite the scars. A princess would own it all as she presented herself to her new family and country without courtiers of her own.

With each step, I channeled my dancing teacher Sky, lengthening my neck and floating in time with the string instruments. Despite the well-attended engagement ball the previous night, nobles filled the cavernous room.

I did my best not to stare at the onyx stone arches reflecting the lamp light. The further in I went, the closer to the royals I came and the more ostentatious the dresses became. Diamonds and gold fought to catch the light while embroidered gowns and shirts barely covered chests. Pastels mixed with metallics. The only exceptions were the military lords in black and sometimes bones.

On one side, delicately wrought glass doors opened into the gardens, dark with the absence of Spirits. On the other side, long tables stretched from the back wall to the raised dais, the heavy stone resembling an ancient altar rather than a high table. There the king sat, next to a woman—older and smaller than the one who licked his lips at breakfast. She must be Inessa Yustina, the Queen of Tal. Then came the prince and five others, all viewing the gathered nobles like unmoving gods facing their supplicants. One stranger was the most beautiful man I had ever seen, though he bore familial resemblance to the prince and Mariska. With his tousled locks, half smirk, regal nose, and artfully rumpled shirt, I recognized him based on rumor alone—Nikolai Alexandre Radanov, the prince's infamous womanizing cousin, who set the fashion for the whole city. Tailors paid handsomely to hear of what he wore at any event, while decrying the expensive fabric and complicated cuts. I could earn a pretty penny by just following him around, selling tales and titbits.

I tore my eyes from Nikolai as his half-lidded gaze swung my way. The focus of one Talian prince was dangerous enough.

As if drawn by the thought, the crown prince's eyes met mine across the expanse. Instead of court dress, he still wore his uniform, a reminder of the enforced isolation in the remote fortress perhaps. I could not imagine resenting days, never mind years, spent as I pleased without struggle or worry no matter the reason I was sent there. From how he spoke this morning, he could clearly not imagine the opposite. But there had been genuine pain and frustration painted across his features instead of the stiff smile he now wore. It reminded me that this was a show.

As I passed between the tables, the whispers grew until some words spread like fire. *The Princess. Oberwalden. Wedding.*

When I arrived at the raised high table, the king stood and silence fell. In contrast to his son's utilitarian clothing, his vermilion coat with heavy, golden clasps and silk pants seemed only suited for pleasure. At least it was an improvement to his underdressed state this morning.

The prince descended and stiffly offered me his arm before guiding me to the empty chair next him. When we were seated, the king finally spoke.

"Welcome to the much-anticipated Helia von Heskin, First Princess of Oberwalden, who arrived early this morning. At her wedding to my son, Dimitri Alexandre Ivanov, on the Day of the Dead, our ancestors will bless their union and she will join our House and belong to Tal. May the Goddess turn away and their days be long." This close, his exaggerated smile held an edge of darkness. "As was once tradition, following the wedding, my son will replace me as Head of the House of Herebov." He raised his glass. The red wine shone like blood. "For Tal," he called.

"For all," the crowd boomed, then drank before offering further blessings.

Like I imagined a shy foreign bride might do, I kept my eyes down, only to notice the prince's clenched fists. Despite his calm smile, he wanted to be here even less than I. *Was he thinking of the woman he really wanted to marry?*

When the king returned to his seat, a servant rushed forward to fill my delicate green glass with spiced honey wine. More cheers and speeches from various nobles followed, each one a version of asking the gods to bless the marriage. I nodded and smiled, raised my glass, and pretended to drink. This was not the place or night for intoxication. I surreptitiously swept the hall twice, but there was no sign of von Lemerch in the celebratory crowd. Would a councilwoman not be expected to attend? Alexei, a few tables down, caught my searching eyes and winked. He did not seem to hold any hard feelings despite me fleeing their company earlier, never mind what else Dimitri might have told him about me.

As one elaborate dish was replaced by the next, I cautiously picked at each, dreaming of sizzling meat straight from the fire and hoping to not be sick from the strange flavors and sheer amount. If you could afford not to, you did not eat anything in Lowtown where you could not identify what went into it. It seemed the rich went out of their way to disguise the food by shaping it into flowers and coloring it with foreign spices.

A middle-aged woman in a stiff bronze dress and graying black hair stood and raised her glass with an overly bright smile in my direction, and I paused to nod politely in return. Seated only a table away, I assumed her to be high nobility, but nothing prepared me for the prince's first words of the night.

"I assume you ran directly to your aunt this morning to argue against the marriage again. Is she the one holding the crown? If I had known she was in the palace instead of her outlying estate, I would have had her rooms searched."

"My aunt?" I bit my tongue. "I also didn't know she was here." At least that was the truth.

The woman still spoke, praising Tal and our union for bringing Oberwalden and the von Heskin family closer to the City of the Dead. She must know I was as fake as a beggar's limp. Still, she smiled. Sweat pearled on my neck. Panic closed in. *Someone is always watching*, von Lemerch had said. Was Helia's aunt in on the ruse or planning to confront me where it did not embarrass her House?

"Well, there is no point," Dimitri continued, unaware of my hidden panic. "Even if she agrees with you, Flora von Heskin might think she holds sway because she married a Talian lord, but she is an outsider. My father would listen to her even less than you."

The woman settled to polite applause and this time, I drained my glass. Before it left my hand, a servant had refilled it. I allowed myself another sip. Inebriation was a risk but so were nerves and currently, my hands shook and my throat was dryer than a stoneworker's in the Talian summer.

Setting the glass down too hard, wine spilled over the rim, staining my blue silk dress purple.

"Breathe and smile." Under the table, the prince's hand settled over mine, his voice calming despite his previously harsh tone. "We're supposed to be the happy couple. Before these jackals, in this moment, our cause is the same."

I was saved from answering by a man in uniform staggering onto a table in the back and raising his glass, spilling more than me in the process.

"Love so sweet, hand holding is a treat, but what does our king do about the peasants clambering to get inside. He goes to his chambers to hide! Death rises and"—soldiers rushed forward to pull the man down, but he jumped to the next table—"whispers of ancient hate. The Spirits turn irate. She—"

They caught him, one clamping his hand over the man's mouth. Muted laughter was the only sound in the previously cheerful hall as the king stood.

Most stared at the madman, but I could not take my eyes off the king, certain that the man I had met this morning, the man who had sent his only child into exile for daring to love the wrong woman, would command murder on the spot. When he finally spoke, his clipped tone was the only difference from how he had introduced me to the court.

"He's lost. You know where to take him."

The soldiers dragged the struggling man outside, the nobles lowering their gazes as they passed. The prince squeezed my shaking hand. The tension of the room seemed to invade me. In Kirill's office it would have led to bloodshed, and anxiety tensed my muscles, not yet ready to accept everyone would return to their drinks.

But I could not react like the cowering stepdaughter with nowhere else to go in the world. Here, I was a princess. The king settled, the music resumed, and glasses emptied. Slowly, happy chatter filled the hall again.

I forced each finger to relax and pulled my hand free of the prince's, instantly missing the warm steadiness of his touch. Any human contact could be interpreted as supportive. I had to remember how precarious my situation was. If the prince found out who I was, I would be the one carried away.

A servant appeared with the next course, and I let myself be distracted. She placed a soup bowl on a plate I hoped was not gold and a silver spoon polished to a mirror shine beside it. If von Lemerch did not hold Lumi's safety over my head, I could rob the kitchen and live out my life in luxury.

As we ate, the prince ignored me. I was happy to follow his lead. Too soon, the dishes were whisked away, and my thoughts returned to what might happen to the raving man while we dined. My stomach cramped around the too rich food.

"How will he be punished?"

Dimitri twisted toward me. "Punished? Only his carers will be. They should have stopped him before he got onto the table, but we don't punish the affected in Tal. He served and through his sacrifice, he saved others. There are already too few mages." Quiet storms gathered in his eyes. "In Oberwalden you would have him hurt? How is his affliction any fault of his own?"

The confusion must have been written all over my face. *Afflicted? What would being a mage have to do with disrupting the dinner and insulting the king?* The prince waited impatiently for my answer. Somehow, I had offended him, his court, and made Oberwalden look bad with one innocent question.

"It didn't seem appropriate," I finally said, choosing the most innocuous phrasing. If there was anything I had learned from growing up with rich, merchant daughters and minor nobles, then a stepfather who held most of the debts in Tal, it was that something inappropriate was always happening.

"Honoring war heroes is always appropriate. As a mage, you know the risks."

I nodded mutely and was saved by the next dish. Eating the succulent pork without tasting it, I turned his words over in my mind. Helia von Heskin had magic, clearly that was what he had implied. Nobles hid their magic, and the lorists told of great reveals in battle where they saved the day. Whatever powers Helia had, I hoped no one would question not seeing them in use. *Could she control the weather? Fire? Move things with her mind alone? How can I fake that?*

The prince sighed. "Will all our conversations end in arguments, Princess? You are a conundrum, changing as often as the fall winds. Caring and lecturing, then judgmental and ignorant."

It's because I don't know what I'm doing. "You seem to assume my every question an attack. I meant no offence." Each word truthful.

I took another bite and refused to watch his reaction to my words. Our quiet conversation felt strangely private. We sat so close his scent of leather and something strange and wild, so at odds with his perfect, princely attire and attitude, wrapped around me. I longed to lean closer and breathe deeply, as if by scent alone I could learn his secrets. He smelt of a world I did not know. Maybe that is why another truth slipped out. "I wish I had the freedom of the wind. To go wherever it would take me."

He nodded heavily. "Others might believe royals have freedom, but we're more controlled than any others. They think only of their daily supper, while we carry the fate of the kingdom."

I looked up, eyes narrowing. He sat a full head taller than me, his back straight as a spear and face imperial. I did not care. "And how many commoners have you talked to, to know of their worries?"

"Many of the soldiers are commoners," he said dismissively.

I should not argue again; should bite my tongue. Lumi's cold mind would have made for a much better princess. "And they tell you of their private lives? You know the worry of your child starving? The hospital rejecting your family due to lack of funds? I might not welcome this marriage, but I would not compare it to the worries of commoners, my prince."

He locked his jaws, and his eyes betrayed turmoil not visible on the rest of his cold face. Anger boiled my blood, returning his words from earlier in the day. *Who was he to talk about people like me while dining on golden plates? Had I forgiven his callous attitude because he held my hand in comfort?*

"And you, Princess, how many commoners do you know?"

"Enough." My smile was as sharp as any blade. "The one I love best in all the world is a commoner. Maybe you should meet more of your own. Then you would care what is happening beyond your palace walls."

He stared at me, and I could almost see the thoughts spinning behind the deepened frown. We faced each other, closer than seemly, but from the outside, we probably looked the loving couple, our words still too quiet to be overheard.

If I had the funds of Helia von Heskin, I would also have stayed away. She had the power to direct her own life and this marriage should send anyone sensible running.

He shook his head in resignation. "We don't have to like each other, Princess. We only have to act our parts to get through this farce. You might prefer a commoner to me, but that's not in the stars. There are no choices for people like us."

He was more right than he knew.

I took a deep breath and, as I had so many times before, suppressed my anger. "We can only do our best with the fate the gods assigned us."

And run as far away as fast as possible after acting the princess and thief one last summer. Looking away, I noticed Flora von Heskin's eyes locked on me, a small smile playing on her lips. A chill ran down my neck.

Dessert had been served and removed while we talked. The music grew louder and couples were exiting into what looked like an adjoining ballroom. At least dancing was something I knew, something I loved.

I turned back to the prince, about to say something to make peace, then propose that a dance or two would show everyone, including the king, we accepted our roles, but he was not looking at me.

While we argued, he flushed with anger. Now, his sun-colored skin paled, his mismatched eyes became unreadable, and his fists clenched as he stared at someone across the moving crowd.

Without a look in my direction, he stood, straightened his uniform jacket, and strode through the room, killing conversations as he passed, ignoring the noble's deep bows and paling faces. Whoever he had seen wiped his future bride from his mind. Alexei met my questioning eyes with a shrug and I could feel the king's judging gaze between my shoulder blades. The last thing I needed was his scrutiny.

I took the prince's abrupt exit as an excuse to escape, mumbling that the excitement of the night had gotten to my head, and I would retreat to my chambers to lie down. It was not like anyone else would dance with the future queen before her groom, and if I could execute my plans for the night before the king and prince returned to their chambers, I would not have to worry about waking them later—a thief knew how to grab an opportunity when it presented itself.

Von Lemerch had demanded I exchange the letters before dawn. For the first time tonight, a genuine smile tugged at my lips. I knew it was irrational—I should have wished to go to bed instead of risking my life and capture—but no matter how much I wanted to escape this life, I loved the rush and the reduction of life's complexities that came with danger.

After a day of sitting pretty and being pulled by other's strings, I now only had my own plan to follow.

I pushed away the desire to sneak after the prince and discover who he was meeting. My night was just getting started, and I had no time to waste. I strode past bowing nobles, praying to the Wishmaker Lana had managed her part.

Chapter Eleven

Dimitri

Like a griffon diving for its prey, I pursued the pale-green dress and ink-blue hair. Each surge of the crowd gave me another glimpse. It could be someone else, but I was a lost man spotting a will-o'-the-wisps, praying it would lead me right. My first night back, I went to her, not knowing what I sought. What I could say. Each day, the need to know she was safe and replace the last image of her broken, in tears, and stained with blood, had grown. While away, I wrote guilt-ridden letters until I realized they were not being delivered.

The green dress slipped into the night through the open garden doors. The outside lacked the numerous lanterns of yesterday, but there were still enough tracing the path to guide me to the hanging willow. Once, we met here before moving on to more secluded spots. When young, all four of us—Alexei, Mariska, Eki, and me—had played and planned our futures under the hanging branches. I missed the Eki of those days as much as what came after.

Barely an outline under the canopy, she stopped, and even after years away, I could read her tense stance. I had cherished her more than half my life, though guilt, not love or longing, slowed my steps.

"You are here," I said, unable to bring myself closer. *Was I supposed to wrap my arms around her? Had she wanted me to follow?*

"I've always been here." She stepped close enough for me to see the hesitant smile. "Waiting."

"I tried to see you at the Tower but was turned away."

She moved even closer. "I needed time. I learned of your return at the same time as your engagement ball. I didn't know if I could stand seeing you at her side or how welcome I would be."

Her words struck like a punch. "If I could do anything to change the past, I would. No one who betrayed us will survive me becoming king. They will all regret their choice."

Blood pounded in my veins, like the blood that had stained my hands since I returned. Revenge and the mercy of the Goddess was all I could offer.

"Still, you will marry the foreigner? Be a dutiful son?"

Her hand hesitated over my chest.

"Eki." It was a plea to understand, though I felt like a beggar coming for forgiveness.

"Did our child mean that little to you? Do I? You promised, Dimi. Saying that together, we would be safe."

Tears strained her voice, and I automatically closed my arms around her. We had the same tutors, shared our first kiss. Shared our first and only time in bed, after which she told me she was with child. I had believed the illusion that my wants mattered and that everything would be accepted after we eloped. Believed Tal was a place for love. I had been a naïve fool.

"I'll only be married in name." I stroked her hair, inhaling the familiar scent. It used to feel like home, but now, I remembered the cries and recriminations, filling me with loss. "I'll make them all pay."

"Then I'll be queen as you promised? Everything will be like it was supposed to?"

She tilted her head up, but I did not bend for the kiss she offered. Instead, I held her, unable to lie or speak the truth. If Tal had a queen when all was done would be up to another. Someone less broken. I would have my revenge, no matter what it took, then I would leave these expectations to someone better suited. If I had learned anything during my years in exile, it was that I had no interest in ruling Tal. Here, my life would never be my own. And the princess had been right: no one needed me, a coddled prince who knew nothing, to tell them what to do.

Eki's demanding eyes pulled me back. "You cannot want that foreigner, Dimi. I know you don't, and she will be all that stands between us and the future we imagined after you become king. We would be safe…"

I hesitated, the words on the tip of my tongue. Maybe I owed her answers even if she would not understand.

Steps scraped against the gravel and Eki leapt away, vanishing into the dark.

A man and woman with the crossed bones of the Roja pinned to their chests stepped forward. I surely only heard their approach because they had wanted me to, probably after they overheard our conversation and decided they would learn nothing of value to bring to von Uster, the royal spymaster. I smiled coldly. The previous betrayal had taught me not to voice my plans out loud.

The woman bowed. "The King wishes to see you."

"Lead the way." He always knew when to summon me.

I had expected it when I rushed out of the dining hall and abandoned my argumentative bride, but confirming that Eki was fine, apologizing to her, had been too important.

After the wedding, Father would step aside—though an archaic custom, it had been my price for agreeing to the marriage—and until then, I would be as dutiful as I could. After the announcement today, even he could not renege on our deal.

I would give Eki an estate, all the gold she desired, for the pain my family had caused her. That was all I had left to offer, because the love I had expected to flood my heart as I held her once more had not come.

No matter how much I might want to, I could not return to the past. I needed to prepare for an infinitely more complicated future.

Chapter Twelve

Vanya

If the king read the wrong letter in the morning, von Lemerch would deliver me Lumi's mangled ear; the image haunted me as I walked through the sparkling palace. The offhanded way the old woman had uttered the words was more convincing than a bloody knife. She considered people like me disposable, barely above vermin. I was not fool enough to trust her offer of freedom and money after the causal threats. That did not mean I had any other choice than to continue as if I did.

In my chamber, Lana met me with her perpetual frown.

"Do you have them?" I asked, already unhooking the corset.

"Remember who you are, cinder girl." She stabbed me in the chest with her finger, clearly having held her words in since I dismissed her publicly. "Just because we are out of my father's house doesn't mean you are out of his debt. How anyone takes you for an actual princess is beyond me."

After years of insults, I longed to snap back, but swallowed my first response. And second.

"So, did you get them or should I tell von Lemerch you stopped me from doing as she asked?"

"Of course I got them. Had to mix with all kinds of people and sneak like a common thief. Don't count on my help again to get you out of the trouble you and your sister have gotten into. At least I got some business done tonight, so it wasn't a total waste of time."

She gestured to the neatly folded clothes on the sofa I previously missed. Lana had many faults, but we never had to clean up after her. She sorted all her possessions by color and other characteristics I could only guess at. If something was out of place, we would pray for the Goddess to save us from her tantrum.

The royal servant's uniforms she stole for me were folded tight enough to fit into a saddle bag, the corners sharp. After rolling up the pants and cinching the coat belt, I should not stand out in the royal wing. The prince's attitude, while off-putting, was not unique. No noble would give a servant a second look.

"And the rest?" I asked.

Svetlana hesitated before handing over a climbing rope and cloth pouch. "They were where you said they would be. Don't make me regret this."

My heart hurt, imagining her rooting through Lumi's possessions. She treasured the picks and had spent months practicing on any lock she found before our first robbery. After we returned from the last one, before leaving for the palace, she placed them under the loose floorboard in our attic room. Asking Lana to retrieve them and expose one of our few secrets had gone against my every instinct.

I tied the rope around my waist under the coat, then folded the too-long sleeves inward, slipping the pouch into the fold. I needed to be both Lumi and myself tonight—collected and able to charm any door, flexible and fleet-footed.

With a last nod, I left Svetlana and the illusion of safety.

It was still early evening, only every fifth lantern was lit. I passed guards patrolling the hallways, but no one looked at me. My purposeful steps and blue and gray livery served as camouflage as I followed the route the prince led me this morning.

Four guards stood unmoving outside the king's doors. No way to get in that way, but luckily that was also not my plan. This morning there had been no guards inside. *Wishmaker, let that still be true.*

Without pausing or looking in their direction again, I turned down the closest hallway to the unguarded doors belonging to the second-highest ranked man in Tal—my fiancé. I was good at casing spaces in one glance, and if I was right, the two apartments were wall-to-wall, hopefully, so were the balconies.

Checking that I was alone, I pulled two needles from Lumi's pouch and tested the lock. Each passing moment reminded me I did not have her skill, and every jiggle, wrong move, and scrape quickened my breath until the final, beautiful click.

Inside the prince's chambers, guilt rose. Not even servants seemed to be allowed in here to clean. I had never had a space just my own. Most days, I loved Lumi being there. She saw the other side of any argument. Backed me when I needed it. Held me when I cried. But sometimes, out of nowhere, came a need to just be Vanya.

I would climb the roof above our mother's apartment—and later, Kirill's house—or disappear up a sacred tree in the Bone Grove, listening to the clanking of our ancestors. These rooms, locked with a key Dimitri carried around his neck, belonged solely to him and I felt like an invader more keenly than at any other break-in. Of course, I rarely dined with my targets.

Despite the summer weather, embers glowed in the great fireplace, casting a low light across the sitting room. The table was still covered in books and papers, as if the prince had left at the same time I did this morning.

I longed to trace the lines on the maps again and dream myself away, as I had so many times before. Tal might be my home, but I owed it no more than it had given me, and a prison cell might come soon enough if the prince caught me here. It was not like he would like to hear about my *commoner's* problems, even if I could tell him.

I passed the half-open bedchamber door. Part of me wanted to slip inside and discover what the place where he let his stern features relax looked like. Instead, I moved my reluctant feet to the last door, where the prince had paced while berating me this morning—the still-open balcony.

Outside, a light summer rain greeted me. As I had suspected, the king's balcony mirrored his son's. Unfortunately, they were both shorter than I had prayed—separated by twenty feet of open air. No matter. I might not be great at planning, but I had come prepared. Hiking up my coat, I unwound the hidden rope.

There was a reason the king's balcony was not watched—it, like my room in the opposite wing, was seven stories up. The roof would have been an easier access point, but I did not know the way and there was a good chance guards patrolled it. I might have had to spend the whole night searching for the right access point. Von Lemerch had not given me much time to work with, so I needed to manage with what little I had.

A small entering hook was tied to the end of the rope. Like Lumi treasured the lock picks, this was one of my few indulgences. The Midtown seller had assured me it would never break. So far, her claim had proven true.

It took two throws and a prayer to any god who might listen for it to catch around the king's balcony railing. After yanking as hard as I could to assure myself it would hold, I tied the other end around a stone pillar on the prince's balcony.

Death Goddess, turn away tonight. Please do not enter my sight, I whispered to the stars, hoping someone out there listened.

Without giving myself time to delay further, I climbed over the railing and used the rope to brace myself against the wall to walk it almost horizontally. Or that was the idea. After three careful steps, I slipped on the slick stones and only my clamp-like grip saved me from a probably deserved death.

The rain soaked into my hair and clothes. My muscles burned and the hurt shoulder protested despite the healing this morning, but this was not the first time I had to push through pain.

Climbing this wall with no preparation in the rain and borrowed shoes was rash, even by my standards—*what would happen if they found me dead beneath the prince's balcony?* Maybe von Lemerch did not trust me after this morning and would use my death to discredit Tal, and I had walked right into it. There certainly would not be a wedding. However this night turned out, it might be a win for her. Von Lemerch might expect me to fail, but she didn't know me.

Swinging back and forth, I clenched my stomach muscles, raised my legs and wrapped them around the rope. In this position, the rough stone wall scraped against me every time I moved, climbing like a mountain monkey to reach the king's balcony.

Inch by steady inch, my goal came closer. Time froze, everything beyond the rain and rope disappearing. The song my mother used to sing when brushing my hair drifted through my mind. I hummed along as everything aligned inside me.

This is what made Lumi call my behavior idiocy. There was nothing to catch me—below me, a straight drop and above, only sky. I should have been terrified, but instead, I came alive. Pushed myself further. Narrowed my focus. There were no questions anymore, no right or wrong, no role I had to play, just me overcoming my own limitations.

Here, above the world, I was free.

My hand bumped the balcony and somehow, I got over the railing. Without allowing myself a moment of rest, I examined the king's closed balcony doors and the dark interior. Despite their inaccessibility, a delicate lock kept them closed. With stiff fingers, I fumbled with Lumi's picks. One fell and rolled off the balcony edge before I could grab it.

"I'll get you a new one," I promised Lumi, imagining her guiding me as I slid the next pick into the lock. The king would be back from the feast at any moment. There was no time to grieve.

When I was ready to kick in the door, it finally clicked open to reveal the same room I stood inside this morning. A golden oil lamp burned by the sofas, as if the king had only momentarily stepped away, but luck was with me as I opened the first door to reveal an orderly study dominated by a massive carved desk.

I closed the door behind me and, in the dark, bumped into what might have been a chair. On top of the desk, paper crinkled under my hands, and I almost wept with relief. Von Lemerch had not given me much to go on and my only plan upon reaching the king's chambers was to search everywhere, hoping for the best—and my relationship with hope was still strained.

There must be unlit lamps somewhere, but in the dark I could not find any. With no other options, I snuck back into the main receiving room. I needed to compare the letter still tucked safely inside my dress to the ones on the desk, to match the stamp. From somewhere further into the royal quarters came raised voices.

After snatching the lit lamp from the outer room and hurrying back into the study, I desperately pulled out von Lemerch's letter and compared it to each one in the engraved silver box on the desk. The sixth one was a perfect match, except mine being crumpled and wet at the edges.

Tucking the authentic letter into my shirt and stuffing the fake into the box, I turned to leave. The voices were closer now, just on the other side of the half-open door. I extinguished the lamp and dove behind the desk as the king spoke only a few feet away.

"You returned, demanding to become king, and all I asked was that you marry the Oberwaldian princess as agreed. That you don't break our word. That meant staying away from *that girl*."

"That girl? Mother used to call her a wished-for daughter." I flinched at the prince's icy voice. "She deserves better."

Steps pacing before the study made my heart race. The prince's rage burned in the back of my throat.

The king snorted derisively. "You dishonored Ekatarina Kuznetsova. Her noble birth no longer matters. Don't do the same with the new one."

The pacing steps quickened, and I could not resist leaning closer to hear the next words.

"She is not what I was led to believe."

The judgmental tone struck a chord in me, though his words were perfectly true. I could imagine his storming eyes as he threw in my face how he wanted to marry someone else. How he had forgotten my existence after dinner.

"They rarely are. And it matters no more now than it did three years ago. You have a role, a duty to Tal. And it is not a hard one." The king chuckled. "I have ordered the seer to measure her power to ensure it matches the marriage contract. That is the only part which matters. She is good looking enough, son. After producing an heir, you can take any concubine you wish. Your bride's opinions should be your last concern, but from the outside we must appear unified. I don't care what you do behind closed doors after the wedding. Have I made myself clear?"

The prince grunted and true anger flared in me, mixing with fear at the mention of the seer. They were not discussing the real me, but to talk so callously about anyone, especially your future daughter-in-law and queen, was despicable. More and more, I believed von Lemerch had nothing to do with the disappearance of the real Helia. She had probably seen the long travel here as an opportunity for a new life, to escape the expectations of royalty, and was far, far away.

"You will have your wedding." The prince's tone was colder than an ice cellar. "Alexei says there is lack of food and robbers on the roads, and the streets full of whispers of rebellion. That we should do something."

"The people are no threat for the army. After the wedding and coronation, you can do as you please, but there is always one emergency or another. If you and Alexei live long enough, you will see that we need to think long-term, not focus on flare-ups."

"The Roja—"

"Enough. The Council takes care of the city, you focus on the wedding and royal line. Leaving your future wife in the middle of a public dinner did nothing to strengthen our position. I will not hesitate to enforce the noble's sigil as long as I am still head of our House."

"Oh, I remember." The pacing footsteps stopped, and my heart stuttered. "Don't worry, Father. My plans haven't changed."

In the oppressive silence, I held my breath until a door slammed shut.

"That boy'll be the death of me," the king muttered, a distance away. "But not of Tal, if he can follow directions this time."

The thuds of heavy steps, followed by a second door clicking shut broke the silence.

Quicker than a rat in Lowtown, I scurried across the room and out on the balcony. The animosity seemed to whisper in the empty room, each breath filling me with their rage and frustrations. My head spun with the alien feelings and the conversation I overheard.

On the balcony, the chill even a summer rain brings cleared my head. If only I could stay here to catch my bearings. But the king could return at any moment.

With a tug, I dislodged my hook and freed the rope. Climbing back as I came would be easier, but there was no way to loosen the hook from the other side, and I was not leaving it behind.

I wound the end of the rope around my waist and between my legs, creating a harness. Grabbing hold as far up on the rope as I could reach, I tied another loop.

A light came on behind me, and there was no more time.

With both hands gripping the loop, I threw myself off the king's balcony. The rope swung like a pendulum—all I could do was hang on and hope the Goddess was busy elsewhere.

The momentum slowed until I hung straight below the prince's rooms. My shoulder did not hurt, despite the abuse I just put it through. Maybe my body was past the point where it thought I cared.

Hand over hand, I climbed up onto the balcony, and leaned against the railing to catch my breath. The night was quiet. Beautiful. Below me, Tal's lights dimmed through the downpour and I could imagine myself anywhere. A harbor city like Sorach. Keskin where the nobles went for summer parties. Oberwalden and its mountains.

Slowly, I untied the rope and rewound it under my coat. I was not free and pretending otherwise brought me no closer to my goal. I had lingered long enough.

As I turned toward the balcony doors, they burst open. Before my brain registered what was happening, someone rammed into me.

Chapter Thirteen

Vanya

I flinched away, narrowly avoiding the attacker.

As one of my mother's favorite clients had entertained her for the night in our apartment, his guard—a grizzled veteran grown heavy from following his noble master from party to gambling den—waited with me and Lumi. After enough bored nights and solitary card games, he'd taken a liking to us and decided that young girls need to know more than dance to survive. After that, he spent the visits teaching us to defend ourselves, not to cause harm but to escape it. Later, those lessons continued in a more practical manner on the streets of Lowtown. Each time I escaped with only scrapes, I was grateful to that nobleman's guard. Tonight, I was grateful again.

Acting on instinct, I caught my attacker by the shoulder and used the momentum to flip over his back into the room.

On my feet again, adrenaline racing, I pirouetted and blocked the arm swinging at me. My own fear and anger mixed with what I had felt in the king's chambers, and something snapped in me. *I didn't deserve this. Could I not have one moment of peace?*

Moving with my attacker, I threw him onto the ground as blue light erupted around us. He pulled me after him, twisting expertly.

But the first, and hardest, lesson I learned was to never end up on the bottom. Pulling my legs up between us, I pushed out and felt a flash of surprise, not my own. Before he could press the advantage, I was back on my feet, and we faced each other in a room blazing with mage lights. My opponent hesitated long enough for me to recognize him. I had hit the crown prince. Again.

Breathing raggedly, I froze. A knock on the outer door filled the silence. The prince's eyes locked with mine. Surprise and anger twisted together, so similar to when he caught me with the crown. Through our childhood, Lumi's emotions had come to me almost as natural as my own, but we were as close as two people could be. I felt her elation before she smiled, her fear before she cried.

These emotions—impossible and foreign—I recognized as Dimitri's.

A second knock sounded, more urgent this time.

"Wait," the prince called out at the same time the door opened and a guard entered. *Would he have me arrested on the spot?*

I threw myself at the prince. Last time we were alone, I had allowed myself to want; this time, I did not pause to think. Digging my fingers into his hair, I swallowed his hot breath and kissed him like my life depended on it—which it probably did—kissed like I had longed to do in the princess's chambers.

My knees weakened, warmth like I had stepped into a furnace spread from his lips to mine and down my body until even my fingertips tingled. He pressed closer, his grip hard as if to prevent me from escaping yet again. Leather and his own scent flooded my senses. Surprise mixed with passion and anger moved from him to me, building as our mouths fought a new battle. It went on and on, until a discrete cough reminded us of where and who we were.

I pulled back, my breaths coming in gasps that had nothing to do with physical exertion.

A chagrined guard stood in the doorway. *Right.* The reason I had kissed the prince. My eyes flickered back to Dimitri as he remembered who I was to him and understood this kiss was a ruse—it was in his narrowing eyes, the rigid posture, and clenched fists.

Face hard, he turned to the guard. "Leave us."

The prince's mind transformed into a wall of obsidian I could not pierce, his voice and anger cold. The guard saluted and retreated, as if escaping a storm about to break.

"I didn't know it was you," I said, facing the prince's cutting gaze with pretend calm. I knew this man would not hurt me. Somehow, I felt part of what he felt, and it was not murderous rage. He had been abrupt and rude when he caught me stealing the crown, yes, but never physically threatening. A small part of me, separated from all the lessons in distrust I should have learned by now, trusted him, despite logic telling me I should do anything but.

That did not mean I liked his stuck-up ways or that he would so much as touch me if he knew who I really was. Not that he had offered to touch me tonight.

He stalked forward until a hand's breadth separated us.

"You didn't know it was me when you broke into my rooms in the dead of night? Did you plan to kill me in my sleep and thus escape the marriage?"

The words stopped me cold. *Was he serious?* I wanted to be affronted, but what did he know about me? Or the real princess? Already the two were getting harder to keep apart. Still, I let some of the hurt show on my face. The mage lights faded along with my anger. The prince waved his hands toward the remaining glittering blobs.

"You could have killed me without lifting a finger. Thrown me off the balcony. I have read the Oberwaldian royal water seer's report included in the original marriage contract, Princess, and know better than anyone the value placed on your powers."

Disgust dripped from his voice, maybe for having to marry someone like me because of my bloodline. Both from what he had told me earlier and how he talked with the king, it was clear Helia von Heskin was not his choice in bride.

Needing to appear unmoved, strong, I approached the still glowing embers and settled on the sofa. Better this than arguing in the dark and I needed a break from meeting his hard gaze to gather my thoughts.

"I came to talk, just us. The dinner…" It seemed like a year ago, but only bells had passed. I forced sincerity into my voice. "I couldn't sleep thinking that I had offended you."

And now I really would not be able to sleep, thinking he suspected me of plotting murder. The stolen letter seemed to burn against my chest, luckily there was no expectation for me to undress.

He added two logs and stirred the fire before leaning against the mantel, leaving me illuminated and him covered in shadows.

"You came here alone, uninvited, dressed as a servant—though I'm sure I locked the door—and waited on my balcony in the rain to apologize. Do you take me for a fool, Princess? I do not believe you have apologized in your life."

I fought and failed to hide the challenging smile that answered his mocking tone. Alone, he made me forget to be the princess, to want to clash blades and words and lips until one of us was declared the victor. *Danger*, part of me screamed, and I grinned. Trading words was too similar to hanging between the balconies—one wrong move and I would fall, but until then, I came alive.

"And have you ever apologized, Dimitri?" I pulled out each syllable of his name, knowing there was a frown on his stern face. He gave me permission to use it, though even in my thoughts I had tried to avoid it. It made him a person. But alone by the fire—after exchanging blows and kisses and barbs—I could no longer think of him as the distant crown prince.

"Why are you really here?" he asked with a sigh.

"Why does a woman ever secretly visit a man at night?" The words slipped out before I could stop them, though my tone mocked the question.

He pulled a hand through his hair, probably considering if he preferred my words to be the truth or another lie. "After arguing with me and, then abandoning you at dinner without explanation, you were in the mood of another argument? Why can you not behave like a princess?"

Because I'm not. "Would you really prefer that I stayed in my room, never looked you in the eye and blushed when you rolled up your shirtsleeves?"

His unexpected laughter took us both by surprise. My lips twitched involuntarily. His laughter was the kind that pulled you along, the kind the popular man at the back of the bar let out, making you want to move closer just to be in on the joke—completely at odds with the stern, buttoned-up prince.

When it fizzled out, he settled on the smaller sofa to my right. A safe distance away, but inside the firelight.

"Rolled-up shirtsleeves? That's what ladies swoon over?" He studied me, and I returned the favor. With his long legs stretched out and without a military coat to hide the rumpled white shirt, he seemed relaxed. Human. "Will I never get a straight answer out of you, Princess? You appear determined to destroy my reputation. What will that guard say?"

"He'll think you were in a fight with a maid. And she won."

"Where did you learn to fight like that?"

Now it was my turn to look away. "A guard thought it best. You never know who your enemy could be." True, to an extent.

He nodded to himself, as if the dangers of royal life were obvious. "I do apologize for leaving you earlier." He grimaced. "I did not think."

Because he had been thinking about someone else. Still, I did not imagine he apologized often. What he thought of Helia, of me, should not matter, but it was too easy to forget when I could still feel his lips on my kiss-swollen ones.

"Thank you." I swallowed. "And I did want a moment to talk."

"As long as you don't suffocate me in my sleep or throw me across the room again, you don't need to sneak in. Just knock next time."

I let some of the previous wickedness slip into my smile. "Practicing hand-to-hand combat doesn't sound too bad. But aren't you worried I will interrupt you with a different woman?"

He rubbed his eyes. "The only one starting rumors here is you, Princess." A smile twisted his lips. "I prefer my practice during daytime."

My goal was not to be good; it was to have a future, but his honest tone crumbled another part of the wall I had built in my mind the moment von Lemerch declared that Dimitri Ivanov had to die for me to be free. It was easier to focus on his arrogance. His apparent reluctance to marry and disinterest in ruling Tal. Otherwise, I might start to care. Still, I found myself reluctant to leave and end this moment of peace.

He did not protest when I got to my feet and walked around the room, studying the drawn maps covering the walls. Even in the low light, I could see some were old but most new, drafted by the same hand. I did not ask again if they were his. Instead, I let my eyes linger on the careful lines.

Turning back to the table, an interrupted game of King's Conquest snagged my attention. The white pieces, three times as many as the black, were more intricate than any I had seen even in the exclusive Midtown boutiques. The marble griffon heads on soldiers' bodies so beautifully detailed I could imagine them moving. I picked up one of the onyx pieces to see it better. One side showed a woman's face, the other a skull. The uniform robe below made it impossible to know what the front was. Only the Goddess in the center had her hair put up with golden bones. In Lowtown she would have been portrayed by a wooden hexagon with a cross on the back symbolizing death.

"Do you play?" the prince asked, and I jumped, only then noticing that he studied me admiring the pieces.

Would a foreigner play? In Tal, every drink hall had tables with carved playing boards where many old men and women spent their days. King's Conquest was the story of Tal, infinitely played out through the city. It symbolized how Herebov had fought for Ealhswip's affections, and through her, the Death Goddess herself.

"You should have taken that priestess already," I said, and lifted a black piece that had been isolated on the right.

He chuckled and reset the board, placing the priestesses on the back central star and distributing the white warriors on the sides. Our fingers brushed as he took the last piece from me, and despite kissing him unabashedly earlier, I blushed at the accidental touch initiated by him in the quiet room.

He proceeded to light an oil lamp, seeming to not notice my sudden awkwardness. The shadow of a beard had appeared on his jaw since this morning, making him even more human and less the distant, chiseled prince. I liked too much, could almost feel it rough against my cheek again and imagine it elsewhere.

"White or black?" he asked as he settled in a chair.

Hunter or prey? Which one of us was what?

"Black." I smiled. "You won't catch me this time."

He opened, pieces rushing diagonally across the square board to trap my priestesses. I answered in kind, luring the warriors into positions where my few pieces could take them out. King's Conquest was more Lumi's thing than mine, but she had forced me to play enough that I put up a decent fight. It did not matter as Dimitri picked off the priestesses with clever ploys and daring moves. He played like I climbed, without hesitation, each leap a joy.

While our pieces battled, we for the first time did not, but instead talked of the weather and the palace, of nothing of importance while sharing innocuous truths. He told me he had always drawn but became seduced by maps while hidden away in the mountains, walking the wilderness to see the land beyond each peak. He dreamt of filling in the cartographers' blanks and complained many maps only contained stylized images of places while he sought facts. I shared the few truths that seemed safe, telling him dancing classes had been my favorite time growing up, that I preferred movement to sitting still, and, like him, longed to travel further.

When only the Goddess remained, and we both knew the game was lost, I picked her up, again marveling at the details. She seemed familiar somehow. I shivered at the audacity of royals, playing with the gods themselves. "How did you get someone to make this? Depicting her brings her attention."

"It's not her face," he said. "But her last divine ruler, Ealhswip."

The same face that decorated the fountain outside. My nerves settled. A priestess, divine ruler or not, was surely not the same as the Goddess herself. "She was beautiful."

"She was," he mumbled, watching me instead of the figurine.

I squirmed under his attention, reminded I had broken into his rooms and stolen from his father. Though what I had shared tonight were truths, I was a lie and trapped in someone else's game as surely as the black chiseled priestesses.

"Does it not seem strange Herebov would take away her priestesses if the purpose was to woo her?" I asked.

The prince replaced the fallen pieces. "Who can say anymore if it was love or war?" He focused on me, the light reflecting in his mismatched eyes, one the blue ice of distant glaziers, the other the brown of warm summer earth. "Sometimes, the two seem indistinguishable, Princess."

With those too-accurate words hanging in the air and the game lost, we bid each other good night.

The walk back to my chambers in the opposite wing was uneventful. A headache drummed up between my temples as the night replayed inside my mind, regrets and worries stealing the moment of peace we shared.

Had I imagined Dimitri's and the king's emotions tonight? Had von Lemerch or the crown changed me? How much remained of the Vanya who had broken into the von Mekeln estate with her sister only days ago? My tired mind had turned foggy and slow. Hopefully, tomorrow would be calmer. I could stay in my chambers and sort out my thoughts. Understand what was happening.

Before falling into bed, I stuffed the stolen letter into Lumi's single shoe in the back of the closet. It could be the leverage I needed. I was not handing it over to Lana.

While I danced to von Lemerch's strings, the world was changing. Something was coming.

To free Lumi, I needed a better plan than the one tonight. I pictured my sister sleeping somewhere safe and could almost feel her beside me. I longed to reach out, to apologize for getting us into this by not being ruthless enough and believing deception and lies could be negated by kindness.

Chapter Fourteen

Dimitri

The nobles, dressed to impress despite the sun still hiding behind the horizon, trickled into the amphitheater. Morovara, High Priestess of Bones, and strong despite her age, struck the brass gong again as I stifled an unseemly yawn.

I had attended morning worship every third-day while away and was determined to continue, but even after the princess left late last night, sleep had refused to find me. Thoughts of her and my father and Eki spun through my mind—how little I had felt besides sorrow when Eki laid her hands on my chest, begging for a kiss; how Helia had claimed it unabashedly, awakening longing better left gone; how my father spoke of women, how he treated my mother; how all three assumed I would keep the throne. How I wanted nothing less.

And, overlapping with it all, how I had relaxed while listening to her talk, how the game had revealed her clever mind. I had not been surprised to win, it was the strategy game of Tal, the origin of our royal house, and I had been trained in it since I could talk. But she had made me work for it, surprising me with unconventional moves. It shamed me I was using Helia to further my plans as much as Herebov, no matter his intentions, had used Ealhswip long ago. In the night, even the wind's whispers had not chased away the thoughts, so I had drifted through the palace like a Spirit unable to find its bones.

The gong rang a final and third time, and Morovara's sharp eyes dug into me. Standing in for the king, I gave her a curt nod to start. Those who had not made it here by now could stay in their beds.

After the worship, I would lose my father's loyal Roja spies in the crowd, and Alexei would lead me to the traitor he found living in Tal, as if nothing had happened. No matter what my friend thought of my revenge, after seeing Eki yesterday, it could not wait. My father might have given the orders, but there were people we had trusted, people who had taken my gold and broken their promises. There was always a choice. They had made theirs, and in the mountains, I made mine. Today, I would cross the first name of my list.

I brushed my fingers over the sword at my side and the dagger strapped to the dark uniform jacket. Soon, it would serve its purpose and hide the blood I spilled. I would wear black until all were avenged.

Morovara, her voice magnified by the amphitheater, called out the familiar greetings to the Death Goddess, patron of Tal. Three centuries-old grieving trees dominated the lowered stage, flanking the high priestess. At most times, the nobles who attended barely filled the stone benches, but this summer, more than usual resided in the palace, and the ones who had not been invited last night surely hoped for a glimpse of their future queen. Thus, people stood in the back while others crowded onto the adjacent palace balconies.

Morovara bowed to someone behind me and I knew Solovyova, my paternal grandmother, the unofficial ruler of the Women's Tower, had arrived. She was the only other royal who came. The wind whispered what was happening behind me—how Solovyova's throne-like seat was positioned just so, how she nodded her permission for the high priestess to proceed. Such was the power of my grandmother.

Morovara continued, but I struggled to focus on the familiar words. Standing alone at the front, I refused to slump. After the wedding, Helia would stand with me to receive the Goddess's blessing. While discreetly rolling my shoulders, I let my eyes sweep the balcony above the amphitheater again, searching for her with the other unmarried women of privilege.

I did not have to look long. Even at a distance she was unmistakable. Where others stood as rigid as me, or turned away bored, she leaned onto the railing as if worried to miss a word. So far, she had always been in movement—a cyclone, unpredictable and wild. Was she dedicated to the Goddess? Or was it because she was a foreigner fascinated by our ways?

Her red dress was as inappropriate for the season and early morning as last morning's dark-blue one had been. It also drew each eye to her, the lilacs and pale blue of the other ladies' dresses lost in the background—like a single rose in a field of wildflowers. Cultivated to persevere. A scent to entice, but with thorns for those not careful enough.

After she left last night, I lit all lamps and inspected every inch of my rooms. My maps were as I left them, my bed untouched. I even searched my closet before giving up. Something was off, but every time I came close, she changed. When she spoke, her words sounded like truth, and there was nothing pretend about her kiss, but why would she seek the company of the man she did not wish to marry? A man she apparently thought entertained other women while preparing for his wedding.

She needed someone she could be herself with, that was what she had implied, and ironically, I was the only one who knew how much she resented this marriage. Despite the shared quiet, I had not dared to ask why she was so set on leaving me after traveling all the way to Tal.

I tore my eyes away as the sun rose high enough to hit the many gilded skeletons hanging in the grieving trees above Morovara. Those most honored among my ancestors watched over us, though the oldest ones had been placed in the crypt to make space.

Under the glittering gaze of the dead, the high priestess spoke of turning points, dawn and eventide, moon phases and equinoxes. How they connected with the Death Goddess. How the dead fed Tal. How our successes are built on those of our ancestors.

The bones above jingled in a breeze that could not be felt below. It spoke of flying high, and I longed to sneak away and join it. Hundreds of eyes rested against my back. I was almost as much of a curiosity as the princess. An outsider in my own city.

Morovara spoke of birth and death, and I forgot the crowds, remembering the swell of Eki's stomach when she returned for our secret wedding ceremony, my amazement that I had been part of creating life. Now, I created death.

The rhythmic pounding of the drums accompanied the ululations of the recently bereft, sharing their grief with all. The same cry echoed inside me, never allowed out as my father had forbidden all mention of the pregnancy. The loss. *His murder.*

A female scream cut through the music, so similar to Eki I first thought it a memory. *Behind*, the breeze whispered, *It's her*. I spun around.

The red dress flapped like a flag, drawing every eye to the woman hanging from the ledge below the balcony. *How did she go over?*

I leaped onto the first bench row.

The lady maid vainly reached down, but the rest stood still. The princess held on by her fingertips. A free fall might not kill her but it would break bones.

I pushed nobles aside as I ran from bench to bench through the overfull amphitheater. Then, as if a spell broke, others rushed after me, asking how to assist. I ignored them all.

With my scraps of magic, I commanded the breeze to catch her. She only swung wider, almost losing her grip. More helpless than a second-rate mage I released the wind and stopped below her.

To my horror I realized I cared what happened to her. The thought of singing Helia's death honor on the next third-day twisted the ice inside, creating cracks like canyons in my emotional walls.

The red dress flapped high above. Someone was climbing over the railing to reach her. Too late. Too slow.

Her fingers slipped.

Save her, I begged the breeze and hoped the Death Goddess listened to Morovara's prayers and turned away.

Chapter Fifteen

Vanya

Svetlana woke me before the sun rose. I would have thought it intentional torture, if not for her tired frown. In Tal proper, few rose before midday; neither of us enjoyed the palace daytime schedule.

"Up. There was a note with the morning mail ordering me to report to my father. Tell me what happened last night while you dress."

"I exchanged the letter and destroyed it," I said, hoping von Lemerch, through Lana and Kirill, would accept my explanation. She had not explicitly said to return with it.

Lana waved a white paper in my face, then threw it on the bed cover. My heart stuttered. Had she watched me return last night and found where I hid it? But Lana would never have risked opening it, and this one had been ripped nearly in half. As I forced myself to focus, I could see it was smaller, merely a note cleverly folded rather than a stamped envelope.

"Who sent it?" I asked, but Lana only stalked out, presumably returning to her own bed.

Helia's name was artfully written on the back.

Dawn, Temple Grove. See Tal as it should be. In the City of the Dead, it is our duty to honor them—D.

A crown, the royal symbol of Tal and a reminder I only had one more day to return it, was stamped below the neat letters.

My heart sped again. Maybe the threat I imagined was not intentional, maybe the informal signature was how he regularly finished correspondence.

I visited Mother in the Bone Grove when I needed guidance but avoided the Temple District with the crowds, the crying, and solemn priestesses. Somehow, the excited tourists mixing with the drifting Spirits seemed a more genuine celebration of death. Either way, this time, dawn worship was not optional. Even without the crown prince's personal invitation, people would want to see the foreign bride. Especially as her arrival had been so delayed.

Bleary eyed, I rifled through layered, uncorseted, light, silk dresses. Most looked like something a twelve-year-old princess in a story would wear—innocent and pure. *Was this how Helia dressed?* The promised baggage had yet to arrive, so I had no way of knowing, but decided I would be more convincing if I felt at least partly at home in my clothes.

In the back, hung a deep-red, form-fitting one. It was light enough to help me survive in the summer heat and partly covered my von Heskin noble's sigil. The less I saw of that, the better. It had the corset with no boning and delicate golden snaps closed in the front, allowing me to dress without help. There was no chance Lana would leave bed again to assist.

When dressed, the woman in the great mirror was both me and someone else—someone I wanted to know better and feared. Someone with magic. I twisted and turned, imagining mage lights erupting around me. Nothing happened. Nothing felt or looked different. *Had it been the prince after all?*

The dress was red like roses and blood. Like the stick figure painted across Tal, calling for rebellion. It was more true to the state of the city than the pale lilacs, dirtied once and then discarded. Part of me insisted I should stay in the background, pretend to fit in, but surely, a future queen would want to be seen. I had a role to play. This morning, more eyes than ever would be on me.

Breaking fast on sweetened red tea and dried dates and apricots waiting in the sitting room, I missed the prince's banter from yesterday. *How can one person switch so quickly between caring, offending, infuriating, but enticing?*

I needed to talk. Preferably to Lumi, who still felt close, like a limb I could not see. But I would even take arguing with Svetlana. She would put my head on straight about the prince. Use or be used, was her motto. Unsure in which category I now belonged, it seemed she would ignore me as much as she could.

Outside, it was still dark, but dawn was quickly approaching. Time to become the princess.

As the door swung shut behind me, Lana caught it, her maid dress and coat in Oberwaldian bronze tailored perfection. Where had she procured that in a day?

"Thought you could sneak away without me, did you?"

Seemed Lana accepted being used after all. Neither of us dared defy von Lemerch. Still, I could not resist pushing her.

"Aren't you supposed to be questioning me about every moment last night?" I asked as I locked up behind us and we started down the hallway.

"Hopefully you're sensible enough to tell me what I need to know. I have better things to do than bother you into common sense," Lana said. "If you want to survive what's coming, you'll do what you're told. There's worse things in life than being a pretend princess."

Her surprisingly direct words stopped me. "What would you know about surviving?"

"That's your problem. You take everything at face value, rushing into places you don't belong and think yourself the victim when it doesn't work out. At least your sister thinks before she acts."

"I know you. I've cleaned for and served you for years. There's nothing beyond face value," I said, annoyed that she's trying to blame me for any of this.

My stepsister passed me, calling back, "If you only see what you expect, you're as blind as all the other fools. Better hurry like a good little princess. You wouldn't want to be late."

We marched in silence the rest of the way, me fuming and Svetlana seemingly unruffled. I knew she was vain and selfish, always following Kirill's lead, ready to carry out his punishments and direct his ire our way. But she was too conniving to be called stupid and her words wormed inside me. Too often I had thought myself victim to circumstance. Weak and poor.

Arriving at the stone balcony overlooking the palace's private temple grove— an amphitheater with towering trees and gathering nobles dressed like pale flowers in the predawn darkness—I pushed away her words. She probably only wanted to mess with me anyway.

In the trees, high above a single white-robed elderly woman alone by a giant brass gong, the gilded royal skeletons glistened, wet from last night's rain. A few feet away stood Crown Prince Dimitri

Ivanov, equally separated from the high priestess in front and the nobles seated behind. An immovable black-clad statue, mirroring Herebov on the other side of the palace—shoulders straight, hand resting on the curved blade at his hip. Indomitable and cold.

Had I truly felt his emotions last night?

That part seemed fuzzy now, like I had drunk too much, though I'd only consumed a glass at dinner bells earlier. It had started already in the king's chambers. Perhaps, he left incense that confused the senses burning.

Stifling a yawn, I leaned against the railing, pushed away the worries, and searched the crowd below for von Lemerch, or my pretend aunt, Flora.

"Princess," Lana sneered next to me and pointed toward the curved entrance, "that is Lady Irina Jovanovich and her brothers."

Two men and a woman with hair curling into halos had arrived. All in fine, pale clothes, the woman, maybe a year or two my senior, hiding part of her face behind a lacquered fan. At midday, I might also wish for one, but now it was needless.

"How do you know?"

My stepsister smiled haughtily. "We hold the debts of several nobles. Their hereditary jewels are locked up as collateral in Father's study. They should have greeted the princess. Seems not everyone is falling over themselves to talk to you."

"Maybe they don't know who I am." *How would a real princess respond to being snubbed?*

Vanya the thief met any problem head-on, often without a thought for the consequences, but I needed to do better. Channeling Lumi, I left my face politely blank.

Lana shook her head but did not contradict me openly. The other nobles, including the lady who had spoken to me by the fountain and certainly knew who I was supposed to be, spared me a glance before turning away.

I'm not here to make friends anyway.

Hopefully the worship would soon start. The morning lightened and more nobles arrived on the balcony. A man in black doublet and pants approached and bowed. Inclining my head in return as I had seen the prince do, I received a frown in response. It seemed frowns were what I specialized in. He covered it behind a slick smile.

"Princess Helia, welcome to Tal. You must be taxed after your long journey, or did you go slow to enjoy the scenery?"

What did the man mean? My eyes flitted to Lana—she knew this world marginally better than me—but she only gave me a fake smile. I was on my own.

"Only delayed by the weather, my lord."

He nodded in sympathy while a woman slipped her arm in his. "Some of us started wondering if you had gone missing permanently, Princess. Or found your way somewhere else." She looked like the cat who got the cream.

To someone else, she meant.

"I'm here now, so no need to worry," I said, and forced a serene smile.

The lady looked me up and down. "Yes, though I hear the prince was so worried, he started searching for a bride anywhere he could find one, even at the engagement ball. I know him *very* well—as did a maid last night."

"I don't see how anyone can mistake me for a servant," I snapped, knowing I should have kept my mouth shut.

Seemed many ladies claimed to know the crown prince. Anger at her implication fought with thinking she could have him and the title. I had not asked for this, could not keep any of it, and Helia clearly was not interested. It would end only in death. My polite smile lost its luster, my confidence crumbling.

Behind her, a golden-skinned middle-aged woman caught my eye. I had seen her before, but that was impossible unless she was another of Kirill's debtees, though Lumi and I had been sent to collect from scum, not nobility. The woman turned to display a slightly crooked nose and hazel eyes. And I remembered them wide in fright with my iron needle at her neck. *Lady von Mekeln.*

Shaking, I spun away. Why had I not expected her to be here? Lumi had told me they were in Tal for the prince's engagement ball, clearly the lady intended to stay until the wedding. Cold sweat covered my hands. She would not recognize me from behind, but I would have to turn to leave, what then? Fortunately, the high priestess's chanted greeting saved me from finding an immediate answer.

The ceremony—echoing words above the crowd, grieving calls with unfettered emotions, pounding drums—carried me away, despite my pressing fears. It was grander than the worships our mother had taken us to in Tal but grief was universal, death nondiscriminatory.

Mother should have been prepared the proper way, like those hanging in the Grove. Her bones picked clean by scavengers in the temples, and then hung, preferably skeleton intact and carved with sacred marks. But the law stated that those who died from the plague must be burned. As the death carriers came, we had chopped the fingers off and hid them in our skirts. A bone worker had carved the metacarpals with too-knowing eyes. We had hung them while her ashes were dumped, mixing with those of a hundred others, in the flowing arms of the Taliell.

The guilt of failing her, the guilt of the living, haunted me.

I let my eyes rest on the prince, thinking of the dark emotions hidden behind his mismatched eyes, when something hit me from behind, blackening my sight, and then I was falling.

Years of climbing made me grasp for purchase before my sight cleared, my fingertips catching on stone sculptured into leaves and flowers under the balcony. And I did what no Lowtown urchin should, what would have killed Vanya the street thief. I let out an ear-piercing screech.

With the scream came a wave of panic, as if silence had kept it at bay for the last three-day. Yet again, I had no rope or safety line. No one here would climb the balcony to pull me up. At least Lady von Mekeln could not confront me as I left.

Lana bent over the railing. Our eyes locked, hers actually wide in fright. She stretched as far as she could, but a good foot separated her hands from mine. Then foreign anger, fear, surprise, and happiness flooded me, and I was lost. Sweat broke out all over my body as more came. *Horror, boredom, love.*

A sudden wind swung me back and forth. My right hand slid. Someone was trying to kill me. They'd pushed me and now used magic to make sure I fell.

People watched from above. A blurry mass of feelings and faces. Then I recognized the dark onyx below me. I had felt it only last night.

Would the prince catch me?

Panic would kill me. It told me to cling to the ledge until the last moment, but if I fell uncontrollably, I could hit the ground head-first. If I landed on my partly healed shoulder, permanent damage was likely, but better a shoulder than a neck.

Aim for the prince, then roll, I told myself. Despite his wish to escape the engagement and love for another, at this moment, I trusted him. I believed in the care I had felt from him last night when yet again, he could rightly have thrown me in a prison cell.

Then I closed down those emotions as well. Fear and hope would not help. Only the part that loved living on the edge, that moment after leaping when you were not falling but flying, remained.

A deep breath, mind empty, I clenched my stomach muscles, raised my swinging legs until the momentum made them touch the stone, then let go.

Like a diver, I fell with my arms pointing directly toward Dimitri. A flash of surprise and fear escaped his mind before I bent my arm and shoulder, hit his chest, and rolled away.

Everything hurt. This time, I was not bouncing up again, but no one was coming to attack or catch me either. The princess-like thing to do was to lie there and watch the brilliant sky—the early sunlight, the gilded skeletons dancing in the wind—while the crowd buzzed around me like a swarm of angry bees.

My mind no longer fit inside my head.

That's the princess. Is she alive? How did she fall? Why is she still alive? She can't die yet. She needs to die. Bring water. Make space. Magic. The crown prince is limping. The king will not be pleased. Stupid girl, a doll could do her job. Leave. Run. Disappear.

Indistinguishable thoughts and words danced around me. The sky a sapphire ready to be stolen, the sun an orange. A bird flew over me, and I knew it was returning to its nest. Lumi was far away, but close like my hand. Next to her, a woman who could be our plumper, straight-haired, bespectacled sister lay as if dead. They were underground, ancient lanterns illuminating black stone carvings too worn to make out.

I fell, Lumi. They pushed me and now I'm flying.

Her head snapped around, searching for me, her usually smooth skin swollen and covered in shades of purple from the beating at Kirill's.

Vanya? The words were barely a whisper, but I caught them. *How can you be here?*

It's magic. Impossible magic, Lumi. She looks like us. Where are you? Are you safe?

"Princess, can you hear me?"

The voice tore me away from Lumi, but I clung to the link between us.

This isn't your battle. Get away, she said, ignoring my question.

I shook my head in denial. *If I leave, they'll punish you. Where are you? Is this real?*

Desperately, I scanned the room for any identifying details. It was most certainly in Tal, the worn images on the ancient black stone walls reminding me of the palace or a temple.

Lumi stood, her green eyes drilling into mine. *I can take care of myself. Leave the magic alone and don't listen to them. If one of us got caught, the other promised to run. Run!*

My body called me back, and no matter how hard I focused, swimming colors replaced Lumi's face.

"Princess? Helia?" Someone was holding me in their arms, caring fingers stroking my forehead. The upsetting thoughts drifted away.

I felt like I was still flying. At some point, the falling would start, and I would hit the ground. A laugh escaped me.

"Besides a possible brain injury, you used too much magic, Princess. You had no build up, and let it rule you instead of you it. Say something."

The sun was replaced by leafy shade. My head rested in someone's very comfortable lap, possibly the same someone hovering over me.

I lifted a hand to trace his cheek. The moment our skin touched, his anxiety and frustration slipped into me. The flying stopped. The falling started—a need to do what was right, mixed with determination and a sea of sorrow pulled me down, down, down.

I jerked my hand away, but the alien feelings remained, and buried deep, anger and grief matching my own rose.

I swam through the sea of grief. Everything I knew disappeared—Mother, home, lessons, fickle friends, and treats. Only Lumi remained, and now she had been stolen as well. Maybe von Lemerch had already killed her.

No.

Only my actual sister would have commanded me to leave. The lifeless woman next to her had not been my imagination. More importantly, Lumi was part of me. I did not need to see her, for she was my other half.

This sorrow was not mine. Those old wounds had long since scabbed over. I broke through the strangling grief, separating the anger and worry from mine.

The world spun as I took in the stone bench beneath me, the branches of a hanging willow above. The worshiping crowds were gone, the swinging sun-reflecting bones replaced by shading leaves. Outside our verdant cave, the palace wall closed us in. The scent of nearby roses permeated the air. Clangs from the smithy and bird-like screeches from stables broke the silence but felt far away.

Dimitri bent over me. *Had he carried me here?*

"We're alone?" I asked, hoping against sense that Lumi was here.

I sat up and bent forward, the grass below seemingly swaying as much as the leaves above.

"I sent your Oberwaldian maid to get a healer, and Alexei is standing guard around the corner. I thought it better to keep others away until I knew what happened. The entire court saw you fall."

"I never fall. The wind tried to kill me."

The thoughts I had heard drifted back to me. Someone had tried to kill me, someone else had thought it was too soon. Another wanted the prince dead.

A headache pounded behind my eyes.

I focused on Dimitri's worried face, for the first time seeing the coldness in his eyes for the deep sorrow he hid.

"The wind... I tried to help. Did someone push you?"

How could I tell him that I knew for sure someone wanted me dead without explaining this strange magic and exposing myself as a fraud? And what if they had tried to kill Vanya the thief and arresting them would lead to my own imprisonment? I pasted on an embarrassed smile and fanned myself with my hand and turned toward the great stones of the palace wall. They kept us trapped while promising protection. The life of a princess seemed remarkably similar. Protection was an illusion, and I was more trapped now than as a street thief.

"It must have been the excitement and lack of sleep causing me to faint."

Dimitri raised an eyebrow. "After last night I wouldn't have thought you the fainting kind."

He clearly did not believe me but was not pushing it. I kept my strained smile in place. Despite a perfectly executed landing, dropping from such a height hurt, and based on my pounding head, so did hearing others' thoughts. "Maybe I prefer it when I'm the one throwing you to the ground. Besides, a crowd is different."

He nodded, face unreadable. "It was a hasty fancy to invite you after so little sleep. You clearly needed rest."

"And you, Crown Prince Dimitri, king-in-waiting, you do not require rest?" I asked, noting the dark circles under his eyes and trying to divert his attention. "You look like you could sleep a three-day, instead you stand alone in place of the king. One could think you care about your people, after all."

His mouth split in a genuine smile. "If you argue, you cannot be too bad off."

I held his worried look and showed some of my inner strength while wondering what he really thought. Despite the role I had to play, I did not want this man to think me weak. If I reached for his hand, I might hear his thoughts, but it seemed wrong to invade his mind to sate my curiosity.

I was ordered to stay near him, to gain his confidence, that is why I leaned closer—there was absolutely no other sensible reason for me to kiss him. Again.

His lips melted into mine, rough stubble scraping my skin. There were only my own emotions this time, the magic seemingly gone. Not that I cared.

He pulled back, catching his breath while grabbing my shoulders as if torn between holding me at bay and pulling me close. Dreams and unfilled wants filled me as I angled my mouth and molded my body to his. Coherent thoughts were long gone as my hands stroked up his hard chest, felt the rapidly beating heart under the stiff cloth, and drowned in his brown and blue eyes. All the barriers I'd built inside, and the guilt that kept them up, shook as an undeniable need grew.

"Princess, it's the magic heightening your feelings. We need to stop," he groaned as if trying to convince himself as much as me.

Damned if I was stopping anything which felt this good. I stroked the uniform, the fine weave distracting. I rubbed my head against it like a cat. His matching longing for nearness to another person, to belong, to find a home, mixed with mine as, despite himself, he pulled me into his arms.

This time, I did not jerk away from his rage-tinged grief. It washed over me, tried to drown me as it surely was drowning him under his stiff facade. He held me like a lover unwilling to part while I cried his tears, shoulders shaking, hands clinging.

Colors danced before my closed eyes, and under the grief, a kernel of hope, a bush that once had been trimmed back too far and then neglected, awoke. Joy and laughter, friendship and lightheartedness locked away deep inside. I stroked it, encouraging new growth and shared my conviction that tomorrow would be better. He pressed his mouth to mine, swallowing sobs that would have brought guards running before, after an eternity or the blink of an eye, he pulled away.

The broken contact snapped the magic like a hair ripped apart, curling back from the broken ends. Frozen, I sat next to Dimitri, unable to meet his eyes. He would never be a stranger again. I did not know what he had felt in return, or the cause of the grief he shared. I did not know how he could live with it constantly.

The world rippled like hot air over Pilgrim's Road in summer.

Dimitri blinked at me, tears clinging to his dark eyelashes. "What was *that*?"

Whatever answer I could offer was cut off by a discreet cough—somehow we were always interrupted. Always watched.

I flinched away and, for the second time that day, fell to the ground. This time, with an embarrassing and less than graceful thud. Dimitri jumped to his feet, instantly stiff and distant, hesitant to offer me a helping hand. Guess the last time we touched had set off warning bells, or he did not approve of how we had been found.

Before the prince made his mind up, I got up and brushed off my stained dress only to see Lana smirking next to a red-coated healer.

There was not much privacy to be had in Lowtown, which was both a protection and inconvenience. When Lumi and I were taken in by Kirill, any modesty our mother had instilled in us disappeared together with our morals. Sitting close while alone or embracing in grief was nothing compared to sharing bathing barrels in a courtyard.

From the prince's stiff back and refusal to look my way, it was different for the nobility. In a social class where holding hands was tantamount to an engagement, what we had just been caught doing was probably comparable to intercourse in the middle of the town square in Lowtown.

Dimitri greeted the man dressed in blood-red, high-necked coat, pressed pants, and leather boots with a complete white skeleton embroidered on his chest—a master healer from the hospital. The cowl ready to hide his face when treating the ill hung loose around his neck.

Alexei and the prince's cousin, Mariska, also in her red coat and dress, stood further away, chatting. She gave me a smile and wave, but there was worry in her eyes. Maybe at the queen-to-be's appalling balance and repeated injuries.

As the healer finished his deep bow, Dimitri gestured to me without turning around. I desperately wanted to see his face, to know if he was suspicious after the magical connection. For a moment, we had been closer than even Lumi and I. Part of me ached to renew the link, for complete understanding and no secrets.

Instead, he strode away without a goodbye, Alexei falling in at his side, and I had never felt further apart while knowing someone's Spirit.

The rejection burned away the lingering passion.

I should focus on running with Lumi and leave the royals to their intrigues, von Lemerch to her scheming. This was not the world for a thief and daughter of a courtesan. Most of the time, I did not even like Crown Prince Dimitri Ivanov, but it was getting harder to convince myself that I did not care, that I could walk away without warning him, because I now knew that no matter what he said or how he acted, at his core he was hurt, but good.

A man who deserved to live.

His black uniform was a vacuum in the Talian sea of colors, drawing my eyes until he disappeared around the stable. Only days ago, it represented danger, now it made my heart race. How could I play his intended for months knowing he was to die at the end? The answer was simple. I could not.

My sister had not seemed shocked at my magic. It appears she had kept many secrets. It did not matter where it came from, for with it maybe even I, the least suitable of us all, could get us out of this. Svetlana had been wrong. I was no victim waiting to duck the next blow.

Lumi wanted me to run, but I was already in too deep to turn away, no matter the cost to come.

Chapter Sixteen

Vanya

When the master healer crouched before me, we were almost the same height. A gray-speckled beard covered his mouth, but lined, kind eyes met mine. I tried to focus on my languid muscles and spinning head, instead of Dimitri's disappearing figure and the strange connection between us. There was nothing I could do about our situation before I had time to think.

"Princess von Heskin, I hear you took quite a fall. The Crown Prince said that you fainted." The healer gently measured my racing pulse with his fingers. "You seem to have recovered. Can you tell me if it hurts anywhere?"

The smile I could see through the beard was indication enough he mistook my fluster as caused by my previous improper nearness to the prince.

This was the kind of man I had been desperate for when my mother started coughing blood, who Lumi and I would have offered everything to if he helped us. We had not gotten past the hospital's spiked iron fence.

This time, I wanted nothing to do with him or his kind eyes. He cared about my supposed rank, about what the royal family thought.

Maybe he was already considering the heirs Helia was required to bear in the near future.

"I'm fine. Use your time to help those who need it," I snapped, forgetting yet again to act like a princess. "I have nothing worse than a headache."

Ignoring my tone, the healer placed his fingers against my temple. Mariska watched with a crooked smile while Lana seemingly ignored us all, though she surely listened to every word.

Magic like tiny star bursts engulfed me, searching for hurts, finding my secrets. I flinched away from the intrusion despite the instant soothing of pains I had not even noticed.

This was why the hospital protected the healers—why anyone, no matter their station, would be trained there. Healing magic was treasured above all. In Tal, we worshiped death, mingled with the dead, and this power could stave off the Goddess of Death herself. It was the magic I had dreamt of as a child after hearing the lorists tell of lost noble children raised in anonymity and discovered when their magic manifested. Other powers found among commoners—rare, though it happened—would be exploited, or the bearers killed, but not healers. They were the truest sign of the Goddess's blessing on a family. I should have known that Lumi and I were not blessed. Whatever power I had, it had nothing to do with the Goddess. Von Lemerch must have done something to me. The timing was too coincidental for anything else.

The master healer tucked his hands back inside his sleeves and looked at Svetlana and Mariska. "I need to talk to my patient alone."

"No," Lana said, clearly ready for this farce to be over.

I put a hand on her arm, probably breaking some "no touching nobles" rule. Somehow, I knew his words would be important. "The healer needs to speak with me alone."

Her gaze traveled from the patient master healer to Mariska's raised eyebrows. "It's not seemly."

"Wait by the palace wall then. You can clearly see us from there and protect my reputation."

The thought that she cared after not objecting for years while her father threatened to sell us to the brothels was so ridiculous I almost laughed. My stepsister looked like she wanted to punch me before composing her face into her normal, aloof expression as Mariska linked their arms together and led her away with a wave in my direction and a quiet word.

Chuckling, the healer settled on the bench next to me.

"Beautiful spot, Princess. Sometimes we all require some calm. I'll respect your decision and not address the tear in your shoulder as I have better things to do than force my powers on those who don't want them, but the magic—I would be remiss if I didn't at least talk to you. It must be under control at all times. I assume your teachers taught you this before you could run, but it seems you need to hear it again.

"Sudden surges can burn you out and destroy part of your brain. Things like today only have short-term effect—for now." His kind eyes turned hard, as if he could see the too-vibrant colors still dancing in the corners of my eyes. "You cannot know when the damage becomes permanent. After that there is a short road to insanity or other erratic behavior usually ending in death—your own and others. Magic such as yours is a tidal wave ready to swallow us all."

It's not mine, I wanted to say. Or, *Take it away*. That something supposedly reserved for nobles ran in my veins did not surprise me. As my father had had enough money to pay for my mother's company, he at least had been rich. But no one suddenly got magic—you had it at birth or you did not—and now I could go insane or worse. Hiding my shaking fingers under my dress, I wondered how far I could trust this man. Probably not at all, considering information on the future queen must be a high commodity, but I needed answers.

"What did it do to me?"

"The usual I expect, though I would have needed to examine you earlier to be sure. Your brain is already healing. If I had to guess, I would say disrupted vision, loss of inhibitions, unstable emotions. Other common symptoms are loss of balance, hallucination, and a wish to hurt yourself or others. There is a reason only mages born from strong bloodlines who are trained from a young age survive until adulthood. You're a princess, there was no reason to spare any expense. The Oberwaldians should have trained you better. Someone of your power going insane would risk us all."

We all believed hardly any commoners had magic—but perhaps they did not have anyone who noticed it early enough, anyone to train them, and were lost among all the children dying from other preventable illnesses. It also confirmed the stories of mages' unpredictability and the death left in their wake.

Unless I got rid of this power somehow, that might be me.

Wishmaker! That was why I threw myself on the prince. And the kiss last night—*had that truly been me? How much of what I heard had been hallucinations?* I felt dirtier than I ever had robbing houses and cleaning muck. Hadn't the prince said something about magic when he removed my hands? Hadn't I promised to never choose a man over Lumi again, and suddenly, I was questioning it all?

Burying my face in my hands, I wished to undo the last bell. To erase every touch.

"When falling I couldn't control it," I said, more to myself than the healer.

"I imagine you didn't train under such circumstances. A spike in adrenaline can override our normal defenses. There might be a lot of stressors here compared to your previous life, Princess von Heskin. Your teachers have been remiss in not challenging you. The Talian Court is a quiet lake, hiding the monsters swimming below."

He was wrong about my life, and I did not need warnings about nobles' intrigues. I needed solutions. "What should I do?"

"You could send for your teachers from home, or you could reveal your powers to one of the sworn instructors here."

"No."

No one could discover that my powers differed from Helia's. That I was unnatural.

The healer stood, his form blocking the sun. "Then I can only recommend vigilance and meditation. Use your powers in small doses to prevent them building up to be released all at once. There is no healing for what magic does to the mind, Your Highness. Nobles' secret keeping will kill us all. Come to the hospital if you reconsider or want someone to treat your mundane injuries. Ask for Gennady."

After receiving my nod, he marched off, clearly not satisfied with my noble ways. Finally, it seemed I had acted like a princess.

Mariska returned without Lana, somehow having gotten rid of my spying stepsister. From her worried expression, I wondered how much she had overheard, though probably my own bleak look said it all. The risk of losing my mind put all my other problems into perspective. If I went insane, everything else would quickly come crashing down. Another reason I could not run. There was no way of knowing if whatever von Lemerch had done to me was temporary. Insanity and hurting those around me would remain a risk until she undid it or I learned to master my strange powers.

"Gennady is one of the good ones," Mariska said, mistaking my worried stare at his back for judgment. "He has treated the royal family his whole life and trained me since I entered the hospital five years ago. You can talk to him. Or me if you prefer."

Her voice carried no further than the rustling leaves surrounding us.

Unable to sit still as thoughts raced through me, I stood and approached the overhanging branches. While the greens and blues were still unnaturally brilliant, the ground remained firm under my feet.

I could trust no one, but I also could not go crazy like the man climbing the tables in the dining hall last night. And if I could use this magic, maybe I could communicate with Lumi again or find out what von Lemerch was after. Why she desperately needed a stand-in to marry the prince without the real crown.

Mariska waited patiently, a stark contrast to her previous energetic presence.

She wanted me to marry her cousin. She wanted Helia to find a home here. She wanted to help. Using that, my stomach knotted as I made a decision Lumi would have agonized over for days. I decided to trust.

"I need a friend." I faced Mariska, who had settled on the bench while I thought. "My powers are different than what you were told, and my training did not take well, or I did not listen well enough. If anyone finds out, I fear what they would do. How it would endanger the relationship between Tal and Oberwalden. Everything is already so fraught."

I gave her a long look, saying, *Neither of us want to be responsible for a war*.

"Why would they let you leave without mastering your powers?"

Her shock seemed genuine, and anger burned in her eyes, though it did not seem directed at me.

"The marriage contract. I stayed away as long as I could," I stammered, pulling lies from the air and sprinkling in truth. "The king wants to have a seer evaluate me to ensure I match what was agreed to."

Mariska waved her hand. "She'll only identify your strength level and House. Surely you cannot be that far away from your line."

I swallowed. *House? As in noble linage?* I had no idea of my strength, though both Gennady and the prince had indicated that from what they felt I matched the supposed level of Helia von Heskin. If von Lemerch had changed me, at least she had not wanted me to get caught.

Mariska grabbed my hand, and fortunately, the magic did not wake again. What would be enough to destroy my brain?

"Thank you for trusting me." She smiled, and the exuberant girl from my room returned. "You're turning out to be much more interesting than I expected. We might have different training methods than those in Oberwalden. I'll try to help, of course I will. I also want to be friends. And then you can still marry Dimi."

I nodded, squeezing her hand. She was so genuine, able to trust, despite growing up among vipers. *What would she think if she heard other's thoughts?* She would probably try to help them. If she got the chance, Mariska might become the kind of healer who answered the pleas of Lowtown. I could only return her trust with a little more of my truth.

"Your cousin and I are very different, and neither desires a marriage. I know he loves another, and I miss my home. I'm not queen material."

Mariska snorted. "I saw you in each other's arms. I don't know what you said to him, but that wonder on his face... You both have a past, that doesn't mean you cannot build a future. Say nothing. There is no point arguing about what has not happened and might bes. The only sure thing is death and love, and in Tal they both come from the strangest of places."

"Then I'll argue with you later." A genuine smile tugged at my lips. "So when do we start? Gennady said the magic spiked during my fall, but I didn't do anything."

Mariska's expression became serious. "First, tell me about your power."

"Swear you'll tell no other."

Everything I had said until now was innocent enough, but even in Lowtown drink halls, where tales of mages were surely exaggerated, people revered elementals—telling of heroes wielding fire and scrying the future in water, while those who affected the minds of others became the villains.

"On my healer's oath, I swear I will not reveal your power without your explicit consent," Mariska answered without hesitation.

"I hear and feel the thoughts and emotions of others. When I fell, I heard everyone." All the vitriol and threats, but nothing revealing who pushed me.

"You're a mind witch! Guess you take after your uncle, did he not want to train you himself? I heard he's a bit of a strange one."

"Mind witch?"

Mariska looked aghast. "I didn't mean to insult you. I shouldn't have called you that. But your uncle is a heart turner, right? It sounds like with a bit of training you could be one as well. I understand the secrecy though. No one wants any kind of mind witch marrying their future ruler. It's like giving away the kingdom if the power is abused. No wonder they wanted to keep you in Oberwalden. Without the betrothal agreement, you would be your mother's heir."

I kept my face carefully blank as I processed her words. *Heart turner. Witch.* And I had something besides my looks in common with the Oberwaldian royal family. This power was real and dangerous.

"Can you teach me how to control it better?" I could not swear to not use the power against the royal family. Not as long as von Lemerch controlled me, and if they discovered I was an impostor, they would surely have me arrested, but I had to offer something. "I intend your family no harm."

"I will try." Mariska sighed. "I think you should tell Dimi. He deserves to know."

"When the time is right."

After throwing myself at him in a magic stupor again, I was not sure I could even look the prince in the eye. Mariska believed I changed something in him, but I had felt the storming grief and rage, and it would take a lot more than a hug to calm.

After Mariska insisted I needed to recover before we tested my powers, she returned to the hospital. Alone, I could have tried to escape again. The debt sigil and Kirill's threats no longer felt unbeatable; instead, fear of my magical ability and the prince's safety steered my steps back to Helia's chambers.

Upon reaching the correct floor, I automatically sidestepped the crowd blocking the hallway. My head was full, longing for a bath. The calm would help me process Dimitri's grief and the healers' revelations, while resisting reaching for Lumi again.

"Niece." A feminine voice cut through conversations and thoughts.

I froze as Flora von Heskin drew me into her too-tight embrace with a calculating glimmer in her eyes, like a street peddler spotting a newly arrived pilgrim. The yellow silk of her dress crinkled as her large body enveloped me.

"Do as I say, and we will get on fine," she whispered, squeezing harder. "We have a mutual friend, and your sister will suffer for any infraction."

She let me go and I stumbled, registering Lana standing smugly among servants and travel chests. My luggage had arrived and there was only one *friend* who knew of my sister.

Ignoring the discomfort from the too-intimate hug mixed with threats, I pasted a smile on my face. This was acting, the hallway only a more intimate stage than the river barge.

"Aunt Flora, I didn't expect you."

She scoffed. "I hurried all the way after your fainting spell. I would have come earlier, but our friend has kept me busy. A young lady cannot be alone in a foreign country." She narrowed her eyes, taking in my dress and hair. "Your maid has told me everything you have been up to. You should rest after your fall, Niece." I knew an order when I heard one. Flora raised her voice, addressing me and the servants, "Well, open your door. We have already stood around waiting long enough."

I had imitated the prince, carrying the key to my door around my neck, and thankfully, no one here was willing to break it open. The little privacy I had remained, the letter still hidden.

As the lock clicked, Flora marched past the servants with a short order for them to unpack. My pretend aunt then ignored them as they swarmed around us, hanging dresses and organizing jewelry. Von Lemerch had thought of everything, even the leather travel chests had the Oberwaldian royal sigil burned into them. The unconscious woman with Lumi flashed before my eyes, and the beautiful gowns became ugly. It seemed Helia had not chosen to stay away after all, and wearing her clothes felt infinitely worse than using her name.

Flora herded me to the breakfast table and settled on the other side, both our smiles equally false. She lifted her hand and, without a word, a boy placed a drink in it before backing away.

"Leave us," she commanded and as one, her servants turned around. "You too. This is Oberwaldian business," she continued, seeing that my stepsister remained.

"Our friend said I shouldn't leave the princess's side."

Flora snorted. "I don't care what deal the councilwoman has with your leech of a father."

Lana looked ready to throw a fit, including foot stamping and screeching, as she would have with her father to get her way. Instead, she surprised me by giving me a long warning look before entering her own room.

Alone, I faced Flora von Heskin and whatever message she carried. Part of me wished my stepsister had raged, taking the focus from me.

The door only partly closed, enabling Lana to listen in. Flora twirled her fingers and it slammed into the frame. There was a muted yelp from the other side. The hairs on my neck rose at the casual show of magic different from anything I had heard of.

With a satisfied smile, Flora drank deep, letting the silence stretch. When I opened my mouth to speak, she raised her hand and my teeth snapped together involuntarily.

Smacking her lips in satisfaction, Flora finally focused on me.

"You, thief, have been given a chance to take my missing, ungrateful niece's place. I have been asked to ensure that you can play your role until the wedding."

"Nobody has questioned me being Helia."

She clicked her tongue. "After being presented to the king, you attempted to leave. At the banquet, the prince found you lacking and left *you*. During three-day worship, you make yourself into a spectacle for the entire court to see. One could think you have a death wish or hate your sister."

I shrank into the rumpled red silk dress, conscious of my wild hair and tear-swollen eyes.

"You'll be happy to hear that I believe you are as ignorant and incompetent as your upbringing would lead one to assume. This means you are trainable. I hope you prove me right without any bloody reinforcements."

She shuddered theatrically, flab jiggling, and raised her hand again when I opened my mouth to reassure her. This time, I shut my lip without magical reinforcement.

"I'll come each morning—Oberwaldians do not sleep until the sun is high on the sky—and you will learn. There'll be little need for you to talk, here or outside your chambers. You will be expected to pay your respects to the queen and dowager at the Tower in ten days, and they will be much harder to please than their useless king."

This time, I only nodded and Flora's pursed lips relaxed a fraction. I would get through this being the perfect puppet, instead of my impulsive, argumentative self. No matter what people thought, I could follow directions when necessary.

"The king informed me that a seer will evaluate my magical ability," I said, to test what she might reveal of my newfound magic.

She waved her hands dismissively but the frown returned. "You smile prettily, and I'll deal with everything else."

Did that mean she knew and was part of gifting me my powers? Or had they bribed the seer?

Flora raised her dress, revealing a large leather satchel buckled to her wide thigh, like something a griffon rider might wear over their pants for easy access while flying. She unbuckled the two clasps and passed it over the table. When I hesitated, she nodded.

"Do not speak of it. I don't feel anyone close enough to overhear us, but in this, I'll take no more risks. If you had not gotten caught, they would simply think they had found the lost one. This mess is yours, so resolve it."

I snapped the central intricate clasp open. Inside lay a crown identical to the one I had stolen, the one still hanging in a courtyard tree. The cold glass, like frost under my fingers, revealed sigils covering the inside. *Who put the decorations where no one could see them?*

"Ensure he gets it before more questions are asked."

"As you command, Aunt."

I stared at my own hands against the ancient symbol of Talian royalty. Remembered how it had looked on my head. How something had shot through me when I touched it together with the prince.

Not willing to linger, I strapped the bag around my thigh under Flora's hawk eyes. After the red silk covered it, she held out her hand as if she wished for something in return. When I did not react, she tapped the table.

"The letter, girl."

Blood drained from my face and I let it. This woman would enjoy seeing my fear. "She didn't tell me to keep it."

"What do you mean?"

"It's gone. If someone had found it on me..."

My statement hung in the air, waiting for Flora's judgment. Sweat stuck the dress to my back and my fingers dug into the creased fabric.

After the silence had gone from uncomfortable to threatening, my pretend aunt finally nodded to herself. "I will inform her. It's not Oberwaldian business anyway."

I suppressed my answering smile. *Stasia von Lemerch and Flora von Heskin had different goals, could I use this knowledge somehow?*

Flora stayed two more bells, directing me in how to sit, which dress to wear when, and what was a seemly smile. Would this build a safe distance between me and the prince? The possibility should have please me. Instead, I suppressed a blush remembering how he reacted to my impropriety.

Finally closing the door behind her, I had never been happier not to be a real princess. The chance of this sham succeeding increased exponentially under Helia's aunt's tutelage, while the freedom I had experienced until now withered away.

As I moved around the room, the crown's weight reminded me of the betrayals to come. Of how I would have to lie to Dimitri's face while remembering his innermost feelings. I no longer wanted a bath or anything to do with this gilded cage. I wanted to run, to jump, and push myself until I was flying free.

Instead, I closeted myself in the bedchamber before Svetlana could corner me.

Despite Mariska's warnings, I tried to find the magic and reach Lumi until the setting sun cast long shadows and my belly rumbled, reminding me I had not eaten since before the worship.

The crown rubbed against my naked thigh with each step as I snuck through the sitting room and out the front door. There was no way I could stomach anything before it was gone.

For the second night in a row, I strode down the brilliant hallways to the prince's chambers, hardly seeing the plush, red carpets and ancient, black stone carvings of forgotten gods watching our every move.

The reasons I could not meet Dimitri's eyes were piling up—there was no other cause for the butterflies flapping through my stomach or to pause to arrange my hair outside his door.

I knocked twice before resorting to the lock picks again. The rewarding click came faster, and I rationalized breaking into his private space—this time I was, sort of, returning something, instead of stealing.

A quick check showed the chambers empty despite the low-burning fire and open windows.

On the mantel, a woman smiled down at me. In the prince's blooding presence, I had been too distracted to notice it. Now, I drifted closer and a chill ran down my back. I had seen her unconscious, maybe dead, next to Lumi. The painted lips a hue darker, green eyes open instead of closed. No glasses and hair perfectly curled. *Helia*. She looked like Lumi and I might have in another life.

Any doubt my sister had been a figment of my imagination disappeared. Von Lemerch had her locked away, and the magic was real. All of this was real, and I had no idea what it meant.

I longed to settle on the sofa and hide away from the world in this room of shadows. The prince's chambers felt more familiar than they had any right to be.

Outside, Rivertown and Lowtown would be roaring but the palace was its own world—alive during the day, the dead blocked from entering at night. How could those who ruled Tal live so separate from what made our city unique?

The day had contained enough excitement and the morning, too little rest. I wanted just a moment to tuck up my feet before returning to my stepsister's unavoidable inquiries. A moment alone to close my eyes while listening to the crackling fire and hoping for a whiff of the wild smell I could not identify.

I opened the central clasp and let my fingers close around the smooth glass crown. With one last fleeting wonder of how Dimitri would react when I handed it over, sleep caught me.

Chapter Seventeen

Dimitri

Alexei fell in silently next to me, sensing my dark thoughts. Together we entered the stables and walked up the creaking stairs. We were late. Not that anything this morning after the princess's cry had gone as planned.

I should not have gotten so close. I should have seen the shine of magic fever earlier, taken her directly to the hospital. We should not have been alone, though a larger audience to our embrace would not have improved the situation. The touch had broken something inside me, cracked the walls I'd built. A tearing midwinter storm now threatened to pull it all down—another moment together and there was no knowing what I might have revealed. The only thing to do was wait until the wall could be rebuilt.

Helia's and Eki's crying faces mixed, past and present. The princess had been so small when I lifted her off the ground and barked at everyone to leave us. So frail compared to the woman who argued and fought me. Part of me wanted to return, to hear Gennady say she would be fine. To kiss her again and breathe in lavender and hope.

It had already gone too far. She wanted out of the engagement, and I would abandon her after the wedding.

In the stable attic, I moved on light feet though my mind was far away. Only the shuffling of the griffons below could be heard. Alexei and I replaced our finery with borrowed stable hand's uniforms of brown and once-black shirt and trousers, as we had when we snuck out as teens. Alexei raised an eyebrow but refrained from commenting at the magnificent bruise forming on my side, a reminder of how my bride threw me across the room the night before.

I stuffed my hair under a wide-brimmed hat and tied a patch over my brown eye. *What would the princess think if she saw me dressed like this?* Laugh? Arch an eyebrow in question? Lecture me on how I should spend more time with my people? It did not matter, and this was not the time for idle thoughts.

We entered as two of the most powerful people in Tal and left as commoners.

"Seemed cozy back there," Alexei said, taking a bite from an apple he had found somewhere. I should have known better than to expect him to leave what he had seen alone.

"None of your business."

He snickered. "In public makes it everyone's business."

I snatched the apple away and stole a bite as he danced after me like when we were boys. How I missed those days.

We walked out the front gate and along the ever-busy Palace Road.

"Have you found anything in the princess's chambers?" I asked, steering the conversation away from recent events as we turned into a mostly deserted side street covered by ochre cloth, the merchant stalls still closed, and rubbish from the night before littering the alleys.

"There wasn't much, as the princess hasn't even received her luggage. There is no sign of the crown. So far, she has not entertained any guests, expressed any interests, or done much of anything besides a walk through the courtyard and the upper ramparts to look at the city. Councilwoman von Lemerch approached her, but I was too far away to hear their conversation. Presumably, von Lemerch welcomed von Heskin to Tal. And Eki left the Tower to speak to her. Has she done anything suspicious?"

Should I worry Eki had approached her? It was not a surprise, but I wished I knew what had been said.

"So what are you holding in? I know you want to share."

I shook my head, but he was probably right. "The princess broke into my rooms last night dressed like a palace maid."

"So that's why you are so worn out." Alexei elbowed me in the side, surely hitting the bruise on purpose. "Now tell me, in detail, what your bride did to you. Please, keep nothing back."

I took one deep breath in to suppress the wince, then let it out. He was my friend, one of only three I still trusted. "I thought she was a thief and tried to apprehend her. She threw me across the room. She has also been very clear about wanting to break the marriage contract, takes every opportunity to challenge me and seems more *experienced* than we were led to believe."

"A princess raised in solitude with her nose in a book, threw you, who used to brag you could beat anyone, across the room? Then showed you how *experienced* she is? How did you find the only noble lady suitable for more than embroidery and sighing? Maybe I should find myself an Oberwaldian as well."

I narrowed my eyes. "Then maybe *you* should marry her. She entered my chambers for something, and interesting though I am, I cannot help to wonder if it was for more than my company. I need to know what she is after. Why she is desperate to get away. Is someone threatening her? Does she have a lover who she will do anything to return to? Why—" *doesn't she want me?*

Even in my head I sounded like the small boy robbed of the only world he knew when at twelve he was taken away from the Women's Tower. My father had given me one look before handing me over to others.

I needed to know if I could trust Princess Helia of Oberwalden before I let her any closer, for I was beginning to enjoy her company too much, despite her unpredictability and earnestness. Even the suggestion of her in another's arms made me want to punch something.

My friend read me with one look and snickered. "On second thought, I think I'm done with women. In less than three months, she will be queen, what else is there?" Alexei asked, echoing my own thoughts. *Who didn't want to be queen?*

"I saw her magic. She lit up the entire room with barely a thought." And on the bench, she did something to me. I was sure of it. I felt lighter, rawer. "She is dangerous."

Alexei led the way, taking us to the border between Midtown and Rivertown, passing shops and stalls still setting up for the evening. Three-story wood and brick houses squeezed in together faced the canal. The humid air flaked pink, green, and blue paint above the waterline, but the residents showed their care by bright flowers hanging from the windowsills and well-swept streets. No pilgrims came here. These were the homes of upstanding tradesmen and women, greeting the day as the midday sun warmed their roofs.

We needed to be out of here before the streets filled. Being caught by the City Guard or worse, other Roja, would infinitely complicate things.

Alexei indicated a black door, and I dug for the cold detachment the princess had robbed me of, suppressed the sound of Eki's tears and grief I could never show, then, cold as the mountain wind, I reached for the door handle.

Alexei put his hand on mine. "You could still walk away. Or command his possessions seized." He squeezed my hand. "This will not bring *him* back. Every death has consequences, even this one, and we cannot foresee them—they say a person is a thread and when it's cut, the weave unravels."

His words registered, but part of me was back there, watching the priestess force-feed Eki the concoction, waiting for our child to be born to screams and tears. Too small to survive. Helpless. A few breaths and the Goddess collected him.

My father had ordered it, but the Council had voted, the priestess had turned us in instead of performing the wedding ceremony as agreed, and behind this door lived the guard who had reported my every move to my father. Who had given us the priestess's name. Who had bought his retirement and this very house with the blood money. Clearly, my desperate curse had achieved nothing.

I pounded on the door and pushed inside. Alexei closed it behind us and blocked the exit. He had located the man, brought me here, but this was my business. My revenge.

The Wishmaker was surely on my side, for there he stood alone and unarmed.

The last years had only increased Zakhar's size. He had towered over me since I started training with the men; now sedentary fat widened his giant frame. I had looked up to this man in every meaning of the words. Had trusted him when he was assigned as my personal guard.

Before he could register who I was, my fist connected with his temple, and he dropped to the floor. My knee hit his chin before my booted foot kicked him down. In moments, a man I had thought unbeatable, obsessed over for years as he haunted my dreams, was incapacitated.

I pressed my knee into his stomach and rested the knife against his throat. Never would I underestimate him again.

"You know why I'm here, Zakhar. You knew I would come."

Seeing that he was trying to talk, I released the pressure and waited for him to catch his breath. It would be over soon enough, and I would be one step closer to making amends.

"I knew," he wheezed. "I've been waiting since you rode back into Tal."

"Eki trusted me. I trusted you. You should have trusted I would not let your betrayal go."

I sounded cold to my own ears. A messenger from the Death Goddess herself. Like the empty shell I had been at the start of my exile.

"I thought he would spirit the child away. Hide it. I had to report it. If you married and I said nothing, the king would take it out of my hide."

"And now, I'll execute the Goddess's justice. An eye for an eye, a hand for a hand, a death for a death. If you had come to me, I would have sent you from Tal. You chose this path."

He did not fight me, did not argue; but closed his amber eyes, tears running freely down his furrowed face to wet his beard. I moved the knife—sharpened on countless sleepless nights for this very occasion—to between his ribs, slowly pushing it through clothes and skin and flesh.

"Say your final words."

He shuddered in pain. "Goddess, bless me on my way. Let my Spirit rattle the bones. Let my life be chanted. Let me rest in Tal."

The words were replaced by gurgling, blood staining his lips, and Zakhar, like my child, died on his third breath.

I slumped to the floor next to him, the drive for vengeance that had guided me here vanishing with his Spirit. With the moon, they would both rise again, but in this moment, I wanted nothing more than to leave Tal prematurely, to run and never look back.

The royal sigil covering my right arm burned—a brand I would never get rid of—commanding me to do my father's bidding until he stepped down. There was no running.

I closed Zakhar's eyes, wishing he had chosen differently, that there was another path for me. The freedom I had felt in the princess's hug returned, unwelcome tears staining my face. *Had she been trying to break or heal me? Did it matter?*

Slowly, I climbed to my feet and Alexei stepped close. Standing shoulder to shoulder with my oldest friend, I breathed out. I could still trust. I still had him.

We needed to disappear before anyone found the corpse, for there was no way to dispose of the body in the middle of the busy city. A murder in Rivertown should not reach my father's ears but I could not risk leaving a trace in case his loyal Roja asked questions. He could not be allowed to how deep my need for revenge went.

More people were on the street outside, calls from children and laundrywomen ringing out. It was time to leave.

I was cleaning the knife on the coat by the door when the ceiling creaked.

"Zaki, is that you with breakfast?" a woman called, the steps above us getting closer.

She appeared at the top of the stairs, curly hair tousled, robe sliding off a naked shoulder, then saw us. Everyone froze to take each other in.

With a tentative smile, she pulled her clothes straight. "I didn't expect guests. Zakhar will be right back."

Her eyes swept the room, maybe to check if it was presentable for strangers stopping by—maybe to find something to beat the intruders with—and landed on Zakhar's corpse.

I could have stepped closer, could have pulled out the knife and threatened her. Alexei could have thrown his own. It would have been clean, safe, done.

Instead, we rushed out, her screams chasing us. Revenge was taking enough; if I murdered without cause, I would be no better than my father. The ice growing inside would never thaw.

Men and women turned to stare as we escaped, but instead of stopping us, they flocked to Zakhar's house. People were always more interested in a tragedy than acting for justice. When I had needed my supposed friends, they had turned away, unable to meet my eyes. All except one.

I followed Alexei through a warren of alleys, never more aware I did not know my own city. If the palace did not rise above the rest of Tal, I would have been completely lost. We crossed bridges into Lowtown and slowed to a walk to catch our breath and blend in.

Alexei steered us to a drinking hall with chipped paint and shuttered windows, the cracked sign swinging in the wind appropriately naming it The Drunken Dead. After looking to see that no one followed, we entered and settled at a table in the back. Despite being just past midday, half the chairs were occupied. Compared to this early crowd we looked wealthy, even in the stable boys' clothes.

King's Conquest boards were crudely carved into the tables, players around us losing what few coins they had. I suppressed the image of Helia in lantern light, brows knitted as she considered her next move.

Alexei tapped a copper against the table, and two cups and a nameless bottle were placed before us without comment by a middle-aged woman. When we were alone again, he poured and clinked his glass to mine before emptying it. I followed suit, the bitter liquid burning on the way down.

"What is this place?"

He refilled our cups. "A place where no one asks questions about the blood on your cuff. The last place they would look for the crown prince and the youngest, most-talented agent in the Roja. And the owner owes me a favor. We'll be safe and undisturbed."

I sipped the second drink. No matter what he said, overindulging outside my chambers was not an option, but the burn served as a distraction from Zakhar's death and my own twisting feelings.

I studied the muddy floorboards, the worn-out men and women drinking to break their fast. *Was this the Tal the princess thought I could not see from the palace?*

On the wall above the bar, I spotted a crude red stick figure—drawn in blood or paint. The dot eyes watched us all, the dripping fingers ominous in a way I did not understand. *Tal was death and death was Tal*, it seemed to say. Even drinking away your worries, you cannot escape it.

"They call it the Spirit of Lowtown, claiming it can control the dead," Alexei said, noticing what had caught my attention. "That despite all the dead in the last plague Spirits have been disappearing. Others say the Spirits will finally be able to move to the next realm if the priestesses are brought back into power. That they stay because the royals and nobles don't honor the dead and are now gathering to right old wrongs. Only then will there be food for all. The rumors seem to have started after the plague five years ago."

I shuddered, remembering the plague bells warning all and being sequestered in the Women's Tower despite my age. For a season, I'd barely been allowed into the garden. The crown prince was too precious. The plague was incurable, and mages most at risk. No matter how careful, nobles had died like flies. I did not know how it had been in the rest of the city.

"Have people seen this *Spirit*? Is it a person?"

Alexei emptied his cup with a grimace. "I cannot find any stories I trust as every description changes. All that remains the same is her power over the dead and call for rebellion. Sometimes she is aligned with the temples, sometimes she wants to burn it all down. They all agree that when the time comes, the dead will walk again and the royals will fall."

I finished my drink and poured another, ignoring the part of me that called for caution. *This has been brewing for years?* I truly did not know my city. Eki and I had been naïve when we whispered plans for the future, seeing only the glitter of the palace.

"When this is done, I'm leaving Tal. Walking away," I said, letting my most-guarded secret out and hoping the liquor offered salvation.

The silence stretched, the crowd grew, and just as I was about to raise my eyes to see Alexei's reaction, he let out a joyless laugh.

"And leave it all to Nikolai? Your cousin will party and gamble away what little is left of the royal coffers and ignore Tal burning around him." Alexei stole away my cup, forcing me to face the anger burning in his eyes. "I entered the Roja to be in a position to help you when you returned. I tell you of farms burning, refugees and rebellions. Of dissent in the temples and rumored saviors." He swept his hand around the room. "These are your citizens, drinking themselves to death. You can help them. Help Tal. I understand why you need your revenge, support you doing what is needed to take the crown—but not to abandon it."

His voice hardened as he talked, the normally easygoing man gone.

I roughly reclaimed my cup, the tumult inside coalescing into anger. "I know nothing of ruling or the real world, Alexei. All I know are the gilded lies of the palace and meditation in a distant fortress. Mountain passes, snow, and listening to the wind—this is what my father sent me to learn while the people thought I was doing some special service to Tal or studying the mysteries of the world. Nikolai might be a vain scoundrel, but maybe all who sees the world for what it is need to drown their feelings."

Alexei shook his head. "So learn what is needed. I have seen you with the princess. She might not be who you would choose, but neither is she what we expected. Give happiness a chance and it might find you. Death and love cannot be controlled by anyone other than the gods. And you cannot refuse either when it finds you."

I met his eyes without resistance. He could not understand the coldness eating me from inside, that the Death Goddess had already found me though I kept walking. I was not the person to bring back

Tal's greatness, to deal with this Spirit of Lowtown, or with the lack of worship among the nobles, or with farms burning and unavenged plague victims. Tal needed someone less broken than me, and so did the princess.

"Then maybe I'll name you king in my stead."

He blinked, and I laughed at rendering him speechless though it did not last long.

"It could be no worse than the chaos you would leave in your wake, Dimi. Give ruling and marriage a chance, a real one, and if you still want to leave, I'll hold you to your word. I would much rather change Tal at your side. Because change it must."

"You sound like a rebel."

"I don't need a revolution, only to convince one man. My best friend, who can do anything if he learns to get up after falling. Tal needs to join this century. It can change, Dimi. Walk through Midtown and see what the foreign merchants bring."

"People don't come to Tal to see the future, they come to make peace with the past."

He rose and slammed a few worn coins onto the table. "Make your peace then."

He left me there with his words hanging in the air. *Get up after falling.* After being torn down? *Find peace.* Did I even want to?

I closed my eyes only to see Zakhar's dead ones staring back at me. He had trained me in sword and bow and spear while claiming he was teaching the greatest king Tal would ever see. Just one among many stroking my ego, hoping to be rewarded by the future king.

I stayed in the drink hall while the day passed outside. Behind the permanently closed shutters and grime, time stood still.

Staggering out when I could no longer stand my own company, I was reminded that outside the palace compound the City of the Dead only came to life at night. Even among the poor in Lowtown, paper lanterns transformed the mud streets into roads of sapphire, emerald, ruby, and starlight white. People moved with purpose between food stalls, cobblers, and produce traders. The broken fountains swarmed with laughing children. On the surface, the dark demeanor in the drink hall belonged to a different world, but as I drifted along, I noticed beggars in cloth tents under the shadows of wash lines, bloody stick figure drawings, and permanent scowls twisting young men and women.

On the iron bridge across the Taliell, one of the hundred separating Lowtown from Rivertown, I paused. Here, the pilgrims and worshipers joined the locals to watch plays, hear the orators, and visit eateries and brothels. Barges with fire jugglers, actors, dance floors, and pretend seers covered the brown river water. Everywhere a riot of color and laughter covered darker undertones.

The closer I came to the temples and holy groves, the more luminous, white Spirits drifted above the streets and houses. Their shine stole away the night. I watched each foggy, androgynous shape, but used my power to gently blow away any coming too close. *Was my son one of them? Was Zakhar already drifting toward the Grove and temples?*

The feelings the princess evoked resurfaced, as if once let out, they would keep trying to escape. On the streets of Tal, anonymous and alone in the masses of pilgrims, I let tears stain my cheeks. They fell like spring rain, light and freeing, melting a layer of the ice encasing my heart.

Pilgrims smiled at me, and a woman offered a handkerchief to dry my eyes. Death had brought us all here, and there was comfort in sharing it, even with strangers.

I returned to the palace at dawn with my cold mask back in place. The loosening in my chest from grieving my lost child, love, and innocence could not get in the way of what I had to do. No matter how hot the kisses and tender the touches, I could not let Helia von Heskin close again before I understood how she had gotten into my head and what her true intentions were. I started on this path years ago, and would walk it to the end, though a growing voice asked, *What then?*

Entering my dark chamber, my blood chilled.

I was not alone.

Chapter Eighteen

Vanya

Someone shook my shoulder. I rolled away, dreamless sleep still within reach.

"Lumi, go away."

What did Kirill want now? Sleep had almost pulled me under again when someone poked me in the face.

"Who's Lumi, Princess?"

I shot up, each scrape and overextended muscle from the fall screaming. A fire illuminated a towering silhouette. Not Lumi. Not our attic room. The prince stepped closer, anger twisting his handsome face.

"Well?" he continued, voice accusatory, and everything muddled by sleep returned like a punch in the gut. "Who are you dreaming about on my sofa?"

"A friend." *My soul mate.* Maybe he heard my thought because his scowl deepened, and I hurried to continue, "I didn't mean to fall asleep."

"But you meant to break in here again? I told you to knock."

I winced and noticed the fresh pain in my side from sleeping on something hard, reminding me why I had come. "You only gave me two days."

As I pulled up my dress, he retreated like I might throw myself at him again. I blushed. Maybe he was right to fear, considering how I had behaved the last times we were alone. *Had it all been the magic?*

As the leather bag clasped around my thigh was exposed and I revealed its content, all thoughts of kissing disappeared. In daylight, the glass crown was beautiful, but in the firelight it glittered like ice. Like magic.

I offered it with both hands like a supplicant, hoping he could not spot the forgery. He snatched it up, minimizing the time it connected us. There was no jolt of energy. No spark. Despite the sigils, this seemed just a crown.

As he turned it over by the fire, I spotted a drop of blood staining his sun-tanned cheek. Despite not wearing the usual black uniform and his simple shirt hanging untucked over loose pants, the night hid any stains. He could be drenched in blood or merely cut himself shaving, though I had noticed no wound earlier.

"Where have you been?"

He spun back to me, crown carelessly in his hand, expression screaming it was none of my business. "Out."

Again, I imagined an obsidian wall, like the palace's, separating him and me, coating his true self like armor. He did not twitch in anger, his cheeks did not color; instead, he stood like an unmovable statue.

I rose from the sofa and he backed away.

"Dimitri, earlier—"

"It's beyond time for you to leave, Princess."

He might as well have snapped "out" again.

I escaped back to my own chambers, not sure how I would have finished my sentence if he had not interrupted. *Apologized for the kiss? Told him I had no idea what had happened between us? That even without magic, I longed to be in his arms again?*

He had saved me, as I did not know which statement was true. I should be relieved, but I only felt lonely.

Back in my chambers, I found my stepsister writing in a small black ledger, similar to the ones Kirill kept.

"He took it then?" she asked without looking up. "After how we found you on the bench, I didn't expect you to return again tonight."

"It wasn't like that." I wished I could tell her of the magic and my confused feelings, that we had become sisters in more than name.

Even Lana's haughty sneer reminded me of home. She snapped the book closed and tucked it into her coat pocket before walking to the front door.

"Where are you going?" I called after her. No matter how little I cared for Svetlana, her taunts reminded me of who I truly was. Vanya the servant and thief, with small concerns. No magic or princes or crowns. She was the only one here who knew me.

"Out," she said, unknowingly echoing the prince. "Don't you think I have better things to do than babysit you? I have aspiration beyond being someone's pawn."

She was gone before I could come up with a retort.

More alone than ever before, I lay awake in the most luxurious room I had ever had and imagined my sister reaching for me. No matter how hard I tried, she only drifted further away.

One of Flora's maids woke me at dawn. She hurried me into the bath while setting the breakfast table, telling me that Lady von Heskin would join me in half a bell. Lana stole the best food while I washed, then settled to watch my every move.

And so started several tedious mornings. Flora would arrive and point out the dress, jewelry, or bag that was wrong with my attire and I would change as directed. She brought a horse whip to rap me over the legs when I displeased her, declaring that even the most willful beast could be broken. Lana watched with a smile.

Then we would eat and Flora would criticize my table manners as we practiced our way through Oberwaldian and Talian courses. The food was always plentiful but she expected me to eat like a bird, leaving at least half on my plate to show that I was not a glutton and provide enough leftovers for the servants. I could never drop the princessly illusion, but rather had to watch my every move even more closely than when in public.

Rap. Rap. Rap. The layered dress muted the pain, but by the end of the first meal, thin bruises were forming.

Then I would walk, talk, and dance. Each step would be accompanied by her scathing remarks. Only the dancing left me without another bruise, despite being paired with my stepsister who tried her best to trip me.

When the grand clock finally struck midday, Flora left, instructing me to do nothing to draw attention to myself. I would nod, smile, and as soon as the door closed, stuff myself on the food I had hidden when she turned away. At least my practiced sleight of hand was being used for something.

In contrast, during the afternoons I paced, waiting for my second teacher. I had to lie to Mariska, but the relationship felt genuine as she guided me through meditations and helped me connect to the diffuse power she called the world's Spirit.

She would stare Svetlana down, then send her on an errand and lock the door. Each day, I made up a new story explaining what Mariska and I talked about. I did not care my stepsister had to report things she surely did not believe. For once, she could deal with her own problems.

Based on Mariska's offhanded comments and lorists' stories, I tried to separate the rumors from facts about mages and magic. Mariska talked of different kinds of elementals—fire bearers were able to bring forth flames from nothing, and wind whisperers could control the weather and listen to the air—and lesser-known mages like telekenetics and death keepers such as the temple priestesses. I learned magic powers were distinct, each with their own rules and secrets.

Only healers and sigil crafters were talked about openly. Their official Guild ensured their services were exorbitantly expensive, their secrets carefully guarded. The Guild was part of a larger network governed from far away Jonesta. Besides crafting unbreakable bonds and contracts, sigils could create a weakened shadow version of the other mage powers. Even Mariska did not seem to know much more about them, though she did confirm something I had thought only a wild rumor: each sigil carried a tiny piece of the crafter's will, similar to a curse that survived the mage's death, like a piece of them lived on. If it had been real, the noble's sigil on my arm would have been a masterpiece, tying me to the Oberwaldian royal House and their sigil chapter. As Mariska spoke, the debt sigil on my upper tight itched—surely Kirill did not pay Guild prices. Everything was available on the black market, even sigils.

The second day of our lessons, Mariska and I sat cross-legged on the floor, knee to knee. I copied how she held her hands in a circle, knowing that each seemingly simple question I asked would raise her suspicions further about my lack of knowledge. Luckily, she closed her eyes, allowing me to study her.

"Bring up your Spirit slowly. Tell me when you have it and I'll do something to distract you. Steady is the aim."

I nodded but felt like a fool. There was nothing inside me that had not been there all my life. If Mariska had not seemed so certain, if a picture of my likeness did not decorate the prince's mantel, I would believe my mage power a fever dream. In our session the previous day, I had pretended a very princessly headache to cover my incompetence.

"Raise a mage light so we can see how stable it is. Tell the world what you want. Magic, no matter what kind, is all about directed will and connecting with the gods-given kernel of power inside. It's part of your emotions. Control them."

Goddess, show me something, I prayed, searching without knowing what I was looking for. The prince had said I raised the lights in his chambers. Then I used magic while falling and after kissing him. I had felt anger and passion, exhilaration and fear. Now I felt only uncomfortable. Maybe the strong emotions—losing control—were necessary.

Sitting here was doing nothing, that was sure, and I had to tell Mariska something if I wanted her help. I swallowed my doubts. Overthinking was Lumi's thing. This required a leap of faith.

"I can only access my power when emotional," I said, and it felt right as soon as the words left my mouth. "That's why I was hard to train."

She raised an eyebrow and leaned back on her hands. "You don't meditate in Oberwalden?"

"Well, others do," I quickly corrected to ensure I said nothing she could corroborate. "But my power is connected to emotions, mine and others."

"Guess it makes sense." She pursed her lips thoughtfully. "People are too secretive about their magic. I will not push you off a balcony—"

As if to complete the sentence, she slapped me. *Hard*.

I had been hit many times and learned to roll with it, or anticipate it early enough to evade, but the tiny noble healer took me completely by surprise.

"What— "

"Raise a mage light, quick."

I swallowed my exclamation, focused on the shock, the red mark certainly forming, and what Flora would say the following morning.

Heat spread from my cheek, tingling and raising the hairs across my body.

Light, I thought, picturing the blue orb the prince summoned when he caught me stealing the crown, the fireflies I created in his room. *Please shine*. Those had been sudden. This was slow, a serpentine power wrapping around me before leaving a chill in its wake as a dozen blue-white pinpricks shimmered to life.

Lumi, what would you say if you saw this?

I touched one. With a burning singe, it absorbed back into my finger. I turned with a proud smile and found Mariska studying me.

"Not sure you should hit me every day," I joked, trying to downplay my obvious excitement at what was probably a very minor show of magic. "Could be a diplomatic incident."

I was not behaving like someone who had power since birth, whose every tantrum had pulled at other's emotions.

"I have to attend dinner in the great hall tonight with your cousin," I said, now truly babbling, wishing I was cold and collected like Lumi. "Think he'll notice a bruise? Or stay long enough to dance?"

Mariska smiled at the mention of the prince. Distracted for now, but how long could I keep this up if she was to teach me?

"I'll heal you in no time, and he never enjoyed the watchful eyes of the court." Mariska fidgeted with the hem of her crimson healer's coat. "Can you feel my emotions?"

Based on her downturned eyes, she had something she did not want me to know. As long as she focused on herself instead of me, I did not mind reassuring her.

I offered her my hand, and she tentatively took it. More naturally than the lights, the foreign feelings overlaid mine.

"You're a little nervous, overall happy. I cannot hear your thoughts."

Or feel your most intimate emotions. That was what had happened with Dimitri, and somehow, he knew it.

When he had seen me the day before as I walked the courtyard, desperate for movement and air, he had looked like he saw a Spirit and turned around. At dinner, he ignored me or gave one-word answers, careful never to touch. His mask never slipped under the court's watchful eyes. I did not dare to break the silence. Each night, I made up a new explanation for what happened between us and tried to put it to paper but failed.

Mariska healed my sore cheek with no more questions, telling me with a wink to say hi to her cousin. Clearly, our stiff smiles were enough for her.

But the following night, the king frowned in our direction, as did Flora, seated one table away from the dais. I forced a smile each time I caught their eyes and focused on applying the rules Flora reiterated each morning, imagining her rapping when I reached for the wrong fork, or dipping my fingers too deeply in the scented cleansing bowl between meals. In short, I was outwardly the perfect princess, while seething inside.

That Dimitri avoided me in private was understandable, maybe even for the best, but he had been born to this life. If I could attempt conversation, so could he. At the end of each meal, he left and I was forced to retreat as well while other couples danced and enjoyed the music. This was the part I had longed for, but sitting alone would be too conspicuous.

Did he spend the evenings with the woman he really wanted to marry? Or drowning in his sea of grief? Was it simply that as he had the crown back there was no need to keep me close anymore?

The third such night, in pure rebellion, I stuffed an unused gold plate into the thigh bag I had gotten used to wearing. If I decided to run, the precious metal would be easier to hide and sell than identifiable gowns. It joined Lumi's shoe in the back of the closet.

Another three-day worship passed, much less eventful than the last—no one pushed me or even said a harsh word, no foreign thoughts invaded my mind.

Again, the prince stood alone next to the high priestess, while I watched from the balcony high above. Flora insisted on staying close enough to catch me if I took one step out of line, to ensure I behaved like a proper princess would. When it was over, she ushered me back into my chambers and Lana's watchful eyes.

The only piece of excitement was an invitation to meet with the queen and dowager queen in the Women's Tower—where I suspected the seer would test me—in three days.

Despite Flora's tutelage and being unable to reach Lumi again, it should have been happy days. There was plenty of food, the finest of everything. There had been no more attempts on my life. I was seemingly safe, at least on the surface. Each day brought me closer to the wedding, freedom, and leaving. But the inaction crawled like ants under my skin, and after the third evening unable to sleep, I snuck past Lana's door in the plainest dress they had provided me.

Wandering the palace aimlessly, seeking the places no one could see, I drifted like a Spirit without bones to the highest tower roof, unknown stars sparkling above. The next night, I walked through the park as it turned into forest, exploring hidden courtyards. I ran from tree to tree, laughing under the rain, meeting no one. Out here I was invisible and free. Then I opened the wood gate and saw him sliding across the cracked stones like an uneasy Spirit.

Perhaps it was inevitable I would run into the only other person who seemed as unsettled as myself. Maybe we did suit each other after all. We both haunted the night, seemingly unable to escape each other.

Chapter Nineteen

Vanya

Soaked from the rain, I stepped into the sweet smelling, rose-covered courtyard. More forest than garden surrounded it, the Taliell ran within earshot, and instead of the ancient, black stones or cold, white marble, the walls were made of crumbling, yellow bricks. The rain darkened the muggy night—wet or dry, a Talian summer was always warm—and I did not mind the reminder of nature's powers, even in this gilded world. An abandoned corner lost on the border of the palace.

Unable to continue or step away, I watched mesmerized by the scene illuminated only by mage light.

Dimitri moved smoothly, as if locked in a martial dance with invisible enemies. Each punch and spinning kick precise. In the dark, I could barely make out his serene face. Around him, a magical wind spun raindrops into whirlwinds.

I should not be here, I knew that. But still I could not leave.

Without thought, my arm moved to copy his, and I pointed my toe and twirled. Movements became a dance of anger and loneliness and frustration. Water dripped down my neck, hair sticking to my face. Did I do it because I was tired of watching others dance each night or because I was also drowning?

First, I followed Dimitri's lead, but soon, my eyes closed and the dance took over. The wind and rain and river sang, accompanied by rustling branches and the creaking gate. I imagined myself dancing through the familiar streets of Tal, neighbors laughing at my antics, Lumi cursing them for mocking her sister. Warm summer rains made the world new.

The downpour washed away my longing tears before they could fall. But there was laughter too. Joy in moving without care, at just being me.

When I stopped, Dimitri caught my eyes. Water dripped from his hair, his muscular chest still heaving from exertion, so he must have noticed me right before I opened my eyes. Since I saw him last, he had changed into the tight, leather armor I had spotted displayed in his rooms, the clasps reflecting the lights. In how many hidden moments did he wear it for the scent to cling to him?

His mismatched eyes narrowed. I could see him considering running away as he had each evening as soon as the last evening meal plate was cleared.

After twice halting his gaze from travelling further down the wet dress clinging to my body, he asked darkly, "Were you dancing?"

"Are you always so serious?"

He frowned as if answering my question. "You shouldn't be here, Princess, gallivanting about. You don't know Tal."

I snorted. What does gallivanting even mean? "And I thought you people in Tal were supposed to be up all night—it's not like you yourself are in bed, and it's perfect weather for a stroll."

He swiped the water from his face and stepped closer, the tiniest of smiles lifting the corners of his lips. "I guess you miss the mountains. I do as well, though when there, I only wanted to escape—the silence and wilderness does something to you. I haven't been to Oberwalden, but I imagine it's similar."

I knew summer droughts and pouring rain, muggy springs, and ever-shifting fall weather which turned into windy winters with rare snow, I but had never left Tal. *What was mountain air like?*

"Is this one of the pleasures you did not want to show me?" I said, deflecting, and spread my hands to indicate the cracked courtyard.

His grin matched mine, as if he could not resist engaging in our banter this far away from court. Clearly, I was beyond the innocent act. "Are you out in the dark looking for hidden pleasures, Princess?"

"You've been avoiding me. So I've been finding my own entertainment, exploring this palace of yours."

We stepped under an overhanging tree, somehow comfortable in the dark despite the distance between us in daylight.

I allowed myself to notice his strong shoulders and chiseled face. Even in Lowtown, dressed in rags, women would have turned to admire him. Especially if he allowed himself to smile, mischief lighting his eyes.

He swept a wet strand from my face. "There is more going on behind the curtains than you know. You stepped into a viper's nest, Princess."

"Does it have anything to do with v—" My throat closed, lungs struggled to expand, as von Lemerch's magic silenced me with ice-cold fingers.

"Princess?"

I won't say it. I won't say it. I chanted silently, pleading with the magic. Bright spots danced before my eyes. *I won't say it.*

Ever so slowly, my vision returned, my lungs expanded, and I registered the prince's worried face. Always, he found me fainting or falling. I shook my head to clear it fully.

"The wedding," I forced out. "Does your problems have anything to do with it?"

A question lit his eyes but there was a distance between us neither would cross again. Still strangers, despite the strange bond growing between us since we both touched the crown.

"My problems are from before I left Tal."

"What were those movements you were doing earlier?" I continued before the silence could stretch and he could ask me more questions.

He gave me a chagrined smile, seemingly happy to switch topic. "It's something I learned while away. One winter, I stayed in a monastery dedicated to the Airmover, one of the forgotten gods still prayed to in small corners of the word. The movements help the priests channel magic and see the greater mysteries. For me, it was a way to process what happened before I left and clear my head."

"Dance works similarly for me."

"It was..." He twisted my loose hair between his fingers as the wind played with his. "Beautiful, wild and free. Does it help you control your magic?"

Unlike last time. I had never reached for the magic while dancing, though nothing made me feel more like myself.

His fingertip drifted to my cheek. Brushed away the rain drops clinging to my skin. I tilted my head, offering—

A piercing griffon cry from the nearby stable split the night. When it cried out once more, the prince grabbed my hand and rushed toward it with me in tow.

"What could have upset it?" I called and increased my pace until we were parallel.

"Nothing should have."

Griffons cost more than a merchant's house and were points of pride among the Talian nobility. The value of the ones in the royal stables would be incomprehensible. They were also vicious creatures who only obeyed their master and trainer. *Could they even be stolen?*

I hurried to keep up with Dimitri's longer steps, avoiding the puddles in my soaked slippers. Based on my wardrobe, princesses did not require proper shoes. They were, after all, not supposed to go anywhere.

The brick stable was attached to the lower wall separating the Women's Tower from the rest of the palace complex. The rain and darkness hid any potential enemies as we ran across the courtyard.

Warm, dry air and deep shadows lit by evenly spaced oil lanterns greeted us upon entering. Rows of griffons ruffled their wings or clicked their sharp beaks. Nothing else moved, but I would have preferred a human enemy to the attention of forty ink-black eyes. Once, when crossing Palace Road, I saw a boy eviscerated by their sharp claws. He had been a street collector, the lowest honest profession in Tal, gathering the droppings of horses, drying and storing it on his family's roof and selling it to burn come winter. The high traffic on Palace Road made it the most desirable and dangerous collection spot. The griffon had ripped into him without it or its rider slowing. Who were they to question the Goddess for placing him in their path?

Beaks longer than my hand reflected the sparse light, like sickles with minds of their own.

The prince, lantern in hand, left me at the entry to inspect each corner of the long stable, including the upper floor, before returning. He'd even bent into the griffon pens. As if anyone would be stupid enough to hide there.

He stopped by a great black beast prancing in the small space.

"Come over here."

"Found something?" I strained my neck, but did not move.

"The stable hand is gone, perhaps he snuck away for a hidden meeting or nap. His pay'll be docked either way for leaving the griffons alone. Their night vision is terrible so they are at their most vulnerable on a night such as this." Dimitri placed his hands on the griffon's neck. "The best we can do is calm them so they don't hurt themselves. Whatever spooked Cherny is gone now, and we're not going to find it stumbling about in the dark."

"Cherny?"

He smiled affectionately. "She's mine and watches over the others. I got her when I left the Tower and spent the next years caring for her as she grew. She gave me the sky. Tal is so small from up there."

The creature calmed to the sound of his whispered voice. I could not blame it, as my own racing heart slowed. I crept closer.

"Beautiful, isn't she?" He petted her beak, and despite his words, I expected it to snap and sever at least a finger or two. Instead, the creature tilted its head, as if to give him better access to her vulnerable throat—not dissimilar to how I had in the courtyard. It seemed the severe prince had the same effects on females of all kinds.

"Is she usually easily spooked?"

Dimitri gave me a boyish smile over his shoulder. "Not a fan of griffons, I take it. The one next to her might seem huge but he is still her foal and she's ready to protect him. No one else should approach her alone. Give me your hand."

There was a reluctance to his stance, a barely perceivable hesitation before our skin touched, but relaxed when nothing *magical* happened. Neither of us wanted a repeat of me diving into his emotions. The least I could do to return his trust was follow when he pulled me closer and placed my hand on the griffon's warm feathers. His leather mixed with the wild scent of the griffon, resulting in something that both exhilarated and calmed.

Cherny turned her head to look at me with her black eyes. I flinched away, but Dimitri held me steady and guided each stroke until both I and the griffon relaxed.

Peddlers sold tame parrots in Midtown. As a child, they had fascinated me, and for my name day, Mother spent pennies she could not afford to let me hold one for a bell. I had petted it, fed it crackers, not minded the claws digging into my shoulder when the merchant allowed me to take it for a short walk. I had wanted nothing more than to bring it home. What would it have been like to be given one of these great creatures?

Cherny's feathers were small and soft on her neck, growing progressively longer until reaching the great wingtips, each one perfectly black like the prince's hair—perhaps the reason she was selected for him. Like the parrot, she cocked her head and studied me with intelligence.

I closed my eyes, and excitement at being close to an apex predator overtook the anxiety. Magic shivered inside me, somehow awoken. Training with Mariska during the last days had brought me closer to accepting it.

Alien feelings traveled from Cherny to me. She enjoyed the petting, trusted the prince—loved him—and was warming up to me. But below the surface, there was a layer of unease. Someone who did not belong had walked through the stable.

Focusing, I delved deeper. There were no thoughts, but impressions of other griffons, leather harnesses, and trusted carers, then a smell that stuck in her nostrils like death.

I flinched away from the poisonous odor. Cherny snorted as if agreeing with my disgust and then warmth spread back into me. *I was communicating with a griffon.*

I opened my eyes. Though he could not know what had happened, Dimitri watched me with a twinkle in his mismatched eyes. When I removed my hand from the warm feathers, he did not let go.

We stood trapped by each other's gaze and a very different kind of magic neither wanted to break.

We did not kiss or embrace. Still, it was more intimate than either. There was no desperation, we were not saving each other or distracting guards. His hand was warm in mine. The light reflected in his eyes like stars. We were people instead of prince, princess, or thief.

I imprinted it in my mind, to carry into bad days sure to come. To remember Cherny's quiet stability, to be grateful the prince had taken me here and put my hand against her flank.

The rain beat against the roof. A slammed door broke the magic, and before we could step apart, the missing stable hand lifted his lantern. When he saw us together, he paled, mumbled an excuse, and backed away.

The prince and I shared an amused smile before leaving. I shook my head to myself. It seemed we communicated better without words.

Stopping under the eaves outside, I felt him about to break the comfortable silence and squeezed his hand. My anger at being ignored the last days had disappeared in the dance, rain, and stable.

"There are a lot of things I cannot tell you, but I need this marriage to become king," he said, facing the dripping rain. "And my father is not a good man. I know you have no more choice than I do, and there's somewhere else you would rather be, but I will try to make the months until the wedding better. I'm sorry for pushing you away."

I had not expected to ever speak to a prince, and now, he had apologized to me twice.

I squeezed his hand in reassurance again, longing to spill my own secrets, or at least warn him of von Lemerch. The thought closed around my throat, like the magic heard my desire and thought I needed another reminder.

We were strangely similar—both in impossible situations, neither having volunteered for our roles in this improbable tragedy. Good actors follow the script and playwright's instructions, playing their part until the unavoidable end. The wedding was a dreaded and wished for milestone treading ever loser. But there was still more than two months until then and the hope inside me seemed impossible to silence.

"Whatever else we are, I don't want to be your enemy," I said, hoping he could read the truth in my eyes. Maybe we were not so wrong for each other after all.

He nodded slowly. "I'm at the same courtyard most nights before bed. If you cannot sleep, and movement helps you too, you're welcome to join me. There are too few places in this palace away from curious—" He squinted into the darkness. "Did you see that?"

I turned, but there was only the night, the fountain, and the black palace.

"What?" The griffon's heightened senses had smelled something dead, but I could not explain to Dimitri how I knew that. Probably there was a lot going on here that had nothing to do with me.

"I thought I saw a Spirit." He swiveled his head searching. "It's impossible inside the palace walls. People from the city sometimes destroyed the protection sigils during the night, but for a Spirit to come in here…"

He shook his head again. I kept staring into the lessening rain.

"Maybe it was a lantern or mage light." No true Talian would make that mistake, but maybe the Crown Prince of Tal had lived so long in this closed off bubble he no longer recognized a Spirit.

He only frowned in response, but as we walked back into the royal palace, he kept scanning our surroundings. Light shone from the gatehouse and a few windows high above. It should have been peaceful; instead, I noticed he tensed at each dark corner.

On the royal floor, we split up with a polite good night. There was no more romance. Still, I closed the doors to my chambers with a reluctant smile. Lana's door was shut, the room dark besides the one lamp I had left burning. The magnificent bed called to me, and I was sure if I closed my eyes now sleep would find me. But I had one more thing to do tonight; the prince had given me the idea.

I always felt the most alive when straining my body, focusing completely on the muscles and letting go instead of overthinking.

The meditations with Mariska were not working, and she was getting more suspicious by the day, even if she did not say so. Hitting me was not a permanent solution, and I had no interest in self-harm.

In the middle of the room, I spread my arms, then fingers, feeling the space. I noted the furniture that I had become used to, building the room in my mind, before closing my eyes. And moved.

Unheard, a slow drumbeat filled me. It was the dance steps of the last ones to leave the dance floor, people too tired to spin and bend but needing the moment to last.

I moved my body as I had learned as a child. It was not the courtroom dance the instructor taught us but the ones I had joined on the dance barges of Rivertown. My feet shuffled and stomped in time with the silent rhythm, my hands silently clapped, and my head swung back and forth.

I focused internally like I had with the griffon. There was a heat in me, a burning core stretching through my limbs, traveling through my blood faster and faster in the dance. Like when I fell or fought with the prince, my pulse quickened; magic tingled in my fingertips.

It flowed out in a jumping stream, a twinkling jet from a happy fountain. Mage lights lit the room. It stretched further, through the crack under the door, and the window left open to air.

Don't let anyone see, I thought to it like I would have a living thing. *Find my sister.*

Then I felt people dreaming in their beds, caught in passion, awake with sorrow. Each one unique. Lana's room stood empty. *Had she returned to her father in Tal for the night?*

Smaller creatures crawled out as the humans slept. A mouse made its way into the kitchen, carefully avoiding the anti-vermin sigils.

Sweat ran down my face as I reached further, never stopping the slow dance. In Tal the party was just getting started, the city full of too much life for me to grasp.

I imagined the face so like my own, the only person I really knew, who had been at my side at each step until now.

Lumi, I commanded the magic, and each of the previously easy steps became a struggle. I slugged through mud and struggled up a mountain. Finally, as if down a long tunnel, I felt her. She was awake.

A scene formed. It was the same underground room, but this time, Spirits drifted around my sister. More than I had ever seen inside a house.

"You're still there. I told you to run. You cannot trust any nobles, Vanya." Lumi waved her hands, dispersing the Spirits as if they were smoke, and looked straight into my eyes.

"What was that?"

"Have they hurt you?" she said instead of answering me, her eyes colder than usual. When was the last time she looked like the sister in my memories?

"No one questions me. I'm fed, taken care of, even Lana is bearable. The prince is... nice. Someone pushed me off a balcony but he saved me."

Lumi tensed. "Royals are not *nice*. Killing them is the only thing von Lemerch got right. The royals deserve no sympathy and if someone tried to hurt you they're probably behind it. They've made Tal what it is, a place where the poor get poorer and the nobility gets away with anything."

I missed a step in the dance, and Lumi's image wavered before I caught the beat again. "Has von Lemerch talked to you? We can't go through with her plan. Something is wrong with her."

My eyes flitted to the unmoving woman next to her. Helia. *What had they done to her and why hadn't they done the same to Lumi?*

"Just leave and I'll take care of the rest. You can get what you always wanted—a life far away from here."

Could I run and leave the thinking to others, as I always had?

"I—where are you?"

Her face twisted like she did not want to answer, and I pushed my worry and need at her.

"By the von Mekeln mansion," she said. "I recognized the way. But Vanya stay a—"

Pain shot through my leg, and I crashed to the floor, all magic disappearing. Blinking through involuntary tears, I found no Lumi or Helia, only the backside of the sofa I had fallen over. My head ached where it had hit a table or shelf, and my body was covered in sweat from the dance. Colors danced before my eyes, the world more real than before, as if to contrast with my vision. My head pounded like drums were still playing inside. The magic aftereffects were lesser than when I fell. Still, I lay on the floor until it stopped rocking.

I knew where Lumi was, or almost, at least. We had a way of communicating, and she had a plan. It should have filled me with the usual confidence. She was the one steady thing in my life. From birth, she had been there to lean on. When she was attacked, my foundation fractured. Since then, the cracks had been growing too slowly for me to notice them until her words filled me with doubt that I could follow where she led.

I could not hurt someone in cold blood nor stand by knowing the Death Goddess was coming for the man who held my hand tonight without expectations—was that why she was trying to send me away? No matter how much I wanted to, I could not see Dimitri as the faceless prince, the enemy of the people, Lumi believed him to be.

Tonight, our relationship had not been a lie, but the start of something impossible. Might he feel the same if he knew he was talking to Vanya? And did I not owe it to myself to find out?

Tomorrow night, after surviving my visit to the Women's Tower and the seer, I would sneak into Tal and free Lumi. We would come up with a joint plan. In person, she would listen to my feelings and find a way to tell Dimitri everything. Surely, she would see having the crown prince on our side would only strengthen our position. He did not seem to like his father any more than she did.

The floor creaked and Lana's face appeared above the sofa. Her mouth twisted into a smile I had learned to fear.

"Well, where have you been, cinder girl?"

I struggled to my feet only to fall again, the magic rocking me. The bedchamber door and safety were impossibly far away. She had waited to find me like this. I should have known better than dismissing her.

"It seems you have forgotten who you are. The nightly excursions, strange dances, and making me take the consequences for your lies are over. As you cannot manage to tell me what is happening or keep me in the room, you're no longer leaving."

She dragged me into the tiny servant's chamber and left me on the floor with a casual kick before slamming the door. Wood screeched against wood as she pushed something to block it.

There was no magic left in me, not that it seemed able to move furniture. I crawled into the narrow cot. My stepsister would have to let me out when Flora came the next morning. There had been moments I thought Svetlana was warming to me, but she would always remain the same selfish person.

If she described my dancing, would my fake aunt guess I had been using magic to unravel her and von Lemerch's plans?

My stepsister's words had implied she would lock me up each coming night. My determination hardened. I knew where Lumi was and had started to understand my magic. I needed to get out and find a way to keep Dimitri safe as well. After the visit to the Tower, I was leaving the palace with enough stolen plates and jewelry to pay Kirill. I would not need von Lemerch to give me my freedom, I would take it myself, and after it all was done, I would leave Tal as well.

Chapter Twenty

Dimitri

The morning brought regrets and duties as a servant I did not recognize informed me of my father's orders to attend the courthouse in his place. With hardly any sleep, in a freshly pressed black uniform and golden epaulettes, I left the ostentatious royal carriage, wishing I could have ridden Cherny across the sky, diving through the clouds until the sun burned away my apprehension. Or that I could wrap myself in the contentedness of the stable last night, in sharing something so simple and watching Helia's face light up.

As the morning's humid heat clung to my face and weighed my every step, I entered Tal's courthouse. The building was painted white for death and the Goddess, and red for luck for those on trial. It was one of the few landmarks built in the last fifty years. My grandfather, preparing for a new Tal, had funded it when he married Solovyova. Already then, Tal had been behind the rest of the world, but why change when death did not? Or so the Council had argued, stopping each development until the plague claimed my grandfather's life and only this one edifice to his vision remained.

Tal was stuck, and somehow Alexei's impassioned speech, together with the princess's wonder, had wormed their way inside, making me see the potential of the ancient city. What would it look like to have one of the thin metal bridges stretching across Palace Road outside? Why were they only for the numerous arms of the Taliell? The last time large scale sigils had been crafted was over two hundred years ago when the palace walls were reinforced. For that, the whole Talian Sigil Guild had come together at exorbitant cost. If brought together again, what else could they do?

I let the musings distract my mind as I strode down halls I had not tread since my exile, willing the images they conjured to suppress thoughts of how my father had gathered those loyal to him on the Council and voted for my son's death. How I might today have to face Heridan and Novikov and pretend ignorance. Worse, how any of the others in attendance could be the unidentified two who voted with my father, and I would not even know it. My stomach churned, ready to reject this morning's meal.

I passed windows with clear glass, wide hallways, and impeccably dressed men and women seated behind neat rows of desks copying out declarations and decisions without pause, appearing as if I belonged. Reaching the still-closed grand doors which simply read "For Tal," I could no longer ignore that I was about to enter the room where my father had condemned my child. Had he sent me to hear cases in his place to remind me? Had I gone to appease him or because I needed the ice inside to solidify?

It did not matter.

I was here, and I would do my duty. Walking the streets, the people of Tal had let me grieve. I owed them my full attention at least in this moment. That should be reason enough.

With a nod, I signaled for the two black-uniformed, skull-masked guards to open the doors. My heavy steps echoed against the arches and glass ceiling high above. A high-backed stone chair composed of chiseled skulls and roses waited. Once, it had stood at the top of the Women's Tower for the divine rulers of Tal. It remained empty unless a royal oversaw a trial—a rare occasion nowadays.

I settled on the hard, cold surface as five Council members, two men and three women, entered through the back door. I only had eyes for one. Heridan. My fingers clenched around the skull armrests as I controlled my breathing, imagining myself moving in the rain to calm. I could not let anyone see the murder in my eyes. Not until it was too late.

After Zahkar's blood stained my hands, I had wanted nothing more than to wash it away. Watching the councilor, I wished all could disappear as easily as my old guard.

The dagger strapped to my arm shifted as they bowed with barely a look my way before seating themselves on the red-and-black-painted pew below, ready to provide advice and judgment at my direction.

Court was in session.

The first two cases were trade disagreements between noble houses, and I nodded for the councilors to give their views, then agreed with their assessment, feeling utterly superfluous. The councilors knew the law better than me, had heard uncountable similar cases and collectively lived several centuries more. Part of the reason royals rarely attended court was simply that we were not needed. As Solovyova once put it when I was no more than six, *In life, the Council ruled the city, the royals the nobles, and the matriarch in the Women's Tower. In death, we all belonged to the temple.*

Despite my initial determination to focus on my citizens, my eyes drifted away from the petitioners as I considered each counselor. Had von Lemerch or Osipov been there? Were they wondering if I knew or had it been such a minor decision they no longer thought of it? I often hated that my very presence instilled fear in most of Tal—from citizens to servants to nobles—but now I wished it extended further. I wanted to see suppressed terror in the councilors' eyes. Wanted them to know, I held their fates in my hands like they had my child's.

I felt councilwoman Stasia von Lemerch's eyes on me and snapped mine back to the petitioner. The least I could do was look the part. My training should have ensured I never let my guard down. I should have learned my lesson. There's always someone watching. Here, that was the whole city, judging the recently returned prince they believed would be their future king.

The court crier introduced the next man as Fyodor Popovanov, and a muscular man anywhere between thirty and fifty years old, his long, gray-speckled hair kept in two braids, was led in by two guards. The prisoner studied me with a face holding enough condescension to be worthy of any royal.

"Who's the accuser?" I asked when no one followed.

Councilor Heridan rose and my gut tightened. "The city stands against Popovanov and asks for death for conspiring against the crown."

"How do you plead?" I asked, knowing I would not let Heridan sentence anyone to death again.

Popovanov smiled. "No more guilty than anyone who dare to speak the truth."

"Guilty," Heridan echoed, and for the first time, spectators who had drifted into the court hall during the last bell made themselves known with dissatisfied rumblings.

I raised my hand and somehow it, or perhaps the power of the ancient chair, was enough to silence the crowd. "What truths?"

"Don't give him a chance to spew his treachery again," Heridan said, fortunately silently enough for it to not reach further than the accused.

I narrowed my eyes. "I asked a question, not for advice."

Thank the Wishmaker, Heridan did not meet my eyes or further test my restraint before Popovanov spoke up.

"That there's more people, Spirits, taxes, and crime, but no food or care. The dead walk the streets of Tal. The poor are sentenced for the noble's crimes, paid a pittance to take their place. We die like the rats while you lock away the healers, ensuring even death reaches you later. No food is coming into Tal because you keep it all to gorge yourself during balls and banquets."

"Your neighbors steal, and you blame the crown?" I raised my hand. This was not the place for a philosophical debate in governance. Nothing had changed, not even the complaints—the nobility ate as much as usual, perhaps even less considering how many faces seemed to be missing since I returned, and there were not enough healers to care for more without risking losing them to madness. One point in his passionate ramblings stood out though. "If you have evidence of bribery, I will hear it."

Hopefully he had something on Heridan, and I would not have to delay my revenge another moment. I leaned forward, my body tense enough to pounce, though I knew any battle in this room would be fought with words, not fists or knives. I could not take out the councilors like I had Zakhar.

The prisoner swallowed, and von Lemerch opened her mouth before I raised my hand to let the accused speak.

"I knew a stable hand working for Lord von Mekeln," Popovanov said, his voice halting. "And an evening two months ago it started.

First the sigils they paid for seemed to peel away, or someone damaged them at night. The lady complained and had them redone at great expense. The next night the first Spirit was seen inside the gates and a boy was sent running for the priestesses. At the same time the lord started coming into the stable at night. My friend would hear him talk to the horses. He slept there you see. The lord didn't seem himself. Talked about death and the Night of the Dead. My friend would follow him, thought the lord might hurt himself, you know. Von Mekeln walked behind the stable, then climbed a tree and over the wall. A man of sixty. Then talked to a Spirit on the other side. But it was larger than they usually are. Solid like. Well, he sort of opened his mouth really wide and it entered him. Like he swallowed a star, it burned out from his eyes before he collapsed. My friend screamed, as any sane person would. A guard came running, thinking there was an intruder. When he grabbed the lord, Lord von Mekeln rose and threw him against the wall. It broke his spine. They arrested and hung my friend the next day for murdering the guard. Now they want to kill me for speaking Orsam's truth."

Popovanov's rambling words stopped, but I could not think of anything to fill the silence with. Crazy. The man might have seen the lord kill a man, but swallowing Spirits and glowing eyes?

The crowd swelled as Popovanov's words traveled through the room. Arguments filled the air, and this time, my raised hand was not enough to quiet them.

"Empty the hall. Take the accused back to his cell," I commanded, and the guards standing along the wall snapped to attention.

As they guided the crowd outside, I knew rumors, each one more incredible than the next, would leap between drink halls, smoke dens, and party barges. For once, the firsthand story might be more outlandish than the tales.

When only the Council and I remained, I had my words ready and spoke before Heridan or anyone else could get a word in.

"We don't hang someone for words, no matter how mad. Change the sentence to fit the crime."

Councilor Florentiy Makariv shook his head. "He ruined a nobleman's reputation, and you gave him the stage to do so again. How could you let him speak openly before you knew what lies he would spew? This is how talk of rebellion brews."

My face hardened as exhaustion and anger made my temper brittle. "If you wanted this discussed in private you had ample opportunity to speak up when the case was read, but if you think what was said here had not already been said outside, you're the one who should pay attention. That man'll have told his story to every guard and cellmate. There is no containing something like that."

Heridan sniffed. "All you had to do was follow our judgment. If you're to be king—"

"If I'm to be king, I'll ensure everyone who judges a man to death at least hear his side first." *I might even listen to yours before I lower the knife.* From his paling face, some of my thoughts must have displayed onto mine.

Von Lemerch rose, leaning on her cane. "What do you propose then, my prince?"

Her eyes too-knowing as they swept over me and focused on the black stone seat raised my hackles. Was she one of the other two who condemned my son? I had only met her a handful of times since she arrived from Denyev and quickly worked her way up the social ladder despite not attending the palace banquets and parties.

Perhaps she quietly agreed with Popovanov in his condemnation of our excesses.

I had made my decision while the guards emptied the room, still, the words weighed like boulders too heavy to lift. This was real power. The throne I did not desire. It was also the last place I could afford to show weakness.

"One month in the prison." A place known for danger and hopelessness. It was the best Tal had to offer its inmates. If he had repented, I could have let him go, but after that public trial, they were right that doing nothing would be seen as agreement.

Von Lemerch's answering smile sent a shiver down my back. This morning could not be done fast enough.

As the doors closed for midday break three bells later, I left surer than ever this life was not for me. I had spoken once more—when a child was brought forth for theft and I could not stomach sending him to prison at an age I had not yet left the Tower. Under the Council's judging eyes, I forgave the crime and allowed him back into his mother's waiting arms.

Part of me longed to find the princess in my chambers again, though I knew I was already getting too attached. The pressing summer heat reminded me the wedding, only two months away, would give me the throne and revenge. Then the councilors who voted to kill children would pay. I could afford no distractions or attachments. Sooner or later, death followed love. I needed to stay hard, not remember how to laugh and live. I needed the missing names, not comfort and wonder. It was not like a sheltered Oberwaldian princess, no matter her beliefs, could understand the cold revenge I craved.

The wind whispered of change to come. Of danger and deceit. I ignored it, already aware of my lies.

The courthouse doors proclaimed "For Tal," but I knew if I let it, the city would swallow me whole, leaving a disillusioned copy of my father in the place of the person I could have been.

Chapter Twenty-One

Vanya

I awoke stiff from tossing and turning in the unfamiliar bed and pounded on the still blocked door. Without a window, it was impossible to know how late it was. Who would they punish if I did not arrive at the Women's Tower on time?

It was not like my stepsister could impersonate me, impersonating the princess. Lana was as blond as I was dark; no one would mistake us for each other. I kicked it and only succeeded in further hurting my stubbed toe.

"Open up!"

Would von Lemerch think I'd run and hurt Lumi?

"You can't keep—"

The door slammed inward, and I hit the bed hard. Framed by the narrow doorway, Flora waved her hand dismissively, pulling me back to my feet with her telekinetic powers. Behind her stood my stepsister wearing a causal smirk and one of Helia's fine dresses. Lana was half a head taller than me and the cream silk exposed her shapely calves. She did not seem to care.

Flora twisted two fingers and launched me forward. I fell before her feet, swearing silently. In her other hand she held the horse whip.

"I hear you've been escaping at night. Who are you meeting with? Did I not tell you to stay in your rooms like a proper princess?"

I gritted my teeth but could not swallow my angry words. "You told me to seek the prince, so I have."

She wrinkled her nose as if I emitted a foul stench. "We all know he has no honor. I don't know why I expected more of you, but you cannot be allowed to drag the Oberwaldian royal name through the mud." She hit me across my ribs without pausing. "Don't think that if you get pregnant, you'll become queen. After our friend is done, there will be no need of one."

"Her mother was a whore," Lana added, playing the evil stepsister before Flora despite how disinterested she was in me when we were alone, though her tone was resigned rather than gleeful.

Flora hit me across the thigh, then wrapped up the whip. "Like mother, like daughter then. Next time you disobey, I will let your sister take a swing. Unfortunately, the Queen expects you. Get dressed."

She settled on the sofa and ordered Lana to pour the tea while I escaped into my bedchamber.

But it was no longer my refuge—the fine bed was slept in, the muslin blanket and two towels left on the floor, and wet footsteps leading out of the bath. Lana, who always kept her space neat, had left it this way on purpose to mark her claim. Involuntary tears ran down my cheeks. The room had not been mine, but it had felt like it. I had not realized how much until it was taken away.

Nothing here was mine. I was someone to be whipped into the shape of a princess. If Svetlana had been in mine and Lumi's room, would any of my things still be there if I returned? I pushed the hanging dresses aside until I saw the shoe and checked for the letter.

Still there. I hugged it close, imagining Lumi giving them to me, telling me I would need to be able to run.

"Do you require another lesson?" Flora called, and I snapped into action.

Dressing in a sky-blue coat over a dress so pale it became inappropriately deathlike, I suppressed my anger and smoothed my face. Emotions would not help me here.

They could try to lock me in, but neither Flora nor Lana was invited to the Women's Tower, which was reserved for Talian noblewomen and their children. After my visit, I would escape them and free Lumi. Together, we would come up with a plan.

I stayed in the bedchamber until a girl no more than ten came to collect me. Flora chaperoned me until the Tower entrance. Her last command was to stay silent, smile and nod, then return directly to my chambers. Following her orders, I only nodded and smiled in answer.

Officially, Inessa, the Queen of Tal, had invited me, but I had overheard enough to know who was behind it. The dowager queen Yelena Solovyova's name was spoken with reverence and fear inside the palace. She ruled the Tower with an iron fist, and as the king's mother, she was the ultimate authority on anything from marriage to local politics.

Solovyova, as she was called, was a woman to respect. Despite the marriage contract and the king's word, if she did not approve, the wedding would be indefinitely delayed. And as Flora had reminded me each morning, if anything interfered with the wedding plans, Lumi and I would no longer be needed.

So as the ninth bell struck high above, I entered the Woman's Tower with a forced smile. My gown was impeccable, coattails hanging almost to the hem, my hair brushed and braided. The perfect bride despite the sharp pain from the lashes and magic exhaustion from last night.

The Tower was gargantuan. A perfectly square black stone building with nine floors and older than the rest of the palace. Maybe older than all of Tal. Before Herebov came here, the high priestess would have stood on the top, watching over her domain. The view must stretch uninterrupted beyond the city and across the steppes. Nothing could hide from death. Or Solovyova.

Black walls surrounded the Tower, at least twice my height, ending in iron spikes, like the fangs of a great maw. Each window was barred with the same black iron. I shuddered, passing below the intricately red-painted great arch—the only way in or out of this opulent prison. This was where noblewomen and children resided, where the prince planned to keep the princess as soon as we swore our marriage vows. Despite his words, it seemed incongruous with how he treated me while alone.

Children ran around me, while women sat on embroidered cushions around teapots and cards. Besides a great black staircase, the bottom floor was one open space, and through an open gate, greenery sprawled. The guards that patrolled everywhere else in the palace were missing; there were in fact no men at all inside the light stone hall.

A smiling woman with the lightest hair I had ever seen bowed to me, and the girl who brought me ran off without another look in my direction. It seemed not everyone was interested in the foreign princess.

"Solovyova is expecting you, Helia von Heskin. Please follow me," my new guide whispered, as if afraid to be overheard. A raven-haired toddler in a blue shift held her hand and watched me with serious brown-green eyes.

I winked at her, and she hid behind my guide's dress. Instantly, another woman rushed forward and comforted the child. What would it be like to be raised not just with a mother but as part of a community and protected from everything outside the Tower walls? Had Dimitri once watched strangers with the same concern?

As my new guide led the way up the deeply worn stairs, the women we passed watched me like I was an exotic animal presented for their judgment.

Unused to so many eyes on me, I imagined the floating Rivertown stage where I had brought the playwright's vision to life. They were not watching me, but the character I was pretending to be—Princess Helia von Heskin of Oberwalden, their future queen, not Vanya, the street thief.

I straightened my back, relaxed my hands, and smiled with a secret. Acting is all about the breathing. Calm breaths and your voice is steady, your heartbeat calm. With the prince and Mariska, I had started to be myself. Here, I needed to remember I was someone else. The painful twitches from Flora's whip reinforced the role with each step.

Part of me itched to reach for my magic and attempt to know their feelings, but Mariska's repeated warnings and the internal fog that refused to completely lift stopped me from even trying. I would not risk my mind for other people's opinions.

Magic was seductive; no wonder gifted nobles thought themselves above others. I studied the ladies we passed, wondering what powers they hid behind their feathered fans and disdainful faces. No noblewoman entered the army and few became healers, but as far as I knew, magic did not differentiate between sexes.

Elaborate mosaics decorated the staircase depicting the scenes of the earth, starting with gold and minerals, roots and caves. On the third floor, we rose above low growing vegetation and reached the stems of great trees. On and on we went until blue and white decorated the walls in visages of the sky. The stairs ended with a golden floor—the world of the gods. An unimaginable show of wealth.

The prince marrying Helia for her money seemed less and less plausible. Sure, if you covered everything in gold you were bound to run out eventually, but Tal did not seem desperate enough to marry with a minor city state for its mines. *Why was the king so set on Helia and Oberwalden that he would hand his rule to the crown prince in exchange of the wedding?*

My guide turned to the right and we entered an airy room. Pale-blue pillars and arched white ceiling disguised the black stone and flowed into the open sky seen through great windows.

Female musicians played string instruments with unworldly skill. The melody lifted the worries off my shoulders, easing my pains and hurting head. Music had always had that power. As often as I could, I dragged Lumi onto the balcony of the royal theater. During intermission, we snuck inside and found an empty viewing room. Each one was owned by a noble or rich merchant family but they often stood empty. To Lumi's dismay, I would dance to the music, dreaming they were playing just for me.

The song built, and I slid closer, a moth to a flame, until my guide pulled at my arm and broke the spell. Blinking, I turned and noticed the stately women sitting at a table on the sun-covered balcony. The younger one I recognized from the evening banquets as Dimitri's mother. Queen Inessa was a short, fine-boned woman with black-and-gray hair, beautiful despite the delicate wrinkles decorating her face, but on a theater stage, the woman next to her would have stolen the audience's attention every time.

There was something magnetic about Solovyova, the undisputed ruler of the Tower. Dressed in a flowing gown of purple dark enough to appear black, she sat straight as a spear upon what could only be called a throne. From there she overlooked the room and her supplicants, rather than the spectacular view behind her. With a gold encircled arm, she waved me forward.

I stopped and bowed at what Flora had taught me was an appropriate distance and angle. Based on Solovyova's face, it was still too close. Elegant seating pillows surrounded a low table, but Solovyova's throne had its own attached tray. She lifted a delicate teacup, the porcelain thin enough for the painted flowers on the other side to shine through.

"Sit, Granddaughter, before you fall," she said and pointed to the pillows at her feet. "I heard you took a tumble straight into my grandson's arms recently. Maybe you think this will raise your position in court. A moon after the wedding, your new husband will be busy ruling and no one will care a wit for what he thinks of you. Men are weak, Granddaughter. Today my son woke up with a cough and remained in bed. The Council rules the city, but who do you think keeps the nobles in line?"

Her clouded eyes caught mine. Rumors said she had been nearly blind since birth, not that it made her any less intimidating.

Nod and smile, Flora had said, but something told me Solovyova would not appreciate it. A servant poured me a cup of tea and I sipped, thankful for the distraction, but forgetting Flora's instructions to stir three times each direction. The too-hot water burned my mouth. I yelped and spat the tea back.

A cane rapped me across the knuckles. The cup crashed to the floor.

The old woman had actually hit me.

"Never show weakness. A queen is strength. Poise. You're no princess."

Clutching my reddening fingers, I mutely watched a servant clean up the mess while Solovyova's unseeing eyes pierced me. Somehow this blind woman saw the truth when all others only saw what they expected.

"Mother, we knew she comes from a backwater state. No use blaming the crow when you picked the egg," Inessa said, without a look in my direction.

She sat on pillows a step higher than me, and her words hit like stones. I do not know why, but somehow I had expected Dimitri's mother to be placid and friendly. During court dinners, she sat at the king's side and rarely said a word, leaving even before me, presumably to return to the Tower.

The dowager snorted and waved her cane in my direction again. "Have her tested. I don't see how this scrawny girl with hips like a boy can bear Dimi a strong heir, but it's the blood that counts. Summon the water seer."

In response to her words, a servant rushed out, and Solovyova turned to me.

"What do you think the purpose of a queen is, Granddaughter?"

I smoothed my face and repeated what Flora told me. "To bear children and support the king?"

"Bear a child, maybe two, ideally sons, and you are done with the first part, then the real work starts. You shape the next king. You decide who he trusts. You rule the women married to the most powerful nobles in Tal. You arrange marriage contracts and control the information. The king has the army, the Council, the city, but behind the scenes, you rule it all. If you can."

Again, I felt myself falling short of her internal measuring stick. I knew she was right; I was no ruler and had no interest in marriage contracts—*why did I want this woman's approval?* The real princess might have impressed them, declared her skills, and already conquered the nobles. Even Lumi or Lana would have made better princesses than I. Watching the floor, I nodded in resignation. All I needed was to get through this without raising their suspicions, then escape into Tal and find Lumi.

The dowager and current queen continued their tea, talking about nobles, the wedding, and the weather, while I sat silently at their feet. No one offered me another cup. Never had I been more glad that this was not my life.

The music allowed me to drift until a fourth woman sat down opposite me.

When I overheard the king talking about a seer, I imagined someone much like Solovyova; instead, a teenage girl with hundreds of braids smirked while waving the servant away as she poured herself two cups of tea. With a hand covered in sigils and a cheeky smile, she handed me one.

"Drink."

I looked up at Solovyova and Inessa, who had paused their conversation. The queen waved for me to get on with it, and I stirred the tea, then carefully sipped the hot beverage. It was something darker, bitter, and foreign.

As soon as I finished, the girl snatched it back. She emptied the remaining leaves onto a gold-rimmed plate and grabbed my middle finger. After pricking it, she squeezed three drops of blood into the black mushy leaves and stirred with the bloody needle.

"Now spit," she commanded, offering the plate.

I obeyed and studied each following step. She pulled out glass tubes filled with azure, ochre, and brick-red powders, and added pinches to the tea until satisfied, then bowed.

"I'm ready to perform the test of power, Mistress."

Solovyova clapped her hands, and the musicians stopped playing. Another clap and everyone, including the servants, left the room.

When only the four of us remained, Solovyova turned to the seer.

"Let's see if the Oberwaldians exaggerated."

She flashed a sharp smile I could not return. Nerves rolled my stomach and chilled my sweaty hands. I might not want von Lemerch to succeed, but I could also not afford to get caught. As the seer rose, I tensed, ready to run no matter what Flora had said. No one in this room would listen to any excuses before locking me up.

Time seemed to slow as the girl lit a fire in a bronze bowl. She threw sweet herbs into the flames, inhaling the twisting smoke.

I could not resist leaning forward. Magic was never practiced openly in the city, and since arriving at the palace, I had only seen the prince create a mage light and felt the healers' power. This was something out of a lorist's tale.

The seer scraped the tea, blood, and saliva into the flames. The smoke swirled around her, mixing with the braids, and though there was no visible magic, I shivered.

The clock ticked and ticked.

"Well?" Solovyova finally snapped, and the seer stepped back, shaking her head as if to clear it.

She bowed, then spoke with her head still lowered. "Forgive me, Mistress. It's true that she is very strong, but something is blocking part of her power and my sight. It's old and deep. I could not pierce it." She swallowed nervously. "The princess is cursed. Since childhood, if I had to guess."

The old woman turned her milky eyes to me. "So, Oberwalden sent us damaged goods. Explain."

My mind spun. *Was this Flora's idea of nothing to worry about?* "I don't know—I always struggled, but no one tested for curses." I focused on von Lemerch and how she hired me to steal the crown, not her curse that choked me if I tried to speak. "There must be someone who wants to stop the wedding and weaken both countries."

"The princess did have trouble on the road," the queen said, and I nodded vigorously in agreement. "*She* could already be back. The wedding must happen or—"

Solovyova clapped sharply, silencing the queen and showing who was in charge.

"Leave," she said to the seer. "Don't breathe a word about this."

"Always, Mistress."

The seer bowed until her forehead was only an inch above the floor before backing out of the room.

As soon as we were alone, Inessa paced back and forth across the balcony. Worry lines marred her face, and for the first time, I saw Dimitri in her features and mannerisms.

"She cannot know how weak our position is, Solovyova."

The old woman scoffed. "This might well have been arranged to stop a wedding which has already been delayed. You should have been here two years ago, Granddaughter. You caused this with your dillydallying."

Would the real princess have known what was going on? I needed answers either way.

"Why would someone want to delay the wedding?" *Or exchange the bride?* The truth felt close, the missing pieces just out of reach.

Solovyova considered me, and I wondered if I had asked too much. "My son married for political connections and stabilizing the kingdom, as did I, but Tal requires magic blood in its rulers. The last generations have been sorely lacking, and we have been hiding it. My son and grandson think they can compensate with worldly power, but it is an offense to the gods. The wedding must happen this Day of the Dead—there can be no more delays."

Her blind eyes shone bright. *Was the old woman not as sharp as I had assumed?* They wanted me—or the real princess—to marry into the family to appease the gods? I, like all others, prayed but that was taking it too far. Von Lemerch was strange, but she was no deity.

Inessa only nodded along as Solovyova continued, "Even your closeness to my son helps. Do not leave his side, Helia. I don't know how but the gods approve already."

I tried smiling in agreement. The gods approved of me and her son hooking up? If they were watching, they likely frowned down on the Lowtown thief scamming the royal family.

"Come," Inessa said and waved me up to my feet. "I will show you what will happen to Tal without a strong royal line to lead."

A fanatical light shone in the queen's eyes as she ushered me out of the room.

I longed to start my search for Lumi, but whatever the queen wanted to show me could be the missing puzzle piece, or something I could use as leverage. I had already known von Lemerch cursed me—had the seer sensed how old her power was and assumed the curse was the same? The lorists said all mages curses related to their power—what kind did von Lemerch have? And more importantly, could the royals and the seer help me remove it?

Hoping for answers, I followed Inessa like the meek princess I pretended to be.

Chapter Twenty-Two

Vanya

The queen rushed down the central staircase and the ladies who stared during my ascent, stepped aside with downcast eyes. With arrogance produced by generations of selective breeding, Inessa noticed none of them.

She led me to the ground floor, then outside, trampling across the grass in the garden until we reached a miniature obsidian ziggurat covered in sigils. After opening the door with a hidden key, she continued down narrower, dark stairs as if we were on a comfortable stroll, and I reached my limit.

"Where are we going?" I asked, imagining the royal dungeons supposedly located under the Tower and rumored to be even worse than the Talian prison. *Did they suspect me after all?*

The queen paused, her cheeks rosy with exertion. "I wasn't shown until after the wedding, but being from Tal, I knew enough. My mother made sure. We cannot talk here. I have other appointments today, do hurry."

She continued into the darkness.

"But where are we going?"

Inessa sighed but did not slow. "The royal treasury. Summon a mage light when it gets dark, Princess von Heskin."

I silently chuckled and hurried down with new enthusiasm. The queen was unknowingly bringing a Lowtown thief within reach of the crown jewels. Despite everything else going on, this, more than anything else, I wished to share with Lumi. There were as many tales told about what was kept down here as roses in Tal.

Lower and lower, we went through a seemingly endless subterranean labyrinth. Inessa knew every twist and turn, while I only knew we continued down. The obsidian tunnels shone like an endless dark mirror.

Despite my troubles previously, I managed to cast the mage light Inessa requested. Maybe my nervous energy and pounding heart was enough.

When we arrived at a straight wall covered in sigils, the queen pricked her finger on a stone shard and pressed a blood drop on the central sigil. Soundlessly, the wall rotated to reveal treasures untold.

In a daze, I trailed the queen inside, leaving the turned stone open.

Each pedestal held impossible jewels. Crowns and gold statues were arranged artfully on shelves. Glass boxes held jewelry I could not have imagined. Nothing Lumi and I had stolen from nobles would have been worthy to enter this room.

The queen marched through the center aisle without a second look, while my eyes flipped from one side to the other, fingers itching. *Would I be able to reach out and put something in my pocket without her noticing?* How often did they do an inventory? Would I, after the wedding, also be able to access this room before von Lemerch enacted the rest of her plan? The temptation was almost enough to see it through. Only the two glass crowns, one real and one fake, elevated in the center brought me to my senses. I had already stolen enough.

Inessa stopped before the back wall. A bookshelf packed with tomes wrapped in ancient leather and gold lettering covered it from ceiling to the floor. I read one. *The Book of Bloodlines, 889.* On a central pedestal lay a similar book, its pages hardly worn compared to the crumbling ones on the top shelves.

The queen carefully flipped through it and waved for me to join her.

First, I thought it was a list of names, perhaps the royal genealogy, then I noticed the symbols next to each entry: crosses, arrows, skulls, and more. The top of the page read "The Blood of Life." Inessa pointed to the second to last name: Helia. Above it was her mother, Elena, and next to Elena was Flora and two men, presumably brothers. Three black squares stood before Helia's name.

Inessa turned the pages again.

"The Talian royal family belongs to the Blood of Elements. The King and my son channel wind. It has been the predominant magic in their line for the last five generations, but the magic has been growing weaker with each child. I come from a small bloodline with no mentionable powers. As you know, the Blood of Life, on the other hand, has only grown in power. There is more. *See.*"

She pointed to names in cramped rows. My eyes moved with her finger until they stuck on an impossible one, one that had nothing to do with magic and royals. She turned the page again too fast for me to be sure of what I had seen. Just as I was about to tell her to slow down, I noticed Inessa was not pointing to the names but black bones crossed next them—death. And there was hardly a name without a cross. The magic bloodlines were dying out.

The queen must have seen my surprise, because she nodded. "Soon, there will be no magic left in Tal."

"But most nobles have it..."

"Maybe in Oberwalden that's still true but in Tal all mages are dying. Some from common illnesses, some from accident, and some from murder, and those who survive are infertile or the plague claims them."

"What does this have to do with the wedding and the royal family?"

I could almost see it. Inessa was providing the missing pieces. It all fit into what von Lemerch was planning, but I did not know how.

"The royal line is connected to Tal. And we are needed to protect it. Marry my son, become queen, and join your House to ours. It'll strengthen the very essence of the city. Tal, the City of the Dead, is needed for the entire world. Worshipers and Spirits flock here. Without magic in the royal line, we're doomed, because our protections are already crumbling."

"What protections?"

Inessa shook her head. "I've already said too much. On your wedding day, you'll know all."

I tried to connect the dots, but there were still things she was not telling me. At least I knew why they needed Helia to marry the prince.

I was trying to formulate my next question, staring at the names, at each skull symbolizing a death, when there was a knock behind us.

I spun, my instincts telling me to flee, and mage lights erupted across the treasury. But it was only Solovyova's servant.

"Apologies, my queen, but you are needed," she said and inched away from the nearest light.

"Solovyova knows this is too important. Tell her I'll be back as soon as I can."

The woman fidgeted. "Forgive me. It's the King. You have been summoned."

Inessa sighed. "I need to hear what my husband wants—it rarely takes long before he tires of me. Stay and look through the pages, count the deaths and know that if the wedding is called off, they will continue. Each child above us with magic in her blood is not safe." She gestured to the treasures without a second look. "Don't attempt to remove anything. This is where they kept the holiest of relics when the Tower was a temple and Tal a theocracy. The sigils on the door will punish any thief, channeling the ancient will of the sigil crafters who made them. I'll be back soon."

Inessa strode away almost leisurely despite the anxious woman half a step behind her. It seemed while the queen could not deny the king's summons, she would not come running. Considering the mistress dining at the king's side, I could not fault her.

Alone and surrounded by glittering gold and jewels, I spun with my arms thrown wide and let out the grin I had suppressed since entering.

With my head still spinning, I brushed my fingers across a ruby so large that anywhere else I would not have believed it real.

Vases painted by long dead masters, silk carpets with a million knots, cuffs, rings, and necklaces—any one item would pay off Kirill and set me and Lumi up for life.

The swirling noble sigil climbing from my wrist to elbow seemed to move when I traced the lines. I was marked for life. The treasures belonged to the true royals, though Lumi would say they belonged to the people. How many trinkets would buy food for the orphans collecting excrement to sell? For more healers to help avoid senseless deaths? First, our baby brother died from fever, then our mother from the plague, and no one cared.

These jewels were not even worn or viewed. The glitter no longer held the same beauty, and keeping up the mage light was making my head pound.

I returned to the Book of Bloodlines—I could not have seen the name I thought I did but could not leave without looking again. Though, as it lay there open and inviting, I hesitated, my fingers hovering over the thick pages and family secrets I had never sought.

Instead of flipping to the correct page, I found myself lingering on each name, slowly moving through the book to the unavoidable end.

I started at the royal bloodline. Dimitri was on the last line, with just enough space left for his children. A tiny blue wind gust had been drawn next to his name. A weather mage, or wind whisperer as the lorists said. I knew he had no siblings, and the book confirmed that of his six cousins only two lived. The king and his brother, Rada, the crown prince, and his cousins, Mariska and Nikolai—the last four people in Herebov's royal line.

Under the Blood of Life, there were three squares next to Helia's name, presumably denoting her kind of magic. Her uncle and a few others had tiny hearts next to them. Were these the people like me—the heart turners Mariska had told me of?

On each page, I read the names next to the crosses marking the end of bloodlines. Each family kept their magic secret so no one besides the royal census knew mages were dying out. If this became public, commoners would stop fearing the nobles' powers and the support for Lumi's rebels would grow exponentially.

Numbly, I continued to read, each page adding to my dread. Maybe it should not have mattered what happened to the noble families, but I could not find happiness in the fall of others. There was already too much sorrow in Tal.

Finally, I could not avoid the Bloodline of Death any longer. It only had two genealogies, one of which died out three generations ago, the second two decades later. Except that was wrong.

Reading the name again, sounding it to myself, it still seemed impossible. *Komara Gorgiana Hereova*—my mother—the space beside her blank of magic markers.

She had always claimed we came from a noble family, and that our grandmother had run away from our controlling great-grandmother. But Mother had told so many stories I had long grown out of believing them.

Hereova.

The names one line above it must be my grandparents, though I did not recognize them, and then a name I did. Last three-day, I had seen her preaching before the crowds—Morovara, High Priestess of Bones, a human skull depicted next to her. A death keeper, though few used that title. Most called her and the other temple mages necromancers. Once, Morovara could have ruled Tal. She was also the person Lumi had told me to seek out in an emergency. She must have known and kept it from me.

Why?

We had drifted apart since her attack, and I borrowed the money for Popova to heal her. I should have been there to walk her home that night and had been trying to make up for it since. I knew she kept her rebel associates away from me, that she no longer spoke her mind, but to find a family member and say nothing? Morovara could have helped us with Kirill. Had Lumi asked and been rejected? Was our great-grandmother as controlling as Mother had claimed?

The mage lights flickered with my swirling emotions. We belonged to the House of Death, and based on the Spirits surrounding Lumi last night, she had magic as well. Had von Lemerch released our magic? Me, she wanted to pass for Helia. Was Lumi more than a hostage?

I paced the narrow room like a caged griffon but found no answers. The darkness hid how much time had passed, and there was no sign of the queen yet. My stress powered the lights, brightening the vault and the gold gained a shimmering halo. I was overusing again. Like on the bench, it was messing with my vision and thoughts. *How much more until it caused damage?*

One by one, I let the lights go out until a single bobbing blue ball remained. Sitting on the floor, I watched it as my headache and fear grew. Silently, I sang the songs my mother had sung to me. When I ran out of songs, and still no one came for me, sweat stuck my hair to my neck despite the chilly air and dread spread from the pit of my stomach. I could not sit here until I ran out of magic.

The place was a labyrinth but as long as I found a way up, I could figure out the rest later; the queen's command be damned. Outside the treasury, the black walls mirrored my frightened face. With the blue light hovering above my hand, I rushed down the hall, ignoring the reflection. There was no hope of finding the way I had come, but any stairs would do. At the fourth turn, I found a shaft, stretching forever up and down.

Pausing to breathe in relief before continuing with dignity befitting a princess, I noticed a chiseled skull at the downward steps—it was identical to the symbol of the House of Death.

Could there be more answers about my family down here?

My mind was fuzzy, vision swimming, but when would I ever get the chance to explore under the Women's Tower again?

As my light wavered, muffled voices I recognized echoed from below.

Chapter Twenty-Three

Vanya

The voices pulled me down into the dark. I recognized Flora's high-pitched exclamation and individual words echoed up. *Oberwalden... cannot... death... Day of the Dead.*

The stairs twisted round and round until leveling out, my mage light unable to reach the cavernous ceiling high above. It made me a target, but in this infinite underground it was my lifeline. If it went out, it might be gone for good.

With a hand raised to block the light, I tested the ground before shifting my weight to ensure no kicked pebbles revealed my presence, finding stone smooth enough to slide across.

With silent steps, I passed gold boxes with cast faces—sarcophagi presumably containing the bones of royals who did not qualify for the Grove above. It might be the oldest crypt in Tal. The last wall contained a twisting depiction of the Death Goddess herself. Only in the temples would they dare to paint her as, next to calling her name, it was the surest way to bring her attention to you. I looked away before a stray thought summoned her. I had enough problems without the attention of the gods.

Before the picture stood Flora, von Lemerch, two white-robed priestesses I did not recognize, and the beauty who had approached me in the courtyard on the first day. The one who claimed to know Dimitri, and I suspected to be the lover the king separated him from. His preferred bride, Ekaterina.

Despite my fear of the dark, I released the light. They could not find me here.

"Just open it. There is no need for her to marry him. There's no need to hurt him. I'll make him see sense," Ekaterina said.

"Quiet," von Lemerch snapped. "Do you think I would go through this elaborate charade if I had not tried everything else over the past centuries? This door and the Gate below cannot be broken from the outside." She gestured to the Goddess. "The wedding must go ahead as planned, and during the ceremony the royal blood will open the way down. Without the real crown reinforcing the magic and with enough dead under my command, the sigils will finally break. You were wronged by the royals and will get your revenge, same as me."

"But he can't marry a commoner and make her queen. Our child is supposed to be the next ruler of Tal."

Flora snorted. "You had your chance and let the king stop you. Proceed as you have, and there will still be a place for you afterward. I'll make sure the thief continues to play my niece. Have you seen enough?"

Von Lemerch stroked the Goddess's face, her own unreadable.

"It's over a century since I last came close enough to feel the Gate. The sigils have degraded enough. It'll work. Without powerful blood to fuel them, they would not last another generation. If you, weak girl, had snared the boy or if the spoiled princess had gone through with the wedding none of this would be needed. Now, the king is set on the Oberwaldian princess, he knows what's at stake, and we cannot delay any further without him finding another strong bride." She turned to Ekaterina, and her demeanor became inhumanly cold. "The commoner has some inherited power, but she's naive and untrained, and at the wedding they will come here to exchange vows. Don't go close to her again. Don't risk my plans for your own jealousy. She'll anyway not survive the night."

The priestesses smiled as if high on smoke, and as one of them turned, I saw the bloody Spirit of Lowtown drawn on her chest. "It's time for the true ruler to return Tal to its holy path. It'll be an honor to serve. When you call, we'll ensure the sigils outside are down and only the dead walk the streets."

Von Lemerch smiled. "The king tried to interfere, but has already been taken care of. Last time I was this close, the crowns blocked me." She focused on the priestess. "Don't fail me. With enough Spirits under my control, the ancient sigils will not hold. No matter how strong the crafter's will and large their powers, they cannot resist death forever. Herebov stole my birthright. With their deaths, his last descendants will return it."

Most of the conversation passed above my muddled mind. I could not understand why they were here or what they were doing. But one thing was clear and that made the rest irrelevant. *They were going to take over Tal and kill me in the process*. My already unstable magic responded to my fear and escaped my control.

Four human lives flickered in this place of death, but when the magic touched von Lemerch, it recoiled—she was alive and dead, burning and freezing. *Wrong*.

Her head snapped up, and despite the dark, met my gaze.

I ran, my pounding steps loud in the silence, but only getting out mattered.

They needed me for now, but Flora's punishments still ached. Allowing them to catch me here would be to tempt fate.

Up, up, up.

The unruly magic reached for the hundreds of women living above, each a song drawing me closer.

The world was no longer stable—I crashed into the walls without feeling the pain. Wishmaker, I needed light, air, and life to wash away the dead feeling of von Lemerch.

What was she? And was the whole temple, including our great-grandmother, part of it? Did von Lemerch know we were related to Morovara? What Gate lay beyond the Goddess's mural? *The dead will walk...*

The questions rushed by without answers, each one more impossible than the last. Only two things were sure: I needed to talk to Lumi, and I did not want to die. Even being sold to the Madam would be preferable.

Lanterns shone above, where hundreds of people and small creatures slumbered. Ten more steps and the moonlight, more warming than the sun, more cherished than all treasure below, hit me.

Outside an unlocked gate, the Tower's private gardens and elaborate greenhouses spread out on one side, the wall separating it from the rest of the palace on the other. Greenery enveloped me as I dropped to my knees and dug my fingers into the moist soil. Insects buzzed nearby, tiny bursts of welcoming life. Moonbeams solid enough to touch twisted around leaves. Part of me knew it was the effect of using magic for so long, still, I tried to grab one.

Giggles interrupted the night, reminding me I was not alone, that von Lemerch and her associates might be racing up behind me. I needed to get away, needed privacy to contact Lumi. I was in no state to launch a rescue mission, but she would know what to do.

On unsure legs, I followed the wall but only found more locked gates. Luckily, the wall was rough stone overgrown with ivy, offering easy handholds for it was built to keep people out, not in.

Seated on the top, the world spread out before me. The lights of Tal danced like fireflies. A city of revelry and death covered by the sweet smell of roses—no matter how much I wanted to escape, down below was home. The bustling streets, colored lanterns, bones, and party barges more real than the gilded world I now inhabited.

Inside the palace complex, Spirits seemed to swirl, like my mind tried to impose the familiar onto the sigil-protected paths. I blinked, and they were gone.

Time passed in fits and bursts. One moment, I was on top of the wall, then the next, clinging to the smoother outer side, before scrambling, falling, and hitting the ground. Once, I had never fallen and now I seemed to do little else.

Unknown stars stared down at me. The lorists told they were long dead gods watching, too far away to interfere, but not disinterested enough to turn away. I wished I knew their names.

On Tal's streets, lights and smoke hid all sins, while behind the sigil-protected palace wall, we became an easily observed spectacle for the gods' amusement. Under their ever-watchful gaze, I somehow remembered my own chambers were no longer safe and made it to the prince's abandoned courtyard. Before Lana locked me up again and Flora interrogated me, I needed my sister.

On the cracked stones, I moved in a formal court dance, imagining the prince as my partner. The delicate notes from Solovyova's reception room played in my mind, and I lost myself in the steps.

The magic traveled throughout my body. I offered my hand to my absent partner and reached for Lumi. In the night, a shadowy form took the prince's imagined role and my hand. We had not danced together since we were girls.

The seriousness and focused drive were there, though she was more Spirit than human. Magic hummed in my blood and sang through our steps as we became one.

Home and love and rightness overwhelmed me. It was the *doleb* cookies our mother baked in the communal oven, the safe embrace during thunderstorms, the knowledge I would never ever be alone. Then Lumi flinched, I stumbled, and the music stopped.

Magic that was easy a moment earlier pulled me to the ground, and she followed. Sitting, our foreheads and knees touched, but the closeness from the dance evaporated and memories of the night came crashing in.

"We have a great-grandmother."

I could feel her spectral forehead wrinkle against mine. "I was—"

"And we have magic," I continued.

"V—"

"And the seer saw the curse. What if she can break it?"

Waves of anxiety washed from normally cold, calm Lumi, and somehow, I allowed her to see the unending sea of love I carried inside. I needed answers, not more recriminations. She was the only one I had in this world. Whatever we decided, we would do so together.

She pressed against me. "It's not what it seemed. Nothing is. Mother paid Popova to curse us a long time ago. I learned of it, the magic, Morovara, and all the lies when you brought me to Popova to heal me after I was hurt. There is always a way to break curses. The attack...what I did...killing or risking my life. Three drunk noblemen tried to take more than I was willing to offer. It somehow opened my curse. The Spirits saved me."

"Why?" There were too many *whys*.

"Someone would have taken us away to use us. Or kill us. Children are unable to hide their powers... Popova only gave me answers in exchange for favors. I didn't know what to tell you..."

"You thought I would indebt us further." *I had broken trust first. I had allowed her to walk home alone.*

"I was so angry, V, and then time passed. It seemed better to leave the past buried."

Weakness spread from where we touched, and I fell sideways.

"You have used too much." Lumi's voice wavered. "You shouldn't have magic. The curse is still in place. Let me go. It's too dangerous."

I tried to focus on her words, to remember what was important.

"Von Lemerch is planning to kill us after the wedding. She never intended to keep her word. I heard her in a crypt. She wants it opened...will kill the prince."

"You must get away. He doesn't matter. You need to do what I say."

Her words were barely audible, but her hand remained locked in mine. Maybe it was the reassuring touch, or the magic's influence that allowed me to voice what I had been feeling.

"I cannot let her have him, Lumi. He's surrounded by lies, if he sees Tal as we do, he'll help. In another life, I could be his. He *must* matter."

She squeezed my hand. "We only have this life, little sister."

I tried to scoff, the courtyard stones cold against my cheek. "You're only moments older than me."

"But I have double the common sense. We'll handle von Lemerch and our debt, but dead or alive, don't care for him. Everyone seems good when living in a gilded bubble. He'll give you nothing but grief."

"Von Lemerch thinks he's the key to getting what she wants."

"Then you must kill him yourself before the wedding. This is your chance to make tomorrow a better day for all."

"No." I tried to rise, horrified she would ask me to become an assassin.

Her other hand stroked my cheek like Mother used to. "You need to choose us. As you said, he's doomed to die."

"Then tomorrow will never be a better day," I mumbled as the world disappeared in a rainbow of impossible colors. "Because he's good."

Chapter Twenty-Four

Dimitri

Alexei entered through the hidden servant's door eating his usual apple, looking as disheveled as me and probably had better cause. Presumably, he had not been pacing the halls like a Spirit. With a nod, he joined me at the table where I had stared blankly at my half-drawn maps for two bells. We had barely talked since he walked out on me in Lowtown. Images of blood and unsettled grief surfaced again as he studied my work. Normally, the steady pencil strokes, the images of the world seen from high in the sky, brought me peace. Frustratingly enough, the only peace I had gotten lately was at the princess's side—another person I was lying to. This needed to be done. I needed to end it.

"Any luck finding the last two names?" I asked, rubbing my eyes.

He gave me a long look before answering, as if considering where we stood. "One. I made careful enquiries among the Roja. Push more, and someone will guess it's not an innocent question."

"Who?"

"Sophina Dorova."

A noblewoman only slightly older than us who inherited an immense fortune as a child. She had grown up in the Tower with us, once wanted to join our group. "She never liked Eki..." I thought out loud. "Could the last one be von Uster?"

Alexei shook his head in resignation rather than denial. "If the head of the Roja voted with your father, you must let him be. He has been loyal to your family for generations."

"And if it comes down to it, who will his people follow?"

My friend gave me another long look instead of the answer that would paint his mentor and fellow Rojas as traitors. Even I would have followed the man who trained me, the brethren I trusted, over a young king who just killed his father. But that did not change what I had to do if the spymaster had been involved. He was the most likely one, for he knew everything that happened in Tal.

"And the priestess?" I asked, dropping the point. I had three councilors on my list. Enough for now.

Alexei ate his apple core before responding. "The temple closes ranks, you know this, Dimi. If you drag someone out of there, someone who only carried out the king's orders—no matter how wrong—it could start a civil war. People are already rumbling, preaching for change. You were wronged, Eki was wronged, but this will not bring him back. You can change things. Give them a reason to stand behind you before making a move."

I needed to do this to get the dreams of flames out of my mind. Alexei would never approve, so there was no point arguing. I could become a good man when I was away from Tal. Better to focus on his other points.

"People always complain in the cities. Those looking for quick money leave the free farms without a plan. It's not Tal's responsibility to care for them all." Most never found what they were searching for in the City of Bones and Roses. It was as it always had been, but maybe the princess had a point. How many peasants had I truly spoken to?

I sighed, seeing Alexei was about to argue further. "Bring me concrete suggestions, and I'll listen. But first bring me the names I need."

"They say poor people are hanged for crimes committed by the rich. There are whispers in the Roja rebels are burning outlying farms with the blessing from the temple. Save the harvest, do something or by winter or there will be starvation and your own people might march on the palace."

"Maybe that wouldn't be so bad."

Alexei pierced me with the look that had made me squirm since boyhood. His words reminded me of the impossible case I presided over. That man had clearly been insane, but sometimes those crazy spoke truth…

Alexei continued, voice rising, "Tal is already underdeveloped and, for the poor, miserable. The world is moving forward while we are left behind—and your solution is to bring back the theocracy while pursuing your personal vendetta, then leaving the city."

"You want me to ride off to stop rebels from burning remote farms?" I asked, both somehow on our feet.

"Better than abandoning everything."

"There it—"

A knock loud enough to not be the first interrupted my words.

I straightened my jacket to calm myself before calling, "Enter."

A boy barely old enough to leave the Tower, a fifth cousin of mine or something similar with the honor of serving the royal family and probably spying for my father, bowed profusely in the doorway.

"Crown Prince, I apologize. You have been summoned by the King."

"Immediately?"

The boy nodded without looking at me. No further explanation. That, more than anything, gave me pause. My father liked public instructions. He liked to talk about his plans, even if they were not always his real ones.

The short walk from my chambers to my father's was enough for me to confirm something was wrong. Servants and guards crowded before the royal doors. Even Solovyova's and my mother's maids had come. My grandmother only left the Tower for three-day worship.

I pushed past them all, answering no questions, as my mind played out the worst-case scenarios. *War? Death? Or was my father missing?* Each one filled me with equal anticipation and dread.

Only Alexei followed me inside, our steps hollow against the stone floor. I knew both my mother and father were inside; still, there were no angry shouts. No drunken laughter, mocking the other. No gaggle of courtesans.

"He woke up feeling unwell," Alexei whispered, as if reluctant to disturb the peace. "Canceled all meetings."

A shiver passed through me, and the air seemed to thicken until I struggled to take another step. *Where were the servants?* Never while my father was in residence had I seen his chambers this empty. Maybe he had escaped to Grigot Manor, our summer estate in Keskin. Surely, he was not sitting in the dark quietly with my mother. Maybe one had finally killed the other.

Opening the bedchamber door, I half expected blood to cover the white drapes, or to see an enemy I could fight. Instead, the king lay in his bed, seemingly asleep.

Until that moment, I would have said there was no love between us. That my only regret upon his death would be that he would not be there for me to punish, but relief filled me when a rattling breath broke the silence.

Strong hands pulled me back the moment before the king coughed. Only then did I notice Gennady and my mother, both in red masks.

"Leave. Now," Gennady commanded and gently pushed the queen into my arms. "Stay in the outer room. The plague has returned."

Without Alexei's support I would have sunk to my knees. Gennady met my eyes with compassion and sorrow. He was not grieving a feared king. Some of his sadness might have been for me, but most was surely for Tal and the days ahead. Healers could cure most ailments, but there were those outside even their powers.

His words had their own magic. During the last outbreaks, the healers could save one in six of those who sickened. My grandfather had been one of the other five. We never learned how it spread. Some became ill after interacting with those already sick, while others walked away with no symptoms. I could already be infected.

Alexei pulled me out and let me fall into a dining chair in the outer chamber. My mother followed as if in a daze and pulled down the red protective mask. The sharp scent of medicinal herbs filled the air, all in the hope of preventing infection.

A serving girl barely old enough to remember the last plague cried in the corner while guards who must have followed me in stood in silence. Gennady's words must have carried.

Like children seeking a parent, one by one they turned to me. I had never wanted to be king, to rule anyone, much less a kingdom, but I could not tell them that as the news of the plague spread. Could not tell my mother, I had planned to escape Tal for good and leave it for her to sort out the succession.

Her empty gaze centered me. She was not outspoken like Solovyova, or harsh like my father. Much like me, she had never sought to rule, but those first twelve years in the Tower she filled with love.

I pulled the song of perseverance the wind sung in the mountains around me like a coat, then stood. A bell ago, I had told Alexei how everyone needed to fend for themselves. A bell ago, there had not been expectant faces turned my way. I could have slunk away in the night, but I could not turn away from the questions in their eyes.

"When the healers have confirmed who is healthy, the call must go out," I addressed a royal guard, Ferki. "Tell the runners to let the country lords and their retinues go—let them protect their lands and the harvest. They cannot wait here for my wedding." I turned to the next soldier, Yahontov. "Order the City Guard to close the gates and segregate the neighborhoods. Morovara is to stop all worships. Curfew starts tonight." I faced them all. "The King is indisposed. Until he recovers, I speak with his voice."

There were more orders. Arguments that Tal was impossible to shut down, that rich pilgrims could not be turned away at the gates after months of travel. Some said the Goddess herself would punish us for interrupting the worships. All I could think was that I could not let it get as bad as last time when the dead lined the streets and too many new Spirits illuminated dark.

I dealt with one emergency through the night until, finally, dawn broke. As the world gathered itself for another day, I managed to escape the people hounding me for solutions to impossible problems.

It was my secret hideaway, but the three of them would always know to find me here. It had, after all, been our courtyard before it became mine. So when, after washing and changing, I found them blocking the broken door bordering the palace forest, I only sighed.

Eki, Mariska, Alexei, and myself—an inseparable quartet before everything changed—hid here after each prank to debrief among laughter and teasing. The four of us had not been in the same room since I returned. The situation was dire indeed that they sought me out as one.

"It seems news travels fast," I said, and Alexei shrugged. I had left him behind in my father's chambers. Clearly he had gathered the others.

"You can tell us to leave if you want to, but we're here for you," he said. "No matter what other differences we might have, you shouldn't sit in there alone."

Eki stepped closer, placing a hand on my arm. "Of course, we're here for you. Whatever you need."

Mariska frowned but did not discreetly look away like she once had. Two days after the princess fell from the balcony, I sat by the window under hers and listened to the wind. I should not have invaded her privacy but had worried Helia was not who she seemed. When Mariska entered her chambers, conspiracies grew in my mind. Instead, I had observed two women growing closer and let the wind go. I had heard enough.

The princess persevered in taming her unpredictable magic and conquered her fear of griffons. Based on her lack of training, it seemed her mother dismissed her the moment she knew Helia would no longer be part of her family or Oberwalden. Still, the princess never gave up.

Mariska's stare darkened as Eki's hand traveled up my arm, confirming my cousin's allegiance. Once, she had pushed for mine and Eki's union while dreaming she would marry Alexei, making us one happy family. I was the one who left, but we all changed.

"Don't you have something to tell Dimi?" Mariska said to Eki as I pushed away her roaming hand.

"This is hardly the time, nor your business," Eki answered and reached possessively for me again.

I retreated through the courtyard gate. Today would be hard enough without their bickering.

A mass of blue fabric lay limp in one corner. Shutting out the others, I moved closer.

A dress.

I knew, even before I turned over her limp body and placed her head in my lap. Dirt covered half of the princess's pale face. My heart beat in my ears like the three-day drums. Black clouded the periphery, my mind threatening to shut down, unable to process more death and shock.

"Helia, wake!" I shook her limp body. "Mariska!"

I fought the terror until the princess, like with my father, drew a barely perceivable breath and the darkness retreated.

My cousin threw herself down next to me and placed her hands on Helia's chest.

"Is it the plague?" Dread covered my every word. Last time, it took the strongest mages first.

Mariska shook her head. "Mage's illness and exposure. We need to get her indoors."

My arms wrapped around the princess's small body, my feet already moving as Mariska continued to speak.

"She visited the Tower and your mother yesterday. Then the king fell sick. Dimi, her magic might not be stable…"

There was something hesitant in Mariska's voice, as if she did not fully believe what she was saying. Once, I would have known what it meant. She had been as close as a sister. Once, I would have trusted her to tell me when she was ready. Now, I could only delay the suspicious thoughts.

We rushed inside, and nobles and servants alike stepped out of the way with drawn faces. With news of the plague spreading, their looks might have little to do with my strange entrance.

Alexei knocked on the princess's door before I could reach it and pushed the Oberwaldian maid out of the way when she opened it.

"What are you doing?" she asked with an affronted look.

I marched past her into the bedchamber and placed Helia in the unmade bed. *Had she slept here last night after all?*

"Your lady is hurt. Run to the hospital and summon more healers."

The woman stared suspiciously at me and then Helia. "Where have you two been?"

The curtains swayed in a sudden unnatural wind, my grip slipping. "Are you questioning the Crown Prince while your mistress lies unconscious?"

She looked like she wanted to argue further but when the wind pushed against her, she hurried away without a bow.

I sat on the bedside, the princess's limp hand in mine, while Mariska worked her magic on the other side. Only when two more healers arrived did I allow them to send me into the outer room.

My eyes locked on the breakfast nook where we ate the first morning. Then, despite myself, I had hoped to enter her bedchamber under very different circumstances. I had not even allowed myself to acknowledge the desire. Though that time, I almost broke down the door to get inside, this felt like an invasion of privacy. She did not even know I was here.

I never wanted to be in her chambers without an invitation.

A bell passed in tense silence and pacing steps, the clock's ticks keeping time, Alexei's and Eki's eyes following me until the healers exited.

I jumped to my feet as hope reared its deceitful head. Mage's illness could be minor or severe. It could be a death sentence.

"Is she recovered?"

The unfamiliar healer bowed. "She's unconscious, but stable. We won't know more before she wakes, my prince."

Despite my reluctance, I reentered the bedchamber where Mariska sat on a chair, staring at her newfound friend as if she could wake her through will alone. Helia lay in a freshly made bed, covered by the finest silk. I took one of her limp hands in mine again. It was warm but not fever hot.

I stroked her cheek. So pale, like she never stepped fully into the sun. The unmoving form seemed lesser, her vivaciousness and wildness, taunting smiles, and lightning-filled eyes gone.

Alexei joined me and Mariska, but Eki stayed away. I could not blame her.

"How can her training be so lacking?" I asked, embracing anger. It was always easier than fear and grief. "Where is her aunt?"

"I told the other healers to send anyone else away," Mariska said. She closed the bedchamber door. "There is more. Solovyova informed the hospital yesterday that the water seer encountered a blocking curse when testing the princess. Grandmother wants us to reach out to Oberwalden discreetly to find out more. No one can know, but it explains why the princess struggles with her magic."

"Why would someone curse her?" Alexei asked, but none of us had any answers.

What had her upbringing been like? I wanted to pull her into my arms and keep her safe from the world. I could not wish to marry her, but I could also not stop myself from caring.

I squeezed her hand, stroking callouses as hard as mine, and knew I should not have presumed anything about her life based on her status. "If she didn't notice, it must have been there since she was a child. We can't trust her aunt."

We nodded in unison, and it felt almost like the old days.

Mariska examined the princess one final time and declared her condition unchanged before leaving to catch up on sleep. Alexei was the next to go, promising to search for answers. From my world having stood still for three years, it suddenly moved too fast.

Alone as we should not have been, I lifted Helia's hand into my lap, trying to not clutch it too tight.

"How can I be what they need?" I asked, able to talk knowing she could not hear. "I told you we were born for this, but you were right to seek your own path. When you wake, I'll tell you the truth because I can no longer pretend. After the wedding, you could rule as queen. Maybe that's what Tal needs. From what I've seen, you're stronger, more open-minded, and more caring than I can ever be."

I pulled my hands through my disheveled hair, wanting nothing more than to lie down next to her. *When had I last slept?*

Determined to be here when she woke—because she had to wake—I staggered back into the outer room to rest on her sofa. When the messengers and officers tracked me down, the day would be full of requests and decisions. Another reason not to return to my own chambers. Unfortunately, the sofa was already occupied.

"I thought you left."

Eki patted the seat next to her, and I obliged.

"I suspected you might still need me. Talk to me like you used to, Dimi."

"We never really talked," I said. "Not when alone."

It had been all four of us planning, joking, arguing. Later, Eki and I met to exchange sweet nothings and fumbled touches.

She pressed against my side. "You just need to remember how good it was. We could be that way again."

There was nothing left of the awkward girl she had been. Despite the exhaustion pulling me down, I lurched to my feet.

"I remember the pain and bad decisions. We were kids, Ekatarina. I've made Zakhar pay with his life—he deserved it—and I'll continue pursuing revenge until the Goddess's scale is level, but we are not starting anything again. Especially not in the chambers of my unconscious bride." My mouth twisted in distaste, imagining Helia waking to find us together. "You should leave."

Anger brought roses to her cheeks. "You think you can trust her? While you languished in the mountains, I had to do whatever I could to survive. If you marry me while your father cannot interfere, this will end well for everyone, but you're too blind to see what is right before your eyes. You should know by now our feelings don't matter."

"If our feelings don't matter, why are you pushing this?"

"Why did I ever? For our child. This marriage is why they wanted it dead, and now you watch over her bed like a lovesick fool, blind to everything else. If only the fall of the balcony had killed her, you might have been able to hear me."

Anger distorted her normally controlled features, the smudged kohl around her eyes an imperfection she would once never have allowed. Somehow, my exhausted mind narrowed on the dark shadows as it processed her words, filling in the blanks, replaying Helia falling from the balcony, her red dress flapping in the wind.

"You pushed her? Tried to kill my fiancée for our dead child's sake?"

Was that madness in her eyes? Mariska had told me Eki had kept to herself, rarely leaving the Tower these past years.

"I'll do whatever is needed to protect my own. Somehow, that still includes you." She tossed her hair defiantly and stalked to the door. "After you recognize this *princess's* deceit, come and see me. Mariska was right, I have something to tell you."

"What do you mean?" I asked, but she was already gone.

Chapter Twenty-Five

Vanya

When I woke, three fuzzy princes sat by my bedside writing in their notebooks. They looked up as I stretched, then merged into one while the world rocked like a river barge during the spring floods. I gripped the bed frame despite knowing the palace could not be moving. Maybe my mind was cracking.

Dimitri reached out as if he wanted to steady me but thought better of it when less than an inch separated his hand from mine. His hesitation snapped reality back into place.

"What are you doing in my room?"

"It isn't appropriate." He searched his notebook for answers before facing me. "I didn't want you to wake up alone. Mariska and I've been taking shifts."

Shifts? "How long have I been asleep?"

"At least three days. We don't know exactly when you passed out." He met my gaze, his blue and brown eyes filled with worry. "I found you in my courtyard. What's the last thing you remember?"

The room resumed rocking. Three days... "I argued with my sister. She held my hand. I'd—"

Dimitri jumped up and interrupted my ramblings. "Princess, you don't have a sister. The healers told me to get them as soon as you woke. They warned me there might be aftereffects. Do you know where you are?"

Princess. I grabbed his hand before he could leave. I remembered too much and could tell him nothing of it. The Women's Tower and the Book of Bloodlines, the extinction of Tal's mages, von Lemerch's plan to kill us after the wedding. That my great-grandmother was the high priestess. And my sister wanted me to kill Dimitri. Real and imagined had intertwined as I stumbled to the courtyard and danced. I was in no state to act like Helia von Heskin.

I pulled the prince back into his chair and put on a vapid smile.

"I'm in my bedchamber, and so are you. I know enough to know this will be frowned upon." I relaxed my grip and leaned against the mountain of pillows someone had provided.

"It might be improper, but this is the only place they'll give me a moment's peace. Seems the only place I'm safe is in your chambers."

Despite his joking tone, the shadows under his eyes and sorrow lines spoke the truth. I liked to think he had started to care for me, but not enough to cause this.

"What happened to you?"

He closed his eyes as if bracing himself before responding. "The real question is what happened to Tal. Never has a three-day been so long."

What else could have gone wrong? If he had learned of von Lemerch's plans independently, maybe I could break my curse of silence. The explanations hovered on the tip of my tongue.

"Tell me," I said, equally surprised at my commanding tone and his acceptance of it.

"It's bad, Helia. Enough that I wish I'd slept through it as well. My father has been too sick to rule. The healers say he might improve but I have not been let in to see him again."

His words shattered my hopeful thoughts. "I'm sorry," I stammered. "You didn't seem close, but it can still hurt."

I knew from experience. My feelings for my mother and childhood were conflicted enough.

"That's not..." He took a breath to gather himself. "It's the Talian plague. I've closed down the city. Put any preventive measures I can think of into action, but the people are either panicking or protesting. There have been riots each night."

"Plague?" My stomach dropped. The word dragged me back to my mother's bloody coughs in our apartment, her rattling breaths, and frail body. When she died, we had been thrown out on the street by men in plague robes and herb-stuffed masks.

Our mother had done a lot of things wrong, but we had soon learned how sheltered we had been. Lumi and I slept outside and lived on scraps until Kirill found us and declared himself our stepfather. The signed marriage contract and inherited debt sigils had confirmed his words. We barely saw Svetlana that first season and I had imagined that while I instantly despised Kirill and the life of deceit he forced on us, she could become family. How wrong I had been. When she finally deigned to interact with us, it was only to reinforce her superiority.

"Princess? I'm getting the healer. I've overwhelmed you."

I blinked at Dimitri. He must have continued talking while the past had me in its claws.

"Don't leave." The last thing I wanted was to answer a stranger's questions. "You're welcome to hide here. To talk, like you offered me."

I had told Lumi he was good and meant it. My chance to improve Tal; to make tomorrow a better day was not through killing, but by listening. My mother had always said kindness would change the world.

"Tell me what's happening out there."

Dimitri watched me carefully but continued. "Tal is low on food until the fall harvest, and the pilgrims sitting outside the city wall are already straining our resources. Everyone is calling for my attention. We had to send the bone soldiers out to keep the peace last night…" He rose again and paced between the bed and the windows. The room which had seemed gigantic to me was barely large enough to contain his frantic energy. "I never wanted to send soldiers against my own citizens. Princess, I want to be honest…since returning, I planned to…"

He stopped to stare out the window, tensing as if what was to come next was even worse than sickness and insurgencies.

Dread filled me at the thought of bone soldiers blocking the bridges between Lowtown and Rivertown. Before I entered the palace, the bloody stick figures had already multiplied, the suppressed grumbles had grown, and food been tight. Plague was not the only thing threatening Tal. Lumi was not the only one who watched the palace and dreamt of blood.

A soft knock on the door sounded and a red-clad healer entered, bowing to us both.

"Forgive me, Majesties, but I should examine the princess. I could hear her awake."

It was the first time someone addressed me as *Majesty*. Either the crown prince's continued presence at my side, or the king's illness had raised Helia's standing. Before I overheard von Lemerch, I would have congratulated myself on how successful I was at playing the princess. Instead, it reminded me of the ever-closing wedding date and our planned deaths. The Day of the Dead was the first day of fall. I had just lost three days, which could have been spent finding a way for us all to see the leaves fall.

Dimitri sighed before nodding. "I'm sure there are several messengers waiting for me outside." At the door he turned to me, eyes hardening in decision. "Rest, Princess. If you feel up to it, come to my chambers tonight. We need to talk."

"I'll be there."

And I would find a way to warn him. I needed to fight back, and not in the way Lumi proposed.

As the healer examined me, I obsessed over my sister's safety and the plague spreading in the city while I had been asleep. I wanted nothing more than to reach out to Lumi and learn what had happened during the last days, but the healer made me promise not to attempt any magic until at least the next three-day. In the end, it was her vivid description of permanent brain damage and the likelihood of losing more time that convinced me to rest.

Lumi had told me she was close by the manor of our last heist, but the palace was in lockdown due to the plague. Somehow, I needed to get to her.

I spent the day obsessing about what to tell the prince, how to convince him to let me into the city while evading Svetlana, and how I might use my power to locate Lumi when I was close enough.

As the sun set outside, I selected a dress and arranged my hair in a way that would have made Flora proud and Svetlana jealous. I needed to look the part tonight. I only had one stop on the way, one game piece that was mine to play.

Lana tried to follow me until I told her the prince had invited me alone. My appearance seemed to convince her. She could spend the night as she pleased or stand outside his doors. Luckily, she chose the former.

During the three days I had been unconscious, the world had changed. The usual bustle in the palace hallways had disappeared. Solitary servants kept their distance and bowed until I passed. Outside, the night air enveloped me. More lights than usual burned beside the guardhouse. Above, the full moon shone.

Settling on the bench I sat on that first day as I contemplated running away, my body vibrated with tension. Last time it had been desperation and fear. It should have been worse tonight—I knew more, my loyalties were a twisted yarn, and the illness I feared more than any other had returned. But during today's enforced inaction, I had arrived at a conclusion. Tonight, I would leap off the cliff of indecision. I would give up on pleasing everyone and take action to atone for my role in von Lemerch's plans. Lumi had not felt her otherworldly *wrongness*. My magic had recoiled, and despite its newness, I trusted it.

I was no princess and had only become a thief out of necessity. If tomorrow was to be a better day, I would have to become a better person. That meant returning what I stole.

When I was sure no one watched, I indecently tucked the ends of my light dress into the waistband, stood on the bench, and leapt.

The crown hung where I left it, the greenery reflected in the opaque glass. Von Lemerch had picked the image of it from my mind and created a perfect replica. The glass remained impeccable, the intricate sigils reflecting the moonlight. Only when I reached for it, did I notice the flaky smudges where my bloody fingers had touched it. It seemed sacrilegious to dirty the ancient glass.

I snatched it up, ready to rub away the blood.

As my fingers closed, something infinitely large pressed down on me, grabbed my magic, and pulled until colors danced before my eyes. I swayed on the branch, trying to let go as my fingers cramped around the crown. If it had a sound, it was an endless gong, its sound expanding until my bones vibrated.

I'm returning you. Don't hurt me, I thought, as if talking not to a crown but the being pulling at the very essence of me.

It stopped a moment or a bell later, the otherness turning from me when it could get no more. The sound of the branches moving in the wind and guards chatting below returned. A breeze warmed my neck and my hand relaxed.

Nothing had happened when I wore the crown, but I remembered Dimitri and I holding it together. The jolt of *something* inside me—what if my magic had not been the only thing waking?

"You're going back where you belong," I told it, noticing the blood that had stayed through rain and wind, was gone. A shiver ran up my exhausted body as I carefully tucked it into the leather bag Flora had so fortunately crafted to perfectly fit a stolen crown.

Just when I decided I was done being a pawn, something happened to show me the game was larger than I had ever imagined.

The prince's chambers were unlocked but empty when I arrived, so I settled on the sofa after placing another log on his ever-burning fire. The half-closed windows tinged everything orange, like the flames had spread to his maps and leapt across the walls.

I owed Lumi more than I could ever repay, but this was the only solution I had seen. Von Lemerch did not want the crown prince to marry Helia von Heskin wearing the crown of Tal, so that he must do. Somehow, I would set it all right.

Ignoring the need to touch the crown again to see what would happen, I watched the dancing flames, wishing to move with them. To dance with the prince like I imagined late at night.

Alone in his rooms, the worries crept back. Playing the princess was unfair to Dimitri. Because he was decent. Because he had caught me when I fell. Unfair to myself to want something I could never really have. I was kidding myself but sitting there in the fine dress and braided hair I still allowed myself to dream one last time.

The door slammed open, knocking me out of my thoughts, and a row of men and women marched past with the prince in the lead. They gathered by the table and bent over the maps without noticing me. Servants rushed after them to light the lamps and candles. A girl no more than ten saw me and shrieked. An overreaction if I have ever seen one. If you screamed like that in Lowtown, you only signaled your vulnerability to worse predators.

The men, servants, and my prince stared at her, some already with knives half drawn.

Imagining myself caught in a theft, a remarkably similar situation to an unmarried noblewoman discovered alone in a man's chamber, I presented a smile promising I knew more than them.

Dimitri had aged ten years since this morning. With his normally impeccable hair and uniform rumpled, his eyes met mine, and I could not even pretend not to care anymore. *He is Helia's*, I scolded myself. Knowing I would forget it again if I let myself.

He mumbled something to the others and approached me. While Alexei studied us with a pensive smile, everyone else turned away politely.

"Princess, what are you doing here?" His voice was too low for anyone else to hear.

"You invited me this morning," I reminded him and gathered my courage. "We need to talk."

He pulled his hand through his hair and looked like he instantly regretted it. "There has been so much today—this is not a good time."

I pointedly looked at the crown I had slipped behind my skirt before rising. Thank the Wishmaker there was no magic or otherworldly presence, still, he paled further, and for a moment, I thought he would sink to his knees, its added weight was too much to bear.

"How did you get it out of the treasury? Why? It doesn't matter. While I speak as king, I'm not holding you to a contract you don't desire. I'll find another way to get what I need." He straightened his back and became the closed off, iron-faced crown prince. He raised his voice loud enough for everyone to hear, "Princess, I'm saddened to inform you that due to the king's condition and the spreading plague, the wedding will have to be put on indefinite hold."

"Do you think I care?" I pointed to the crown again to remind him how we first met—though von Lemerch would certainly have something to say about a broken engagement. I had chosen my path by returning the crown. As soon as he brought it to the treasury, he would discover the fake one. His public rejection could not matter, still a hand squeezed my heart. I lowered my voice, "How many dead so far?"

"One hundred eight confirmed infections and twenty-four deaths."

I clenched my fingers around the too-cold glass. *What if Lumi was one of them?* If there was any fairness, our stepfather would be struck by the bloody coughs. What about everyone else who helped us through the years?

But Dimitri's resigned look when faced away from his men worried me as well. His voice had been strong but he looked like someone who had given up just as I decided to fight.

"The wedding doesn't matter. We still need to talk," I said, proud of my calm voice.

"Later."

Making myself stand as straight as him, I glared. We *would* talk. This was my last chance before leaving. I flashed the crown again. "Tell me where I can wait."

His face softened an inch. "It'll be late."

I strode to his bedchamber door, rumors be damned. I was not Helia von Heskin, and maybe this way, von Lemerch would be convinced I was still doing my part, because despite my outward confidence, part of me was panicking thinking Von Lemerch and Flora might act as soon as word spread. I needed time to put my plan into action. Would they punish Lumi for my perceived failure?

Would they move up their plans to kill Dimitri and put someone else in his place? Or in mine? My only chance to protect us was to stay until I could convince him to temporarily change his decision. And then leave him when I could return the real princess. Life had never been fair.

In his bedchamber, I closed the door behind me, placed the crown on the mantel and settled on a stuffed chair to watch the oil lamps burn. The even flames calmed my mind as I sought arguments for why Helia von Heskin could have reconsidered her stance and how to convince the prince that the wedding was best for both—or at least to pretend for another three-day.

Could I tell him how I enjoyed his company? That I wanted more quiet moments between us?

I would do to anything protect him and Lumi, no matter how impossible it seemed. Dimitri might not think he was suited to rule, but Tal needed him. I needed him to be safe, even if he could not be mine.

Despite my days in bed, I stifled a yawn, slid further down, and drifted off listening to the muted voices in the other room discuss the lack of a spread pattern and experimental treatments.

Screams haunted my fitful sleep. Men from my childhood. My mother's pained face when she thought we were not looking. Her begging for death at the end.

Outside, the curfew bells rang, locking me in nightmares of plague and our first year at Kirill's until a hand shook me awake.

Trapped in the drafty attic and a life filled with physically and morally dirty tasks, I rolled to the side and sought a moment more of sleep, but the usual sloping wall was gone and instead I hit the floor with a thump.

"No need for another fight. Tonight, you would win without breaking a sweat, Princess."

The prince's exhausted voice drifted through the dark and part of me relaxed. If he had ever wanted to hurt me, there had been more than enough occasions. Instead, he kept carrying me to safety.

"Could you light a lamp? I don't like the dark," I said and reached blindly without success. It was the truth. I did not mind the dark of the night—it was when Tal came alive—but this absolute darkness, like that in the tunnels under the Tower, held no possibilities of illicit meetings, dancing, and thieving.

Dimitri threw a log on the embers and blew on the coals until a flame illuminated a grand bed, two chairs, and his tall form. How strange to see the crown prince do something so menial. At Kirill's, tending the fires had been one of Lumi's and my tasks. If the flames died in winter, our stepfather would not have hesitated to bring out the cane. But I was learning the prince let others do very little for him.

I drifted closer, not sure if I sought Dimitri or the flames. We stood there in comfortable silence, and slowly, the tense muscles between my shoulders relaxed.

In the end, he spoke first.

"I didn't mean to wake you. You shouldn't even be here… I'm sorry I announced it like that, but the engagement was based on falsehood and our parents' contracts. In Tal, marriage used to mean love."

He settled into a chair, and I sank down on the floor, leaning against the fireplace. The dry heat from the flames spread through my back. For a city so obsessed with death, love was almost as sacred, though its goddess long forgotten. I had next to no experience, but even I knew love could not be built on lies, and lies were all I had. He had caught me. I could not let it doom him.

"Your mother showed me the Book of Bloodlines—she and Solovyova think we must marry to protect Tal and its mages. That the royal line is connected to magic itself."

He scoffed. "Old superstitions. I cannot believe they told you that." He pulled his hands through his loose hair and shook it out with a hard laugh. "We have enough real-world problems without thinking we can influence the Death Goddess herself. I'll fight with the tools I have, but in the end she decides who to take. Everything else is hubris."

I thought of my mother and the infant brother I lost before he was old enough to receive a name. If those under one died, they were not grieved, not spoken of or honored. They only lived in our minds. The Goddess might have the last word, but the rich had tools others did not. If the healers had treated either my mother or brother, they might have lived. But I no longer wanted to argue about past hurts he had no influence over.

"Then delay any decision regarding the wedding. That's using the tools you have, and it costs nothing."

"The decision is made. I'm sorry for how I said it—I never meant to hurt you—but it's for the best. Neither of us wanted it."

That was a third impossible apology, but it did not fill me with the same joy the others had. His sloped shoulders, half-closed eyes, and crumpled clothes spoke of defeat. I wanted to ask him how he was doing, but that seemed too intimate.

"How did your meeting go?"

The firelight deepened his sardonic smile. "Bad. It's worse than during my grandfather's time. Six more cases, noble mages, confirmed inside the palace tonight. The healers are doing everything they can to keep it contained. If it spreads among the Guard, we will not be able to keep the peace. I can't..."

His voice drifted off and he shut his eyes, like he could not face all the things he could not do. Without thinking, I squeezed his hand. We had fought and kissed, laughed and smiled, but to show weakness implied a trust I wanted, even if I would break it if everything went as I planned. He needed someone at his side tonight. Where would I be without Lumi to lean on? He had friends and advisers, but from what I observed earlier, he kept up the facade even before them.

After a moment, his fingers closed around mine. I hardly knew this man, but I had never respected him more. Despite claiming not to care for his people, he was good in a way I was not. In his position, I would run, then danced to forget.

"You can," I said, answering everything left unsaid. "And now off to bed. No one can think without sleep. We'll talk tomorrow." Because I could not make myself add more onto his shoulders tonight. It was a coward's way. Soon, the crown would expose the lies I could not speak.

A shadow of a smile answered my words. He got up, rolled his head, and stretched his arms toward the ceiling before flinching. How long had he sat by my side before I woke this morning? How many more bells bent over maps and letters? I doubted there had been time to practice the fluid fighting stances in the courtyard.

He belonged to Helia. I should leave. Inside me, a voice whispered, *If the wedding was off, was he not free to do as he wished?*

Focusing on the open gold buttons on his jacket, I fought the heat rising in my cheeks as I spoke. "I could massage your shoulder. I used to do it for my mother. She often ached in winter."

"That's not appropriate, Princess."

Despite his words, the soft tone and eyes glittering in the firelight pulled me closer. I rose and he retreated, like a dance without touch. Another step and he bumped against the bed post.

"A dozen people saw me step into your bedchamber," I said softly when barely an inch separated us. "I think my reputation is thoroughly ruined." And the only opinions I cared about in this palace was that of the man in front of me and von Lemerch's, neither who would disapprove.

He sat on the bed, too far away for the flames to show his face. "Why would you offer to stay?"

I was so sick of lies. "Because I'm not very good at behaving like a princess. Because I want to. Ask me to leave or roll over."

The moment stretched. *I'm no princess*, I reminded myself. *But also no hero. Come morning, I'll disappear and somehow find answers. Tonight, neither of us deserve to be alone.*

Still he said nothing, until I mentally prepared myself to face Lana again. To be locked into her room. For Flora to beat me for smearing Oberwalden's reputation. Perhaps, I would sleep in the courtyard. The night was warm.

As I inched backward, Dimitri lay down and the hard knot in my stomach loosened.

I settled next to him on the bed, our thighs touching. It felt like the mage light had as I absorbed it—pleasant and dangerous, scorching and wild.

He lay perfectly still while I wiped my moist hands on my dress. This was silly. My mother taught Lumi and me to give massages, perhaps quietly thinking the massage house was better than the whorehouse. In the evening, I would rub her hurting hands, feet, and back. There had been nothing sexual about it—but she had been my mother and not an infuriating, caring, too-handsome man I had to let go in the morning.

But there were few things I hated as much as allowing fear to rule me, so ignoring my reluctance, I placed my hands on his wide, shirt-clad shoulders and imagined them my mother's, no matter that they felt nothing alike.

His muscles were hard boulders with pebbles trapped between them. Soon, practice overcame awkwardness as I worked my fingers into the knots. He let out something between a moan and cry, and I froze.

"Don't stop, Princess. Please, just—"

Before he could finish the sentence, I pressed hard under the shoulder blades. At least he could not see my flaming face. Slowly, the locked muscles split into individual knots. He kept making the most delicious noises, and I pretended not to seek them.

Moving down his spine, I slid my hands under his shirt. It was only practical, as it had definitely been in the way, and it was not like I had never touched a man's back before. In the firelight, I could barely see the sculpted muscles as my fingers ran over each one, savoring the nearness I had denied myself so long.

"Princess?" he said, his voice rough. In response, I pushed my fingers into the hard muscles of his lower back and he let out a yelp.

"See, it only works like this. Now lay still."

He obeyed without further protests. I could get used to this.

I pushed the shirt up until it was collected around his shoulders. His warm skin slid under my fingers, and his breath caught. I had forgotten to breathe completely.

At least I would remember the warm touch of his skin, catalogue each sound of pleasure and treasure them more than gold. Nothing I planned solved our debt to Kirill or erased the sigil on my thigh, because the only way I knew out of the locked-down palace relied on me being nimble and light, and would not allow me to bring anything to sell. It did not remove the danger of having magic and little training. I could only run and hope the dust settled before my stepfather caught me.

Pressing and stroking until Dimitri moaned in my hands, I tried to dispel the dark thoughts. His muscles turned soft under my fingers, until I continued as much for my own benefit as his. A stolen moment I hoped he would not come to regret.

His breathing deepened as he drifted off to a peaceful sleep despite the burdens he carried. Satisfaction at helping him opened inside me like a spring rose—no princess would have done the same. For once, being me was the right thing.

The nearness had lit a fire inside me. I longed to continue the exploration, to kiss and press closer in the dark, but today had been long. Every day had been since this started.

I pulled his shirt down and rolled up against his side. On the mantel, the flames painted the glass crown warm orange like the outer rooms. It had never been mine and soon it would adorn another brow. Would it fit her as well as it had me? Would she feel the same presence pull at her very being?

Soon, I would make myself leave to find Lumi and Helia. But as my eyes closed listening to Dimitri's peaceful breaths, I convinced myself I would stay just a bell more. For the first time in years, I felt safe.

Chapter Twenty-Six

Vanya

The brightening light pulled me out of perfect contentedness, and I blinked awake in a stranger's room and arms.

Dimitri's long limbs held me tight, the silk, summer blankets a mess at our feet. He seemed larger like this, his head above mine, my feet resting against his calves, and his arms easily long enough to cover my torso. The scent of leather and sun and man filled my nose. I could not help inhaling it. This was what safety felt like.

He mumbled in his sleep and pulled me further into his heat. Now that I was awake, I should move away. Instead, I rubbed myself against him, hoping to carry his scent with me. Needing to get even closer.

His hands clenched in my dress, one on my abdomen, the other on my thigh, feeding the pulsing warmth inside me.

Taking a deep breath, I tried to think of other things than how good this forbidden moment felt, but it had been two years since my first and only experience with a boy, both partying despite the spring rains. That night, I let Lumi walk back alone and returned bells later, flushed and giggling, to find her bleeding and broken in Kirill's courtyard. Now I had again spent the night in someone's arms instead of going to her.

Outside this impossible cocoon, the plague had returned and food was running low. Von Lemerch and Flora undoubtedly knew of the broken engagement. No matter how many guards patrolled the palace wall, I should have left during the night to search for my sister and Helia. It should all have mattered more than the body pressed against mine. Shame burned, and still I did not leave.

And now, here I was, and Dimitri, the Crown Prince of Tal, was certainly no boy.

Either I was not as still as I thought, or the sun woke him as well. He nuzzled my neck, sending thrills down my back. I should beg him to take back the broken engagement to appease von Lemerch for a few more days; instead, all I wanted was to pretend I belonged in his arms. He buried his fingers in my hair and gently turned my head until our eyes met, breaths mixing, lips parting.

Kissing like this would hold weight the previous stolen moments did not. His eyes held a question I could not answer. I was the one planning to leave, but he was the one who finally inched away until only our hands touched, his thumb stroking my palm as if refusing to let go no matter what he had decided. While his words were so often wrong, his actions were all right.

"I'm sorry I fell asleep," he said, as if hearing my thoughts. It felt like he was apologizing for so much more.

Unable to hear him ask for forgiveness from me, a fraud, yet again, I turned away. "Can't we just forget who we are for another bell?"

"You make me forget myself too often." He allowed me to rest my head on his chest. "I'm not the man you think I am."

I could barely contain my laughter—oh, the irony. "Well, I'm not the woman you think I am. So I would say we are a match. What would you do if tomorrow we would never see each other again?"

When he did not answer or move, I slowly placed his hands on my waist and threw my leg over his.

He tensed as I inched up, defined muscles hard.

I let my fingers stroke his arm through the wrinkled shirt, burning to feel him without it. I was weak and strong.

His lips fondled my neck, triggering fully body shivers.

I placed a hand on his hip, feeling like I would catch fire and craving the burn, as I eased my fingers under the untucked shirt, finding smooth muscles tense like coils.

My breath caught. Body ached.

"Princess," he said, his voice strained. I moved higher and he cursed, pushed against me, and ran his hands over my midriff. "You should leave."

His breath on my neck, lips almost touching skin, contradicted his words. It sent shivers dancing down my spine and erased all thoughts. A moan escaped my lips as I struggled with his buttons. One tore and his restrain snapped.

He yanked up my dress, hands roaming my flesh. "Tell me you want this, Princess. Tell me you're mine," he growled in my ear, trailing kisses down my throat.

I could not say I was his. He did not even know my name. And I did not want to lie anymore. I twisted until I caught his hungry eyes. Our breaths and hands slowed, as if both knew after this there would be no going back.

"If I wasn't a princess, I would be yours," I whispered. "I could love how much you care even when you think you don't. The person you let me see when we are alone."

"And if I wasn't a prince? I returned to Tal, seeking revenge. You're making me feel too much." His fingers clenched around my arm. "I only planned to hurt those who hurt me, to make amends, then leave. We cannot marry, because I don't plan to be king."

My mind spun. And no longer just with desire.

He did not want to rule. Again, I felt like I was falling. I made my choice yesterday, knowing it left me worse off than before von Lemerch entered my life. Would the prince disappearing before the wedding stop von Lemerch's plans? If the queen was right, would it affect other mages? This way, Dimitri and I would live. We could run from Tal and all its problems. The city had not changed for centuries, it could take care of itself. For the first time, I saw a possible life.

"What if we both leave?"

More possibilities than the Taliell's arms were opening before me. We could get to know each other away from lies and conspiracies. Kirill would be able to track me through the debt sigil, but with the prince's resources and my newfound magic, I must be able to find someone who could remove it or the money to pay it off. I could free Lumi and then we would all leave together. Fresh problems arose in my mind, but I pushed them aside. They could be solved when they came. Everything was better this way.

"You would leave all this behind?" the prince asked.

I relaxed into his arms. "In a heartbeat, but no one can know beforehand—the wedding must go on as planned until we are ready to leave."

"I still have unfinished business, but perhaps I don't have to wait..."

I nodded, despite not quite understanding what he was talking about. "Let's not wait."

The excitement triggered my recovering magic and his disbelief mixed with my hope. I wanted this future. Wanted him. My mouth met his, our passion a tidal wave pulling me away from sensible concerns.

I buried my fingers in his disheveled hair, ready to let it all go. Dimitri unhooked my corset and tore the twisted bands of the dress. I let it pool around my waist as the bedchamber door slammed against the wall.

Alexei rushed inside before either of us had time to react.

He smirked at me. "Up."

Dimitri threw himself between us. "Out. Unless someone is dead, you can wait."

Alexei ignored the angry glare, and threw open the curtains, then the balcony door. "The Princess and you can work out your relationship problems later. Your city is on fire."

The prince swore and stepped outside. Panic squeezed my chest. It could be the Gateways, many warehouses were dry from the summer heat, but part of me already knew what I would find when I stumbled outside wrapped in the bedsheet instead of struggling with my dress.

An orange glow—like the prince's chambers last night, like the crown, like the world had tried to warn me—tinted the morning and if Alexei had not said anything, I would have thought it only fog colored by the early dawn light. But Lowtown was getting darker, not brighter. The wind blew the smoke away from us; otherwise, we would have smelled it. Hopefully only livelihoods and livestock were being eaten by the flames, but I knew better. The narrow alleyways and old apartment buildings leaning against each other were a death trap. People would refuse to leave their homes. When you had so little, you clung to it because starvation in winter would take you as surely as the flames today.

The longer I watched, the clearer it became. The easternmost houses, flush against the city wall, were hidden by smoke while the northern part bordering the palace seemed saved by the wind. Were the mothers lugging water from the fountains where they normally chatted and washed, trading food and gossip? Was Popova, who had healed Lumi and cursed us, trapped? People like Kirill could burn, but somehow, they always seemed to be the ones who benefited in the end. At least Lumi should be in North's Place, safe enough for now, but if the wind turned, she could suffocate from the smoke.

Still feeling the kisses we exchanged while my sister and friends fought for their lives, tears streaked down my cheeks. How many new Spirits would there be when the sun set tonight? *The only one happy would be von Lemerch*, I thought, her words in the crypt replaying in my mind. She needed the recent dead.

The magic slipped my tenuous hold, exploding outward.

Their screams rang in my ears, broken bones and singed skin tore through me. A sea of emotions where each wave pulled me under like an acorn adrift in the storm that tore my world apart.

Dimitri and Alexei were talking next to me, sending runners with orders. Words like "fire street" and "flood level" passed through me while I lived and died with the people below. The prince tried to pull me inside, telling me to go to my rooms, that I did not need to be here. His touch snapped me back into my body. The magic churned under my skin but could not pierce his obsidian walls. Swallowing my emotions until only endless dread remained, I locked eyes with him.

"Are you sending mages to flood the river?" My voice was hoarse, as if I had screamed my anguish instead of standing silent and safe on a balcony overlooking the destruction.

There was compassion in his eyes but no grief. "It's too dangerous down there, and with the Taliell at its lowest it probably wouldn't be enough anyway. I cannot risk them now and leave Tal unprotected."

Anger bubbled up, and it was easier than horror and helplessness.

"Your people are dying, and you rather care about preventing a potential future threat? What can invaders do that is worse than burning them and all they know? But that is how kings are, isn't it? Only caring about battles and conquering, not about the people living so far down in the dirt that they wouldn't catch their hand if they were falling. Seems you would make a good king after all. *Children* are burning."

The last came out as a sob. Once, I would hide to watch those children—the ones with happy families who laughed. The mothers who stroked chubby cheeks. The siblings playing tag through the streets. Secretly seeing how they threw themselves around their father's neck when he returned from the backbreaking labor in the fields or tanneries, how he carried them home. Then when older, I watched over them as their mothers worked, all to belong, if just for a moment.

The wind shifted and I could smell it. See the gray snow—it rained ash.

The prince swore and pushed me at one of the guards.

"We must protect the rest of the city. Take the princess to her chambers."

And so, before nobles, guards, and servants who had stared as I broke down and screamed at their prince—a man they hardly dared to look at—I was carried away, still wrapped in his bedsheet, and in Helia's chambers, was left more alone than ever before.

I sat unmoving on my balcony, wanting to do something but hope had escaped me again. I would have prayed but Tal was the City of the Dead, and the Goddess had never listened so far.

Lana joined me silently. For the first time, we were both just girls from the bustling streets of Lowtown. From the nobles' perspective—from Dimitri's—it did not matter her father was rich and my mother a whore. We were both ants, not worth risking their lives to save. Expendable. Von Lemerch, whatever she truly was, had seen the same. It did not matter what came before or after this, what words or fists we had lugged at each other, as Svetlana and I both watched our world burn.

How had I imagined I could run away from it all with a prince? Would I never have told him the truth in that absurd fantasy? Inside, crazed laughter met unshed tears. Outside, my face was finally as blank as my sister's.

By afternoon, the smoke choked the city. Lowtown and most of Rivertown were lost behind the black shroud. Familiar houses had burned while I soaked up the smell of a man who could look at it and not care. The thought transformed his sheet, still wrapped around me, from comforting to revolting. It also shook me out of my passivity and self-blame. Out of the overwhelming emotions.

I was no princess. I did not belong here.

I put down the tea someone had brought and noticed Lana had left. Alone, I dropped his sheet over the side of the balcony and entered the princess's chambers without watching it fall. For the first time since I arrived, I saw the finery as Lumi would and knew the disgust she would have felt had she seen me dance away the time in this gilded cage, benefiting off others' labor. I had accused the prince of doing nothing to help, while I sat safe behind the palace walls. No more. Better to try and fail than do nothing at all.

A quick check confirmed that my stepsister had locked the front door when she left. It did not matter. I changed into the servant's clothes I had worn when breaking into the king's chambers, and found my climbing hook and Lumi's trusted lock picks still hidden in the sleeve. Lana must have forgotten their existence and never told Flora.

With a grim smile, I teased open the lock and left with no intention of returning. My time as a princess, spy, and thief was over. I packed nothing else. The way I planned to leave, I needed to be as light as possible.

Dealing with the threats of fire and plague, no one questioned me as I rushed by, the servant's clothes more effective than any magic.

Outside, I entered the park and then the woods. Kirill had instructed me how to leave when ordering me to steal the crown. While playing the princess, I had not dared act on them. That no longer mattered. Trees enveloped me and lazy insects buzzed through the air. There was no sign of fire, nor guards blocking my path. No reason for my steps to slow.

I should have felt free, like finally flying. Instead, I was still falling. Falling for Tal. For a prince who was never mine.

I should have left the previous evening before he caught me in his arms a final time. Putting one foot in front of the other, I swore there was no going back. He would be safe either married to another or far away from here. What did my bruised heart matter when von Lemerch, Flora, and the temple planned to take the very city and kill us in the process?

Chapter Twenty-Seven

Dimitri

I should have done the sensible thing, but somehow, the princess made me throw caution to the wind.

As the smoke coated my throat, her accusatory eyes and words haunted me through meetings until I pulled Alexei aside and asked him to quietly gather twenty city guards. The Council did not need me to nod at their suggestions. No matter how I despised them for their support of my father, they knew how to evacuate the hospital, clear the wide Palace Road to ensure the fire did not spread to the west side of Tal, and segregate those escaping the east outside the city walls. Helia had been right—any royal would make the same decisions. I was interchangeable, expendable, and could no longer sit in safety while children burned.

In borrowed guard uniforms, Alexei and I marched out, hidden among the soldiers before the Council could miss me. The smoke hit my face along Palace Road. For the first time, the busy thoroughfare was empty. The same could not be said as we entered Rivertown's narrower streets.

Streams of people crossed the hundred bridges, carrying everything from food to tables between them. Soot-stained faces squinted in the unnatural dusk. Children cried, chickens cackled, and everywhere, coughs sounded above the cacophony. If the plague had infected anyone in Rivertown, it would be unstoppable tomorrow, my orders for segregation and curfew useless.

On the Rivertown side of the Talliel, ever-entrepreneurial merchants sold food and drink, secure the fire would not jump the river. But the wind was turning; I could feel it in my blood. If the fire spread over the waterways, if it somehow crossed Palace Road, only the palace and temples would remain come morning. An unending sea of desperate Talians poured over the bridge before me. How I wished for an enemy I could meet with a blade.

I pulled on Alexei's arm to get his attention.

"We need to get closer to the fire." Because my pitiful powers could not reach far.

"Helping is right, Dimi, but you cannot risk your life. Carry water and sand to stop it here."

"You told me to care," I snapped, accusing green eyes blazing inside me. "I can leave Tal, but I cannot stand here and watch my city burn."

Before he could answer, I dove into the fleeing masses.

Our guards struggled to keep up as I pushed against the flow. The fleeing people cursed and shouted, but getting away took precedence over beating up an anonymous guard for an elbow in the ribs.

Alexei called for me to stop. It did not matter. The whispers of the wind filled my mind. The years in the mountains had helped me bond with it, listen, and open myself. It sang of smoke and hot air, flames pulling it in, and—stronger than anything else—the wind whispered of growing heat coming my way.

I allowed only a moment on the other side for Alexei and the guards to catch up. Of the original twenty, eleven had managed to keep with us through the pushing crowds, and together we moved from the colorful houses of Rivertown to the mud alleys of Lowtown. Even before the smoke, I had found the towering apartment buildings claustrophobic. The ash-filled air turned them suffocating. Wind whisperers desired open spaces, not a warren with more rats and bats than people.

The crowds lessened as the screams increased. Even without the wind telling me where to go, the thickening smoke informed us we were getting closer. My throat and eyes itched, lungs not filling, despite the wind moving to clear the air around us at my bidding.

Two streets away from the nearing flames, I raised my fist. This had to be close enough because if I failed and the wind turned, the fire could be here in moments. Eight guards remained—I had no idea where the other three had gone and had no time to search for them.

On the next street, brave men and women poured buckets of water over the dry wooden buildings. The rain a few days ago would be long gone under the hot sun. If I had the time and manpower, I would tell them to tear the houses down instead to create a fire street. Water and prayer were the only things they had, but it would do no good. The Goddess would welcome too many Spirits tonight.

The wind twisted around me. The fire was coming.

"Make them leave," I commanded the guards, pointing to the water carriers. "They can across the bridge. Here, they risk their lives for nothing."

The commander hesitated. "Our duty is to protect you, my prince."

"Today your duty is to save as many as you can. Make them leave everything they cannot carry with ease. Your swords won't protect me from the flames."

The wind pushed, begging for my attention, and I ignored the people around me. Alexei could deal with the guards.

Mages rarely displayed their powers openly, and never had I imagined calling the wind in the cramped streets of Lowtown. It was too exposed, almost indecent. Still, I moved my fingers to wrap air around them.

When firmly under my command, I stretched the power down the alleys. The fire inhaled the air and me, consuming with limitless hunger.

Each flame ate flesh and wood, feeding it as it reached for another. And another. The scale overwhelmed me. How could I fight this endless beast? Dark memories threatened to swallow me whole. The guards holding me back as they carried Eki into the hospital to force our child from her had been the first time I understood the power I wielded as the crown prince was a mirage, a pretty lie told to me since birth.

But Helia had asked me to try as she cried for a city not her own. I needed to focus on the present to change the future. The past had no place here.

In fits and bursts, I sang to the fickle wind of the clear sky, luring it away from the city and flames. *Up, up*, I told it. *Fly high from here*.

Little by little, it resisted the pull of the fire. The blaze shrank because everything suffocates without air. *Clear the smoke*, I hummed and moved my hand. *Blow down the alleys.*

Sweat stuck my hair to my forehead, shivers moved from my arms to legs, smoke choked my throat, and the fire sucked the air back, roaring to life.

My eyes snapped open, each smoke-clogged breath a struggle. Alexei and two guards remained on the otherwise empty street. The fire was no nearer, but neither was it burning out—if kept from spreading, it would soon run out of fuel. If I had been stronger or joined with other wind whisperers, we could have choked it. But there were so few mages left that we protected those who remained—those who should have been out helping—above all else. The healers would not walk the streets; probably, they had already been evacuated by griffon and sat in the Red Manor waiting for the city to be declared safe.

"Are you back?" Alexei asked. "Only stragglers too stubborn to leave remain here. Time to go."

"And the rest of Lowtown? Of Tal?" Still open to the air's whispers, I knew there were more people in the buildings around us. "We're not leaving. The canals are not wide enough. If it spreads the rest of the city will be beyond saving."

"Well, I can only lug a bucket, and not for very long if the smoke returns."

We were surrounded by houses built wall-to-wall, blocking the sun and sky. "Magic is easier to direct if you can see the target—I need to get closer. Higher."

"You're not going in there. Even unburnt these houses are a day away from collapsing."

I ignored Alexei's sensible words, already pulling open the closest door. Luck was with me, and no one had locked behind them when escaping.

"You can leave or follow. As you said, there is nothing you can do to help," I called behind me and entered the grubby hallway. "You and the princess told me to care about people, to do something. The plague, I can do nothing about. My father, I can do nothing about. The grief has twisted Eki, and perhaps me as well. Maybe today, I can make something better."

Rushing up on the creaking, uneven stairs, it swayed under our pounding steps.

"I didn't mean for you to throw yourself into an inferno. Dimi, are you listening?"

"No." I could not. Nothing scared me like the flames. They had come to represent my failures, become the way I tortured myself. If I could not escape the past through blood, maybe I could through saving someone from the fire.

"Slow down! Don't rush in blind!"

It's coming, the air sang.

I sped up.

Dirt and darkness pressed in, but the higher I got, the more daylight pierced the narrow, soot-stained windows.

On the fifth floor, the stairs ended and a locked door blocked our path. I struck it with my shoulder only to bounce back. Had they kept their best wood for the roof or had the weather petrified it?

"Kick it down," I said, glad the guards had followed.

Precious moments passed before the wood split with a loud crack, the wind whispering of the ever-closer flames. If caught here, we were doomed. Three more steps and the smoke-covered city spread out before me, unnatural heat pressed in, and I had no regrets. I had dreamt of leaving but never formed a concrete plan for what came after abandoning the crown. In the far distance, the wind whispered of a summer storm, but by the time it reached us we would all be dead.

Maybe I had always known I would never leave Tal alive. Alexei and the guards still had hope though.

"Get out of here. There is nothing more you can do."

Alexei pushed aside the boxes of hallucinatory gunna plants—probably the reason for the reinforced door—and stepped up next to me. "Three years ago, I let you leave on your own and you returned broken. I'm not leaving again."

"My mistakes were never yours."

"I swore to warn you the next time you did something incredibly stupid."

I could hear the smile in his voice. "This is you warning me?"

"This is me being stupid with you."

And somehow, despite where we were, what was to come, and watching my city burn, I smiled back. "I would rather I knew there was someone sensible back at the palace when this is over. When I said I would leave you and Helia in charge, I meant it."

"Let Nikolai rule in name. Solovyova can hold his hand."

The wind pressed against me. If I was to do something, it had to be now.

I waited until the guards reached the street below. They would stay unless the fire consumed the building, and then have the unenviable task of carrying the news of our deaths to the palace.

We stepped onto the roof's edge. The smoke, an enveloping cloud, blew into our faces. My eyes teared and lungs ached, but I did not turn away. I needed to see.

Removing all mental defenses against overuse, the walls I learned to build before I left the Tower, I threw my magic wide, imagining myself back on the mountain tops, and invited the wind in.

Since birth they tell us our three curses are to be treasured and feared. One for your last breath, two to get there. Three years ago, I used the first one in grief and nothing came of it. I had expected death to be further away than this. It did not matter. Alone, I could only hold the fire, not extinguish it. Never had I felt my lack of magic more. There was no time for careful words or holding back.

"Drown in rain. May the fire die and Tal live." I raised my arms, pushed outward, and a part of me followed out into the world, making me forever lesser than I had been.

Praying to the Wishmaker that this curse turned blessing would work better than the last, I gathered my remaining magic.

I would stay as long as I could, until the fire burned out or consumed me.

For me, like my son, there would be no gilded bones above the worshipers on three-day.

I imagined Helia's approving smile, the challenging twinkle in her eyes, and smirk on her lips. The feel of her in my hands. If I had let her, she would have stood next to me.

I had told her of my plans to leave, and without asking a single question, she had understood. She deserved someone without a past weighing him down. Perhaps, she would return to Oberwalden where other arms would hold her like I had last night. Her skillful hands would help another forget his burdens. Her hard words would make someone else a better man. It should have reassured me, but instead, it fueled my anger. This morning had been a dream, lost before it could become reality.

Now, the wind sang.

Channeling the grief and pain I had kept inside for three years, the fury at a future that would never be mine, I screamed my rage at Tal and held nothing back. At my side, Alexei shouted his own defiance at the world.

We could not let the fire pass us until the first raindrop fell.

Chapter Twenty-Eight

Vanya

I trekked alongside the palace wall. Kirill's instructions had been clear when he sent me to steal the crown. That thrice-damn oak must be here somewhere. The faint scent of smoke was enough for horror images to dance in my mind, pushing me until I was running over the uneven ground.

Lumi was out there, but she was not alone. Despite exchanging pleasantries with the neighbors, my sister and I had seemed to exist in a bubble—only our struggle to get away from our stepfather completely real. One catastrophe following another burst that illusion. I belonged out there.

What did an oak look like? Each tree I passed seemed the same. Show me the corner of a roof or alley, and I could tell you where in Tal you stood. Blindfold me, and my feet would still betray the streets. How could I, who had never left the city, recognize one tree from another?

Fortunately, it did not matter because while I did not know the name of the giant growing before me, I recognized an escape route, and the branch leaning against the top of the wall high above was just that.

I shrugged out of the coat and threw it together with my shoes into the underbrush. The earth was moist and comforting under my toes. To get up and over the wall, I would need every sense and bare feet offered better grip than soles.

With a running start, I jumped and gripped the stem. The climb to the lowest branch was harder than any rose trellis. Twice, I fell only to be caught by the undergrowth.

By the time I clung to the first branch, bark stuck to the sweaty servant's clothes. If anyone caught me here, proper attire would be the least of my concerns. I climbed from one branch to the next until I was eye level with the wall.

Seated high above a sea of green, I caught my breath and studied the partly attached branch I was about to risk my life on. It split where it rested on top of the wall, like fingers clinging to the worn parapet too far away for my rope and hook.

The black stone met the gray sky, and I dreaded what I would see from up there. *Did any of Tal remain? How could Dimitri allow it to burn?*

I had been so excited when he held my gaze and body, confessing he wanted to leave Tal, that my problems and common sense had evaporated. I had not considered what would happen to Tal if the king died and the crown prince ran away. But he must have weighed the chaos sure to follow his disappearance against his own comfort and found it worth the price. Maybe Lumi was right in her judgment of him after all.

I shook my head. Even here, he took too much of my focus. I had decided to leave, now I had to follow through. My sister and the real princess might be choking on smoke as I sat fuming.

I inched forward and the broken limb creaked ominously. Maybe talking my way past the guards at the gate like last time would have been the better option after all. But climbing down held more than a fair chance of breaking my neck. I was running out of time—magic and instinct both told me to hurry.

On my hands and knees, I crept a foot, then another. Despite moving smoothly and distributing my weight equally, the branch rocked like a river barge. Then it slid, barely noticeable at first—a few leaves falling, smaller offshoots breaking—until I was halfway across and one of the supporting limbs snapped. The branch dropped a foot, and I dug my nails into the bark to keep from losing my grip as it rocked. If I fell this time, there would be no prince to catch me. *Was it this unstable when Kirill ordered me to use it the night of the ball?* No way of knowing now, though if I had ever doubted he cared if I survived, this confirmed it.

Sweat rolled down my back. *You don't fear heights*, I told myself. *The Goddess will call you when she wants, but you cannot sit frozen. You'll not stand by like a bloody useless royal.*

The tree steadied, and I shifted my weight. It swayed precariously, then slid down, and this time, it did not stop.

There was no time for second thoughts. I sprinted along the branch with my eyes locked on the top of the wall.

With a loud *crack*, the branch split from the stem, and I threw myself into the air.

It crashed to the ground as my fingers wrapped around the rough stones. I pulled myself up and saw the devastation below, confirming this was a one-way trip. Carrying the realization like a stone in my stomach, I turned to face Tal.

This lonely segment of the wall bordered the poorest part of Lowtown. Normally, it would be teeming with life between the tightly packed buildings, grimy drinking halls, and stinking tanning pools. Instead, a world painted gray greeted me. The smoke even covered the reek of the tannery.

Did Kirill's house still stand as the greatest among the poorest? I had hated living there, dreamt more than once of torching it myself, but now that all I knew was disappearing, I hoped it had been spared and that the last of Lumi's and my possessions remained—the last proof Vanya and the innocent girl I had once been had existed.

Further away, the fire burned its way toward Rivertown's barges and markets. Beyond that lay Palace Road and North's Place with its mansions untouched—and Lumi locked in a basement. If the fire got that far, it would be a death trap. The temples' black tops were barely visible through the haze. Hopefully the Goddess's vision was blocked as well.

On the other side of the wall, the high tenements of Lowtown leaned, having used ancient, immovable stones to save on building material and reach high enough to escape the stink below.

With my hook secured in the wall, I shimmied down the rope and landed on a roof covered with laundry lines. There was no way to loosen the hook, so squashing my reluctance, I left it behind and snatched one of the unbleached dresses—torn and leaf-covered palace servant's clothes would be too memorable if I needed to disappear. Stripping in the open felt strange after the imposed propriety of the palace, but in the beige, Lowtown dress, I felt more myself than I had in previous month.

I leapt from roof to roof until I spotted an open door. After taking the abandoned stairs two steps at a time, I could finally feel the familiar muck under my bare feet. Since my mother's death, the Lowtown pebbles and dirt had become home. Now, they were covered in ash.

Despite the unnaturally silent alley, the melody of the streets played in my mind. The rattling bones, chirping bats, cheering crowds, wailing mourners, merchants, children and mothers, fathers and animals—my feet hit the ground in time to the song of Tal and the magic spread across the streets in response.

There was life everywhere—people and animals terrified of smoke and plague, but with nowhere to escape. People in doorways and windows called out for news as I passed, asking if the fire was approaching, if the Guard would force them from their homes. With no breath to spare, I shook my head. Some cursed me for not stopping but most watched silently, unable to process how their already hard lives had changed in a matter of days.

Their worries and desperation threatened to drown me. *Lumi*, I thought to my internal music, focusing on her voice and too-rare laugh while shutting out the rest. I could not risk falling down unconscious again by overusing the magic. Someone found on the streets of Lowtown would not be cared for during the best of times. They might burn me with the plague victims rather than ask questions, especially as there was already a convenient fire going.

Lumi, sister, half of my Spirit, I sang to my pounding steps and felt a tug at my heart. I needed no magic instruction to tell me I was getting closer.

Worn stones replaced the mud of Lowtown as I crossed the first bridge. Merchants should be setting up their wares in the sprawling Rivertown markets, calling out the first bargains of the day while betting who could sell the most before the sun set and the real crowds appeared. Instead, the colorful awnings flapped abandoned above empty stalls. Was the wind increasing? Praise the Wishmaker it did not speed the flames.

By the time I crossed Palace Road and entered the wide streets of North's Place, I had slowed to a fast walk. Despite the fine food of the last month, I was no distance runner and had entered the city close to Kirill's but far from the noble house we robbed the last time Lumi and I were together—where I now hoped to find her.

Griffons circled high above, sometimes diving for their riders to deliver news of the fire's progress. Undoubtedly, the finest possessions were loaded onto carts behind the private walls I passed. If you could afford to fly away, you could wait until the last moment. Still, it reassured me the rich were not yet running.

Roses sprawled up the buildings, their sweet scent covered by smoke, and the purple night lilies remained closed. I hoped when the sun set, they would bloom again.

In daylight, Third Street seemed worse off than I remembered. Lumi had picked the house to rob, telling me no good people lived there. I had laughed at her because she often said no one with money in Tal was a good person. *What made these nobles any different?* Could it be a coincidence I found myself back here, or that we broke into the von Mekeln mansion the night before von Lemerch hired us to steal the crown? Was my similarity to Helia more than serendipity?

A nagging voice in the back of my mind said everyone else knew more than they let on, and I—impulsive, peaceful, ignorant, and wild Vanya—was the only one who had been tricked. I needed to talk to my sister.

Standing in the middle of the street under the ash rain, I focused on my magic, but now that I needed it, it slipped away.

With closed eyes and controlled breathing, I sought the elegant song of North's Place—of garden parties, closed coaches, and scraping servants—and moved. If anyone saw me, they would have thought me insane, but today, there were no guards to spare for a crazed dancing girl.

The song became a lament for Tal, the accompanying movements slowing and rolling, allowing the magic to run through me in waves. This time, I recognized the strain. *How much could I use without permanent damage?* It did not matter. I was too close to freeing Lumi and Helia, and returning my world to what it had been before this started. To—no matter his ignorance and callousness—save Dimitri. Come Day of the Dead, he would marry the right princess with the right crown, and whatever von Lemerch planned would fail.

The magic responded and again, I felt all life around me. The mansion we had robbed stood empty; the residents presumably returned to their country estate because of the plague. Lumi had said she was close to here.

Several houses further down the street had residents, but none had Lumi's cold, sharp energy. I had not known this magic for long, but I knew my sister. The memory of her stiff movements worked their way into the dance.

There.

I had climbed that wall, watched the Spirits congregate in the abandoned house, and turned away. Now it pulled me closer. *Down.* There she was, together with another. The magic flinched away from the second—*Helia?*

I climbed the dilapidated wall again, sliding down into the overgrown garden on the other side. The front door gaped, daring anyone to enter. Below, Lumi paced while the other felt more dead than alive. With equal longing and apprehension, I entered.

Inside, the boarded-up windows turned day into night, but Spirits illuminated the cracked walls.

Great thinkers and street frauds all had theories of where the Spirits went during the day. One thing everyone knew—they were not seen in Tal. Still, here they hovered, their unearthly light revealing worn, flowery wallpaper.

When my magic touched a Spirit, I flinched. They were empty holes ready to drag me in, cold where my magic was warm, but Lumi and answers were too close to turn around.

The entry hall floorboards creaked ominously under my bare feet as I inched around the nearest Spirit. Below, Lumi paused. Could she feel how close I was? Had our preternatural sense of each other been blocked magic all along?

Something almost tangible pulled me to her. I could not have turned away even had I wanted to. I hurried my steps. The Spirits hung unmoving, as if waiting, and death thickened the air. They had been a nightly presence all my life, and while passing through them tingled and dishonored the dead, they had never scared me before. With my new magic swirling around me, despite the interrupted dance, I knew these Spirits were *wrong*.

I squeezed against the wall to pass their diffused forms as a primordial fear shook my knees and my teeth chattered.

Hurry. Hurry. Hurry, my heart drummed. The smell of smoke remained a constant reminder of the closing-in fire.

The ground floor had been abandoned long ago and the staircase consisted of more holes than wood. There were no signs anyone had entered for years. Even to my new senses it felt dead—no rats scurried behind the walls; no bats slept above. And there was no sign of a basement door.

After a second round, I leaned into the corner furthest from the drifting Spirits. There must be a way down. Below, Helia had not moved. This close she felt even more wrong. Half dead. Lumi was back to pacing, her steps almost close enough to hear, like Dimitri paced when stressed. Nothing in my old life should remind me of him; still, even the faded blue wall brought back his hard eyes. Had he already checked on his princess, only to find her gone?

The abandoned living room, large enough for parties, spread before me. Once, I would have dreamt of living in a place like this. The Spirits must have scared away thieves and squatters, for each inch in North's Place was worth its weight in gold. Someone had been paying a lot for a long time to keep this a hovel. It made no sense.

My footprints marked my path through the dust and debris. I squinted in the Spirit light, then bent to study my steps closer. There was something strange about them.

The style of the house was no older than eighty years, all light river stones and wood, but my steps exposed black stones. I brushed away more dirt. I *knew* this stone. Had lived surrounded by it for the past month.

Standing on an exposed slab with dirt-stained hands, I was sure. The mansion stood on the same obsidian as the ancient death temples and palace. And in my corner, I noticed a swirling sigil. Where the rest of the stone was worn down by uncountable steps, the sigil looked well taken care off. It reminded me of the ones in the crypt under the Tower. I traced it with my fingers, but it gave me no clues as to what it was for. Few outside the Sigil Guild could read the sigils, and those that could guarded their secrets close. I rubbed against the debt mark on my thigh.

Lumi was locked below temple stones. I cleared more of the floor. Each corner held a sigil.

After crawling across every inch, painfully aware of the passing time, I found nothing more. Next, I knocked on the walls, hoping for a hollow one. Rotted bookshelves lined them, but one was better kept than the rest. With renewed energy, I examined each section. Hidden behind the fourth shelf, I finally found a lock but elation was soon replaced by despair. Even with the picks, it was well beyond my skills. Lumi might have been able to open it.

I kicked at the lock. Attacked it with the lock picks anyway, hoping for a lucky click. Then finally, I rested my head against the shelf, conflicted, unable to give up or go any further. I could not beat it, climb it, or charm it. I could certainly not dance through it. If my magic had been physical, telekinetic like Flora or a fire bearer able to burn it down, I could have waved my hand and nothing would stand in my way. Instead, I could feel my sister so close and still not free her.

Help me get to her, I begged the magic inside.

I needed to talk to her and at least tell her I would be back after checking the progression of the fire outside. For once, I did not feel like dancing, but the magic vibrated with Tal's death lament. The song said outside, people fought for their loved ones, watched the ashes fall, and drew their last breaths, and part of me was with each one.

Maybe for trained mages, magic manifested in other ways and obeyed their every whim. Maybe it was the curse blocking mine from flowing freely, but since the prince mentioned using movements to focus, something had unlocked inside me and the ever-present music demanded I move.

The gliding motions started slowly, then sped to match my angry heartbeat. Why was this happening to Tal? To me and Lumi? Why was this goddess-forsaken lock separating me from my sister?

Dum.

Dum.

Dum.

My heart and feet pounded together. There was an echo, another set of feet matching mine, a heart that beat with mine since the womb, and I was no longer alone.

I opened my eyes.

"You shouldn't be here," a dirtier, paler Lumi with fading bruises said.

She stood where the bookshelf had swung out like a door. My feet paused and my heart missed a beat. A moment later, we were laughing and crying in each other's arms, thanking the Goddess and Wishmaker and any other god we could think of as the previously stationary Spirits swirled around us.

Lumi stepped away from me and raised her hand. As one, the spinning Spirits sped outward, until we were alone. It seemed I was not the only one with strange magic.

"They'll tell me what is going on," Lumi said, as if the Spirits and the open door required no further explanation, and picked up her discarded lockpicks. "Thanks for returning these, but I told you not to come—as you see, I didn't need your help. I'm right where I need to be."

I stared, unable to process her matter-of-fact words. "I'm here to save you. The city is in flames, and you expected me to stay in the palace while you burned?"

She scoffed. "I was perfectly safe here, though von Lemerch will surely know the door has been opened. That pushes up the timeline."

"You want to be here?" My world rearranged itself as I watched my sister's cold eyes.

"The rebels knew von Lemerch and her tame priestesses were doing something. The dead speak, though she is pulling them away. Then she came to us with promises of a better tomorrow. I don't know why she thought we would trust her words. The royals are enough. We don't need a new ruler."

We as in the rebels, but not Lumi and me. The robbery that went wrong, von Lemerch's eyes drifting between me and Lumi, her lack of surprise at my likeness to Helia… "You placed us in her way to get closer to her?"

Lumi nodded sharply. "She cannot be killed. We already tried. No Spirits of the recently dead walk the streets anymore. When she spotted me from a distance and asked Kirill who I was it was an opportunity too good to pass up."

"Since when do you talk to Spirits? Why did you hide our magic?"

"First, I didn't keep your magic from you, just the knowledge of my own, and it took a lot of time after the attack before I even accepted it was magic. For months, I heard the Spirits' whispers and thought I was going insane."

"And then?"

"We weren't talking. I blamed you too much. Nothing like being locked in a basement for a month to help you get over the past though." She gave me a sad look and the twisted scar reminded me of the pain she had been going through at the time. "I'm a death keeper, I later learned. A necromancer. You?"

"Heart turner, I've been told," I said, unsure how to react to her opening up so calmly.

The silence stretched until three Spirits returned. Lumi tilted her head as if listening.

"Come, there is someone you need to meet," she said, and led the way down hidden stairs into the obsidian basement below.

Mage lights appeared to guide us, and they were not mine. Still, I followed my sister down without hesitation. The black walls were covered with figures in worship, carved in scenes of human sacrifice appearing untouched by time. If I was right the foundations were as old as the palace and this had been a temple before Herebov's time.

At the end of the staircase, a room stretched longer than the building above, perhaps all the way under the street and the von Mekeln manor on the other side. The bobbing lights revealed two tunnels leading even further away, and, on what used to be the altar, lay a woman.

Lumi swept her arm over the body and more lights appeared.

She was the same age, shared similar features as us, just shorter, with rounded cheeks and straight hair. Her left wrist showed an identical noble's sigil—I could see why someone who had not met either could mistake us, but she had less sharp edges, an innocence and peace Lumi and I did not share.

"Helia von Heskin," I said, half expecting her to open her eyes. She looked dead, but I could still feel a glimmer of life in her.

Lumi nodded. "She was here before me and has not moved since I arrived. Not sure if they planned to wake her after switching out the crown, and thought better of it when they saw us, or if she was never meant to arrive."

"I heard von Lemerch say Helia came to Tal to refuse the marriage." *Why had I not thought about how to wake her?* Again, I knew I was not capable of making the plans. *Why had I thought this would work?*

"Is that so?" Lumi asked, considering the unconscious woman. "Perhaps away from here, I can wake her. Von Lemerch's magic stinks of death. Bringing Helia to the palace could at least stall the marriage plans."

My mind spun. What if Helia was not a good person? I could never offer Dimitri an explanation. Could not see Mariska again. What if I was not ready to give up the life of the princess? Panic raised my voice to a squeak. "What if she leaves Dimitri directly? I could return until the Night of the Dead, while you find someone willing to remove the debt marks and a way to break von Lemerch's curse. Find a way to tell him everything. No one will die."

"Dimitri is it?" Lumi said, narrowing her eyes and seeing too much. "Of course, you care for the misunderstood prince who has had everything handed to him. This plan of yours puts us at risk while von Lemerch has two months to find a new solution. She might already know you left the palace and that I'm free. Do you really think the Crown Prince of Tal would look at you twice if he knew your real name? He thinks you're *her*." She pointed at the unconscious woman, her face serene and hands unmarked by labor.

"He cares." It sounded empty even to my own ears. The words of a girl who had longed to belong her whole life. I had decided to do what was right, but standing here now, I could not walk away. "I'm not leaving him. Not yet."

"You were supposed to run and live for both of us. Dance and bring joy. I told you from the start. You're not suited for plots and the sacrifices that must be made."

Lumi's hard face was unreadable. The temple muted my magic as well, blocking any attempt to read her emotions.

"No," I said. How could she think I would walk away?

We stared each other down until Lumi nodded, seemingly reaching a conclusion. "As usual you won't do anything until circumstances force you to. Von Lemerch needs the prince. They won't have time to anoint another heir before the wedding. If Helia arrives suddenly, it will distract von Lemerch and her allies enough for us to *manage* him. It's the only way forward. And you will need to run. No matter what you wish, you'll be safe. Help me get her out of here." A Spirit drifted toward Lumi. She listened with a smile. "It seems the decision is out of our hands. That prince of yours was useful after all."

"What?" It was the last thing I had expected her to admit.

She waved toward the Spirits. "Did you know he is a wind whisperer? They tell me he shaped the wind in Lowtown and stopped the fire from spreading further."

Pride filled me, and the wide grin was impossible to hide. Unknowingly, Dimitri had saved my home.

"If we could tell him the truth, he would help find a solution."

Lumi pursed her scarred lips. "It's doubtful he'll still live until midnight. The building he was in collapsed. Seems no good deed goes unpunished in Tal."

Hearing her calm statement, I did not understand at first. *He could not die*. He was the crown prince. A great conspiracy would kill him—plots and poisons—not a roof.

"Tell me where he is." He was still alive. I had freed Lumi, I could free him as well.

She glared. "He needs to die, later would be better but this works, and we need to carry Helia out of here. No matter her noble birth any fool could tell we are related. Blood comes before all. We promised to stand by each other, V."

"Like you stood by me? I'm no fool either. You've been hiding things for years. Tell me where he is, and I'll forgive it all."

Lumi threw an inscrutable look toward Helia's prone form. "When you refused to kill Lady Meklen and we didn't get the contents of the safe, I was sure we'd failed." Her face softened. "I always planned to pay off the debt with those jewels, then you could dance away to your happy life, and I would do the next part alone. Then you were the one they wanted while I was left here to guard a sleeping princess."

"Why didn't you tell me what was going on?"

"You could never understand." She swallowed. "When those noblemen attacked me two years ago, I made them pay for thinking they could take anything they wanted. The world is cold and hard, but for you it's a pretty show. No wonder you fight for a prince and the palace instead of the real, rough world. Today Lowtown burns, but it's just the start. In the end, the royals, von Lemerch and the temples will all pay. Then tomorrow will be a better day."

The vehemence in her words coated me despite my reduced magic. How had I missed all this hatred? "Better through kindness, that's what Mother taught us. I never turned away from you. You're my other part."

She smiled and it was not pretty. "Then prove it. Dimitri Ivanov lies close to Torik the butcher, a block from Popova's apothecary shop. You can work with me with your eyes finally open, or try to save him and then run away, because either way, I'll bring Helia to the palace at sundown tomorrow. Sooner or later, he needs to die and your time as a princess is done. Staying out of it will cost you nothing."

I wanted to argue until she saw reason, but there was no more time for words. Instead, I embraced her stiff form and pushed all the love from my heart into hers.

"No. Turning away would cost me everything. I'm not leaving you by saving him. Love is not finite or reasonable. It cannot be turned off because you lied to me or stopped from growing because he might not deserve it. Trust is a leap of faith. I trust he'll make tomorrow better, and I need to know if I'll fall or fly."

I turned and ran, leaving my sister and the unconscious Helia in the abandoned mansion.

I had told Dimitri to stand for something, and he had listened. He could not die for it. I would not let him.

Chapter Twenty-Nine

Vanya

The streets flew past under my feet. Behind the smoke-stained clouds, the sun was setting. If Lumi's Spirits were right, there was not much time left.

Dimitri could not die because of me. Our last words could not be accusations. Everything about me was a lie besides who I was when we were alone. The knife twisted in my heart at the thought of arriving too late.

I crossed Palace Road as the curfew bells rang, calling, *Plague, plague, plague,* despite the fire. Closed shutters blocked any lit lanterns and the regular Spirits had yet to rise. Tonight, no one was lighting the street lanterns. Tal was unnaturally dark.

Ash flakes like the winter snow covered my soot-stained dress and face as the first drops of rain smattered against my cheek.

What had the prince thought entering Tal himself? I had wanted him to *send* help, never had I thought he would risk himself for Lowtown.

I blinked away tears as I entered Rivertown. People milled around with blank faces and singed clothes, their possessions in piles on the street next to them—they had run from the immediate danger, perhaps had no homes anymore, so despite the bells, they stayed.

Children with scared, gray-stained faces clung to their parents. Somewhere lost among the masses were my former neighbors, fellow theater troopers, and nameless dancing partners. Having no time to spare, I did not look too close at anyone I passed because I could not stop. They turned their faces to the sky, let the shower wash them clean, and whispered it was a miracle the rain arrived before the fire spread. That the Death Goddess and Wishmaker both blessed Tal today.

Their resilience spurred me on. Lowtowners were knocked down by life but rose again and again until the Goddess took them. Hopefully, the same strength had grown in me since my mother died and I was torn from the pretend finery.

I crossed the last bridge. The people were right—it was a miracle that the fire had not spread this far—but from what Lumi had said, they could thank their crown prince instead of the gods for each house still standing. I did, while praying his interference had not attracted the Goddess's attention.

At Popova's sooty windows, only two blocks from Kirill's fancy house, I paused. Cinders had burned furrows into the wood and the ash lay thick against the walls, the rain turning it into black muck. At the end of the street, only burned-out husks remained. In between was the fire line, buildings partly burned but still standing, including the butcher Lumi mentioned.

Returning people milled about while others cried in pain and loss for possessions and loved ones. *How will I ever find the prince?*

Above in the drizzle circled griffons while further down the street shouting increased, attracting a crowd. Their building emotions surged and like a leaf lost in the Talliel, I drifted along in their wake.

Closer, their emotions buzzed like angry bees as we swarmed around one of the burned-out shells. I heard grumblings about how the Guard caused this, how without the curfew, the fire would not have gotten away. That they had protested the lack of food when someone torched a bridge. That it was time for revenge. Traces of the bloody stick figure remained on house walls and was embroidered on huffing chests.

"Get help!" a familiar voice called.

I pushed through the crowd to reach the front before this blew out of hand. The people of Lowtown had lost everything in the fire and the Guard had never been appreciated here. From each sleeve I brushed against, anger clawed at me.

"Please. We didn't cause this. We stopped it. The hospital—" Alexei continued before a coughing fit interrupted his words.

I could only see the broad back of the man who answered him. "And where should we take our hurt? Will the hospital open their doors to those as well? You forced us to close the stores when your master yapped. Blocked the bridges, hoping the plague would burn out among the poor and didn't care if we starved."

Emotions swelled into a wave ready to crash down as I broke through the front of the crowd.

My first thought upon seeing Alexei, *How is he still standing?*

Blood dripped from his hairline, masking his normally carefree face. The guard uniform was in no better state. But what almost brought me to my knees was the blackened wood stake piercing his chest. Only drops of crimson surrounded it, as if it was keeping it all in, keeping him on his feet.

Then the first stone flew.

It bounced against the doorframe above Alexei's head and burnt flakes rained down into his eyes. He staggered back blindly.

Frozen, I stood at the front of the mob with damned ash and blessed rain falling on my face. There would be no explanation for me being here. Nothing a fake princess could say to halt the crowd. Stepping forward, I might well be throwing my lot in with his. Speaking highly of the Guard was not good for your health, even under normal circumstances.

A second stone soared past me. This one flew true, striking Alexei's head.

He fell to his knees, and the risks did not matter. Alexei had been nothing but nice to me, he was Dimitri's best friend, and standing aside, watching, I might as well be throwing the stones myself. I had told Lumi there was a cost to walking away, talked to her of kindness. I had known better than to expect either to be free. Still, the moment stretched as I fought my natural self-preservation.

With a leap much shorter, but more decisive than those I had taken so far in my life, and I covered Alexei's normally imposing body.

"Stop!" I commanded with pretend confidence at faces unrecognizable by rage. "Killing a man on his knees, someone who came to help despite cause to stay away, achieves nothing."

The mob's feelings pressed in until they became a physical force I braced against, one hand on Alexei's shoulder to anchor me. Tears ran freely down my cheeks as I absorbed the rage and loss and pain behind the twisted faces before me. Grief and helplessness seeking an outlet, like what I had felt inside Dimitri on the bench but expanded until it became identity and community. If the curse muted my power, it might also save me now as I could barely hang on to my sense of self under the onslaught. Almost lost among their feelings, I did not notice the second pain behind me at first. The prince's energy flickered, like a candle about to burn out.

The crowd had momentarily paused at my words, and I waved my arms, drawing their attention further. "They only came to help because I asked them. Hurting them won't bring your homes back." People grumbled but no further stones flew, and my confidence grew. "Help me get them out."

"Who're you to talk for guards?" someone called as Alexei grabbed my hand to pull himself up. Again, the anger grew from the crowd, and I pushed him down.

"I'm no one, just a Lowtowner. I've lost family because I was turned away from the hospital, have indebted myself for those I love. When I walked these streets some of you saw a starving girl and shared the little you had."

"Princess?" Alexei asked from behind, maybe recognizing my voice, because my disheveled soot-stained appearance could not be further from Helia von Heskin's fine dresses.

"The man is addled. That's no princess," a voice I recognized said and some of the anger dissipated at the preposterous statement. "That's Vanya, Kirill's girl, I saw her play Queen Tatiana last summer. I still remember how she seemed to fly."

I found the speaker. Despite his burned clothes and bandaged hand, I recognized him as one of Popova's numerous grandsons.

"Yes, maybe you should call the girl queen," someone further back said, and laughter followed.

I smiled with my neighbors.

"She helped me once."

"She cared for my kids when I was sick."

"What will Kirill say if we hurt her?"

The voices continued and the tense mood relaxed. For the first time, being just me, the bastard-born urchin adopted by the murderous moneylender, was an advantage. I had thought myself a nobody my whole life, but they had seen me anyway. I had become a part of this place without noticing it. *Why had I always believed myself an outsider when they had not?*

"You know me, and I know them. They came to help," I said, while I felt Alexei and Dimitri weaken behind me. I needed to hurry.

The first speaker pushed those around him aside and Popova herself, short, dark, and unbent despite being at least seventy, stepped to the front.

"I know your sister well, girl. What have you gotten yourself into? Messing with those from the palace leads only to heartache. Even your mother learned that."

Despite the wrinkled black skin and almost-white hair, calculating eyes took me and Alexei in before she nodded and turned to the crowd.

"Go rebuild your houses, care for your children."

She did not raise her voice, but no one argued. *Witch*, people called her behind her back, and I wondered if I would have found her name in the Book of Bloodlines had I read each line, or if it also denied the existence of commoner mages. One thing was for sure, the mob dispersed as if by magic.

Judging the threat over, I dropped next to Alexei. Burns left bubbling skin and flesh exposed on his arms. The blood at the corner of his mouth stood stark against too-pale skin and coal-blackened cheeks, but his eyes were clear as they met mine.

"What are you doing here?" we asked each other simultaneously.

He shook his head and swayed. "No time," he bit out. "It doesn't matter—not who you are or what you're doing. I've seen how you look at Dimi, how your words moved him. He used to be different. Thoughtful. Hopeful. Help him find it again."

I swallowed. *Who was I to help someone find hope?* But Alexei saw me as me without judgement and my doubts were not important. Not now. "I'll get help for both of you."

The hospital was on the other side of Tal. Even if I could get there, the healers might not have returned. Mariska might not be there and no one else would listen to someone looking like me. There was no time to sneak into the palace, wash and hope a servant believed me. Von Lemerch needed the prince alive. Where was she now?

"Grieve later," Alexei said, seeing my falling face. "Keep him safe."

Inside the house, the prince's energy fluttered. The sun was setting, and Lumi had said he would not survive the night. I did not know if the Spirits felt when the Goddess came for the dying, but I could not risk it. I had to do something, but what?

The crowd and Popova, including her strong grandson, were nowhere to be seen. A grieving girl bent over a dying guard was no longer interesting. Grief was all around, a blanket muting Lowtown's usual evening bustle. The first Spirit illuminated the street.

A man stepped out from the nearby alley, like he had been waiting for me to turn. I swallowed, then stumbled to my feet. I needed help, no matter where it came from.

"A runner said my stepdaughter was making a nuisance of herself," Kirill said. "That cannot be so, I thought, because she has a job to do."

"I'm doing it. Help me get them to a healer," I blabbered, hating my subservient tone. Princess Helia had probably never sounded like this.

"Now, what do we have here?"

With a kick to the shoulder, Kirill knocked Alexei to the ground, and I shouted for him to stop as the prince's friend cried out in pain. Kirill ignored us both and flicked open the torn guard jacket. Below was a pin that set all Lowtowners shaking in fear. How could the smiling, joking man be *Roja*?

"As I thought. Two men recently killed a debtor of mine, a former palace guard, before he could repay. People in the know claim one of them was Roja, but my friends also tell me no such killing was sanctioned. This man fits the description of the perpetrator and owes me a debt. And I always collect."

Before Alexei could answer, before I could process the words much less act, there was a blade in Kirill's hand. With a practiced movement, he stabbed it into Alexei's chest twice, seemingly unconcerned by the spurting blood.

The man I had barely known and still wanted to call friend collapsed, blood soaking his clothes and staining his unnaturally pale lips. I wanted to press my hands over the wound though I was no healer. Wanted magic that could keep the Goddess at bay.

Before I could act, Kirill turned to me, wiped his face clean, and smiled. "Let that be a reminder of what happens when you don't pay your debts, Vanya. Your mother understood, your sister understands no matter how much she hates me, but your face still lights up when you see me, thinking I'll help." He laughed. "Now you don't need to worry about finding a healer willing to talk to one such as you—so I did help after all."

Inside the building, the prince let out a faint cry, like he had felt the death of his friend, though I did not think he had such power. Kirill turned toward the noise.

"Is there another one? There were two, and though they only stole one life, both should pay, don't you think, Stepdaughter?"

Before, it had been too fast for my fear to rise. This time, it tried to swallow me whole as I stepped over Alexei's body to block the doorway.

"No. Von Lemerch needs him. I'm repaying my debt, as you said."

Kirill tilted his head. "You claim the prince himself lies in there?" He spat on the ground. "The royals deserve no sanctuary, and von Lemerch won't ever know what happened on this street. You wouldn't be stupid enough to tell her, would you?"

As usual, Lumi had been right. There was no loyalty between von Lemerch and Kirill. It seemed the only one who had been loyal and trusting at all was me.

Kirill stepped closer and I refused to flinch. Dimitri had come to help because he cared, despite the front he put up, and somehow stopped the fire. Despite not moving or dancing, my feelings grew with those of Lowtown. The colors were already smearing, my magic strained, but I did not care. The rage I had suppressed by convincing myself others knew better, by telling myself that if I did what Mother and Lumi and Kirill said one day I would be free, filled me.

Kirill stood close enough to reach, sneering at my futile anger. My so-called stepfather, who had used my mother's debt to enslave me and Lumi, who had forced us to serve him and his daughter, who sent us to spy on his enemies and collect his debts no matter the danger. Who had watched us steal and scrape to pay back and still been ready to sell us to the brothels. Who intended to kill the man who held me in his safe arms last night, who made me feel wild and free.

"No." The word was quiet, barely a whisper.

"What was that, Stepdaughter?"

"No. Leave," I said louder. The anger beat with my blood, pumping through my body until it buzzed inside me.

Kirill came closer.

"You will not hurt him." Inside me, the beat of the death priestesses' mourning drums and a call to war sounded, a plague bell rang for all I had lost. "You will go no further."

Kirill grabbed my shoulder to push me aside. Thinking only to keep him from Dimitri, I moved with the motion, spun around him, and slammed my hands into his back over his heart.

He staggered and I followed, pouring my desperation and rage into him. My blood pumped it out, my breath exhaled the wrongs held too long. He struggled under my hands, his heart racing faster and faster. I left Lumi to come here. It would not be to watch my stepfather murder a prince. He would not reach Dimitri.

Kirill hit the ground with me on top.

His heart silent, unmoving. My stepfather was dead.

The only person I had hurt in anger, but there had been no intention to kill, only to protect, and the debt sigil had let me. Mother had wanted us to meet the world with kindness, and I had tried, but it seemed the name heart turner was literal.

I staggered into the burned-out building, leaving two corpses behind. Lowtown would take care of them, their possessions redistributed, their bodies added to the flames or sinking into the Taliell before morning.

The world swam. I moved like a drunk, but at least I was conscious. The magic inside me felt different, a river where there had been a stream. All thoughts evaporated when I saw Dimitri on the floor.

Most of his coat was burned off, and the remnants had been wrapped around his hands. He mumbled but did not react when I touched his shoulder.

He seemed smaller, his overwhelming presence gone, but still far too large for me to move any distance. Avoiding his bandages and burns, I wormed my hands under his shoulders, braced, and lifted.

The weight immediately threatened to bring me down on top of his prone form. I locked my knees and prayed to the Wishmaker. The Goddess was not getting the prince tonight. I had not come this far to fall. Alexei had not failed to save his friend.

Each muscle straining, I pulled. And pulled again.

Inch by inch, Dimitri slid over the floor, leaving a sootless wake. He moaned in pain as he opened his mismatched eyes and somehow focused on me.

"Princess?"

I shuddered. Alexei had accepted my presence without accusation, but I had not slept in his arms. And he had known he was dying.

Another few steps, and we would be outside. I looked away, unable to meet his pain-filled eyes, fearing the lies he would see. This was not the time for explanations, and von Lemerch's magic would block the most important words anyway.

Luckily, his head fell to the side, seemingly unconscious.

Outside, Spirits lit the street.

After laying Dimitri next to his friend, I felt his pulse, unable to trust my new magical senses. With the pale skin, slack face, and barely visible breathing, the prince and Alexei looked too similar. Had the sun completely set? It was impossible to tell with the clouds and smoke tainting the air.

I could not drag Dimitri the entire way to the hospital or palace, and I could not leave him here to the charity of Lowtown. No one walked the street, the night uncommonly empty. Fire and plague had killed even Lowtown's nightlife.

Tears mixed with the rain drops before I brushed them all away. I had stood up to Kirill. Killed him. And it did not matter. The prince would die anyway.

I pulled his head into my lap and placed a hand on his chest and felt the irregular heartbeat inside. My magic flowed from me to him, but all I felt was pain. Bringing up my best memories—how my mother used to brush my hair, how Lumi and I hid away to enjoy a rare treat, the freedom of dancing, the shared joy when Dimitri placed my hand on the griffon, the excitement of fighting with him, verbally and physically, how alive I had felt, how seen—I let them all flow from me to him, soothing the pain. Where my magic previously had required movement, it was now effortless to share my personal treasures. I was no healer; all I could do was make his last moments comfortable.

His eyes fluttered open again, and this time, I did not look away.

"All will be right soon," I lied, like I had lied from the start.

I pushed away my grief, that was not what he needed, and forced a smile. He placed his hand on mine and feebly squeezed it.

"The Goddess is here."

Unable to keep more tears from falling, I turned my face toward the sky. High above where the dark clouds reflected the sunset, something moved.

I squinted, tracking the figure until it swooped lower, as if to get a better look at the destruction. A griffon, maybe relaying the fire's progress to the palace.

An impossible hope awoke inside me. When I fell from the balcony, I heard the thoughts of the crowd without touching anyone. I had reached Lumi from the palace. I had communicated with the griffon in the stable.

I squeezed Dimitri's cold hand. More magic might kill me, especially after what I did to Kirill. Even if I survived, lying unconscious on the street I would be buried with the other corpses.

I should walk away, run like Lumi said. Without the prince, von Lemerch might well let us go, and with Kirill dead, no one else would come looking. I could be free. Lumi had spoken true. He would most likely die anyway. But where she had torched his home in anger, he had risked his life to save hers. Hope told me to try and despite all the times it had led me wrong in the past, I listened.

Under our joint hands, his heartbeat slowed. The last daylight fled.

Focusing on the spot I last saw the griffon, I let go. There was no dance. No pain or excitement. No passion or kisses.

There was just me, accepting myself, though I no longer knew who I was. That was fine. If I got out of here, I would have time to figure things out. Poor, noble, bastard, sister, liar, and thief. Possibly in love and worthy of love. Killer and heart turner.

There was a melody to the street, a dance in my mind.

Far above, I felt the griffon turn around, ready to fly back to its rich masters.

I swept my free hand up, as if throwing my power outward—reaching, searching.

Pain and grief, joy and love, anger and hate, the feelings of those around me filled me. Then too many thoughts, whispers and screams, wishes and curses. I ignored them all for the speck high above in the black clouds.

Help! Return! I screamed internally, and something responded. The griffon seemed to pause, but then continued.

I placed the prince on the ground and pushed myself up, raising both hands.

"*Come.*"

The command echoed in multitudes of minds. They turned, watching.

"*Help me.*"

People approached, but I ignored them. Maroon, emerald, and sapphire spots danced in my vision. Mage lights, such as might never have been seen in Lowtown, lit the street in unearthly blue.

I fell, catching myself on hands and knees.

The people of Tal filled my mind. Beautiful and ugly—I embraced them all, telling them tomorrow would be better.

"*Come.*"

The still warm, rain-slick stones met my cheek, the prince's breath stuttered, then a creature as wild as the wind responded.

I shut my eyes, remembering how the feathers felt under my fingers, how its heart was brave and true.

Something slammed into the street next to me, and a sharp, cold beak brushed my cheek. This time, I felt no fear.

The rider cursed, but it seemed far away. I pushed myself onto my back, trying to see her.

"The Crown Prince. *Save him.*"

I do not know if I spoke out loud or in her mind, but surprise and acceptance bloomed. The prince's body moved away from my side, then strong hands lifted me and, finally, I flew.

Chapter Thirty

Dimitri

I awoke in my sweat-soaked bed and could, for a moment, pretend it had all been one of my fire-filled nightmares. My last memories were a confused tangle of pain, smoke, and fantasy, but I remembered what came before too well to trick myself.

My power had been flailing, the fire slowly suffocating. I could not put it out, and every time I relaxed my hold on the wind, it fed the fire again. We climbed from one roof to the next, ever closer, and magic overuse made me rash. On the wind, I heard the cries of those trapped, urging me on. Further away, the hope of rain hung in the air.

Standing on the brink of my burning city, Alexei held me steady while I pushed everything I had at the flames. I suffocated them, feeling like my own breath was sucked out. The first drop hit my face as the roof gave out.

It was a mess of smoke and terrible heat. A beam fell on Alexei, pinning him to the ground. The world swam as I freed him, hardly feeling my scorched hands. As he staggered to his feet with a splinter the size of my forearm piercing his chest, the knowledge he'd been seriously hurt hit me. The lack of air stole my strength and consciousness threatened to escape.

We supported each other down stair after stair, coughing worse and worse.

Then there was nothing until I rested in the princess's lap, memories of dance carrying me away through the air. I closed my eyes, trying to find the real memories behind the dreams, but came up blank.

Clearly, the healers had somehow found me. Only a vague ache remained in my chest, and my previously burned fingers were now only stiff, like when I had gripped a pen for bells on end. Knowing the extent of my injuries, they must have spent the night healing me.

A rustling broke the silence. Twisting around, I found Mariska sleeping in the same chair the princess had rested in during my meeting—two days ago? That day, Helia had woken up to me waiting at her bedside.

My cousin moved in her sleep again, and a slight frown passed over her smooth forehead. I had promised to visit her at the hospital, and instead, she had been summoned to my sickbed.

As if feeling me watching, her eyes blinked open.

"You're awake," she said as she placed a magic-tingling hand on my forehead. "How do you feel?"

"Like new." Hating the weakness, I brushed her away and pulled on the shirt hanging on the chair next to the bed. "What have I missed?" When the silence stretched, I sought her eyes again, finding worry and pain. "What's wrong?"

Had I failed after all? I remembered the fire going out, the rain on my face, but perhaps the magic was playing with my mind by then. Maybe I just wanted to be the savior for once. I fought to remember, but there was nothing but darkness and the princess's impossible presence.

"Is Tal still burning?"

Mariska quickly shook her head. "You performed a miracle. How could you put yourself in such danger?"

"The princess said something, and I couldn't do nothing. The only wind whisperers in the palace are my father and me. For a fire bearer, I would have had to search the records and then track them down. There was no time. It worked, right?"

Her anger made no sense. Of everyone, she should know our ancestry did not make our lives worth more than anyone else's. It had been more curse than blessing to both. Then I registered her red-rimmed eyes with tears still hiding in the corners. She was not angry, she was grieving.

"Who?" I asked, dreading the answer. The smiles upon waking were long gone. If only they could have stayed longer.

"Alexei did not make it."

What? "No."

There was no other answer. Despite my memory of his injuries, it could not be true. If the healers could save me, they could save my oldest friend. My only friend. *That* was why Mariska was here. After Alexei, and Eki's insane confession of attempting to kill Helia, of our quartet, only the two of us remained.

Mariska reached for my hand, but I flinched away. I did not want comfort. This too was my fault. Alexei had promised not to leave. He could not be gone. "How?"

"Only you and the princess returned. All she said was that he was gone, and the searchers found no trace of anyone else when they returned. You were both in a bad state, Dimi."

"The princess was there?" Seemed my impossible dreams held truth, after all.

There was more, I could see Mariska held something back, but it was enough for now. I needed to move. Throw something. Scream. Grieve. "I need to be alone."

She stepped away. "Your father is awake. They say he might live."

The door clicked closed behind her before the words fully arrived in my magic-addled mind.

I twisted and pounded a fist into the stone wall, pain tearing into the recently healed flesh. *Alexei's gone, and so is my chance to run.* I would be trapped in this place until the wedding. Longer if I cared about the city Alexei had given his life for. I could not leave Tal to my irresponsible cousin, and Mariska would not take the crown from her older brother. And never would I give the old men and women on the Council the power they sought, nor marry Helia and leave her to their scheming.

I needed to get out of here. To know everything that happened after I blacked out. To hear the wind and honor Alexei's Spirit. Was his body perhaps brought to the temple? Were his bones being prepared at this very moment? I shrugged into a coat and tied my hair back when there was a knock on the door.

Opening it, I expected Mariska to have returned, and hoped I could welcome her comforting embrace. She was as alone as I. Instead, my father's Roja spies stood on the other side. They must have watched for my cousin to leave. Maybe she had informed someone I was awake. I knew what the spy would say before she opened her mouth—wanted to protest but knew I could not.

"The King has summoned you."

I closed my eyes and allowed the stillness in the air to calm my breaths and stop the threatening tears, then nodded. Duty never ended. It would take everything from me until my gilded bones dressed the Grove.

During the short walk to my father's chambers, nobles and servants stopped to watch. Some bowed lower, others snickered—I had done enough the last days to feed the rumor mill for years. It no longer seemed important to save face before people I cared nothing for. Grief clawed at my insides, but I kept my face a blank mask. It seemed when I was close to lay one body to rest, another died. Tal and the Goddess took all I cared about, binding me ever tighter.

My father sat in his normal chair propped up by pillows—slimmer, older, but with the familiar cruel twist to his lips.

Anger and grief twisted inside me. Why did he still live when so many in Tal had died? When the best man I knew was gone? My father looked me up and down, dissatisfaction painted across his face.

"At least you still come when summoned. Seems you played king—badly—in my absence."

"I've been a better king in days than you were in decades. I care about—"

His wheezing laughter cut me off.

Before I knew what I was doing, my hidden dagger was in my hand. My hand at his throat. His Adam's apple bobbing and rasping against the blade. The two servants standing against the wall did not even twitch.

He had been dying. Would anyone question his death when so much had happened? I would be king and could pay off or threaten the corpse carriers and servants. Only family attended the preparation of the body.

And I had always planned to kill him.

As I pressed the blade closer, he grabbed my arm, hand overlapping with the royal sigil and—though physical touch was unnecessary—I knew I had been too slow.

"STOP!"

His voice wrapped around my Spirit, squeezing until my body felt like it was submerged in water, the pressure about to crush me. He was the Head of House Herebov and a direct, simple command could never be disobeyed. Only a master sigil crafter could transfer the power from him to me when the time came.

He leaned back in his chair, unconcerned about the blade still close enough to shave.

"Well, *finally*. There is some fire in you after all, son. When you learn to hone it instead of it ruling you, you'll make a fine king."

I could not answer. Frustration brought tears of anger to my eyes—at him and at myself. I had a plan when I returned to Tal, but everything was unraveling.

"Step back and don't threaten me again," my father said, his voice still laced with magic.

This command was less precise, would only hold a day or two, but his show of power was enough to make his point—he always held the winning move.

When I returned to my original position and put away the knife, he continued as if nothing had happened, as if he could not see the murder in my eyes.

"A few days of absence and my city is burning, citizens rioting, lords leaving, wedding canceled, while my heir throws his life away in the hopes of saving peasants and brings down a hailstorm that damages half of the crops."

"Yes," I said, knowing it was futile to argue I had not brought the plague. That I had done it all to save lives. I swallowed my resentment. If he wanted to pretend, so could I. "Do they know how the fires started?"

"I've been told people heard coughing from bakeries in Lowtown—like those people don't always cough—and people panicked. They tried to escape to Rivertown where the Guard, following your orders, blocked the bridges. The fools waved torches and houses caught fire."

The king looked like he wanted to spit on the floor, and my self-righteous anger suffocated. While I had not lit the fire, I had rung the plague bells, and protocols declared infected stay inside until assessed. I had caused panic by trying to save everyone and underestimated their desperation Alexei had tried to show me. Five days in charge, and I had caused only death.

"I did not—"

"Your actions have further increased the food shortage. Even the merchants in Wall now grumble. We cannot afford to let the dissent spread to the nobles. And I hear impossible tales of you and the princess in Lowtown, either starting or stopping the fire, and attacking citizens. I thought you would be ready to take over as king and Head of our House after the wedding."

"I am." After his show of power, I wanted nothing more. Never would anyone control me like that again. At least my impulsive attack had not changed his mind. Undoubtedly, he thought he somehow could control me even then.

My father scoffed. "Prove yourself before the Day of the Dead. Learn to think like a king."

Despite my determination to be free, part of me wondered if he was right. I had been so focused on enacting my vengeance I had not considered how my plan would affect Tal. What had my decisions led to? And all I had wanted was to give the responsibility to someone else after taking my revenge.

"What do you command?" My voice was dead, even to myself, but my father seemed satisfied by my renewed obedience.

"We need an act of strength while solving the lack of food and keeping you out of the public eye until the talk disappears. A fed man is a happy man." A coughing fit interrupted his speech. Now the servants rushed forward with warm beverages and cloths while I was the one who stood still, waiting for it to play out, hoping he would choke.

When he stopped gasping for breath and waved everyone away, he rewarded my stony face with a considering look.

"Despite the consequences you made hard choices. Find where the food is before the wedding, command the riders as they scour the countryside and search the city. If we cannot provide for the celebrations, the nobles will conspire no matter how powerful your bride. Bring me the heads of the brigands burning crops and attacking farms. Denyev and other outlying cities have been ignoring my letters. The steppe clans avoid Tal. Rebellion is brewing and we need a show of strength. Show everyone Tal cares and kills. And keep your distance from the princess. We need no more controversies."

"As you command, Father," I said, and bowed my way out while he descended into another coughing fit.

Alexei's death had forced my father to order me and our riders to do precisely what Alexei had argued for. Somewhere, I hoped his Spirit knew. I could honor him by finding the food and helping the people. He had cared too much for Tal and me, had given his life, but I had wanted nothing more than to throw mine away.

Already, I longed to be in the air, though I mostly would be commanding others. Until now, I had avoided taking my place in the hierarchy of the army and nobility. The promise to run away with Helia was now impossible, the wedding back on. I would have to disappoint her too. My gut clenched and a different kind of pain mixed with the grief. I did not want to leave her smiles and witty retorts, her comforting touches or fiery kisses. The glimmers of hope and happiness.

Before I started on my new tasks, I would tell her everything. Tell her I would not hold her to her wedding vows if after the Day of the Dead she preferred to leave. Only one of us need be trapped here. I would bare my wounds like Alexei would have wanted.

In Lowtown, Alexei and I had been alone at the end. Would he have survived if we kept the guards with us? I would not lead others into danger without preparation again. And so, the day disappeared in meetings and logistics edged by ever-present grief. By keeping me busy, my father had given me an unintentional boon, because at every corner and meeting, I expected Alexei's crooked smile to meet mine.

As the sun set again, I could no longer put it off. All day, my heart had wanted to seek distraction and comfort in the princess's arms and lips, while my mind told me to stay away—for once, our upcoming conversation would be neither comforting nor distracting.

I should have been open with her when I caught her stealing the crown the first night. Maybe if I had dared to bare my heart then, if I had trusted her instead of arguing, and listened to her counsel, everything after would have gone differently.

Chapter Thirty-One

Vanya

Dimitri was safe.
Lumi was safe.
I was safe.

I paced the length of my locked sitting room, repeating the words at each turn.

I had not planned on returning here, but after regaining consciousness in the princess's bed with healers fussing over my state, I discovered Flora had ordered my rooms locked for my safety and recovery. Now, here I was, trapped. And tomorrow at the latest, Lumi would bring the real Helia to the palace; I had to disappear.

Kirill drawing the knife replayed in my mind and each time, I imagined how I grabbed his hand, used my power earlier, and changed how the night ended. The rider had left Alexei's body on the street, her griffon already tired from bells of circling above Tal as it burned. I had used more magic than ever before, but the recovery was easier. Maybe it was like a muscle, and I was growing stronger. Only this time, I wished I had blacked out and could forget.

Dimitri was safe. Lumi was safe. Safe. Safe. Safe.

At least until von Lemerch found my sister and the real princess missing. Would she come directly for me? I should climb out the window again, but still I stayed—for the prince. Alexei had told me to keep him safe, and somehow I, a street thief and fake, wanted to do just that. I could not leave before I knew for sure they had healed him.

Dimitri was safe. Lumi was safe.

A knock on my front door was followed by someone trying the handle. It seemed my time was already up.

"Helia? Can we talk? Dimi is awake," Mariska called. There was pain in her voice. She had cared for Alexei. Known him better than I ever would. Grief tore through me as I again saw the knife enter his body.

"Let me in," Mariska said through the door.

I leaned against the other side. "The door is stuck."

"I'll get a guard to open it."

I could already hear retreating steps.

"No. Please, don't." I could not get her involved. Mariska had been nothing but nice to me. The first night in the palace, von Lemerch had paid off several of the guards. None could be trusted. The choking curse awoke inside me as I thought of all I wanted to say. How I wished to tell just one person the truth. If Alexei had lived, perhaps he could have guessed the rest. "I can't explain but nothing is as it seems."

Mariska's steps returned and I could feel her on the other side of the massive door. "Can't or won't?"

First, I did not understand her, then wondered how far I could push von Lemerch's hold. "Can't."

I did not choke. Maybe I could warn her before leaving the palace. Even with Helia back and Dimitri planning to leave, the more they knew the better.

"Did they put a sigil on you?" she asked.

I focused on Kirill instead of von Lemerch when I answered, "I have a sigil restricting my actions."

My debt sigil itched as soon as I focused on it—although, it was already fading. In a few days, the debt would be gone with the lender. Luckily, it seemed he had not paid the Sigil Guild enough for one that transferred to his heir.

"I knew you weren't Helia von Heskin! With each delay it became clearer Helia didn't want to come, then you show up with strange injuries, no training, and bad manners. Are you a maid or bastard the von Heskin's forced into this?"

"You knew? And didn't say anything?"

I wanted to laugh. She had guessed from the start I was an imposter, but was not one step closer to the real perpetrators.

I almost saw Mariska wave her hands in dismissal. "As long as you and Dimi care for each other, and Oberwalden keeps up the ruse, I don't see how it matters. You need to tell him, though. He should know who he is to marry and I'm sure he wouldn't care. Especially not after last night." She hesitated and the enthusiasm was replaced by the grief Tal seemed to drown in. "Alexei would have been happy knowing Dimi had someone more practical than a cloistered princess."

My forehead fell against the door. "The wedding is called off." And I was leaving them all.

"I told you to give him time."

With the new sense I had managed to mute but not turn off, I felt someone else approach.

"You need to leave." I closed my eyes, knowing this was the last time we would speak. "Thank you for being my friend despite it all. Know that I'm sorry."

"Don't worry, your secret is safe with me." Mariska reeled in her emotions and stepped away.

Soon enough that my visitors must have passed each other in the hallway, a key turned in the lock and Flora, followed by Svetlana, entered. *Did they know Kirill was dead? And Helia and Lumi gone?* From their smug looks, I guessed not. Unless they let me out, I would have to attempt the window again.

"I hope the rumors of the Oberwaldian princess running around Lowtown are exaggerations," Flora said.

I backed away. "I'm here." *For now.*

"I wouldn't be so glib, if I were you." Svetlana closed the door behind her but neglected to lock. "After what you have been up to, no one will question if the healers missed a bruise or two."

"You need to learn to behave, girl," Flora said and handed her walking stick to my stepsister. The polished wood reflected the afternoon sun. It seemed my recent actions were beyond the correction of a whip. Hatred as hot as the fire yesterday spread through me.

"And spending the night in the prince's chambers. How was he, Vanya?"

Her words sounded rehearsed. Still, bile rose in my throat at the thought of telling my stepsister of the precious moments I had shared with Dimitri before it all went wrong. When I stared mutely back, she swung the stick at my legs.

I danced away. I was not letting her abuse me again. No matter how meek I appeared, kindness was no longer an option.

She lifted the stick again.

"Stand still, or we will deliver you your sister's ears in a box," Flora said.

I laughed. Lumi was beyond their reach—had probably never been in danger. If I had misbehaved enough, would they have cut off a stranger's ear and hoped I could not tell the difference? I had tried playing the princess for them, tried to be the nice girl mother had raised to marry well. I tried so hard, I no longer knew who I was.

My magic expanded as I evaded Svetlana's second swing, and I felt a fourth person approach my chambers—never had I been so popular before. Time was running out.

Yesterday, I had raced the way back to my old life, but the role I had once had no longer fit. It was time to make my own decisions. I would not escape beaten out the window.

Another step, and I snatched the stick from Svetlana and finally let the hatred show on my face.

"And what do you think you can do to a princess?" I taunted and waved it as she had.

Flora laughed. "You are no princess. Von Lemerch can dress an urchin in silk, but it does not make you more royal than any other Lowtown scum."

"So, that's all I am?" I asked, backing toward the bedchamber door. "It's clear as day that we are related."

They followed me, as I knew they would. Almost there.

"You're only a stray my father was forced to take in," Lana said, though it lacked her usual passion, like she was playing out a role she had lost the taste of, but played nonetheless.

The banter's for them, not me, I reminded myself and dropped the stick, surrendering. I did not want to kill again, had never wanted to, but I would fight. The familiar presence was almost at my door.

Hurry, I thought, forcing myself to concentrate on Flora as I entered the bedchamber. She exuded anger and superiority, unknowing I could invade her mind.

They stalked after me.

Whatever curse Popova had placed on my magic, it seemed lighter since yesterday, like not only the debt sigil was fading. Time to put it to the test.

Flora and Lana took one last step, stretching to grab me. I threw myself at them and kicked the bedchamber door closed.

In me lived the pain of losing my mother, Kirill's kicks, days-long starvation and broken bones, Flora's whip, and Lana's dismissive sneers. Like Lumi, my stepsister thought me someone to be used or ignored. Last night, I gave Dimitri my best memories. These women deserved my worst.

I pushed the ever-present magic into them, and they cried as I forced them to relive my pain.

Someone knocked on the front door, but I kept up the emotional barrage until the women whimpered on the floor.

I bent over Lana. I was a stranger to Flora, an interchangeable impostor. With her it had never been personal. When I was sure my stepsister was incapacitated, I pressed my lips against her ear, remembering her hurting me and Lumi for years. Remembering all the opportunities for kindness she had not taken.

"I'll always be sorry for what I did to your father, and I hope others are kinder to you than you were to me, but this I'll never regret." The power inside me swelled, as if sensing my intention.

The lorists said a mage could speak three curses in their lifetime, and when they did, they surrendered parts of themselves. For my vain stepsister, I would use one of mine.

"Until you love someone above yourself, all who put eyes on you will turn away in disgust."

Magic rushed out of me as the knock came again.

"Just a moment," I called out.

I hog-tied them to the bed with the silk ribbons they had thought too good for me and gagged them with pillowcases. There was no time for anything more. I was not leaving without answers.

By the time the third knock came, I straightened my dress and closed the bedchamber door behind me.

"Come in."

My hair hung wild, my cheeks flushed, and all thoughts of hatred evaporated when I saw my guest. Dimitri's walls were back up, his face an icy mask, but I could read his grief and anticipation, then insecurity and starbursts of joy in his eyes when they met mine. How had I ever thought him unfeeling?

This was my chance for a goodbye. The truth of how Alexei died sat on the tip of my tongue. He deserved to hear it from me.

"Dimi—"

"No." He placed a calloused hand against my cheek. "Let me talk before I lose my nerve."

I swallowed the words, my treacherous heart galloping at the warmth in his eyes.

"I told you I planned to leave Tal after the wedding, but I did not tell you why." He hesitated, and I enveloped him in my arms. I wanted to tell him it did not matter, but could feel he needed to get it out. "When Alexei and I were ten, we caught toads in the pond and hid them in the girls' beds. All except one screamed—that's how I noticed Eki. Since that day we became inseparable. Mariska joined a year later, making us four."

"And then?" I prodded, wondering where this was going. His pain swelled. I did not use magic to attempt to ease it, it did not seem right without his knowledge; instead, I hugged him tightly. "Whatever it is, it's fine."

He shook his head. "For so many reasons, it's not fine. We got older, teenagers sent out of the Women's Tower. Alexei and I practiced the sword and spear while Eki and Mariska became ladies. Maybe it was proximity, maybe it was love, I no longer know, but Eki and I snuck away alone. We were stupid. My first kiss—first everything—was with her, before she left to visit relatives for the summer three years ago. By fall, she wrote me, saying she was expecting my child."

"You have a child?" I asked in shock. Even in Lowtown, we would have heard. "A bastard?" *Like me.* Someone hidden and shunned. At least it made more sense for Eki to hate Helia, to help von Lemerch, if she was fighting for her child.

"Kings have no bastards. It risks the succession," he said dully, like repeating another's words. "We planned to marry in secret, then Father would have had to accept it. I arranged for a priestess to meet us at a temple in Midtown. I had not seen Eki for months when she arrived, large with child."

"But you did not marry?"

"The priestess and my guard had shared our plans with my father. They only waited that long because Eki's family would have hidden her until our son was born, because her family knew and wanted the child on the throne. Father wanted to share the blame for enforcing laws no one has looked at the last century. He took it before the Council and people I trusted testified the child was mine. I thought we'd been so careful. What a fool. There's always someone watching."

I stroked his back, longing to make it better. Inside, the sea of grief I felt previously stretched, but it seemed shallower than before, calmer.

"Rather than letting me marry my childhood love, my father killed my unborn son—forced him from his mother's belly—for being a bastard."

"Being a bastard is no crime." Vehemence filled my voice. My mother might have done a lot wrong, but never had she blamed us for our father's absence or treated us as less than.

He continued without acknowledging my words. "The baby was sentenced to death without last rights, Eki to the Women's Tower with no future prospects, and I was sent to the mountains to reflect on my ways. They gave her something to give birth. He was too small to live—those tiny hands, lips. A few more months and he would have been ready for this world. Instead, he was another death to haunt Tal without even drawing breath. Father made me watch when they burned his body to ash so the Goddess would not find the bones. Told me to remember the smell, and never disobey again. Because of the noble's sigil, I cannot challenge him directly, so instead I decided to play the perfect son until I had something to bargain with."

Ice filled me. "Marry the princess of Oberwalden and get the crown."

"All for revenge and freedom. I used you, Princess, but I don't want to anymore. I don't want the darkest moment in my life to drive my actions. Eki...she cannot move on..."

"Through kindness, tomorrow will be a better day," I said, because my mother had been right. Hope lay in the future.

I pulled his head down. Our lips met tentatively at first and then with hunger, and I tried to show how much his trust mattered to me, that this was real, despite me living a lie. Passion built between us, and if my bedchamber had not been otherwise occupied, I would have pulled him inside.

Instead, we fell together onto the sofa, our breaths mingling. He belonged to another, and still, I opened my mouth when his warm lips pressed against mine. Our tongues clashed and hands roamed. His fingers slid between my curls and his other hand wrapped around my waist as if he knew I thought of running and needed me close as our mouths moved together.

This time, no one would interrupt us.

I had not let myself be with someone since the night Lumi was attacked and refused to speak of it. Had not even let myself look. But since Dimitri caught me, I had been ready to throw caution to the wind. The impossibility of the situation had broken down my self-imposed barriers until I could no longer think straight. He had infuriated, frustrated, and pushed me away—showed me through actions rather than words who he really was. He thought me another, but I had never been more myself than I was with him. If the Wishmaker could give me one thing, it would be for this moment to never end. But the gods had never listened to me.

My breath hitched as he brushed against my breasts. And when he hesitated, I slipped my hands under his shirt and, instead of burn scars, found smooth skin across taunt muscles. The amazing powers of the healers were enough to make me pause.

Alexei and Mariska had not condemned me. Tomorrow he would meet the real Helia and know the truth. Would he think himself a fool again? Would he come to regret these very kisses? And could I share my body without letting him see the rest? Could I ignore it when he moaned the name of another?

Von Lemerch had cursed me to never tell her secrets, to choke on my words, but with magic I had been able to share memories that spoke for themselves. He had bared his heart, deciding not to let the bad ruin the good. If he could be brave, so could I.

I wanted nothing more than to let his hand creep up my thigh, to unhook the corset and let the regrets come tomorrow. But I was done with lies. Done stealing things that were not mine. I would not take his heart as part of a ruse.

As I felt the magic beat beneath my palm, I gathered what it meant to be me. The tutoring in Midtown, the bells spent dancing alone to perfect each step, climbing ever higher to see the stars or steal, and acting on the Rivertown barges. Then everyday things like teasing and watching the children of Lowtown while their mothers washed and chatted, memories of cleaning soot-stained hearths and emptying chamber pots. The dark parts were harder. The pain of beatings, hunger pangs, and plague bells. My mother's death and the days that followed were broken shards in my mind. The only thing I kept back was Lumi. She hated the royals, and her secrets were not mine to share.

Dimitri brushed the hair behind my ear and pressed his lips against my neck, his whispers just below my ear.

"What are you thinking?"

Meeting his tender eyes, I imagined offering all the parts of me, memories no princess would have, and made the furthest leap of all, not into the air but in trust, knowing it could also be my most dangerous fall if he did not catch me. A quiet stillness opened inside me. Faith in myself. Fall or fly, I willed the gathered memories to flow from me to him. Finally, he would see the real me.

His eyes widened in surprise, brows furrowed, and hands clenched. There was no way of knowing how he experienced what I shared. No way of mincing words or twisting the truth.

"This is me," I said when he finally blinked out of his stupor.

"The memories in Lowtown during the fire... You're not Helia. Who are you?"

The suspicion landed like a slap. "You saw. That's me."

"Why?"

It could mean so many things. *Why lie? Why am I here? Why did the real Helia not arrive?* Von Lemerch was the answer to it all. She was also the answer I could not give. My throat was already closing, the magic feeling my intentions. Even the thought of sharing her face clenched invisible fingers around my windpipe.

"It wasn't my choice," I said, focusing on how Helia had not agreed to the marriage either.

Dimitri had told me from the start. None of us had a choice.

He retreated to the door. The rejection hurt, but the lies had been replaced by unanswered questions, and there was a chance, no matter how slim, that he could finally find the answers. That they could save him.

"What wasn't your choice? To pretend to be my bride? To lead me on and—" He snapped his mouth shut and pulled his fingers through his hair as I had moments earlier. "I cannot be here."

"Everything the night in your chambers was real. Me wanting to see the world...I want you to know the truth. I'm leaving ton—"

"No." He raised a hand to stop me. "My father can never know you're not Helia. From tomorrow, I'll be hunting bandits and the missing food. Gone from the palace most days. Stay away from me and nothing needs to change. I don't know what will happen after the wedding, but that doesn't change that it *must* happen."

Death, betrayal, and worse, I thought, then registered his other words. He wanted me to hide away. Alexei had asked me to keep his friend safe but Dimitri could no longer look me in the eye. Was he thinking about his revenge again?

It's better this way, I told myself. This way we can let each other go. Surely, I could figure out how to reveal the rest to him before the Day of the Dead, still two months away. Perhaps he would even be safer without me.

I gathered my hurt feelings. The coming months would give me time to plan instead of reacting. Time to decide what I wanted. I knew I had to go, that Helia was coming, but still I could not resist questioning Dimitri. "You'll leave me until the wedding?"

He nodded slowly, taking another step away. The proper distance for a noble. Further than it had ever seemed before. "That seems best. I need to think, to..." He hesitated, his eyes traveling up my disheveled clothes and messy hair to the sofa where we had kissed and fought, then met mine. "You'll be here?"

I had opened myself so that there would be no lies between us before I left; still, the easy words sat on my tongue. I swallowed them, then tried to find a truth I could live with. One that did not make this goodbye.

"I'll wait for you."

He gave a curt nod. Had I not known him, I would have thought he did not care. Would not have seen the anguish in his eyes. The unanswered questions he bypassed for he had been taught a royal did not show their weaknesses. He would mull over what I had revealed. Formulate a plan. While I was impulsive, he was the opposite. In King's Conquest, he retreated before my wild moves, then returned to beat me every time.

In the doorway, he paused, and for a moment, I thought he would return and let me explain what I could. That we would kiss again. That he would dare to let me close. Instead, he spoke so quietly I barely heard the words, "What's your name?"

It was a plea. How many times had I wished to hear him say it? Tears gathered in my eyes as sorrow and magic clenched my throat.

Before it let me go, he was gone.

I should have hurried to pack and escape before he decided to expose me. Instead, my legs gave way and I fell to the floor in a tumble of skirts, allowing myself a moment. Allowing the tears. The pain.

Too many emotions had passed too quickly. But I could at least find Lumi again and hear her out. Figure out my next step and what my sister really intended.

As I finally got to my feet and reentered the bedchamber, ignoring Flora's muffled protests, packing was quick. Once, I had dreamt of reselling all the fine dresses, but I was leaving like I had come. A thief in the night. And the debt sigil on my thigh was almost gone. If I was going to live my own life, I would do it with honest money. I would take nothing more from Helia.

Despite feeling her eyes dig into my back, I felt less bothered about claiming one of Lana's dresses. I had served her for years. She owed me.

When there was nothing else to take, I pushed aside the Oberwaldian dresses and shoes until I saw the single, worn leather boot. Hiding it had been a silly way to keep the last thing Lumi gave me close. Taking it with me now, even more trivial. That did not change that I could not leave it.

As I pulled it out, I noticed the crinkled letter sticking out from the top. I had forgotten all about it. Or perhaps I had not wanted to think about what I had done.

I closed my fingers around the fine parchment. I should leave it here for whoever came to look for me but what could have been important enough for von Lemerch to send me into the king's chambers?

Before I could question myself, I pried open the seal.

The letter inside was addressed to the king.

I read it twice. My legs threatened to fold again.

She had wanted to hide this.

My world shifted and the fight became personal.

Would Dimitri get the letter if I left it here? Would anyone believe it when the real Helia arrived?

No. He might not want to see me now, but I would have to convince him. To regain his trust somehow.

I removed Lana's dresses from my bag, leaving them on the floor, and changed into her too long Oberwaldian maid's dress, knowing no one would give another servant a second look. I was no princess—would no longer pretend—just a girl from the streets in love with a prince, but there was no way I would let any more of the people I cared for die at von Lemerch's hands. I needed to retreat and plan before I saw him again. If I had broken out of the palace, I could break in when the time was right.

He would talk to me. My heart ached, but it was the least important thing I was risking.

In my bedchamber, I tested the bonds holding Flora and Lana. It would not do for someone to discover them until I was gone—a prison cell was still a too-real possibility—but the night was long, and I planned to find out everything Flora knew before I left.

Because when returning to Tal during the bell before dawn—when both nobles and commoners slept—I would no longer be acting blindly, dancing at someone else's strings. Lumi had been right; there were things worth fighting for—but through my own means.

The princess was gone, but the prince must live. Somehow, I would find a way to answer his questions, no matter how he judged me when he learned it all. Tomorrow would only be a better day if we made it so. Kindness and wishes were not enough; I needed to act, and hope when it was all over, Lumi understood what had forced my hand.

I was done running, for the Talian plague was not real.

Epilogue

Lumi

The sun set and the ever-present Spirits became visible to all as the palace guards stopped our hired carriage. Plague protocols said no one without a pass was to be let through, but I offered none. Instead, I demanded entry, declaring loudly that Princess Helia von Heskin of Oberwalden had finally arrived.

As the guards sent a runner for someone with authority to disprove her identity, I pulled the curtains closed and removed the blanket covering the unconscious woman. This was for the best. Time for her to wake; Vanya had enough time to disappear.

After hiding all day to study the magic stasis, I had confirmed my previous theory. From the start I'd felt von Lemerch's powers were similar to my own, but the ancient temple stones had limited my magic. Fortunately, it had also given me time to study the woman before me.

I placed my hands over Helia's unbeating heart, bent until our lips touched, and breathed in the death coating the other woman from inside out. Simple, but it took enough magic for me to sway on my seat.

Color returned to Helia's cheeks as her heart stuttered to life. Green eyes met my own. While Helia resembled Vanya and me, after so long with only her unmoving face for company, I no longer noticed.

"You were there," Helia said, her voice raw. "After they trapped me."

Hurried steps approached outside.

"Blame your aunt and Councilwoman von Lemerch." I pulled a scarf up to cover my face. "I've delivered you to the palace. My sister was forced to pretend to be you, if she is caught, know she had no choice. Watch your back, Princess."

I might be angry at Vanya for choosing to save the prince, yet again picking a dalliance over blood; still, I did not want my sister to suffer for von Lemerch's plans. The rebellion had brought the opportunity to infiltrate von Lemerch's rebel priestesses to me. We needed to know their true intentions for Tal. And their weaknesses.

My sister should never have been involved, and the mistake of saving the prince could be fixed with the edge of a blade easily enough. When it was all over, Vanya and I would make up.

As the right carriage door opened, I slipped out the left, leaving the real princess to handle the questions.

I strode back down Palace Road. As I passed, Spirits whispered that discontent was growing, that my friends were gathering, and that the prince had left Tal. *Interesting.*

Like the royals, von Lemerch was too strong and ancient to face head-on, but every plan had a weak spot. I had overheard enough to know it—the crown prince. Neither of his cousins were prepared to inherit or marry. The path was clear. He could not be allowed to return to Tal, no matter what it took.

I felt Vanya move further away from the palace. My sister cared too much, was willing to forgive and not pay the price for progress. The world needed people like her, but it also needed people like me.

Reluctantly, I blocked our connection as I had been doing for years, though it was harder now that Vanya had gained access to her magic. She could not be allowed to sense my intentions.

Better Vanya ran far away and when the danger was over, I would help her grieve.

Tomorrow would only be better if we wiped the slate clean.

VANYA AND DIMITRI'S STORY CONCLUDES IN
CLAIMING GLASS in Feb 2024
Can't wait? Want the first chapter now?
1) Pre-order
2) Forward your receipt to livstromwrites@gmail.com
3) Read it today!

Did you enjoy Stealing Glass?
Please share your thought on **Goodreads** and **Amazon** and help make this book a success

The Tale of Cinderella

Cinderella has a thousand versions and many different origin tales. Some claim the original came from China to Europe, while others say it's the ancient Greek story of Rhodopis. The most famous ones today are derived from the French version by Charles Perrault published in *Histoires ou contes du temps passé* in 1697, or *Aschenputtel* by the Brothers Grimm in their folk tale collection *Grimms' Fairy Tales* in 1812.

Some just think of Disney—blue dresses, pumpkins, and talking mice.

No version is truer than any other; that's what I love about fairy tales. They are oral tales that travel through time and space, morphing to their surroundings but—mostly—keeping the moral. Cinderella is the tale of rags to riches, of the kind, downtrodden girl catching the eye of the prince, and the hardships of blended families—for some, the ultimate fantasy.

While I always enjoyed the tale, I minded how shallow the prince was and how unsuited Cinderella was to become the future queen of Fairy Tale Land. I minded how the three sisters never grew past the roles their parents cast them in, and how, in the end, having small feet was the deciding factor (I have rather large ones).

In Vanya and Dimitri's tale, I tried to take the parts I loved and, by mashing them together with a fantasy city on the brink of change, transform the parts I didn't.

I hope you enjoyed it.

About Liv Strom

Liv is raising three children on fairy tales.

For the last ten years, she has lived in Zurich, Switzerland, and works as a management consultant reorganizing Swiss banks, using her planning and goal setting obsession both professionally and privately. Her main writing companion is her wild beagle, Amazing Louis of the Whispering Hunters (he came with the name and a long and proud pedigree).

Her stories have appeared in *Mystery Weekly*, *Hexagon SF Magazine*, and *Timeless 2 anthology* by Dragon Soul Press—and many more depending on when you are reading this. Her debut novel, *The Last Spiritwalker,* is an adult dark contemporary fantasy for readers who enjoy mythology and don't mind a bit of gore.

You can find Liv's latest publications and posts about her publishing journey at http://www.livstromwriters.com

Acknowledgements

No book is created in isolation. Besides my wonderful family who are always my first readers, critics and cheerleaders, I would like to thank my editor at Evermore Editing and wonderful beta readers. You made this Vanya and Dimitri's story so much stronger, and any errors are my own.

A specials shoutout goes to the most awesome group of writers out there at the 11:59 Workshop. They have made me a better writer, reader and inspired me when the going got tough. Thank you!

Made in the USA
Coppell, TX
14 December 2023